B[illegible]

the

Dark Oceans

Best wishes
Alison Huntingford
x

Beyond

the

Dark Oceans

ALISON HUNTINGFORD

Lupin Publications

A CIP catalogue record for this title is available from the British Library.

ISBN: 978-1-0683885-1-4

DISCLAIMER

This story is a work of fiction based on true events and people from the author's personal family history. No disrespect is intended (nor should be inferred) to the persons or organisations herein. Some characters and incidents have been fictionalised for dramatic effect.

Dedication

In 1906, a total of 211,700 immigrants arrived in Canada, the vast majority of these coming from the United Kingdom. This novel is affectionately dedicated to them all.

ATLANTIC COAST OF CANADA

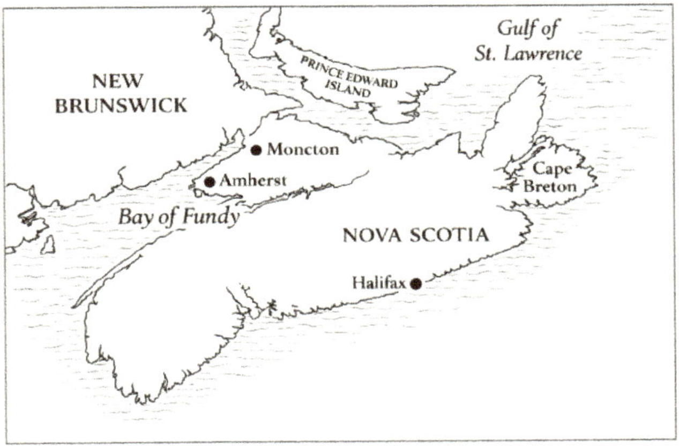

Map illustration created using AI tools, for illustrative purposes only.

Contents

Acknowledgements

With thanks to:

My husband Nigel for patient proof-reading and advice, as well as his love and support.

The descendants of Ethel, who supplied vital information and invaluable family anecdotes.

Lyn McCulloch, founder of the Huntingford 'one name study' and newsletter.

Credits:

Text formatting: Alison Smith

Cover design: @Rogue Debby CIC

Title and quotation taken from '*Canadian Railroad Trilogy*', Gordon Lightfoot, 1967

'Behind the blue Rockies the sun is declining
The stars they come stealing at the close of the day
Across the wide prairie our loved ones lie sleeping
Beyond the dark oceans in a place far away'

Gordon Lightfoot, 1967

Chapter 1

Middlesex, England 1904

Georgy's mother screamed as her waters broke, and she went into labour.

'Georgy! Quick. Fetch the midwife. The baby's coming!'

Though he was only eight years old, young Georgy Huntingford had seen all this twice before with the births of his younger brothers William and Gilbert. He'd been too young then to be of much help but this time he'd been given an important role. He pulled on his boots hurriedly and dashed out the door as his mother continued to cry out in pain.

'George, hurry, please!'

He knew it must be serious as his mother nearly always called him by his 'baby' name, Georgy, to avoid confusing him with his father, who was also called George.

Rushing along the main road in Long Ditton, past a line of small, terraced cottages, Georgy dodged horse and carts and the occasional new motorised carriage with equal speed and dexterity. He was used to the hustle and bustle, but this time he was annoyed by it. Couldn't they see he was in a hurry?

Having found the midwife, Mrs Triggs, luckily at home, they attempted to make a similarly fast return, but the narrow high street was busy with deliveries, and it took some time to negotiate their route. By the time they got back to Georgy's mother she was screaming more loudly than ever.

'Please help me,' his mother, Ellen, begged. 'It's never been this bad before; I can't stand it!'

The midwife took one look and went smoothly into action, taking Mrs Huntingford off into the main bedroom out of the way. After a few minutes, however, she came out looking concerned. She looked at the three boys, who were huddled by the fire looking worried.

'George, fetch your father. He should be here.'

'Father will be working,' Georgy told Mrs Triggs. 'He won't be able to leave just for a baby. He'll lose money.'

'Now you listen to me, young man,' she said sternly, 'this is a serious case and could be a matter of life and death. You tell him that and say he is to come immediately.'

Georgy felt his heart quail. Surely, they wouldn't lose their dear mother. He couldn't bear the thought of it.

The midwife saw his face and softened. 'There, there, don't take on, sonny. It may not be as bad as that, but we should be prepared. Now go, please.'

Something was different this time, Georgy realised, something wasn't right, though he didn't know what. Anxiously, he darted off.

Whilst he was away, William, aged six, looked after their youngest brother, Gilbert, who was only four. It was lucky that it was the weekend, otherwise the two older boys would have been at school, leaving just their little brother at home.

Their father was a busy builder and decorator, with his own business, who rarely took any time off except Sundays. Consequently, Mr George Arthur Prideaux Huntingford was not best pleased when his oldest son arrived with the message. He scowled at the boy.

'Look here, my lad, I can't just leave, you know. This lady's house still needs a lot of work, and I gave her my word that we'd finish it this week. It's my reputation on the line. A promise is a promise.'

Young Georgy begged him again, telling him what the midwife had said.

'Please Dad. She said it's real serious and that you're to come at once.'

Reluctantly his father put down his tools, and after a brief conversation with his employees, he packed up and followed Georgy home to their small semi-detached villa. Long Ditton was a pleasant rural village situated near the river Thames, though divided in two by the railway line. The hedges and fields around the area gave it a countryside feel, quite different to nearby Surbiton which was fast developing into a prosperous urban town.

Today there was a cold March wind whipping around them as they hurried along, but they scarcely noticed. The two of them shared the same dark Huntingford hair and eyes, with Georgy's hair as black as coal, but it seemed as if this family trait had become diluted as time went on, for William had brown hair and Gilbert's hair was like golden sand.

Unlike their fresh young complexions, their father's face was weather beaten and tanned by frequent exposure to the open air. Now, in spite of his protests, it was lined with worry.

Arriving home, Georgy heard the unmistakable screams of his mother piercing the air. His father turned quite pale at the sound and hurried into the bedroom. Georgy was then firmly shut out with the younger boys, and it seemed like the end of the world was coming. Gilbert, only four years old, was crying, not able to understand any of it. William too, looked scared. They were relieved to see their older brother who gave them both a hug and tried to calm them down. This was a hard job, as he was close to tears himself, but, being a practical and resourceful boy, he made some generous helpings of bread and jam which temporarily eased the situation.

After a short time however, their father reappeared, having also been turned away from the delivery room by the midwife.

'This is no place for a man,' Mrs Triggs declared. 'Give your wife a kiss, then leave, Mr Huntingford. This is women's work. I'll call you when it's over.'

The boys were relieved to see him and ran towards him, but he recoiled as if not knowing what to do. They were strangers to each other, if truth be told. Their father worked long hours and barely saw them. By the time he came home at night they were often in bed. To them he was a stern-faced figure who occasionally passed through their lives. To him, they were a responsibility to be shouldered. It's not to say that he didn't love them, but he scarcely knew them. They were his offspring, his family, but not his friends. He patted them gingerly on the head now and told them gruffly not to worry.

'Your mum's been through all this before. She'll be fine. Now get yourselves outside to play.'

Confused and scared they obeyed, though they had little inclination for fun and games. Their father was left to pace up and down, outside the bedroom door, nervously waiting for news.

It was more than three anxious hours later that they all heard the feeble cry of a newborn. Mr Huntingford started up, a mixture of joy and fear on his face. He went to the door but was met by the midwife.

'Mr Huntingford, your wife has given birth to a baby girl, but she is very small. Not only that but I have to inform you that there is more to come!'

'More? What do you mean?'

'Another baby, or maybe even two.'

'Twins! Surely not. We've never had that in the family before. Let me see my wife.'

'Please be patient, sir. I must ask you to wait, I'm afraid.'

Another hour went by and another infant cry, followed swiftly by a third. Triplets! None of them knew what to think any more.

At last Mrs Triggs came out and beckoned to their father. His wife lay there exhausted beyond belief, and in the cot beside her, three tiny babies.

'They're all girls, sir. Congratulations.'

'But, but…' he stammered in disbelief, 'what do I do now? How can we feed three?'

'Well, if they all survive, sir, you can always apply for the Kings Bounty.'

'I don't know what you mean,' he said.

The midwife then explained that when triplets were born, there was an amount payable from the crown to assist the parents.

'Our dear late queen set it up and His Majesty has kindly agreed to continue it, but you only get it if they all live, I'm afraid. I can help you apply for it.'

Looking at their tiny bodies, so frail and delicate, Mr Huntingford felt a rush of love and pity. Poor little mites. Would they even last the day?

His wife stirred slightly. 'My babies. Let me hold them.'

Her husband moved close taking two of the little ones with him, the midwife taking the third.

'Girls,' breathed Mrs Huntingford. 'I've always wanted girls. We will call them Ethel, Gladys and er….'

'Ellen,' finished her husband. 'We must have one named after you, my love.'

In a rare display of affection, he stroked his wife's brow, damp with sweat, and kissed her gently.

'You have done so well. You must rest now and get strong again.'

Ellen's blue eyes closed again, so they quietly returned the infants to their cot.

Mrs Triggs took their father aside.

'Your wife has been through a lot and has bled badly. She's very ill and needs complete rest. Have you got anyone who can come in and lend a hand? I can get you a wet nurse for the new arrivals, but you will need some help with your sons and around the house.'

Mr Huntingford thought for a moment.

'Well,' he said, 'my brother Dick and his wife live nearby but they've just lost one of their own children so I don't think it's a good idea to ask them, and Ellen's mother hasn't been very well recently, but my wife's sister-in-law might be able to help. I'll find out. They live north of the river, in Tottenham, but it doesn't take that long to get here, really.'

The midwife nodded. 'Good.' She looked serious. 'I have to warn you, Mr Huntingford, that the babies are underweight and very weak. They might not make it, I'm afraid.' She sighed. 'Life can be very hard at times.'

Their father gazed at them, now swaddled in warm blankets but pale and barely moving. Tears came into his eyes, but he blinked them away. Abruptly he left the room.

Outside he was met by a congregation of his sons, all enthusiastic to know about the new additions to the family.

'Dad, Dad, how is the baby? Is it a boy or a girl?' cried William eagerly.

'Is Mum all right?' asked Georgy.

'I want Mummy!' wailed little Gilbert.

'Boys, boys, please!' he said, trying to calm them. He could see that they needed to know what was going on. 'Let's sit down and have a chat.'

It was on rare occasions that he talked to them like this, but now he sat down on a low stool, facing them. The boys squatted on the floor by his feet, gazing up at him.

'Is it a boy or a girl?' asked William again.

Georgy felt worried seeing his father's face. 'How's Mum?'

'Look lads, your mother has given birth to three little girls.'

There were oohs and aahs of delight, but George Huntingford held up his hand.

'Yes, it would be wonderful but three babies at once is very hard on both the mother and the babies. Your poor mother is exhausted, and we need to look after her. As for the babies, well, we don't know if, if….' his voice trailed off …. 'if they will all survive. They're very small and fragile, after all they've had to share your mother's tummy, and they haven't had much room to grow.'

'Will they die?' asked William bluntly.

'They might,' his father admitted.

'Will Mum get better?' asked Georgy.

'She should do, I hope, with lots of rest and care.'

'I want to see them!' declared young Gilbert.

'Yes, me too,' said William.

It was obvious that their father wasn't going to be able to persuade them otherwise, so he led them into the bedroom with strict instructions to be very quiet. Georgy, who had seen both William and Gilbert at their births was shocked by how tiny and delicate they were. The babies' skin was translucent, with blue veins showing just below the surface. Somehow, they looked unfinished, incomplete. He reached out one hand carefully and felt the minute fingers of the little girl nearest to him. They curled gently as he touched them, and he felt in awe. What precious bundles and yet how fragile.

Ellen, their mother, lay in a deep slumber, her face ashen and her light brown hair soaked with sweat. Georgy felt quite frightened at the sight. She'd never looked like that before.

'Come along now,' Mrs Triggs said, 'that's enough visiting for the time being. Be off with you!'

After they had left, the midwife busied herself with going into the street and collaring several teenage boys to run urgent messages for her. One was despatched to the doctor, one to the woman down the road who could be used as a wet nurse, and one to the parson.

'Just in case,' she explained to Mr Huntingford. 'They should be baptised, you know.'

A message was also sent to their Aunt Mary to come and help. In the meantime, they waited.

The first person to arrive was the wet nurse, Mrs Richards, a kindly lady from down the street who had not long given birth to her fifth child. She promptly attempted to suckle the newborn infants.

The next to arrive was Doctor Gordon who took one look at Ellen and said she really should go to hospital.

'She is badly in need of a blood transfusion and medicines,' he told them. Mr Huntingford turned pale at the thought.

'No, it's so dangerous. I won't let you do it. It's too risky. People die, I've heard.'

The doctor tried to explain.

'It used to be very risky, it's true, but now that they know more about the different types of blood it is much safer. If she doesn't get the blood she needs, your wife will almost certainly die, I'm afraid. We must try it.'

Reluctantly George Huntingford agreed and let the doctor arrange transport. Only a few years earlier, George and Ellen had watched in amusement as the new horse drawn ambulance service had started in London and then slowly spread out to their area.

'Fancy that!' Ellen had laughed. 'It'll never catch on.'

Now the family were only too grateful for it, despite its slow speed and the ability to take just a single patient. Today it was invaluable to them.

Doctor Gordon sighed as he looked at the babies. Mrs Richards was struggling to get any of them to feed. It seemed that they just didn't have the strength. Even a bottle was barely noticed.

'I'm sorry,' she told them. 'I'm trying everything I can think of.'

Half an hour later their worst fears were realised when first one, then another faltered and failed. The tiny flutter of their hearts ceased to beat any more, regardless of everyone's best efforts. The third baby lingered on for a short while and they were hopeful she might pull through, but it was not to be. Within two hours of their birth the little ones had perished, their brief lives but a smudge of smoke on the horizon, a glimmer of light on the sea, a sad case of what might have been, but never was.

The parson arrived an hour later, too late to save their immortal souls, but he blessed their tiny bodies and arranged an appointment with their father to discuss the funeral. Ellen was taken to hospital, still unconscious, not knowing her infants' sad demise, and the rest of the family were left to mourn. The three boys were forlorn and quiet, their father sunk in silent gloom.

Night came on and the rain started to fall. It went on and on. Georgy lay in his bed next to his brother William, wondering if he would ever see his mother again. His tears matched the deluge outside, and a storm raged in his young heart. If she died, what would become of them? Would Father send them to an orphanage – a place only spoken of in hushed tones of dread? He didn't know what they were like, but he knew he didn't want to go there. He wanted his mum, and with that he cried all over again.

Chapter 2

All was not lost, however, for the next day their Aunty Mary arrived. She bustled in like a galleon in full sail, her two young children trailing in her wake. Ellen, known as Nellie, was a bright and bubbly five-year-old, with fair hair in pig tails and a mischievous grin. Her younger brother Billy, only three, merely smiled angelically like a fat faced cherub. A carter followed them in, carrying their baggage.

'Excuse me, Mrs Goddard, ma'am, where do you want these put?'

Having indicated a place and paid the man, Aunty Mary turned to give them all a big hug. Georgy had met them before and liked them, so he was happy to be enveloped in his kindly aunt's embrace, and despite his mum's absence he felt cheered. Surely everything would be all right now. Gilbert on the other hand, came over all shy suddenly and hid behind the nearest chair. William dragged him out and thrust him at Mary.

'Here's Gilbert,' he told her. 'He needs some breakfast!'

Aunty Mary laughed and the sound felt like sunshine after the rain.

'I expect you all do, my young gentlemen. Let's get you all sorted out then.'

Father had tried his best to get them up and breakfasted, in a vain attempt to get them to church on time but he had no idea where anything was, or what any of them liked to eat. 'Chaos' was putting it mildly! The morning church service would have to go on without them for once. Secretly Georgy was quite pleased about that. All those boring hymns and the vicar's slow drawl nearly sent him to sleep.

Now Aunty Mary set about putting things right. After a decent (though late) breakfast the two older boys helped her tackle the washing up and usual chores, such as fetching the coal and laying the fires. At the same time, Nellie made the beds, helped and somewhat hindered by the youngest two. George Huntingford was amazed at how easily everything fell into place. After expressing his thanks over and over, Mary finally packed him off to the hospital to visit Ellen.

'Find out how she is and bring back all the news,' she ordered.

Then she organised games for all the children to take part in. Nellie ran, jumped and threw balls as well as any of the boys, and they all played happily for the afternoon, with little Billy watching from the sidelines. Finally, they collapsed in a heap and chatted.

'Where's your dad and brother Charlie this time?' asked Georgy. He was a naturally curious lad, always asking questions.

'They've both got to work in the morning,' Nellie explained, 'so as we're staying for a few days Mum told them they'll have to look after themselves. She said it's about time they did.'

'She never! You're a liar, Nellie Goddard,' exclaimed William. 'She wouldn't have said that!'

'She did, too!' Nellie retorted. 'I heard her.'

'What did they say?' Georgy said. 'Our dad would have been very annoyed.'

'I don't think they minded too much,' replied Nellie. 'Dad's a softy, really. Anyway, he's not far away from Granny and Grandpa if he really needs any help.'

'Why is your brother so much older than you?' asked William in his usual direct manner. (Charlie was eighteen now and working as a carpenter).

'He's Dad's son from his first marriage,' she said. 'His wife died and then he married Mum.'

This made Georgy remember their own mum in hospital. For a few brief moments of fun and games, he had almost forgotten.

'I hope *our* mum doesn't die,' he said, his voice trembling at the thought of it.

Tears came into little Gilbert's eyes. 'When will Mummy be back?' he asked.

'She'll be home soon,' William said and put an arm around him, comfortingly. 'Don't worry.'

Georgy hoped in his heart that his brother was right, and that their emotional, highly strung but loving mother would be with them again very soon.

Nellie saw his face, leaned forwards and gave him a quick hug. 'It'll be all right,' she told him. 'Now come on, let's play another game.'

Georgy was thankful for her kindness and shrugged off his worries as best he could. 'I must stay strong', he thought to himself, 'for the sake of the others.'

Father came home late, after the youngest children had gone to bed. There had been much excitable 'to-ing and fro-ing' about where everyone was going to sleep, and this had helped distract them for a while. Now with Billy and Gilbert sound asleep, Georgy, William and Nellie waited quietly for the news. They were all in their night clothes, well wrapped up in a pile of blankets, having undressed by the fire as usual. The bedrooms were never heated because it cost such a lot, so were too chilly to do anything in, other than leap into bed as fast as possible.

Mr Huntingford's face was solemn when he returned.

'Dad, Dad, how is she?' the boys clamoured.

Their father shook his head sadly. 'Not good boys, I'm afraid. She has a fever – a high temperature that is – from all the struggle of giving birth.'

'And the transfusion?' enquired their aunt quietly. 'How did that go?'

'It helped, I believe,' he replied. 'Thank goodness. Now she just has to fight this infection, but, oh Mary, I don't know if she's strong enough.'

'You must be strong, brother George, for her sake and for the boys,' she told him. 'The Lord will provide; I am sure. We must all pray for her recovery.'

Young Georgy had never been much of a one for praying, but now they all bowed their heads together as a family and sent up whatever silent pleas they could to the Almighty.

'Dear Father in heaven,' prayed Georgy, 'if you can save our mother, I promise I'll be very good every day, and I'll even try not to get cross with William when he's being annoying. Thank you. Amen.'

What prayers the others sent up were not known but there was scarcely a dry eye in the house that evening.

It seemed that the heavenly powers were turning a deaf ear, however, as three days went by, and little changed in poor Ellen's condition. Aunty Mary did her best to get Georgy, William and Nellie to school as normal, despite William's tantrums and Georgy's tears. Nellie had to walk further than normal whilst they were away from home, but she didn't complain. Meanwhile Mary kept house and looked after young Billy and Gilbert.

On Monday, Georgy fidgeted at his school desk, trying not to break down in front of his class of fifty boys. He knew he'd only be called a 'sissy' if he did. The other pupils wouldn't give a second thought as to *why* he might be upset. They were all brought up not to show too many feelings. It wasn't the done thing.

The teacher, a stern-faced Mr Jenkins, seemed to know that Georgy wasn't concentrating today. The man seemed determined to show him up in front of the class.

'Master Huntingford – would you tell us all how to do the arithmetic sum I just set you, please. You seem to be *so* interested in it!'

Mr Jenkin's sarcasm stung him and brought his stifled tears to the surface. A sob broke through in spite of all Georgy's efforts to stop it. His face turned crimson with shame.

'Boy! Stand in the corner now!' the teacher ordered, 'and you will stay there at breaktime as well. Now class, can someone tell this imbecile how to do this?'

A multitude of hands went up, eager to please the master. None of them wanted the same kind of treatment, or worse. Georgy's tears now poured down his cheeks as he stood facing the wall, but at least, he thought, no-one could see.

Breaktime came and everyone else went out to play. Georgy stood there alone until the end of it, when Mr

Jenkins returned to the classroom just before the children.

'Well, boy - what have you got to say for yourself?'

Georgy tried to apologise.

'I'm sorry, sir,' he mumbled. 'It's just that my mum is in the hospital, and they think she might die...' His voice broke and the sobs returned, huge choking gasps of distress.

Mr Jenkins swallowed hard, looking uncomfortable.

'Oh lad, I'm sorry to hear that. Well look, run and wash your face, then come back and sit down. Let's say no more about it.'

Georgy did as he was told, grateful to escape for a short while. When lessons resumed, Mr Jenkins no longer hounded him, but made a point of ignoring him completely, much to Georgy's relief.

At the end of the day just as he left, Mr Jenkins came up to him.

'Give my best to your family,' the teacher said gruffly.

'Yes sir, thank you sir,' muttered Georgy and he sped off to find William in the younger class. His brother had had an equally trying day, and after throwing one of his tantrums had ended up with the usual punishment, a caning. It was two very subdued boys who made their way home that afternoon.

Monday, Tuesday, Wednesday went by and each night Father went to the hospital after work and came home looking drawn and haggard. There was no change. The children begged to be able to go and visit but their father refused.

'There's no point at the moment, boys,' he told them. 'She won't know you're there.'

One evening Georgy was in bed, not able to sleep when he overheard his father and aunt discussing matters.

'It's so hard, every day,' Father said, 'seeing her like that. Not only that but the fees are mounting up.'

'Surely you have a subscription though?' said Aunty Mary. This was how most working families paid for their medical costs these days.

'Yes,' replied her brother-in-law, 'but the doctors are grumbling that it will barely cover it all. I wouldn't mind if she was getting better, really, I wouldn't. It would be worth every penny. Then there's the shilling and sixpence to find for the midwife, plus the funeral costs. It's all too much, Mary. I can't take it any more!'

Georgy heard a sound like a sob, but he couldn't believe it. His father wouldn't cry. He just knew he wouldn't. The voices grew quieter, and he lost the thread of their conversation. Eventually he dropped off into an uneasy sleep, where dreams of hospitals and crying babies tormented him.

Friday evening came and Mr Huntingford returned wearily to the hospital for yet another bedside vigil. Every night he sat there, hoping for a miracle. Over and over in his head he replayed the scenes of their love and life together. He knew he would be nothing without her. Yes, she could be difficult at times, over emotional and demanding, but she had opened up something in him that no-one else ever had. To others he was a closed book; stern, cold, dutiful, repressed – but she had reached inside his very soul and lit a flame that could never be quenched. It seemed to him that he had always loved her, and he knew that he always would.

Tonight, there was better news at last. A doctor approached him as he entered the ward.

'Mr Huntingford, can I have a word please?'

George felt himself go cold with fear.

'Please sir, do not worry yourself unduly. I have encouraging news.'

He let out a sigh of relief. 'Really?'

'Yes sir, your wife has turned the corner I'm pleased to say. The fever has nearly gone, and we think she will recover.'

George's fear turned to joy.

'Oh, that's wonderful news. Thank you!'

'She may regain consciousness soon, possibly tonight, so if you can stay by her that would help. I'm sure it would do her a power of good to see you when she wakes.'

'I'd be happy to,' he replied.

'There's just one thing,' added the doctor, 'she mustn't be distressed by anything at the moment. It wouldn't be good for her.'

'No, no, of course not.'

'So that means that she should not be told that the babies have died. It would be too much for her at present.'

George felt stunned. What was he to do? His wife would be bound to ask. What could he say? He was silent, thinking it all through.

'But doctor, how, how….?' he stuttered finally.

'Mr Huntingford, you must keep it from her for a day or two. It is best for her sake. Change the subject if she asks. Try to focus only on her.'

'But our children will want to see her, and they're bound to tell her.'

'Keep them away for a couple of days until she's stronger,' advised the doctor, 'then break it to her gently beforehand.'

3am and George Huntingford had finally dozed off at his wife's bedside, after many hours of watching and waiting. He was roused by a murmur from Ellen, barely more than a whisper, which brought him round very quickly.

'George – are you there? What's happened? Where am I?' Her voice was croaky and fragile.

'My darling!' he said clasping her hand. 'I was so worried. Just rest now. Everything will be all right.'

He bent and kissed her cheek gently.

'You're in hospital my love. You were very ill but you're getting better now.'

'George, take me home. My babies need me.'

'You just need to rest and get well,' her husband told her. 'Please don't worry. Now sleep.'

His wife closed her eyes and drifted away again, but the colour was coming back to her face and her breathing was steady.

'I'll visit again soon,' promised George and then he got up and wearily made his way home. After telling his anxious sister-in-law the good news, he collapsed into bed. The next couple of weeks would see the dreaded funeral of the ill-fated little ones, which he must somehow find the strength to face, but at least now, he had some hope.

Chapter 3

At breakfast the next day there was much rejoicing and cheers from the whole family at the good news.

'When can we go and visit Mum?' asked Georgy.

'Can we go today?' piped up Gilbert.

'Yes, please Dad, can we?' pleaded William.

'Now look lads,' their father told them, 'You know what is happening today. Your Aunt Mary is going to take you all out for the day, and you'll have a fine time down by the river. Maybe tomorrow.'

Georgy, being the oldest, thought he guessed why.

'Is it about the babies, Dad?'

'Well, yes,' admitted Father. 'I need to see the vicar about the funeral.'

Nellie's face clouded with tears. 'It's so sad,' she whimpered. 'Poor little things.'

Her tears soon spread to the two youngest, Gilbert and Billy, who joined in. They weren't totally sure why, but it seemed like a good idea at the time.

Aunt Mary managed to stop all the emotional scenes however by briskly rounding them up and getting them sorted out for the day ahead.

'Now Nellie, stop that. Go and make some sandwiches in the kitchen. William, you can go to the shop for some lemonade. Georgy – please get Gilbert cleaned up ready to go out. Billy, come with me. Your face needs a wash.'

In no time at all she'd organised them and they were soon on their way, cheerfully. All of them were looking forward to their outing, now that they had heard the good news about Ellen. Georgy's spirits had lifted, and he happily led the way towards the Thames. Although it was only the middle of March the cold wind had dropped, and the early spring sunshine was doing its best to warm them. A few flowers peeped out here and there, hinting at better days to come. All along the banks of the river, primroses raised their faces gaily and welcomed the light. Elegant ladies strolled with their parasols on display, though they still had woollen shawls wrapped around their shoulders.

The five children ran freely along the path, though Mary kept a watchful eye on the youngest to make sure they were safe. Later they stopped for a picnic, watching small pleasure boats go by as they ate. It was a lovely day, and Georgy felt very glad that his aunt and cousins had come to stay. Remembering the reason for their visit, he briefly felt guilty, but with the innocence of youth, he dismissed this and just enjoyed the moment.

After lunch the children attempted to sail their flimsy wooden toy boats down a little stream that flowed briskly next to the river. It was a small tributary rushing and leaping as it went to join the main body of water. All was going well until Nellie's boat got caught in a sudden current and went dashing off downstream towards the Thames. They dived after it along the bank, but too late – it was swept out into the river!

'Oh no!' cried Nellie in great distress. 'My boat!'

'I'll get it!' shouted William. 'I can swim.' Impulsively he started to take off his jacket, but Mary stopped him.

'No William. It's too dangerous. There are nasty currents there. No!'

They ran beside it, keeping pace with the disobedient boat. Nellie's face was covered with tears. Georgy hated to see anyone cry and was keen to help his cousin. Being a practical boy, he cast around quickly in the nearby bushes for something – anything – he could use to retrieve it. After a moment or two he found a long stick with a fork in it which he hoped he might just be able to hook around the toy. It wasn't as easy as it looked, as the water was moving swiftly, and the boat (though not far out) was bobbing along at a fair lick. Georgy reached out, splashing the stick in the water, gradually drawing the item nearer. Eventually he managed to hook it and bring it close enough to grab. Nellie was over the moon and flung herself at Georgy, planting a big kiss on his cheek and declaring him to be her hero.

'Ugh!' said Georgy, wiping his face with his sleeve. 'Girls! Why do they always have to be so soppy?'

But Nellie's eyes were shining with admiration for him, and she took no notice of his rebuke. Secretly Georgy was pleased. He was fond of his younger cousin, her giggles and her sense of fun, and didn't like to see her upset.

With a sigh of relief, Aunt Mary took them all away from the river to a nearby stall to find some ices.

'Five penny licks, please,' she ordered, 'oh and a good strong cup of tea!'

Georgy loved the little glass cones that the ice-creams came in, and he was always reluctant to hand them back to the vendor, but it had to be done. After enjoying their refreshments, they started for home, and Mary was able to relax at last. What a big responsibility five children were!

Meantime, her brother-in-law was having his own problems. His mid-morning appointment with the vicar had not gone well. The Reverend Hughes was a kindly man but fixed on sticking to protocol. Oxford educated and twice married; he had been at Long Ditton a long time. He knew the Huntingfords well, as he had baptised all three sons and was aware that they were a respectable, hard-working family. They could usually be relied upon to attend his sermon on Sundays, and though he had a feeling that the boys were none too keen, Rev Hughes could tell that Ellen, in particular, was quite devout. Now he was having to give Mr Huntingford some unpleasant information.

'It's like this, sir; because the babies were not baptised then they can't be buried in the churchyard, I'm sorry to say.'

George stared at him in disbelief.

'Not baptised! But that's not their fault. You didn't get there in time!'

The vicar looked embarrassed.

'Well, yes,' he admitted. 'That is most unfortunate, but those are the rules, I'm afraid.'

'But why?' exploded George. 'What have these little ones done? Nothing! They have never sinned. Why should they be shunned?'

The Reverend tried to explain. 'The thing is that unbaptised individuals cannot go to Heaven, or even to Hell. Their souls are in limbo and therefore cannot be counted by the Lord, or by the church.'

‘That’s rubbish!’ declared George angrily, ‘and so unfair. They’ve done nothing to deserve this treatment. Well, I will not be bringing my family to your church again if that’s the case.’ He stood up to leave.

‘Now please don’t be hasty, Mr Huntingford,’ Reverend Hughes pleaded. ‘Sit down. Let’s see what we can work out. It does seem, as you say, that it’s not their fault, and that it is unreasonable to punish them.’ He paused. ‘What I could offer would be for them to be buried on the edge of the churchyard, by the north wall.’

‘Where the suicides and ‘unfortunates’ go?’ asked George in a hostile tone. ‘I don’t think my wife would like that at all.’

‘I understand,’ said Reverend Hughes, ‘but regrettably, it’s all I can do. They would all be buried together in one coffin.’

George considered for a few minutes.

‘I suppose if that’s the only option, we’ll have to take you up on it. Will there be a ceremony?’

The vicar shuffled uncomfortably in his seat.

‘Er, yes, a short one. Unfortunately, there won’t be a marker, or a headstone allowed either. It’s against church policy, you see.’

George sighed but couldn’t see a way around it. Reluctantly he agreed a date for the following week and then left, feeling absolutely disgusted about the whole affair. What a way to treat such innocent babies. There was something quite wrong, somewhere, he thought.

During a brief stop at home for a bite of lunch, George Huntingford wondered what he should do next. He was desperate to see his wife and to know how she was progressing but the burden of the secret that he bore, was a heavy weight. If she asked, he knew he wouldn't be able to hide it any more. He dreaded her reaction, knowing how much she had wanted a baby girl. She would be devastated.

The other thing he needed to do was to visit his brother and sister-in-law, who were mourning their own loss at present, having lost their little girl, Irene, only a couple of weeks ago. Her funeral was arranged for the following Monday, and George needed to tell them about their own unhappy ceremony which was to take place on Friday. He doubted that they would want to attend, but they should at least be given the option. In the end, he decided that, as the hospital was on the way to his brother's, then he should go there first. Luckily, both were in Surbiton and therefore only a half hour walk. He headed to the hospital with a heavy heart.

He was delighted to find his wife sitting up in bed, looking much improved. He greeted her with a peck on the cheek, so unlike the demonstrations of affection he had displayed whilst she was ill. Ellen expected nothing more, however, and was quite content.

'How are you, my dear,' George asked, smiling. 'It's lovely to see you looking so much better.'

'I feel fine,' replied Ellen, 'but for some reason they won't let me see my babies. Surely, they are here in the hospital as well, aren't they? Or are they at home? Did you get a wet-nurse for them?'

He felt himself go hot under the collar.

'We did have a wet-nurse, yes,' he muttered, looking down at his hands.

'Well,' said Ellen, 'you don't need one now. I can feed them. Let me see them, please.' Her voice was pleading.

George took a deep breath. As gently as he could he said: 'I'm sorry, my love. They didn't make it.'

There was an ominous silence whilst his wife digested the news.

'What? I don't know what you mean. Where are they? I want them!' Her voice rose in pitch.

Her husband looked her directly in the face and took one hand in his.

'I'm sorry to tell you that they didn't survive, my dear. We did everything we could.'

'No!' Ellen wailed. 'No! It can't be true! What – all of them? Surely one must have survived. Why didn't you tell me before?'

She was beginning to sound hysterical.

'Calm yourself, my love, please. It's not good for you to get upset. Yes, I'm afraid all three died. They only lived a couple of hours. They were so tiny and very weak.'

Ellen started to sob wildly, exclaiming: 'No, no, it can't be true. No.' Then she started to try and get out of bed. 'I want my babies. Where are they?'

'Nurse!' called George, struggling to restrain and calm her. 'Please help me. My wife is very distressed.'

A sedative was swiftly administered, and his wife lapsed into an unhappy slumber. George then left the hospital feeling broken and exhausted. He doubted that the worst was over, but at least the dreadful secret was out at last.

His next visit was equally sad. Sister-in-law Minnie opened the door of their small two-up two-down cottage to him looking pale and fragile. Her fair hair hung down limply instead of being delicately arranged as usual. Her eyes were red from crying.

‘George, dear brother, how are you and how is poor Ellen? She must be feeling the same as me, devastated by so much loss. Why is life so unfair?’

George had no answer but patted her hand sympathetically. His older brother Dick (Robert Richard Prideaux Huntingford to give him his full name), came up to greet him and offer his own condolences. They exchanged the mournful details of funeral arrangements and commiserated with each other. Then Dick took George off into the small garden of their terraced house to talk privately.

‘Minnie is broken hearted,’ he told him. ‘Irene was such a lovely little girl and was doing really well, then infant diarrhoea just swept her away. Ralph is so unfeeling as well; he doesn’t seem to care one way or the other.’

Ralph was Dick and Minnie’s eight-year-old son, who was turning out to be moody and difficult at times.

‘Maybe he is just hiding it well,’ suggested George.

‘I wouldn’t bet on that,’ grunted Dick. ‘How is Ellen?’

‘Her health is improving, but I’ve just had to tell her the news about the babies, and she didn’t take it well. You know how she can get, sometimes.’

Dick had seen Ellen’s tendency to hysteria at close quarters on various occasions, so he well understood. He patted his brother on the shoulder in a manly attempt at consolation.

‘She’ll get over it, old chap. Don’t worry.’

George sighed. ‘I hope so. These things are so upsetting, and she is very fragile.’

‘Have the boys been to see her yet?’

‘No, not yet. I’ve been putting it off.’

‘Well, I would take them in if I were you. It will do her good to see them and it’ll help take the pressure off you. And don't worry; I'll be along on Friday to support you, though I doubt whether Minnie will be up to it, what with Irene's funeral on Monday.'

George thanked him and promised to return the favour. Then, weary beyond belief, he made his way slowly home.

Chapter 4

Georgy sat listlessly on the chair in the hospital corridor, swinging his legs back and forth for want of something to do. He was bored. His two younger brothers were with him, equally dejected. They'd all been delighted the night before when their father had told them he would take them to visit their mum the next day. When they arrived, however, he asked them to wait there.

'I just need to have a chat to your mum first. Then I'll come and get you.'

But twenty minutes had gone by, and they were still waiting. William was engrossed in his new book, the Just So Stories, and Gilbert played quietly with his wooden spinning top, but Georgy couldn't find anything to distract him. He was an avid reader and was currently enjoying a fabulous story of King Arthur and his knights, but he just couldn't settle to it. What were they doing? Why was it taking so long? Surely their mum wanted to see them.

Another ten minutes passed, and Georgy, though normally a patient boy, had had enough. Putting his book aside, he decided he would find out what was going on. In a commanding tone he ordered his siblings to stay where they were – 'no matter what!' and then headed stealthily down the corridor to the ward.

As he got nearer, he could hear his parents talking – no - arguing! He overheard bits and pieces.

'Why didn't you tell me? .... How dare the vicar be like that? … There's no way I'm staying here!'

Georgy quietly crept closer until he could peer round the corner and see his mum at last. For a few moments he hesitated, unwilling to disturb the emotional scene, but then his desperation to see her brought him just a bit too far out into the open, and his mother noticed him.

'Georgy!' Ellen exclaimed and held out her arms towards him. He ran to her and was enfolded in a warm embrace.

'Mum, Mum!' was all he could manage at first, but then he remembered his brothers still waiting.

'I'll get William and Gilbert,' he said and rushed off to fetch them before he could be stopped.

It was a joyous reunion for them all. They clambered on her bed with cries of delight and were hugged and kissed until they could hardly breathe.

'Well,' said their father grinning, 'it's good to have all the family together again.'

Ellen smiled through tears of joy.

'My boys,' she murmured, 'my dear boys. You've made me feel so much better.'

It was three days later when the children came home from school to find their mum waiting at the front door to welcome them. Ellen still looked pale and fragile but with Aunt Mary's help she had made dinner for them all. What a celebration they had! Five children and three adults all happy to be together. Their father had fetched home a joint of best beef, Aunt Mary picked vegetables from the garden, and a slap-up meal was produced. They even had it in the dining room, instead of around the kitchen table as usual. Proof, if any were needed, that it was a very special occasion indeed. Georgy couldn't remember ever having had a finer dinner, though it was the company that made it.

The doctors had recommended that Ellen take it easy for a few more days, so Mary, Nellie and Billy would be staying until the weekend. Georgy realised that he would be sorry to see them go. They had all become such good friends.

Poor little Irene's funeral had passed by unnoticed by the children, as was only right, but their father and Aunt Mary had taken time out to be there. It was a sad event but at least she had a proper burial in a well maintained and visible part of the cemetery, unlike the pitiful funeral for the triplets which was due on Friday. Dick and his wife were both there, though Minnie leaned heavily on her husband's arm and looked quite ill. George hoped that his own wife would be strong enough to cope with their mournful duty. She was insistent that she wanted to attend, and there was no arguing otherwise.

Friday morning came and the children were all packed off to school, blithely unaware of what the adults had to face that day. Georgy wondered briefly why his father hadn't gone to work yet, but he soon forgot about it. Ellen was still frail, but she dressed solemnly in her best black jacket and skirt and took her husband's arm to go to the churchyard.

'Ellen, my dear,' he tried in a last-ditch attempt to persuade her, 'surely it would be best if you stayed home. You're still not strong yet.'

His wife glared at him. 'George,' she said in a voice like ice, 'no-one would be able to stop me paying my last respects to my dear children, so you needn't think you can.'

George fell silent, knowing how strong-willed his wife could be. It was going to be an upsetting enough day as it was, without making it worse.

Slowly they made their way to the north side of the cemetery, where they were to meet Reverend Hughes. Aunt Mary accompanied them, and they were shortly joined by brother Dick and Ellen's mother Martha; a sensible, pragmatic woman. She had travelled all the way over from their home in Edmonton, the other side of London. George was grateful for her making the effort and hoped that this would help her daughter to stay calm.

They gathered around the pathetic little hole in the ground and waited. It was gloomy and cold there. Ten minutes went by. Eventually the vicar arrived, hurrying along and looking flustered.

'My dear folks, I'm sorry I'm late. The business of the day, you know. It never stops.'

He smiled apologetically and then before they had a chance to say a word, he went straight into the service.

'Dearly beloved, we are gathered here today to mourn the loss of these three babies – er' (and here he consulted a piece of paper in his hand) 'Ellen, Gladys and er… Emma.'

Their anguished mother shrieked at him: 'Ethel! Her name is Ethel!'

'Yes, yes, of course, that's what I meant. Apologies.'

The Reverend continued the ceremony hastily, obviously in a rush to be elsewhere. The Lord's Prayer was conducted at a brisk pace; the bearers lowered the coffin and that was that. Ellen was becoming hysterical, partly from anger and partly sorrow.

As the vicar started to bid his farewells she cried at him: 'You don't care, do you? Tiny innocent little babies – but because they're not baptised you don't want to know! Not part of your flock, are they?'

'Now, now, Mrs Huntingford, it's not like that at all,' the vicar mumbled. 'Anyway, I must be going as I have another service shortly.'

As he left rapidly, Ellen continued to shout abuse at his retreating form. Her husband tried to pacify her.

'Now come on dear, you'll make yourself ill again.'

'Yes', added her mother, 'this won't do any good you know. Pull yourself together.'

Aunt Mary simply put her arms around Ellen and hugged her tight, whilst the tears flowed. Meanwhile the two men looked embarrassed.

'Please dear, everyone's looking,' said George. 'Let's go home.'

But Ellen threw herself down on the ground beside the grave and sobbed. Grief had overcome her reason.

They half carried, half dragged her out of the cemetery back to their house, where she retired to bed, faint, dizzy and despairing.

As always with her outbursts, it passed eventually, and she had composed herself by the time the children came home from school. Despite this, Georgy noticed that his mother was very pale, and her eyes were red rimmed.

'Are you feeling all right, Mum?' he asked, concerned.

'Yes, of course, my dear,' she replied, trying to smile. 'Just a bit tired, that's all. Now what shall we do on Saturday? Shall we go out somewhere?'

'Can we go to the shops, Mum?' asked William enthusiastically. 'I want to buy some sweets.'

'Yes, please,' added Gilbert.

'Very well,' said Ellen. 'We'll all go into Surbiton tomorrow. Your Aunty and your cousins will be going home on Sunday, so maybe we can treat them to a nice lunch out, to say thank you for their help.'

Georgy's face fell.

'Can't they stay longer?' he pleaded. 'Please!'

'Now be sensible, Georgy dear. They need to get back to their own home,' his mother explained. 'Uncle Will and brother Charlie will be missing them. Anyway, Grandma Goddard will be visiting us next week as well, so that's something to look forward to.'

Georgy sighed. He was a bit in awe of his gran. Martha Goddard was a tough, no-nonsense woman with a heart of gold, but she seemed very fierce to him. He couldn't remember his other grandma as she had died when he was very small, but he had a vague recollection of Grandpa Huntingford who came to live with them for a couple of years. He seemed to be a gentle but distant old man, somewhat lost in a world of his own. Georgy didn't know what had happened to him. He just disappeared one day. He supposed he must have died, but nothing was said.

In fact, Grandpa Huntingford bequeathed his estate to be divided equally between his two daughters-in-law who had looked after him, when his wife Jessie passed away. His sons had felt snubbed at the time, but in reality, it avoided Dick having to use it to discharge the debts from his previous bankruptcy, and they had all benefitted. Their own family had been able to move to a better house, with one of the new-fangled indoor toilets and a proper garden. It was built of solid red brick and even had a small front parlour with a bay window, which Ellen was very proud of.

Saturday was a joyous day. Ellen was very tired but with Mary's help they took all five children to the town. Georgy loved his mother, even though he knew a storm could brew in a minute, but when Ellen's mood was sunny, she was the greatest fun. Lively, witty and entertaining, she would play games endlessly with them, often behaving in a delightfully childlike manner herself. Ludo was their favourite, but making scrapbooks also filled many happy hours.

After a trip round Surbiton shops, followed by lunch at a local café, she took them to the recreation ground, where they all played on the swings, slides and merry go rounds until, exhausted but happy, they made their way home by omnibus.

The children were so excited to see it was one of the new 'double deckers' as they still weren't very common at that time. William insisted on going up on top, and Georgy and Nellie felt they simply had to follow. There was no way they wanted to be thought cowards. The two mothers and youngest children stayed below, Mary declaring that it was not natural to be up so high in the air. Ellen secretly agreed and made an excuse of looking after little Gilbert. It certainly wasn't very warm up there with the wind rushing around them from every side, but it was exhilarating none the less. Afterwards, William said it felt like flying and was the only way to travel.

Sunday was melancholy for the children. Georgy had grown very fond of his younger cousins, Nellie and Billy, and was sad to see them go. Nellie shed a few tears at parting from her new best friends and William went into a sulk, though really, he was quite upset.

'It won't be long till you see each other again,' Aunt Mary consoled them. 'We're not far away really, just a couple of short train journeys. Maybe you can come and visit us in Tottenham sometime.'

'When?' asked Georgy brightening up. 'Soon?'

'Very soon,' reassured his aunt, 'but we have to go now, so say your goodbyes.'

Several hugs and some tears later the family finally left, waving as they went. Ellen put her arms around the shoulders of her two oldest sons.

'Come on now boys. Chin up! Why not go and play in the garden?'

But the weather turned damp and drizzly, so instead they gathered around the family piano, where Ellen played old time songs and nursery rhymes, whilst they sang at the tops of their voices. Their mother could always make them feel better, Georgy thought, and he was glad.

Chapter 5

May 16th, 1905

The lusty wail of a newborn infant heralded a welcome arrival, so long prayed over. Baby Ethel had come into the world, strong and healthy, with mother doing well. The family heaved a collective sigh of relief and prepared to celebrate. What a few months it had been!

Compared with last time, this birth had been a breeze, though they had all dreaded it. Ellen had announced she was pregnant again at Christmas, the previous year, and it had been a difficult time since then. Their father had sunk into a gloomy brooding silence and Georgy often noticed him watching their mother intently. Ellen herself had been a nervous wreck, refusing to run around or do anything manual – just in case. Both their aunts and their grandmother were drafted in to help out, taking it in turns to do the laundry, scrub the floors, clean the grates etc. All the groceries were delivered where possible, and Ellen hardly left the house. Mrs Richards also popped in to help out when she had time, though her large family kept her very busy.

For Dick's wife the extra chores were as much as she could bear, not being of a sturdy disposition. Fair, slight and delicate, Minnie was a weak and sometimes foolish woman but devoted to the man she loved. She'd first met Dick when he'd had to sell his tobacconists shop in Southampton, to her father, in order to settle some of his debts. She'd fallen in love with him at first sight. Dick had had his fair share of tragedy; his first wife having died after a long battle with cancer, which broke his heart. Their only child also perished within a year, and he was left to try and pick up the pieces of his floundering business, only to find it was too late.

Heartbroken and bankrupt, he turned to Minnie for comfort, and she was only too eager to respond. Realising her youthfulness and not wanting to take advantage of her, Dick returned from Hampshire to Middlesex, to the bosom of his family and found work painting houses but was shortly followed by Minnie. Travelling on a train without the means to pay for a ticket, she was caught and prosecuted. Only her father's ability to pay the costs saved her from a prison sentence. Dick felt bad about this. She had come there purely to see him. It seemed to him that he owed her something, and later that year they were married. Minnie had never regretted it, and what Dick thought was anyone's guess.

George and Ellen knew all this of course but kept most of it from the children. As far as Georgy knew there had only ever been Aunt Minnie with Uncle Dick, and never anyone else. He was happy to see her when she came to help his mum through her pregnancy, but less pleased to see her son Ralph. Minnie was not very good with children and didn't really know what to say to them, but at least she tried. Her feeble efforts to amuse them usually fell flat, but Ellen's boys were polite enough to pretend to enjoy them. Ralph however was a different matter. Minnie's attempts at child rearing had resulted in an awkward and angry boy. Though he was much the same age as Georgy, they didn't get on. He was a bully – rough and aggressive to them all. Georgy particularly disliked it when he picked on Gilbert. Being the youngest he couldn't defend himself and inevitably Georgy and William would step in to protect him. Fights ensued and they often seemed to get the blame, with Ralph looking smugly on, claiming they'd started it all.

'It was two against one!' he cried. 'It just isn't fair. I didn't do nothing!'

During her pregnancy Ellen's moods fluctuated wildly. One moment she was singing and happy, the next in tears. Lying in bed at night Georgy and William overheard dreadful arguments between their parents that they didn't understand.

'You don't know what it's like - it's all your fault! How will I cope if it happens again?'

One afternoon in the garden after a particularly bad night the two boys sat down in their secret hideout (an awning supported by some planks, round the back of the shed) and discussed it all.

'You don't think Mum will leave, do you?' William asked in a worried voice. 'I couldn't bear it if she did.'

'I don't know,' replied Georgy. 'She sounds so cross with Dad.'

'I don't know why he doesn't answer her back,' said William.

'Perhaps he's just trying to take no notice and hope she'll calm down.'

Georgy was nearer the truth than he could have imagined. Their father was doing his best to try and ride out the storm. He knew, (which his sons didn't), that Ellen rarely meant what she said when she was in that state of mind. Pregnancy had always played with her emotions, but with the bad experience of the previous time, she was more vulnerable than ever. Paranoia and fear gnawed away at her. Only her mother, Martha, seemed able to reason with her.

'Now stop this nonsense, immediately, Ellen,' Georgy heard him say one day, and to his surprise their mother pulled herself together, though the effect was only temporary.

Martha Goddard and her husband Bill were tough, hard-working, practical folk. Now in their early sixties, having successfully brought up six children, they showed no sign of slowing down. Bill was a bricklayer by trade, but he was an intelligent and capable man who dreamed of a different life, where he could be his own boss. His wife was a force to be reckoned with, and no-one dared argue with her. Georgy found her quite terrifying at times.

Despite Ellen having so many siblings, she was closest to her older brother Will than any of the others. Her two sisters had both married and moved away so she rarely saw them. Will was the closest in age to her and she had enjoyed playing with him whilst they were growing up. He was an easy-going man who had made a good match with Mary; a jolly, cheerful, (though outspoken), woman who everyone loved. They lived near Martha and Bill in Tottenham, an area which was steadily becoming part of the Greater London sprawl. Whenever they visited them, Georgy always returned feeling thankful that his own family lived in the country.

Every time Aunt Mary, Nellie and Billy came to stay the Huntingford boys were delighted, especially

Georgy. Nellie was even permitted to join his and William's gang, but no-one under five was allowed, so Gilbert and Billy had to stay away. The adults secretly smiled about it and pretended not to notice.

In March that year Ellen became very depressed when the anniversary of the triplets' death came round. Father, however, had his own problems. The building trade had hit a slump, and his business was suffering. At the weekend Georgy asked his dad if he could go to work with him on the Saturday. Their grandma was coming over, and he dearly wanted to escape for a few hours.

'Please Dad! I'll be ever so well behaved. I can help.'

His father wanted to refuse but hadn't the heart. His son was so enthusiastic. William scowled when Georgy told him that their dad had agreed.

'That's not fair! I want to come too. I don't want to be stuck here with Grandma Goddard all day.'

In spite of his desperate entreaties his father was adamant. It would be Georgy, and Georgy alone. There was no room for anyone else.

'I'll take you next time,' he promised, but William stomped off in a bad mood, refusing to listen.

Georgy enjoyed accompanying his dad to the building site, but he was surprised to find it very quiet. Where was Jim, the painter and decorator, and Stan, the carpenter?

'I've had to lay a few men off,' his father told him. 'Business has been a bit slow of late. When it picks up again, I'll give them more work, but as it is, there's only just enough for me.'

Georgy was worried.

'It'll be all right, won't it, Dad? I mean, it won't be like when Uncle Dick lost his shop, will it?' (He'd heard about this from his mum, recently).

'No, no, of course not,' his dad replied smiling. 'There's no need to worry.'

The two of them spent a happy morning working together. Not that Georgy could really help very much, but his father gave him a paint brush and some paint, and he felt very important splashing whitewash all over the place. George Huntingford smiled to himself. He would have to spend most of his next working day cleaning up again, but he was pleased to see his eldest son getting involved.

They returned to an angry and miserable household. William had gone on the rampage in one of his moods, upsetting Gilbert in the process and incurring the wrath of their grandmother. Ellen was in tears and Gilbert was bawling his eyes out. William had been sent to their bedroom without any tea and was moping. It was a sorry scene.

Taking it all in, Father decided enough was enough, and for once, took charge very decidedly. Firmly but politely thanking Martha for her kindness, he managed to pack her off home, then retrieving William and pacifying the others, he gathered them all together.

'Now then,' he said, 'Georgy and I have worked hard all day, and this nonsense from all of you has got to stop. Ellen, Gilbert – stop your tears right now! William – cheer up! Let's get some fish and chips and enjoy the rest of the evening.'

Everyone was so shocked that they did exactly what he asked. The unexpected treat was enough to calm everyone down and the day ended in songs and laughter. Georgy thought later as he fell into bed happily, that his father was an absolute hero, and he wondered why he had never realised it before.

The months slowly passed until the big day came with the safe and speedy delivery of a beautiful baby girl. Ellen christened her Ethel and began to live normally again.

The large cumbersome baby carriage took up most of the hall, but they were all happy to see it, for it meant that the new arrival was well enough to go outside for some air. It was a sunny day in mid-June and the whole family were enjoying taking Ethel to the recreation ground.

George and Ellen sat down at a nearby tea booth with the pram and took some refreshments. Meanwhile the boys ran happily enjoying the fair weather and the freedom. Gilbert was getting more grown up now and it would only be a few months until he started school. Georgy and William had been considering co-opting him into the 'gang' but these things couldn't be rushed, they decided. The timing must be right. It's true he wasn't the baby of the family any more but there was no need to be hasty. Gilbert was keen, however and followed them around like a pet dog, so that they could hardly move without him.

'Please let me join!' he begged again. 'You said when I could when I turned five, and it's been three months now. Please!'

Away from the adults the two eldest boys finally gave in and announced that Gilbert could join the gang, but it had to be top secret, or he would be banned.

'Cross your heart and hope to die,' said Georgy solemnly.

'Swear it on our mother's life!' William demanded, always prone to over-dramatise.

'I swear!' replied Gilbert in awe.

They joined their hands together, palms up and swore a brotherly oath, then they all went off to play.

The visits from the family went back to reasonable proportions again and things began to settle down. They still saw a lot of Aunt Mary and her children and were even able to go and visit them, though it took an hour and a half to get there. The children were very excited to see the house and garden and played for hours whilst the adults talked. They had great fun with their cousins.

Not so happy was their Uncle Dick's visit. It seemed to unsettle both their parents for some reason. Gilbert said he had heard them all talking about travelling on a ship overseas, but Georgy didn't really believe him, and William was downright scornful.

'Don't be silly! Why would they go over the sea? It doesn't make sense. You don't know what you're talking about.'

The truth, however, was that indeed the adults had been discussing just that. Dick had come up with a new idea – emigrating to another country to start afresh. Maybe Canada or America – he wasn't sure, but he was keen for the whole family to go, and he was busy trying to persuade them.

'It would be a great chance for us all,' he persisted. 'Lots of work. Money to be made. A change of scenery. What could be better?'

'You must be joking,' said Ellen. 'I'm not leaving everything behind to go off into the unknown. It's a ridiculous idea.'

George was in two minds.

'I can see your point, Dick,' he said, 'but I agree with Ellen. It's too much to ask. It could all go wrong so easily. We don't know anything about these places.'

'Besides we would have to travel overseas, which is very risky,' Ellen pointed out. 'These ships take months to get there, and so many are lost on the way.'

It was this comment that Gilbert had overheard on his way past the kitchen.

'Overseas travel is much safer and faster these days,' Dick continued, 'what with the new steam ships. It's the future.' He continued to try and persuade them.

The three boys crept along furtively to eavesdrop on the conversation to find out whether Gilbert had been correct. As they got there, they were just in time to hear their mother declare: 'Well, you can forget it. I'm not doing it, and that's that.'

'Told you!' whispered William to the others. 'We're not going anywhere.'

Chapter 6

February 1906

It was chilly as Georgy and his brothers made their way to school one early February morning. Their breath steamed in the frosty air as they hurried along.

'Don't you think Mum and Dad are in a funny mood at the moment?' remarked William. 'Dad really snapped at me yesterday.'

Georgy considered for a moment. 'Yes, I have noticed something,' he answered thoughtfully. 'Not sure what it is, though.'

Gilbert chipped in. 'I heard them talking about that election thingy, whatever it is. Dad said it wouldn't help at all.'

'That's odd,' said Georgy. 'Why would it worry him? I mean it's nothing to do with us, is it?'

'I heard it was a 'landside' victory,' said William knowledgeably.

'You mean 'landslide', corrected Georgy.

'Oh well, whatever it is!' William retorted crossly. 'I didn't know you were such an expert!'

'The teacher was telling us about it at school,' replied Georgy. 'That's all I know.'

'Mum said she didn't think it was fair that she couldn't vote,' Gilbert added, 'but Dad said women aren't allowed because they don't understand it all. She went off in one of her huffs after that.'

Georgy sighed. This seemed fairly normal for their mother, but even so, they still wondered – what was wrong?

Meanwhile the adults were struggling through their troubles as best they could. The truth was that the Liberals winning the election didn't really seem to be changing anything at present. There was much talk of reform but little definite action. George Huntingford was at his wits end. His business was failing, and he knew it. With a wife and four children to support he worried night and day. What could he do? He had kept it from Ellen so far, hoping things might improve, but there seemed little hope of this. His reasons for this were mixed. He felt ashamed of the thought of not being able to provide for his family, and fearful of how his wife would react. The work contracts continued to evaporate and the bills to mount up, until one evening in February George had to confess. The children had gone to bed, and he sat there trying to make his business accounts add up. No matter how he tried the figures wouldn't balance. His employees had all been laid off weeks ago and yet outgoings were still decidedly more than incomings. Despair overwhelmed him and he sat with his head in his hands. Ellen looked up from her darning and noticed.

'Whatever's wrong, George?' she asked. 'You've been there all evening, and you look like there's been a disaster.'

'There has!' George told her gloomily. 'We're finished. The business has had it. Oh, Ellen, I'm so sorry. I've let you all down.'

Tears came into his eyes, but he wouldn't let them fall. He didn't normally give way to emotion if he could help it.

His wife put her arms around his shoulders comfortingly. 'Is it really that bad? Isn't there anything you can do?'

Touched by her kindness he buried his face in her apron, holding her tight.

'I'm sorry,' he said again. 'There are so many bills for materials, and the work has dried up. I don't know what to do.'

For once Ellen supplied the strength he needed. 'Look,' she suggested, 'let's have a cup of char, then we'll have a look at it together and work out how to pay the debts. We can borrow from my father if we have to. Then we need to think of what you can do next. A new job perhaps, working for someone else?'

George smiled gratefully at her. 'The other day, Stan Simmonds told me of some opportunities in plumbing, but it means starting all over again from the bottom. He is looking for someone reliable to train up, but the wages wouldn't be much at first.'

'Plumbing, that's new, isn't it? Surely, it's just a passing fad?'

'It's the future, I'm sure,' enthused George. 'All the new houses have indoor privies now like ours, and some even have built-in baths.'

'Imagine that!' said Ellen. 'Well, if that's what you think is best, then you must do it. I could get some part-time work now that Ethel's a bit older. Maybe take in some sewing or mending, that would help out.'

'But I don't want you to have to work!' George cried. 'It's my job to take care of you all.'

'I know my love,' she said, 'but money will be tight whilst you re-train. It would only be temporary.' She paused. 'You know I'll back you whatever you decide to do, George,' she said seriously.

For answer all he could do was to hold her close, caressing her, so thankful that his wife would stand by him in his time of difficulty.

The children groaned when they heard they were all going to visit Grandma and Grandpa Goddard at the weekend.

'Do we have to?' asked William petulantly.

'Now William,' scolded Ellen, 'don't be so rude. You know Granny and Grandpa love you all and enjoy seeing you.'

'But I wanted to go to the park to play football,' William sulked. 'It's not fair!'

William's temper often got the better of him, and it wasn't the first time (and probably wouldn't be the last) that he was sent to his room without any tea. Even so, his mother always relented later and took him up a late supper.

'You shouldn't do that,' Mr Huntingford told his wife. 'You're just encouraging him.'

But Ellen loved her temperamental son, maybe because he was most like her – emotional and demanding, but lovable – and she carried on regardless.

Now that Georgy was older, nearly ten years old, he had started to see that Grandma Goddard was not quite as fearsome as she made out. Though he too had sighed at the thought of the visit, in his heart he felt that he quite liked her. She had spirit and was not afraid to speak her mind. For that she had his admiration.

Their grandparents' house in Edmonton was part of a long terrace of compact houses which stretched up the road as far as the eye could see. Georgy thought that they looked like little boxes with roofs on, unlike their own home which had a more individual character. The back gardens were narrow strips of lawn with high fences all around. This seemed very boring to the three boys who were sent out to play whilst the adults talked. Not only that, but the weather was chilly with a brisk wind.

'It's all right for baby Ethel,' moaned William. 'She gets to stay inside. I'm cold!'

Gilbert stood there shivering and looking forlorn whilst William complained. Suddenly noticing, William put a brotherly arm around his shoulders in an attempt to keep him warm.

'It's all right, Gil,' he said. 'Here; take my coat.'

Privately Georgy agreed that it was indeed very cold, but being the eldest it was left to him to amuse the others.

'Let's have an obstacle race,' he suggested, with as much enthusiasm as he could muster. Inspired by his idea, the three of them dragged various items of garden and household equipment into use, and spent the next couple of hours happily racing, jumping and scrambling around it all. This certainly warmed them up and they forgot their blues. William even let Gilbert win the first race, just to cheer him up.

Indoors was another matter, however. Ellen had finally found the courage to broach the subject of money with her parents.

‘It would only be a loan,’ she pleaded, ‘just until George gets trained up and has a new job. We can’t let him end up bankrupt.’

‘Like his brother Dick, you mean,’ interjected her mother.

George Huntingford cringed with embarrassment.

‘I know Dick was careless, but he was going through a lot at the time, what with losing Bertha and the baby. He’s been working hard ever since.’

‘Well yes,’ conceded his mother-in-law. ‘I give you that, but even so….’

Her husband Bill had been silent until now but suddenly spoke up.

‘Listen, we don’t want you all to be in difficulties, so we will help you out on this occasion, but on a strict re-payment agreement. We have our own outgoings too, you know.’

‘Of course,’ said Ellen. ‘Oh Father, thank you. We’re so grateful.’

‘Enough of that,’ Bill said gruffly. ‘Anyway, we have some news of our own.’

They looked at him, surprised. He hesitated then Martha took over.

‘We’re moving,’ she said bluntly. ‘Bill’s got the opportunity to run a pub in Wendon Ambo, and we’re taking it.’

‘A pub!’ exclaimed Ellen. ‘But why? You’re a bricklayer.’

Her father tried to explain. ‘Ellen dear, we’re both in our sixties now and it’s time we made a change. Bricklaying is too heavy for me now, and I’ve always dreamed of having my own place.’

‘But you don’t know anything about it!’ protested Ellen.

'We all have to learn sometime,' he replied, 'and your brother Fred's coming as well so it'll be the three of us working together. How hard can it be?'

'Anyway, we've put our money into this and we're not backing out now,' added Martha. 'Surely it's just the same as George here re-training as a plumber?'

'Well yes, I suppose so,' admitted Ellen. 'But where are you going? Wendon Ambo – I've never heard of it!'

'Oh Ellen, really!' said her mother. 'Have you forgotten where I was born?'

'Essex! But that's miles away!'

'It's true it's a fair distance, but for me it's wonderful to be going back to the area I grew up in.'

'We'll never see you,' her daughter whined, getting tearful.

Bill put an arm around her shoulders. 'Come on, old girl, of course you will. Buck up now, it's not the end of the world.'

George had stayed quiet during this conversation, but now added:

'Ellen, my dear, it's a new start for them, just like us. Can't you see? I think it's a brave thing to do and I wish you well.'

Bill shook hands with him gratefully, exchanging similar thoughts.

'I'm sure you will do well at your plumbing, George. It's definitely a growing trade.'

An awkward peace descended. Ellen was still unhappy, and Martha was still angry, but they choked back their differences and ended the day in a precarious ceasefire. Their two husbands talked cheerfully of all the new experiences coming their way, affecting to ignore their wives' emotions, though very much aware of the under-currents.

Gathering up the children, Ellen and George finally took their leave.

'We made an obstacle course, Mum. It was great,' William told them enthusiastically.

'Did you, dear? Well done,' said his mother, thinking to herself that they'd had their own obstacle course of a different sort that afternoon, one without any clear winners or losers. She only hoped there wouldn't be more hazards further down the road. Time would tell.

Chapter 7

Early April 1906

Georgy felt irritated. Uncle Dick and Aunt Minnie had come to visit and talk about something 'important and private' according to his mother. In the meantime, the Huntingford boys had been left to entertain their cousin Ralph, and to mind baby Ethel who was just starting to crawl. No matter how hard he tried, Georgy couldn't seem to keep up with her. She was interested in everything and everywhere. Who knew babies could move that fast, he thought, retrieving her yet again from the kitchen. If only she would go to sleep for a while -but it seemed she had no intention of this. William was reluctantly trying to keep Ralph occupied, but the sullen and angry boy was bigger and rougher than him, and trouble was brewing.

Trouble of a different kind was to be found in the front parlour where four adults were deep in thought.

'The problem is,' said George, 'that I've had training in plumbing now, but it's difficult to get any decent paid work. There are so many other people, all more experienced than me. I hoped Stan would be able to keep me on, but his brother has joined the business now and there's just not enough work for both of us. He's told me that he'll have to let me go.'

'Well, there you are!' said Dick persuasively. 'As I told you, they're crying out for plumbers in Canada. I saw it in this newspaper.' (He passed it to them). 'There's money to be made. As it says, there's '*room for all*'. Even the wages are higher! You can't lose.'

'That's all very well,' Ellen interrupted, 'but it's the other side of the world! How are we supposed to pack up and leave everything? We've the children to think of as well.'

'There are good schools in the area and a decent standard of living. And it's not like leaving Britain, it's still part of it. Why, it's got to be better than this country,' Dick continued.

'Times are very hard here,' piped up Minnie in a small voice. 'Dick is convinced it's the right thing for all of us.'

'And you wouldn't be alone,' said Dick. 'We'd all be there together.'

'But what about the cost of getting to Canada?' asked George. 'Steamship voyages aren't cheap, you know. Money is tight at the moment.'

'Didn't you hear what I said? They're offering vouchers for travel to skilled workers like you. You just have to apply. And they help you once you arrive as well.'

George wavered. 'Well, it's true that I've heard that registration for plumbers is coming in this year, and that it will be difficult to get unless you have lots of work experience, and that doesn't look very likely at the moment.'

'There you are then. Go to Canada and make the most of your new skills. You don't have to stay if you don't like it. Just make some money and gain some experience. Then when you get back, they'll have to register you.'

'What are the houses like over there?' wondered Ellen.

'Just the same as here, only better,' enthused Dick, 'and there's lots of help for immigrants. They are looking for families. Here – read the article. It's in all the newspapers at the moment.'

They studied the newspaper.

'It certainly looks interesting, I have to admit,' said George. 'It could be better than being unemployed here. I would hate to lose the house if I couldn't earn enough money to pay the bills.'

'The countryside sounds lovely,' agreed Ellen. 'It would be good for the children to get some fresh air, away from London. All this what do they call it – Smog? It can't be good for them.'

'I heard Ralph coughing his head off the other day,' said Minnie. 'It's not right.'

Ellen nodded. 'I know. It worries me, especially with little Ethel.'

'It's not like you'd be in the wilds. These days they've got towns with all the things you'd need,' Dick persisted. 'Those days of struggle are gone now. It's a good life, a new opportunity.'

The adults pondered long into the afternoon. Dick's enthusiasm was convincing, and his brother and sister-in-law began to be persuaded.

Trouble had erupted among their offspring, however. Ethel had finally escaped from Georgy's clutches when he needed to use the privy. Asking Ralph to keep an eye on her he sped off, only to find upon his return that she had crawled around the back of the stove and was now covered in soot and grime. Her face, her hands, her clothes – what a disaster!

'You were supposed to watch her!' he shouted at Ralph, but his cousin just shrugged.

'Ain't *my* job.' He sniggered. 'Your mum's going to kill you!'

Georgy thought that he was probably right and decided the only option was to bath her. Desperately he started to fill the iron bathtub by the fire.

'Go outside and play, won't you?' he ordered the rest of them and reluctantly they went, William complaining all the way and Gilbert being dragged along.

Twenty minutes later, having just about got baby Ethel clean again, Georgy heard an almighty rumpus coming from outside. Swaddling her in some clean, dry towels, he went to the back door to see what all the fuss was about. There he saw William and Ralph rolling around on the ground, punching and grabbing at each other, whilst Gilbert stood there bawling his eyes out.

'Stop!' roared Georgy. 'Stop. Whatever is going on?'

The two combatants continued, oblivious. Shoving Ethel into Gilbert's arms with an imperious 'Take her!' Georgy leapt into the fray. He pulled them up from the ground and thrust them apart.

'What are you doing?' he demanded, feeling older than his ten years, almost like an adult in fact.

'He started it!' cried Ralph. 'He hit me!'

'Only `cos you started on Gilbert,' shouted William. 'Georgy, he took his special blue train, and you know it's his favourite toy. Then he wouldn't give it back. He hid it and said he was going to throw it away!'

'Is this true?' Georgy asked his youngest brother gently. Seeing his tears he guessed it was.

Gilbert nodded tearfully. 'I want my train!' he sobbed.

Georgy turned to his cousin.

'Give it back now or I'm telling your dad.' he said forcefully.

'It was only a joke,' Ralph said snidely. 'Some kids are just babies. I'd have given it back sooner or later.'

He produced the toy from under a nearby bush. William snatched it off him, and passing Ethel back to Georgy, returned it to Gilbert.

'He hit me!' accused Ralph, pointing at William. 'He's a bully!'

William would have flown at Ralph again, but Georgy intervened.

'It's you that's the bully, Ralph. Don't you know better than to torment a young child? Shame on you! William, Gilbert – come with me. Let's go indoors.'

'He deserved all he got,' William told Georgy later. 'He's so mean, and it makes me mad to see him pick on Gil. He can't defend himself.'

Secretly Georgy felt proud of his brother for his actions. William was never one to take injustice lying down, and for that he loved him. Gilbert adored William too and looked up to him. The incident only served to make the three of them closer, but as far as relations with Ralph went, the bad feelings continued to simmer like a pot on the stove.

Just as they went inside Ellen came out of the parlour to make some tea. Seeing them all she was horrified. William and Ralph were covered in bruises and scratches, their clothing torn and dusty. Gilbert's eyes were red from crying and Georgy struggled to contain a newly bathed Ethel who was not at all happy at having her movements restricted.

‘What on earth have you been doing?’ she exclaimed. ‘Look at the state you’re in! Have you been fighting?’

William and Ralph hung their heads in shame, but Georgy attempted to smooth things over.

‘It was just a game outside,’ he said. ‘No harm done. It got a bit rough, that’s all.’

‘Hmmm,’ Ellen said suspiciously. ‘It looks like more than that to me. And why is Ethel only half dressed? What happened?’

‘She got herself all dirty by the stove,’ said Georgy, reddening. ‘I’m sorry. She just crawled off. I had to give her a bath.’

‘You were supposed to look after her!’ his mother exploded. ‘Really Georgy, you need to be more careful. Give her to me. I’ll sort her out. Obviously, I can’t trust you at all.’

The boys fled to the safety of their room upstairs. Ralph stomped along sulkily behind them. At least no-one had spilt the beans. They may have had their own disagreements, but they weren’t about to tell the adults. It just wasn’t done.

Over the next few days George and Ellen reached a momentous decision after hours of soul searching. They would get the forms and apply to go to Canada. The chance of a new life was too tempting to resist, and they decided to give it a try. After all, what would George do when his plumbing work ran out? The family would struggle if he was unemployed.

‘We can always change our minds,’ said George. ‘We might not even get accepted, but we’ve got nothing to lose by applying.’

The children were confused by their parents’ lack of interest in them that weekend. Normally their mother would have taken them out somewhere but this time she was shut away in the front room with Father, and they had strict orders not to disturb them. After the last unfortunate incident baby Ethel was safely in her pram with Ellen, so at least that was something, but the boys moped around and quickly got bored. They ended up playing a game of Ludo, but an argument broke out when William (allegedly) started cheating.

'You only got four and you counted five,' declared Georgy. 'That's not right!'

'Didn't, so!' retorted William.

'Yes, you did. I saw you!' chipped in Gilbert.

'Shut up Gil, you don't understand!'

Just at that moment Mother and Father emerged from the front room, smiling.

'Let's go out now,' said Ellen. 'We've all had enough time indoors.'

Joyously they agreed and all was forgotten.

Towards the middle of April, a large, important looking letter arrived. William snatched it up gleefully and raced in to give it to their mother. A letter was a big event.

'Look Mum – a letter. Open it!'

'Later,' said Ellen, looking pale. 'I need to wait until your father comes home.'

To Ellen and George's utter surprise the letter was offering them a place in Canada, with a voucher towards their travel and advice on accommodation.

'Well,' said George to his wife, 'fancy that! What now?'

They both felt stunned but excited too.

'I think we should go,' said Ellen firmly. 'It's not often you get such a chance. Let's hope Dick and Minnie have heard good news as well. Should we tell the children?'

‘Not yet,’ replied George. ‘Let’s wait to hear what Dick and Minnie have to say.’

They didn’t have long to wait. Dick and Minnie appeared that weekend, but their faces were gloomy, and it was clear something was wrong.

Ellen opened the door smiling broadly, saying ‘We’ve had some good news,’ but then she saw their downcast look.

‘What’s wrong?’ she asked. ‘Come in quickly and tell us.’

Ensconced in the front parlour, Dick broke the news.

‘We’ve had our application for Canada rejected. Being just a painter and decorator, it seems that I don’t have the skills they want, and not enough money due to my past bankruptcy. They won’t take us.’

George stared at his brother. ‘What? I don’t believe it. Surely you misread it?’

’No, it’s true,’ said Minnie. ‘We’re so sorry. Have you heard anything about yours?’

There was an awkward silence. George swallowed hard.

‘Well, we, er, we’ve been accepted, I’m afraid.’

Amid the gasps of astonishment Dick expressed the opinion that obviously George and Ellen wouldn’t go now, without them.

‘Well, I don’t know,’ said George hesitantly. ‘Ellen and I have thought about nothing else recently and we really think it would be good for the family.’

‘Surely you won’t go without us!’ exclaimed Dick. ‘I mean, it was my idea!’

‘You’d be all on your own,’ added Minnie.

‘Well, we’ll have to consider it carefully,’ George replied stiffly. ‘It’s up to Ellen and me to decide for ourselves. Obviously, this will change things, but we can't just dismiss it. I need to work and provide for my family. This would give me the chance to do that. It sounds like just the thing.'

The afternoon ended on a difficult note. Dick and Minnie left, barely containing their anger and surprise. George and Ellen were embarrassed but stubborn. Whatever decision they made would be theirs alone. As the door shut behind their in-laws, George let out a deep breath and turned to Ellen.

'Now what, old girl?'

He held out his hands, and she took them in hers.

'George,' she said seriously, 'once I've made a decision I stick to it, so, as far as I'm concerned, we still go, but you have the last say.'

She gazed intently at his face. For a moment he was silent, thinking hard. Then he said:

'I'm with you, my love. Canada, here we come!'

Chapter 8

Late April 1906

'Boys,' called Ellen, 'come in here and sit down. Father wants to talk to you.'

That sounds ominous, thought Georgy and his stomach tightened in a knot of anxiety. What had they done? They must be in trouble.

The three of them shuffled nervously into the front parlour – a room rarely used except for formal occasions. To their surprise their mother was smiling, and what's more there was cake – a rare treat.

'Tuck in, boys,' she said. 'It's a special occasion. There's no need to look so worried.'

With relief and some bewilderment, they fell to, demolishing most of the plateful before their father entered the room.

'What? None left for me?' he teased. 'Well, that's healthy appetites for you! Now lads, I've got some important news.'

'Is Mummy having another baby?' asked Gilbert.

'No, nothing like that,' Father told them. 'We're going to move house.'

Their mouths still full of cake crumbs, they were ready with their questions.

'Where to? Will we have to change school? Is it a big house? Is there a garden?'

Their father smiled but held up his hand to pause the onslaught.

'I don't know all the details at the moment,' he explained. 'We won't see it until we get there.' He hesitated. 'We're moving to Canada.'

There was a short silence whilst the children tried to digest the news.

'Canada,' said William, 'where's that?'

'Is it over by Aunty Mary's house?' asked Gilbert.

Georgy thought that he had heard of it and was a bit worried. 'Isn't it a long way away, Dad?' he said.

'Yes, it is,' replied his father. 'It's over the sea. We will be travelling there by steamship.'

'Brilliant!' cried William. 'I've always wanted to go on one of those. Will it take all day?'

'It will take a few days,' Father admitted.

William was impressed but Georgy wasn't so sure.

'I hope it won't be too rough,' he said. 'I've heard people get sick.'

'Nonsense!' Ellen told him. 'That's just old wives' tales. There's nothing to it.'

(In her heart she hoped that this was true but wasn't really sure).

'Will we have a garden?' asked Gilbert.

'Of course,' replied his mother, 'a nice big garden for you all to play in.'

'Spiffing!' exclaimed William. 'When do we go?'

'We are planning on the middle of May,' their father told them. 'That's the best time for travelling, and it gives us time to get packed.'

Georgy tried his best to join in with the celebration but felt uneasy. What would it be like there?

A few days later they all went to visit Aunt Mary, Uncle Will and their cousins. It was normally a very happy occasion as the two families were very close, especially after the tragic demise of the triplets. This time, Georgy sensed a certain trepidation from his parents, though he didn't know why.

Sitting comfortably in their front room, Ellen began brightly, though she was feeling quite nervous if truth be told.

'We've got some exciting news,' she announced, catching all their attention.

Aunt Mary smiled encouragingly. 'Really? Tell us all about it.'

Ellen's brother Will laughed.

'Not another baby, is it sis? What does that make – five now?'

'Nothing like that,' she answered and hesitated. 'George, you tell them.'

George took a deep breath. 'Well, we're moving house,' he said, 'to Canada.'

'Canada!' exclaimed Aunt Mary, 'but that's the other side of the world!'

'Have you lost your minds?' asked Will. 'What on earth are you doing that for?'

The children all sat there, confused.

'Is it a long way?' asked Nellie.

'It certainly is,' replied her mother. 'We won't be able to visit, that's for sure.'

All of a sudden, it hit Georgy – he wouldn't see them again for a very long time, if ever – and he felt he wanted to cry, the pain was so great.

Tears came into young Nellie's eyes as well. 'But who will we play with now?'

'Do you know what you're doing?' persisted Ellen's brother Will. 'You're taking four children all the way across the ocean to an unknown country. Why, there could be all kinds of dangers there!'

'We've looked into it very carefully,' said George, 'and there are lots of opportunities for skilled workers there. I am likely to be laid off soon if I stay here. After all Canada's not primitive any more. It's the future. There's a railway, good schools, lots of well-paid work.'

'And ferocious wild animals!' interrupted Mary. 'They have bears and all sorts out there!'

'We'll be in a town,' explained Ellen, 'and they even help us with accommodation and travel. It's all very safe. Haven't you seen the newspaper advertisements?'

'We'll never see you,' Mary continued. 'The cousins will lose touch. Doesn't family matter to you?'

'Of course it does,' Ellen replied. 'You know how much we care about you all, but we have to take this opportunity.'

The argument continued for some time but reached no conclusion. All the children felt lost and scared. Raised voices and tearful exchanges were not a fun way to spend an afternoon.

Eventually Ellen and George got up in a huff, gathered their offspring and said their goodbyes. Georgy just managed to give Nellie and Billy a quick hug as they were being dragged away. His last view of them was of them standing there, tears in their eyes.

'Mum, I don't want to go,' he pleaded but Ellen took his hand firmly in hers and hurried him along. There was no turning back.

Days went by rapidly and there were more farewells. Grandma Goddard merely grunted when told, then said sarcastically: 'And you said *we* were moving too far away!'

The pub in Wendon Ambo was flourishing and they were all busy serving customers, too busy to spend much time chatting to family. Georgy and William amused themselves by petting the huge shire horses when they came to deliver the ale to the pub. Gilbert was a little scared of them though. They towered above him and so he sheltered next to his mother, with little Ethel. Georgy thought he had never seen such magnificent animals. The driver kindly let them both hop up onto the cart for a few minutes, whilst their Uncle Fred unloaded the barrels, and they were delighted.

The adults seemed to have said all they had to say, and the time came for them to depart. Grandma Goddard approached the boys, and Georgy detected a certain huskiness in her voice as she wished them well. To his surprise she kissed each of them tenderly.

'Georgy,' she said to him earnestly, 'you're the eldest, almost a young man now. Take care of them all, especially your mother.'

She turned away, fumbling for a handkerchief. Then she was gone, swallowed up in the hustle and bustle of the busy pub, leaving Georgy at a loss for words.

Packing and organising took up most of their remaining time. A booking was made on the steamship Norseman, leaving on the 15th May from Liverpool. Train tickets were purchased to get them there and belongings were packed. The children cried when told they could only take some of their toys with them.

'There isn't room in the trunk,' their mother said firmly, but she squeezed in as many as she could anyway.

Temporary housing had been booked in Nova Scotia for them, a place which sounded very exotic and exciting.

'I've been looking it up,' Georgy told his brothers. 'There are mountains there, and forests, and it's near the sea!'

'Fantastic!' exclaimed William. 'We can go to the beach.'

Despite his initial misgivings and the sadness at parting from loved ones, Georgy was starting to look forward to it now. If only they had been able to take the family with them, then it would have been perfect.

'Will there be wild animals there?' asked Gilbert.

'Yes, but they're quite harmless,' William told him confidently. 'No need to be scared.'

He didn't know this of course, but it made Gilbert feel better.

The house got emptier by the day, giving it a sad and unloved look. New tenants came to look round and suddenly it all felt like it was really going to happen. Ellen had a sudden pang. How could she leave her family like this? Were they doing the right thing? There was no-one she could confide her fears to. Mary was barely speaking to them, her mother was busy dealing with the pub, and as for Dick and Minnie – well they hadn't seen them since the argument. They didn't even know that George and Ellen were actually going.

'I think we ought to tell your brother,' Ellen said to George that evening when the children were in bed. 'He's a right to know we're moving, at least.'

George agreed. 'Yes. I suppose we should. I just hope they can understand our decision. Let's visit at the end of the week. It's our last chance.'

Ellen felt sudden tears come into her eyes. 'We are doing the right thing, aren't we?' she said in a trembling voice.

For answer George encircled her in a huge, reassuring hug.

'My darling, it will be fine. It will be a wonderful new life for us all.' He paused and looked at her seriously. 'Are you having second thoughts?'

'Not really. It's just so close now and it scares me.' She tried to smile. 'It's such a big move.'

George stroked her cheek and brushed the tears away. 'I understand my love, but we will be strong together.'

'I know,' Ellen replied and nestled against his shoulder. 'I'm just being foolish.'

It was agreed that they should visit Dick and Minnie on Saturday that week. The family were due to travel to Liverpool on the following Monday, so time was short. The three boys were all wildly excited at the thought of the adventure to come and were full of restless energy. Ellen arranged for them to go to Mrs Richards (the lady who had acted as wet nurse for the ill-fated triplets) to play with her children for the day. She guessed that their visit to George's brother and his wife could be stressful. The boys were delighted and spent the day happily at the rec' with the five lively Richards children. They were a joy to be with – happy, healthy and cheerful with an easy-going mother. Much fun to be had all round.

Minnie opened the door to George and Ellen and gave a little cry.

'Oh, you're here! I'm so pleased to see you. Come in.'

Encouraged by such a welcome, the couple entered the front parlour readily enough. Nevertheless, they felt awkward standing there whilst Minnie fetched Dick. For a moment when he came in, no-one knew what to say, but then Ellen blurted out:

'We've come to say goodbye. We leave on Monday. Please say you forgive us!'

Tears came into her eyes, but she was not the only one choked with emotion. Amidst hugs and sobs, they all somehow resolved their differences.

'I understand,' said Dick in a husky voice. 'We've been thinking it through, and we don't blame you. We just wish we were going with you.'

'We wish you were, too,' George told him. 'And hopefully you will be able to join us in the future. Of course we might not even stay. It just depends on how it all works out.'

More cheerfully they revealed their plans to Dick and Minnie who were enthusiastic about it all.

'Sounds like it's all sorted out,' Dick commented. 'Well done. I told you it would be fine, didn't' I?'

'You were right,' admitted George, 'but I can't say we're not a bit scared as well. It's a long way from everything and everyone we know and love.'

'It will work out well for you, I'm sure,' his brother assured him. 'You deserve this. You've earned it. What have you got to lose?'

With such a positive and happy reunion George and Ellen finally left feeling fully optimistic about the adventure waiting just ahead of them. One more day and they would be off into the great unknown, for better or worse.

Chapter 9

May 1906

Ellen shut the front door for the last time, with a sudden pang of sadness. It had been a good home, she thought, though life had been difficult at times. Still, a new chapter was ahead.

Swallowing back her emotion she headed out to the cart where her husband, baby and children were all waiting, surrounded by as many trunks and belongings as they could take on voyage. The horse clip-clopped slowly but relentlessly to the railway station where they were to catch the train to Liverpool. The family were silent on the way, the enormity of what they were doing having finally caught up with them. Even William could find nothing to say.

The station was a different matter, however. All the children had travelled on before was the underground and occasional short trips to the coast. The pure grandeur of Euston Station overawed them. The cart pulled up alongside a huge archway, the columns simply dwarfing it by their majesty and size. None of them had ever seen anything like it before. The Huntingfords unloaded their baggage, having found a willing porter with his trolley, and proceeded into the ticket hall. Here was another surprise. A more gracious and beautiful hall was rarely to be seen. A pair of sweeping staircases led down to an elegant ground floor, embellished with Greek style statues and potted palms. They stood and stared, scarcely believing their eyes.

'This isn't quite what I was expecting,' remarked Mr Huntingford, expressing what they were all thinking.

'It's brilliant,' cried William. 'Amazing!'

'I've seen these statues in the books at school,' said Georgy. 'I think they're Greek.'

'Well, they're certainly very fetching,' agreed their mother. 'Now, let's go and get checked in.'

After a short wait their train was announced at Platform One and they got up to go and find it. It was then that they had another pleasant surprise, for there was Minnie running along, out of breath and panicking, desperate to see them before they left.

'Minnie dear,' said Ellen warmly. 'We weren't expecting you.'

'I wanted to wave you off,' she gasped, 'and tell you how much we wish you good fortune. Dick wanted to be here as well, but he has to work, and Ralph's at school, but I felt I had to come. Here let me help you with your bags.'

Her frail, slight frame struggled with even the smallest of the luggage, but she was keen to help so they let her. Proceeding out to Platform One they found the enormous engine waiting impatiently, sending up bursts of steam as if wanting to get going.

Finding their seats in the third-class carriage they disposed of their trunks and bags and prepared for the long ride to Liverpool. Minnie stayed with them until the last possible moment, then leapt out and waved frantically from the platform as they departed. Eventually her tiny figure was lost to view as they rounded a bend, and they were on their way at last.

The train rattled along, reaching speeds of nearly 35mph. Gilbert started to feel sick with the motion of the carriage as it lurched backwards and forwards, and when they finally stopped for a ten-minute comfort break, they were all glad to have a stretch.

'My legs feel all wobbly,' Georgy told his father. Mr Huntingford just smiled and said he would get used to it soon. 'We've a lot further to go yet. It'll get easier.'

Ellen and Gilbert both looked a bit pale, but a few gasps of the smoky station air soon brought the colour back to their cheeks.

The guard blew his whistle and reluctantly they returned to the hard wooden seats that were reserved for them. In spite of the lack of comfort in the carriage, they were pleased to find it was heated, gas-lit and even had a toilet nearby.

'All these modern things,' said Ellen, impressed. 'It's so much better than when we got married, isn't it George?'

Her husband agreed, remembering the cold, dark, cheerless compartment of the train which took them, newly married, to their honeymoon destination. He smiled to himself though, recalling them wrapped in each other's arms, barely noticing at the time.

A few hours went by, and dinner time arrived. The boys were all feeling hungry and William complained his stomach was rumbling.

'Well, we've got a treat for you all,' Ellen told them, smiling. 'How about a meal in the dining car?'

They agreed enthusiastically and leapt up at once. Making their way along the tossing and pitching corridor of the train was not easy and Gilbert was scared of crossing over the join between carriages.

'What if it comes apart?' he cried. 'I'll fall down the hole.'

'Don't be silly,' said William scornfully. 'You're such a baby sometimes, Gil.'

'William!' reprimanded his mother sternly. 'Gilbert's much younger than you. There's no need for that.'

'Sorry Mum. Sorry Gil,' William mumbled, and peace was restored.

They had a fine dinner in the dining car and were much amused by the waiter bringing them their food.

'Chops,' said Georgy, impressed. 'My favourite.'

'And suet pud,' exclaimed William. 'Super!'

It was well into the evening when they arrived in Liverpool, and they were mightily relieved to get there.

'Now,' said Ellen, 'there should be someone to meet us and show us where we are going to stay tonight.'

A smartly dressed middle aged man stepped forward on the platform, calling their name.

'Huntingfords! This way. Huntingfords.'

He introduced himself as Mr Hardcastle, the representative from the Dominion Line. They went with him gratefully to a nearby lodging house, which had been arranged by the steamship company. The accommodation was basic but clean, and they fell into their beds without a second thought.

Next morning Georgy woke in his new surroundings and for a moment couldn't remember where he was. Then it came back to him. They were in Liverpool and today would be the day they would board the ship. How exciting.

After a breakfast of porridge, Mr Hardcastle arrived to give them their tickets and take them to the docks.

There seemed to be a problem though, for when Georgy came back into their room having been to the outside privy, he heard his mother say:

'Third class? No, this is a mistake. I ordered second class tickets.'

'No madam,' said the rep. 'You're on the assisted immigration plan, aren't you? That's what you get, I'm afraid. Third class. The authorities won't pay for more than that.'

'That's not right,' she protested. 'I've heard dreadful things about third class, and we've got three children and a young baby.'

'Madam, conditions in third class are much improved now,' the man assured her. 'You don't need to worry.'

'Can we pay the extra to go up to second class?' interjected their father, George. 'We might be able to scrape it together.'

'Sir, even if you could, I couldn't help, I'm afraid. The Dominion Line has scrapped second class at present. They are only taking cargo and steerage…er… I mean third class, so it's that or nothing.' He paused. 'Of course, it's no skin off my nose if you don't want to go. You can just go home again. There are always people wanting passage on a ship like this.'

'Wait,' said George. 'Let's not be hasty. Can you give us a few minutes to discuss it, please?'

The representative took out his pocket watch and checked it. 'Well, five minutes maximum, because then we need to leave. I have other people to collect as well, you know.'

'I understand,' replied George. 'Please just wait outside for a minute and we'll be right with you.'

Mr Hardcastle huffed but removed himself,

‘Look my dear,’ George said to his wife, ‘it seems the only way is third class. Can it really be so bad? It’s only for a week after all.’

Ellen was nearly in tears. ‘But it will be so unhealthy for the children. I’ve heard such stories. We can’t put them through it.’

‘We must,’ George told her firmly. ‘If we want to go, we’ve no option. After all, we can’t go back now. The house is let. Our things are packed. We’ve come this far, don’t let’s back out now. Like I said, it’s only for a week, then we’ll be there.’

Ellen sighed but gave in. ‘I suppose you’re right.’

George patted her arm affectionately.

‘Chin up, old girl. It won’t be so bad. You’ll see.’

Mr Hardcastle escorted them to the steamship offices, collecting two more families on the way, then he departed to do the same for others. After signing a contract for the voyage, the Huntingford family were led off to separate rooms for medical checks. They were prepared for this, as they were aware that they needed to be certified healthy and free from disease before being allowed to emigrate. All went smoothly and they were then allowed to board.

Liverpool Docks was enormous, bustling with people, horses, carriages and goods. There were so many ships lined up along the quayside that if the Huntingfords hadn’t been accompanied by another steamship representative, they would never have found the right one. There it was, the SS Norseman, part of the Dominion Line fleet, looking fine in the spring sunlight. It had four masts and a gigantic funnel, presently quiet but just waiting to burst into action.

Gingerly they climbed the gangplank dragging their trunks and baggage with them. Mr Oliver, a friendly ships officer, showed them the way and it wasn't long before they were descending into the bowels of the ship. In the dim light they were dismayed to see lines of bunk beds, crammed together, stretching the length and width of the ship.

'How many of you are there, now?' said the officer. 'Oh, six, including the baby. So, here are three beds.'

'Three?' asked Ellen, 'but there are six of us.'

'Two to a bed, I'm afraid. That's the rule. No room, you see. Have you got your bedding?'

'Bedding?' Ellen repeated, confused.

'Yes, passengers have to provide their own. The Dominion Line cannot supply everyone, you know. Stands to reason.'

Raiding their carefully packed trunks Ellen found what was needed for the three beds. Then after a few more brief instructions, the cheerful Mr Oliver left them 'to settle in'.

They sat down on the beds, feeling rather gloomy. It was a depressing place, dark and bare. Sunlight did not penetrate here. There were no windows and little fresh air. It smelt of damp and sweat.

As the day wore on, more and more people filtered in – couples, families, solitary travellers – every sort and age of person all squashing into this confined space. Georgy was beginning to feel quite claustrophobic and badly needed some exercise.

'Please can I go up on deck, Mum?' he asked. 'I won't go far, promise.'

'Me too!' cried William. 'It's boring here.'

'Yes, all right then but make sure you know your way back. Be careful not to get lost.'

They'd been shown a public lounge as they came down, which Georgy badly wanted to explore. William and he went off in search of it and found a large, bare, whitewashed space filled with hard, wooden benches. At least there were some windows and light. They could even see the water when they looked out, which was exciting.

It was smellier here, though in a different way to below. It smelt of grease and soot, for it was close to the funnel and the furnaces. The boys ran around quite happily, pleased to have the chance to let off some energy of their own. After a while, William suggested they go up on deck to see the rest of the ship. Eagerly, the two boys climbed the steep metal stairs up to the level where they came in. Dodging the endless stream of people descending was difficult, but they were small and flexible and able to squeeze in between. An elderly man swore at them as they tried to get past.

'Damned kids! Look where you're going.'

'Sorry sir,' cried Georgy as they dashed off.

They got to the top of the stairs, but no further. A steward refused to let them through.

'You can't go up there, lads. They're loading the cargo now. It's too dangerous.'

'We just want to have a look,' pleaded William, but his words fell on deaf ears.

Defeated they descended again to the public lounge, which was now filling up fast with passengers. Returning to their family they told them all about their explorations, which cheered everyone up a bit.

'So, we don't have to stay here all the time,' explained Georgy. 'We can sit up there, and we'll be able to see where we're going.'

By 9 o'clock the next morning the ship was full of people, over 2000 to be exact, as Georgy found out from Mr Oliver. The sleeping area felt uncomfortably warm. Exposed pipes and vents pushed out hot air in places, whilst even in cooler sections the sheer volume of bodies made the temperature rise. It had been three hours earlier that the noise and smell really started, as the furnaces were lit to make the steam required for departure. The fumes drifted down into the bows and lingered there, making the occupants cough and choke.

'Let's go up to the lounge,' suggested Ellen. 'We'll be leaving soon, and we may get a view, plus it will be fresher there.'

Fresher air, it certainly was, but the area was so crowded that they found nowhere to sit. Remaining standing they watched through the port holes as the ship finally started its journey. It was with a mixture of fear and excitement that they saw the land slip away from them and knew that they had finally left everything behind. Ellen had tears running down her cheeks and her husband put his arms around her shoulders soothingly. The three boys were silent, gazing out, lost in their own thoughts.

As the ship got out onto the open water it began to roll and shake, causing them to feel quite ill. None of them had been on any kind of boat before and were unprepared for this. Returning to their beds below they hoped this would give them some relief, but if anything, in the twilight depths the motion was felt more keenly and the lack of light only served to make it more intense. Baby Ethel started screaming, but her cry was lost amidst the general noise and chaos of the massed humanity below decks.

Food came and went. It was basic but plentiful and wholesome, though none of them could stomach it at first. Hours went by and slowly the two older boys recovered, as did their father, but Ellen and Gilbert remained indisposed. Baby Ethel was fractious and was refusing to settle.

'Father,' asked Georgy, 'can we go up to get some air? I feel too hot down here.'

Father agreed, so somewhat shakily Georgy and William ventured upstairs. They had hoped to get up on the top deck but there were iron gates barring their way, so it was the lounge once again. This time it was eerily quiet, most passengers in their bunks struggling with sea sickness. A couple of other boys were up there, and they soon made friends. Seamus and Finn were from Ireland originally, travelling with their widowed mother to try and find long lost relatives in Canada. Georgy found their strong accent hard to understand at first, but during a game of football around the lounge, any language barriers were soon overcome.

The days went by slowly, the cramped monotony of the sleeping quarters only relieved by regular visits to the cold and uncomfortable public lounge. On the third day the rest of the family felt able to join them, though seats were hard to come by at times. But anything was preferable to the hot, sweaty half-light of below. Many passengers were still being sick, and the sound of retching and the smell of vomit did nothing to enhance the atmosphere downstairs.

Georgy counted the days. Father said it would take seven days to get there.

One, two, three, four, five… then a storm blew up like a demon. The ship tossed like a cork on enormous waves and the wind howled. Everyone was very scared and stayed huddled downstairs. Many were praying. Seamus and Finn came over to sit on Georgy and William's bunk. Their mother, Finn told them, was quite distressed and was seeking comfort from a catholic priest who was holding a mass for his shipboard flock.

Ellen lay cuddled up to baby Ethel in her bed and their father was trying to distract Gilbert over on his by telling him stories. Seamus suddenly started to sing a lilting Irish ditty, which Finn joined in with, called '*Leave Her, Johnny, Leave Her*'. Georgy thought it the most wonderful song he'd ever heard and very quickly he and William were singing along as well. '*For the voyage is done and the winds don't blow, And it's time for us to leave her.*'

Around them folk stopped to listen, and others joined in. When the song stopped it seemed that the winds had eased, and everyone relaxed. Things were going to be all right again.

Six, seven.... The seventh day dawned clear and bright. All the passengers on the ship were full of excitement at the prospect of arrival. Bedding was repacked, trunks and baggage gathered together, and everyone was in a good mood. Georgy and William said a sad farewell to Seamus and Finn. They would be travelling on to British Columbia, whilst the Huntingfords would be staying in Halifax for the time being. Friends can be found anywhere, thought Georgy, and he was grateful for this.

Finally, the heavy metal gates were unlocked and the ocean of people surged forward as the ship docked, eager for a glimpse of their new life. The Huntingfords were swept along with the tide of passengers, more than ready to face the future. Canada at last!

Chapter 10

Canada 1906

Their first glimpse of Halifax was impressive. A mass of elegant waterfront buildings surrounded a bustling harbour, with ships coming and going like bees round a honeypot. Above the lively city loomed a huge hill, wearing a large star-shaped fort like a crown.

Georgy, as usual, couldn't help asking questions:

'What's that?' he said to the ships officer as they queued up to disembark.

'Why that's Citadel Hill, lad,' the man replied, 'where the army have their garrison. Fort George, they call it.'

'That's my name!' exclaimed Georgy.

'Well, they must have called it after you, then, lad,' the officer said smiling. 'Mind you live up to it. Listen out for the noon day gun. They fire it every day. Have done since 1857.'

'Cor,' said Georgy, 'that's nearly 50 years. Amazing.'

The SS Norseman nosed its way gently between the various small islands which dotted the harbour, until it finally came to rest at the docks. The line of passengers edged their way slowly forward, but it takes a long time for 2000 people to get off via a few small gangplanks and progress was slow. Eventually Georgy and his family came within sight of the exit. Ellen was exhausted, having had to carry little Ethel in her arms the whole time, and the rest of them half carried, half dragged their baggage along. Their arms ached and their backs were sore, but still their excitement mounted. As they got on the gangplank William could contain himself no more and ran forward, dodging between the legs of cursing passengers, and cheering as he reached the shore.

'William, wait there!' commanded his father. 'We don't want you getting lost.'

Finally, they were all together in a new land, hardly knowing what to do or think. In the distance the hills were green, the sun shone, and birds sang. Even the water was sparkling. It was a perfect moment. Sadly, it was all too brief, for they were called upon by officials to enter the immigration shed to be processed.

This was an enormous, unfriendly looking, metal building on the waterfront. Entering it, they could see rows of bare wooden benches where they were told to sit. As far as the eye could see were people, some at desks talking to officials, many sitting, waiting patiently or so it seemed. People progressed into different areas so there were constant movement and a clamour of voices. The Huntingfords waited, and waited, and waited. An hour went by, and they were getting hungry and thirsty. William started to complain and baby Ethel was crying. Georgy felt his stomach rumble. How much longer?

Another twenty minutes went by and finally an officer approached them, clipboard in hand, looking very important. After taking some details about themselves and where they had travelled from, as well as which ship he frowned and went off to a desk to consult with a colleague. There was much shaking of heads and worried looks. Their father was getting annoyed by now and decided to find out what was happening.

'Look here,' he said, 'we're tired and hungry. I've got a wife and four children here with me and we need to rest and recover. Just tell us what we need to do and then we can get on with it.'

'There is a problem with your ship, sir. A suspected case of disease on board. We need to take precautions. Please be patient.'

Shortly after this they were all led off for health inspections to decide whether they were fit enough to enter the country. They were also minutely examined for skin, eye and ear defects or disabilities of any kind. Ellen and Ethel were taken off to a separate area, and it was another hour before they were all reunited. Gilbert started to cry. He was frightened of the men in uniforms with their stern voices and cold looks. It took all Georgy could do to comfort him.

To their relief no health or physical issues were detected and so their parents were then allowed to complete the necessary paperwork. Progress at last, they thought. Not long now.

'Please stay here,' an official told Mr Huntingford sternly, after this, directing them to a holding area. 'Do not move.' He went off.

They waited anxiously. Many other people joined them, and it began to get cramped.

Then the official returned and made an announcement.

'Passengers from the SS Norseman: due to possible smallpox contagion from a fellow passenger, we need to send you all to a quarantine facility on Lawlor's Island. Boats will be arranged to take you there shortly.

Whilst you are waiting, we will provide you with some refreshments. Your stay will be a minimum of two weeks. We appreciate your co-operation. Thank you.'

Quarantine! They felt stunned. What would that be like?

The journey to the island only took about twenty minutes but it seemed a world away from the vibrant city of Halifax. In the boat, Mr Huntingford tried to encourage them.

'It'll all be worth it in the end, you'll see. At least it means they are strict about keeping disease out of Canada. That means it's a healthy place to live. We'll soon be able to settle there.'

'What if we're infected?' cried Ellen. 'I couldn't bear it!'

'Come on, old girl, we're all fit and healthy now, aren't we? It's just a precaution.'

'It's not fair,' grumbled William. 'We've only just got here and now we have to go away again!'

Georgy watched from the boat as various islands came into view. They appeared green and beautiful in the sparkling sea, almost idyllic.

'What are the islands called?' he asked the boatman. 'Which one are we going to?'

The man grunted and pointed to one. 'That's Lawlor's, where you'll be staying. The others are McNabb's Island and Devil's Island.'

Georgy didn't like the sound of the last one. 'Is it nice on Lawlor's?' he asked innocently.

The man laughed sardonically. 'Depends on yer point of view, lad!' he replied, then turned his back on the boy. He preferred not to talk to his passengers.

The boat pulled into a small rocky cove, and they piled out onto the slipway. Uniformed officials were waiting to check them in and escort them to the appropriate place. The island had appeared a lush green from a distance but now Georgy could see some low-lying buildings not far away, large and forbidding, a depressing sight. They felt like prisoners as they were marched along up to the reception hall to be dealt with. This was when they found out that they were to be separated!

'Women, babies and female children over here please. Men and male children in this section.'

'But we're a family,' protested their father. 'We need to stay together.'

'No sir, sorry. Rules are rules. Mrs Huntingford - you and the baby come over here. No, no good arguing. Sorry madam. It's just the way it is. Same for everyone. Prevents cross infection, you know. Sir, bring your sons along now. Come on.'

Ellen was crying and pleading,

'But that's not fair! We've done nothing wrong. How can you do this?'

The authorities refused to listen and took her and baby Ethel off to the women's quarters whilst the rest of them were sent to the male area. Gilbert started crying at being separated from his mother, and though Georgy and William were trying hard to be brave, it must be admitted that a few tears came into their eyes as well. Mr Huntingford attempted to stay positive, shepherding them along and trying not to hear his wife's protests as she was led off in the opposite direction.

'It won't be for long, boys,' he said as confidently as he could manage. 'We'll all be together again soon.'

The grey, stone barracks that they were taken to did nothing to raise their spirits. Inside was bare and cold, but it seemed they had fared better than some, for single men without children were housed in tents. The huge building was teeming with people, and they found little privacy or comfort there. Yet in spite of the crowds, they were very much alone, each family restricted from socialising with others for health reasons. Isolated and yet together – the irony was not lost on Mr Huntingford, but he did his best for his sons. Days of monotony wore on, broken only by regular medical examinations. Food was basic and did little to enliven their days, consisting mostly of salted, canned and dried goods that could be easily stored. Fresh food was rare. Sanitation was also limited, and with the overcrowding, long queues at the privies were common.

The family were allowed one brief excursion outside each day where they breathed the fresh salt air of the island and glimpsed a greener world. Most of the time they were cooped up on their bunks, dismally trying to amuse themselves. George Huntingford was no storyteller, unlike his wife, but he did his best to distract the boys with anecdotes from his working life. He ended up teaching them all about plumbing, which Georgy, with his natural curiosity, found fascinating. William got bored quickly and Gilbert didn't understand most of it, but Georgy thought that one day he might like to do that himself and listened with rapt attention, asking endless questions.

A mile or so away Ellen and Ethel were enduring similar conditions. The worst thing for them all was not knowing when the quarantine would end, and they would be reunited. Nobody seemed to know. The officials could tell them nothing in answer to their enquiries and the waiting and wondering went on.

Two weeks after they had first arrived the good news suddenly came. The passengers of the SS Norseman were free to leave. It seemed the suspected case of smallpox had turned out to be nothing after all. There was a mad rush from the barracks towards the shore, but how would the Huntingfords find the girls? Would they be released at the same time?

George Huntingford gathered his sons tightly around him and attempted to make his way to the women's quarters, but the multitude of people slowed them down. Suddenly, they realised that William wasn't with them any more, Frantically they cast around for him, shouting anxiously. With the density of the crowd, it was almost impossible to see, but by a small miracle a tall man moved out of the way and there was William, looking scared, which was unusual for him.

'Dad,' he whimpered, 'I thought I'd lost you all! You wouldn't have left me behind, would you?'

'Of course not,' his father replied. 'We'd have searched until we found you. We would never have given up.'

Slowly the four of them progressed towards the women's barracks where they were pleased to see a similar mass of people emerging. But where were Ellen and Ethel? Would they find each other?

A frustrating half hour passed, struggling through a morass of humankind, all trying to reunite with their loved ones. At last Georgy's keen eyes spotted their mother, baby in arms, being blown this way and that by the crush.

'Mum!' he shouted and waved like his life depended on it. An emotional reunion soon followed. Much relieved and overjoyed the whole family now made their way towards the waiting boats by the shore. The queues were immense as the boats were small and the numbers very large. Yet more waiting ensued but this time they felt happy and enthusiastic. They would be leaving here soon.

They felt a tingle of excitement as the small boat arrived in the harbour of Halifax at last. A thankfully brief trip through the immigration shed and then they were out, their papers finally stamped and approved. The city of Halifax stood before them in the spring sunshine, waiting to welcome them to their new life in Canada.

Chapter 11

Summer 1906

The butterflies in Georgy's stomach refused to lie still as he walked down the echoing school corridor to his new class. Three weeks had passed since the Huntingfords had settled in Halifax and it all seemed a bit of a blur. For the first few days they had needed to rest and recover. Though their temporary abode of the boarding house had been no palace, it felt like luxury after the rigours of the ship, followed by quarantine. A real bed, privies without queues and hot food – pure heaven.

They stayed in the boarding house for the first week, then set about finding somewhere to live. Father quickly found that his skills were indeed in demand here, and offers of employment came flooding in. Meanwhile their mother was frantically trying to get their new home habitable. The three boys did their best to help, fetching and carrying, running errands. There was no end of things to do.

But now here they were, all about to start a new school in a new country. How would they fit in?

Georgy was relieved to find that the school was not so very different to the one he'd left behind. Up to 30 pupils were squashed in there, in cramped conditions, but the teacher, Mr Norman, though strict, seemed fair. Much of the learning was by rote, merely memorising facts and figures and Georgy soon found it quite boring. At break time he discovered that there were several other English immigrants like himself in the class and that made him feel better. In particular, he made friends with a boy called Edward, Ted to his friends, who had a head of dark curly hair, an impish grin and a lively disposition. By the end of the day, they were the best of pals. Ted and his family had come over from London and had been in Canada about a year now. He promised to show Georgy around the area.

Meeting up with his brothers again after their day in different classes they all agreed that maybe it wasn't such a bad place after all.

As the first week wore on however, Georgy discovered a certain amount of resentment from the French speaking Canadians in his class. These pupils kept themselves very much apart and spoke in a language that he couldn't understand, even though they could all speak perfectly good English as well. Georgy got the feeling that he was being laughed at, even though this might not have been the case. Ted told him to just forget about it, and he tried, but it wasn't that easy. The teacher did his best to be fair to both cultures, frequently breaking into French, which Georgy found confusing. Was he missing out on something important?

At last, the weekend arrived and with it, the prospect of spending some more time exploring the city. They'd all been so busy settling in that they hadn't had much time before. Halifax was an exciting place. Their new home was a modest but respectable house in an unremarkable neighbourhood. Georgy had heard that many people (including Ted's family) lived in much poorer conditions than them, in tenement blocks and he was grateful for what they had. What fascinated him most were the tantalising glimpses of the sea and the forests which were not far away.

From the ramparts of Citadel Hill, where visitors were allowed to wander, the views of the countryside were breath-taking. The contrast with English suburbia could not have been greater. The family went up there in a rare break on one of their first weekends. The weather was glorious though the breeze up there was mighty. In the clear air Georgy could see for miles and he never forgot it. At that moment he fell in love with Canada.

The three-storey tower and dome of the Town Clock stood out like a beacon, gleaming in the sunlight. In the harbour he could see huge ships of all sorts – steamships like the one they had travelled on, military vessels, cargo ships and more. Looking further, he saw the islands clearly. Recognising Lawlor's Island, he shuddered briefly, but with the resilience of youth he shook it off and just admired the beauty of the islands from afar. Someone had told them that there was a pleasure ground on McNabb's Island and Georgy was keen to visit. Apparently, there were fair rides and games of all kinds just over the water. It sounded great fun.

On June 21st they were surprised to learn that there was a public holiday.

'It's Natal Day,' their mother explained, 'which means it's the anniversary of the founding of Halifax.'

'Who founded it?' asked Georgy in his usual enquiring manner.

'You always have to know everything!' exclaimed William. 'Isn't it enough that it's a holiday?'

'Yes, but I want to know,' his older brother replied.

Their mother got flustered as she didn't really know the answer.

'You'll have to look it up,' she said, much to Georgy's frustration. 'Natal means to be born and so that's when the city was born. That's all I know.'

'Wasn't there anything here before that?' Georgy continued.

'Well yes, there were native tribes, I think,' replied Ellen.

'Natives? Were they '*Red Indians*', like in the stories?' asked William.

'I don't know,' said Ellen, getting a bit hot under the collar.

'What happened to them?' persisted Georgy.

'They live somewhere else now,' she said.

'Why?' he asked. 'Don't they like us?'

'I'm not sure, dear. Now come on. Let's go out.'

The day was great fun with the whole city involved. It was the first time that Halifax had joined in with the neighbouring city of Dartmouth in celebrating it. There were parades, a regatta, fireworks and even a concert in the evening. The shops all shut at noon, and everyone took some time off. Their father stopped work then as well and joined them in the afternoon watching the boats in the regatta. The whole family had a wonderful time, and the boys were even allowed to stay up later than usual to see the fireworks.

July arrived and today their pleasures were somewhat more sedate but just as nice. Ellen packed up a picnic lunch and took them all out to the Halifax public gardens. Their father was working, it being a Saturday, and he was away early before they had even had breakfast. The most exciting thing was that as a special treat they travelled across the city on one of the new electric street cars. As they rode along at an exhilarating speed, they could see all the other transport on the roads. Horse drawn carriages were still around, though slowly going out of use, being replaced by the automobile which looked very strange beside them. Ellen was nervous on the streetcar, clinging on as it rattled and swayed its way through the streets.

'It's not natural,' she muttered through clenched teeth and held on tightly to Ethel. Since her husband had now brought home his first wages, Ellen had managed to buy a second-hand baby carriage, but it was bulky and awkward to get on the vehicle. Nevertheless, it would be a great help when they alighted.

They got off at the public gardens and were instantly calmed and enchanted by them. There were flowerbeds full of dazzling summer colour, the insects buzzing crazily around each bloom. In the ponds there were sparkling fountains and everywhere a sense of peace and tranquillity. The hustle and bustle of the city streets seemed a world away. They wandered the paths happily before settling on a bench to enjoy their lunch.

'Can we go and look at the harbour after lunch, please Mum?' asked William. 'I want to see the ships.'

'I'd have thought you'd have seen enough of all that recently,' remarked his mother, smiling.

'Please Mum. I think I want to be a sailor one day.'

It was William's latest craze, but Ellen was always happy to indulge him, and so after they had eaten, they headed towards the waterfront.

The city was busy, packed with people of all nationalities and types. Many wore uniforms and Georgy guessed they were either army or navy.

'Why are there so many soldiers, Mum?' he asked.

'They are the British troops, my dear,' his mother replied, 'because Canada is one of our dominions; but they are leaving soon.'

'Why?' he asked.

'They are letting Canada use their own soldiers to look after us all,' she replied, 'then the British can go home again.'

It was a simplistic explanation but true to the sense of the word. The navy had already officially 'left', though there were a great deal of personnel still coming and going on naval vessels. The army were due to leave within the month.

The family wandered through the busy markets to the harbour area where they spent a great deal of time watching the ships. Then Ellen bought some fresh fish from a stall for their supper, and they took another streetcar to get home.

'I've had enough walking for one day,' their mother declared. 'I'm quite worn out.'

The weeks sped by and soon it was the end of the school term. Georgy was relieved. They had been learning French recently which he wasn't too keen on. He couldn't get the hang of all those verbs. Not only that, but it meant he could now understand some of the playground talk from the French-Canadian pupils, and it wasn't too complimentary. One boy in particular, Jean-Baptiste, seemed especially to despise him. Georgy wondered what he had done to deserve this and hoped things might improve after the long summer holiday.

Their mother had promised to take them all out to the coast for a few days and they were really looking forward to this. Ethel was a year old now and was beginning to babble a few things that sounded like words. She was also trying to stand up, though she hadn't quite managed it yet. Georgy felt that she was getting more interesting. She seemed to be developing a very determined character, with a strong will of her own, and if she didn't want to do something they soon knew about it.

One fine morning in August they set off by horse and wagon to the nearest beach, Cow Bay. Father wasn't with them, he couldn't take the time off work, but he kissed them fondly and wished them well. Ellen had booked a couple of rooms in a boarding house in the area for a few days, and they were all very excited.

The horse clip-clopped slowly along out through the suburbs of Halifax into the countryside to the east. The first views of Cow Bay were awe inspiring. The shining silver sand stretched endlessly into the distance, with the sea lapping gently at its shoreline. The children had never been on a beach before and as soon as the wagon stopped, the boys jumped down and raced off before Ellen could stop them. She smiled to herself. She'd been expecting this. Settling down at a nearby picnic table with Ethel she waited patiently. Her sons were out of breath and covered in sand when they finally returned. Their voices were an excited clamour.

'It's brilliant, Mum!' cried William.

'Can we go for a paddle?' asked Georgy.

'I've got some shells, Mummy,' said Gilbert.

'Lunch first, then you can go in the sea,' promised Ellen.

Those were wonderful days. The boarding house was clean and bright, with good home cooked food. The sun shone and they were able to paddle, swim and explore all angles of the beach. Then when they wanted a change there was the lake just behind the trees to discover. All manner of wildlife was present. They caught glimpses of deer, pheasants, rabbits and all sorts of birds. Georgy thought he saw a large, dark animal moving around which could have been a bear, but William was sceptical, and Gilbert seemed scared, so Georgy said no more about it.

On the last day they went for tea at the pavilion, an elegant, open work building right by the beach. Waves rolled back and forth in perpetual motion and the sand glistened like diamonds. Georgy thought that he had never been so happy. Little Ethel must have thought the same, for she suddenly managed to pull herself up to her baby feet for the first time and toddled a few steps onto the sand before she sat down again, looking surprised and pleased with herself. They all laughed. What a lovely holiday.

Chapter 12

Winter 1906

The first serious snow started to fall on November 29th, floating like ghosts in the air. There had been minor flurries before but nothing to get excited about. This time it meant business. The boys danced up and down with delight at the sight of it. Even Ethel gurgled and babbled appreciatively when they lifted her up to let her see out the window. The temperature had been falling rapidly all month, and their small suburban house was chilly and damp. No matter how many logs Ellen burnt on the fire, they didn't seem able to keep warm. But today it seemed milder due to the snowy arrival. The number of flakes steadily increased, and the wind got up, so the whisper turned into a roar. Blizzard conditions soon ensued, and Ellen became anxious about their father getting back safely. There was no need to worry however, for he returned home a bit earlier than usual, cheerfully stamping his feet to remove the snow from his boots.

'My, it's a wild one out there,' he remarked.

'Can we go outside and play?' asked William.

'Certainly not!' exclaimed their mother. 'I've already told you. Besides, it's getting too dark now. Maybe tomorrow.'

The children had all been let off lessons early that afternoon as the weather began to worsen. They'd been hopeful that when they got home, they would be able to enjoy themselves outside, but Ellen had put her foot down. They were cold and wet upon their return, though with the enthusiasm of youth they hardly noticed. Ellen made them sit by the fire with hot drinks and warm blankets until she was satisfied that they weren't going to catch a chill.

'But we're dry now, Mum,' protested William. 'Surely just a little while outside wouldn't hurt.'

Their mother wouldn't be swayed, but she promised they could go outside in the morning.

'But we'll have to go to school tomorrow,' complained William, 'and all the snow will be gone by then.'

Their father laughed.

'I wouldn't worry, my son. When it snows here in Canada it's a bit more than at home, in England I mean. I doubt the school will open tomorrow if it carries on like this. There's six inches out there already.'

'Really? That'd be brilliant!' cried William, and his brothers agreed. Georgy was particularly happy to be missing school as he wasn't having a good time of it at the moment. He was still good friends with Ted, and he'd become popular with many of the English-speaking Canadian boys in his class. His relations with the French-speaking pupils, however, seemed to go from bad to worse. They'd taken to calling him names openly now, and items seemed to disappear such as his schoolbooks, his pen and his lunch box. Georgy was a patient boy by nature, but he was beginning to get annoyed.

The next morning dawned bright and sunny with a clear blue sky, but the snow lay two feet deep, and the air was bitterly cold. It wasn't going to melt any time soon. From the neighbours, Ellen gleaned the news that all the schools were closed. Most roads were impassable, except on foot. The streetcar had stopped running and even the horse and carts struggled. The boys were delighted. A day off school – and then it was the weekend. What fun!

Once they had wrapped up warmly, Ellen allowed them outside to play. The snow was pure and white, and they loved it. Most of the neighbourhood children were also outside playing and they made many new friends that day. Snowmen were built and snowball fights begun. Gilbert found some new young pals a couple of doors down and spent most of the day with them. Georgy and William had a ferociously brilliant snowball battle with next door's children – Henry and Anne. They were all quite exhausted by the end of the day.

Their father still went to work, travelling on foot. The plumbing work never stopped, even in the bad weather. Ellen tried to dissuade him but, as he said, if he didn't work, he wouldn't get paid, so off he went.

Over the weekend the snow slowly turned to a disappointing grey slush. Georgy wondered if there was more to come. 'Last winter was really nasty,' Ted told him, 'So I doubt it will be as bad this year. Everyone says we get it milder here than the rest of Canada because of the ocean.'

Georgy didn't think it seemed very 'mild' to him. It certainly hadn't been like that in Long Ditton.

Occasionally they had seen a few snow showers and often had frosts but nothing like this.

Christmas came and the chance to relax and have some fun. The weather continued very cold with regular snow and freezing rain. The family were grateful to be able to spend some time indoors.

Just before the big day they all went to a carol concert organised by the Halifax Fire Department. This worthy organisation often did things for the community, it seemed. It was a fun evening, with lots of singing followed by hot chocolate and mince tarts afterwards. Heaven.

Georgy enjoyed their traditional Christmas dinner of roast turkey, potatoes and vegetables, followed by figgy pudding, unaware of the struggle his mother had had to obtain it all. With all the bad weather, food supplies were slow to come into the shops, and Ellen had to hunt high and low to find some of the items. They all exchanged gifts as well, though they were mostly handmade by themselves. Ellen had knitted everyone new scarves. With Father's help, Georgy had created some small wooden boxes, and Gilbert had made sweets. He liked helping in the kitchen and was now being allowed to do some simple cooking under his mother's supervision. William simply bought them all some nuts, as he couldn't settle down to make anything. He didn't have the patience.

Over Christmas it snowed hard again, and the family all went out sledging. Father's Christmas present to them was two wonderful wooden sledges that he had been secretly making for weeks. They all took turns to use them. In the city they saw people tobogganing as well, a sight they'd never seen before. William was keen to try it but was firmly told no. 'When you're older,' Ellen said, 'not yet.'

If they'd thought the weather had been bad so far, this was nothing compared to the dark days of January. Now the snow took on a wilder, meaner character and no-one wanted to play in it any more. The house was very cold, and heating supplies were running low. In desperation one day, Ellen sent the two oldest boys out to find firewood wherever they could. Coal had run out in the neighbourhood and wood was scarce. Another storm had been forecast in the newspapers and people were trying to prepare.

'Don't go too far, though,' their mother said. 'Just do the best you can.'

The sky had an angry pink hue to it and Georgy knew that snow was imminent. He hurried along the streets with William calling at every possible supplier. Nearly everywhere had run out.

'I'm tired,' said William. 'Let's go home. We don't want to get caught out in the storm.'

'Just another couple of streets,' pleaded Georgy. 'We can't go home empty handed. If we don't have a fire the house will be freezing.'

'I'm freezing already,' grumbled William, but he tagged along with Georgy anyway.

In the distance Georgy spotted a small wood yard.

'Come on,' he said. 'They'll have something, I'm sure.'

It was the furthest they'd ever been from home, but they bravely carried on. Their efforts were rewarded by a kindly man from the yard who sold them as much wood as their arms could carry. Georgy had also brought one of their sledges and they piled it up as well with lots more. By now the sky had turned to a sombre grey and the first flakes of snow were whirling in the air.

'Quick,' said William, 'let's get home while we still can.'

The going was slow and hard. Carrying and dragging piles of wood was heavy, back-breaking, arm-aching work and they struggled along. The air was becoming thick with snow, and it was blowing against their faces, making it difficult to see. Suddenly Georgy realised that he didn't know where they were any more. Everything looked so different, and visibility was down to only a few yards. They stopped, both unsure of their way.

'We're lost!' cried William. 'This is your fault, Georgy. *You* said we should carry on.'

'I'm sorry,' muttered Georgy, trying not to panic. 'Look, let's just have a think.'

He felt miserable and cold.

'Do you see that building over there? That tall one with the spire. Do you think that's the church near our school?'

They didn't know but headed towards it hopefully. It *was* a church but not the right one. Georgy didn't recognise it at all and felt scared.

'Let's go in and ask someone,' he suggested desperately. 'At least we can shelter for a minute.'

They entered the dimly lit church, thankful of some respite from the weather. A few candles burnt inside giving a cosy glow, but they could see no-one.

William dropped his pile of wood with a clatter which echoed around the building.

'My arms hurt,' he said.

Just then a friendly voice behind them said: 'Can I help you, boys?'

They turned to see the vicar of the parish.

'We're lost,' Georgy told him. 'We were getting firewood for our mother, but we can't find our way home.' His eyes filled suddenly with tears.

The clergyman smiled. 'Well, that's a great thing you have been doing. Don't worry. We'll help you find your way. Just tell me your address and I'll get one of the vergers to take you home.'

Half an hour later they were finally home with their precious cargo of wood. Ellen was profuse in her thanks to the verger, who then went on his way.

'Oh boys,' she said, 'I didn't mean for you to go so far and get lost. What a scare you must have had. I knew something was wrong when you were so late back. Thank goodness you're all right.'

'It was fine,' said William nonchalantly. 'Nothing to worry about, was it, Georgy?'

'No, nothing,' his brother mumbled, but he was relieved to be home.

The winter wore on with no let up. On top of more snow came a big freeze with dangerous ice and arctic blasts. The children went to school when they could, but opening times were erratic. Mr Huntingford still went to work each day although Ellen constantly worried about him. Plumbers were in demand as much as ever, especially with the number of burst pipes from the low temperatures.

It was early one Saturday evening when there was a frantic knocking at the front door. One of George's work colleagues stood there, pleading for him to come and help.

'There's an old lady over in Creighton Street, whose water pipes have all burst,' he explained. 'The house is flooded, and she really needs our help. She's got three orphaned grandchildren living with her as well. I'd do it myself, but it's a two-man job. Please say you'll help.'

'Please George,' begged Ellen, 'don't go. It's dangerous out there.'

'I must, my love. These people are desperate. We have to help them. Don't worry. I won't be long.'

The snow was falling fast on the frozen ground, but George gathered his tools and followed his workmate Jim out into the blizzard. It was nearly dark already.

'Oh dear,' said Ellen to Georgy, 'I hope he'll be all right.'

'Don't worry, Mum,' Georgy replied. 'I'm sure he'll be home again soon.'

But the hours went by, and Mr Huntingford didn't return. It was now night-time and quite wild outside. Ellen sent the children off to bed and sat up waiting and worrying.

Georgy struggled to get to sleep knowing his dad was out in the storm. The wind howled around their house and the windows rattled. His brothers were all sound asleep, but he tossed and turned. He heard his mother pacing the floor below and he could stay in bed no longer. Pulling on a warm jumper he went down to her.

'Oh Georgy, you shouldn't be up,' Ellen declared, but he could see she'd been crying. 'All the same, I'm glad you're here. Come and sit with me by the fire.'

They huddled together, trying to keep warm, listening to every sound in case it was George returning. The night dragged on. As daybreak came the wind subsided and the snow finally halted. Ellen and Georgy had dozed off for a while, but now the quiet light woke them.

'He's still not home!' Ellen exclaimed despairingly. 'Something's happened to him. I know it has.'

She was beginning to get hysterical. Georgy did his best to calm her, even though he was equally worried about his dad.

'It's just the weather,' he said. 'He's probably staying somewhere overnight, that's all, until he can get home again safely.'

'No, no, he's had an accident. I need to go and find him!' She started pulling on her coat, but Georgy stopped her.

'No Mum, listen. You mustn't go out there. It won't help. You'll only get lost and cold.'

'But I must find him,' she cried.

Patiently Georgy tried to explain.

'You can help him best by waiting here. Dad would want to know you're safe. He wouldn't want you going out in this, you know that. And who's going to look after little Ethel and the rest of us? Now come on, Mum, be sensible.'

Slowly Ellen's reason returned, and she took off her coat, much to Georgy's relief.

'Let's get some breakfast and hot drinks ready,' suggested Georgy, 'then when Dad comes in, he can get warm again.'

It was nine o'clock in the morning when the front door finally opened and Father returned, looking cold but none the worse for wear. Having fixed the pipes, the two workmen were forced to stay the night due to the storm, and had in fact, been warm and dry the whole time. As soon as the streets became passable George and Jim had made their separate ways home. Ellen was overcome with emotion and relief.

‘Oh George, I thought you were lost or dead. Don’t do that to me again, please. I can’t bear it!’

Her husband soothed and calmed her as he always did, and peace reigned once more in the household. Georgy left them to their reunion and returned to bed. It had been a long night.

Chapter 13

1907

Slowly, oh so slowly, the winter crawled away to hide under the spring flowers. March and April that year were still very cold, but the snow eased off at last and life began to return to normal. Supplies came back to the shops, transport ran normally, and the schools were open again, much to Georgy's dismay.

The situation had not improved in class. Georgy was a naturally intelligent boy who was often able to answer the teacher's questions. This earned him praise from Mr Norman but disapproval from Jean-Baptiste and his gang. 'Swot!' they called out when they saw him. 'Teacher's pet!' In the corridors he was frequently jostled and even shoved around at times. In sports they refused to pass him the ball, or they attempted to 'accidentally' trip him up.

'Oh, pardon me. So sorry!' said Jean-Baptiste sarcastically when he managed to send poor Georgy flying to the ground one day. Georgy nursed his grazed knee and muttered: 'It doesn't matter.'

On another occasion, Georgy found his exercise book had been scribbled over with rude drawings and dirty words. Mr Norman saw it and frowned but said nothing. Georgy went red with shame and embarrassment.

He took to trying to avoid the ones who so despised him, going a different route out of the school at the end of the day just so that he didn't meet them at the gates. He made an excuse to William and Gilbert, who he always walked home with, and met up with his brothers further down the road. They didn't know about the bullying. Ted knew Georgy was having problems, but he didn't realise just how bad it had got.

Georgy became quiet in lessons, stopping himself from answering the teacher's questions. Mr Norman often tried to encourage him, but Georgy pretended he didn't know the answer. The teacher was disappointed and felt something was wrong.

One day Georgy's coat disappeared, even though he knew he had hung it on his peg. He had to walk home in the cold without it and Ellen was very annoyed.

'How can you have been so careless?' she demanded. 'Surely you know how much these things cost.'

'Sorry,' mumbled Georgy. 'I don't know where I put it. I forgot.'

It was a feeble excuse, and he knew it. Ellen looked at him keenly, sensing something was amiss.

'Are you all right, Georgy?' she asked, concerned. 'Is something wrong?'

He was shivering from the cold, so his mother took pity on him.

'Come and get warm by the fire,' she said. 'I'll make you a hot drink. Hopefully your coat will turn up tomorrow. You can wear your old one for now. It's a bit small, but it'll have to do.'

When he arrived at school the next day, his coat was on its peg, as if it had never gone astray. He clutched it and took it into class with him, gripping it tightly throughout the day.

'Are you cold, Master Huntingford?' asked Mr Norman. 'Why do you need two coats today? They should be on your peg as you well know, not in the classroom.'

'Sorry sir,' Georgy replied but he didn't let them out of his sight.

The other boys laughed at him as they passed by.

'Two coats! What a mother's boy!'

Things came to a head one day in early May. It was breaktime and everyone was outside enjoying the better weather. Georgy was with Ted happily kicking a ball around and trying not to catch the attention of Jean-Baptiste or his mates. Suddenly he became aware that a group of boys were surrounding them, watching with intent.

'Come on,' said Georgy to his friend softly. 'Let's move over here where there's more room.'

Their way was blocked, however, and wherever they tried to move there was no progress. Georgy looked around desperately but there were no teachers in sight. They'd all gone in to have their lunch.

'Scared, are we?' Jean-Baptiste called out.

'There's no-one to protect you here,' teased another of the gang, a boy called Joseph.

'Leave us alone,' cried Ted.

'We've done nothing to you,' said Georgy.

'Oh, so you think so, do you? Just being here's enough! Soft little English boys, both of you. Go back where you belong.'

The gang came closer, and the two friends tried to make a break for it. Ted slipped through their lines and made for the other end of the playground, but Georgy wasn't so lucky. A well-aimed kick to the shins sent him sprawling on the ground. Then all the rest of the boys piled in. Georgy was not a weakling. He was sturdy and strong like any ten-year-old boy, and he gave back as good as he could. Punches flew and he felt one land on his eye. Ouch! That made him really angry, and he turned on Jean-Baptiste with a fury that surprised himself as much as his opponent. He was laying into his enemy just as two teachers came running up, having been fetched by Ted. Unfortunately, all they saw was Georgy fighting like a demon, and not what had led up to it.

An hour later four boys stood gloomily outside the headmaster's office to receive their punishments for fighting at school. Georgy, Ted, Jean-Baptiste and Joseph were all there; most of the others had managed to flee before they could be identified.

'I'll get you for this, Englisher,' Jean-Baptiste muttered under his breath. 'You'll pay.'

One by one they went in and came out crying. Georgy's turn came.

'We don't allow fighting in this school. Hold out your hands,' said the headmaster.

'But it wasn't my fault,' he protested. 'They started it.'

'Don't talk back! I don't care who started it. Rules are rules. No fighting. You're lucky I don't expel you. Three extra lashes for being impertinent!'

The pain was as much as Georgy could bear. He returned to class with stinging hands, so sore that he could hardly pick up his pen. His eye was turning black, and his lip was split. His legs felt bruised and aching. Mr Norman looked at them all sternly.

'Let this be a lesson to you, class. Fighting is not right and will only lead to severe punishments. Remember that!'

Tears poured down Georgy's face. What on earth would his mother say? He dreaded to think.

Walking home with his brothers, he refused to answer their questions. Gilbert was very concerned about him and kept asking if he was all right, until Georgy got annoyed and bit his head off.

'Just forget it, won't you! I'm fine.'

William was impressed. 'I heard you've been in a fight,' he said, 'who with?'

'I don't want to talk about it,' replied Georgy. 'Leave me alone!'

William and Gilbert fell silent, and it was an awkward journey home. Georgy knew he was being unfair, but he couldn't face telling them what had happened. His mother would be a different matter, though.

As soon as Ellen saw him, she was horrified.

'Georgy, my darling, what happened? You're hurt!'

Georgy fell into her arms in tears then. He could hold it back no further.

'Mum, Mum, I'm sorry! I didn't mean to.'

Ellen turned to William and Gilbert who stood there, staring.

'Boys, take your sister upstairs and amuse her for a while. I'll bring you up some tea in a bit. I need to talk to your brother.'

Obediently they went off, although William was dying to know the details. Then Ellen gathered Georgy to her, and finally he spilled all the beans. Everything came pouring out – the teasing, the bullying and then the fight. Ellen was shocked.

'I shall go to the school and speak to them,' she declared. 'This is not right.'

'No please Mum, don't,' begged Georgy. 'You'll only make it worse.'

'Well, you can stay home from school for the rest of this week,' said his mother. 'You're not well and you need to recover.'

Georgy was thankful. A few days of peace; but what would happen after that? he wondered. Would there be more of the same?

Later that evening there was a knock at the door. A woman they had never seen before stood on the doorstep. Her clothes were worn and shabby, though appeared clean. She seemed embarrassed and awkward. Ellen invited her in.

'I am Jean-Baptiste's mother,' she began, 'and I've come to apologise on behalf of my son. He has behaved disgracefully.' She had a strong French accent, but they could understand her easily enough.

'Well, I should think so,' Ellen said. 'My son is battered and bruised. From what I hear your son has been a bully throughout.'

The woman looked ashamed. 'I'm sorry,' she said, 'it won't happen again. I've told Jean-Baptiste that I will be keeping an eye on him now and that if I hear anything at all he will be severely punished by his father.'

Georgy listened to what she said, hiding behind his mother for safety. Could it really be true? Would things be better now?

She turned to him. 'I'm sorry, Master Huntingford. The family has had a hard time lately. My husband was laid off at work, and the job given to an English man instead, so Jean is very angry about it, but it's not your fault and I shall tell him so.'

Georgy just nodded and clung to his mother.

At school the following week, all was silent. Jean-Baptiste avoided him and told his friends to do the same. It was an uneasy ceasefire, but Georgy was grateful. He began to take part in lessons again and he regained his teacher's respect.

In the middle of May, the family celebrated Ethel's second birthday. She was turning into a lovely little girl, able to toddle around now and say quite a few words. They had a little party for her which they all enjoyed. At the end of the afternoon when Ethel had been laid down for a nap, their parents called their sons together into the drawing room.

'We've been thinking it over, boys,' their father said, 'and we've decided to move out of the city. Do you realise we've been here a year now?'

'Where to?' asked William enthusiastically.

'Your mother and I have found a house in a place called Amherst. It's still quite a big town, but it's out in the countryside more. You'll be able to enjoy the forests and hills nearby. Plus, the coast is beautiful around there. I've been offered a good job as well.'

'Will we have to change schools?' asked Georgy hopefully.

'Yes, of course,' replied his father. 'It's too far away from Halifax for you to continue here. It'll be a new start for us all.'

'I'll miss all my friends,' said Gilbert wistfully.

'Yes, that's a shame, but you'll make new ones. We'll move over the summer holidays and then you can start school there in September with everyone else, at the start of term.'

Georgy was delighted. Though he liked his friend Ted, a change of school was just what he needed, and he looked forward to discovering more of their new land. Roll on summer!

Chapter 14

Amherst 1907-1908

It appeared that moving to Amherst was a good idea. The boys started school at the beginning of the academic year and found no problems in settling in. Georgy made lots of new friends and there was no resentment from the locals.

Amherst was a most agreeable town with lots of attractive brick and sandstone buildings, many boasting late Victorian grandeur, including their own home. Though not one of the very finest houses, it was still large and elegant, with a decent sized garden which the children loved to play in. Gilbert finally got the swing he'd been after for so long, though it was rather makeshift and tied to a tree. Ethel toddled around the lawn and spent ages digging in the dirt, until Ellen nearly despaired of getting her clean again. There were several trees in the garden which Georgy and William loved to climb, and they spent several happy days creating their own treehouse. Gilbert was nearly seven years old now and was allowed to join them if he wished, as long as he gave them the secret password, but he spent a great deal of time amusing his little sister instead. They seemed to have formed a close bond.

The town was prosperous, with new industry springing up everywhere. The main trades seemed to be shipbuilding and lumber. Because it was near to the Bay of Fundy, this meant that many of the occupations were related to the sea, though it was also surrounded by lots of good farming land, where both crops and animals flourished. The area was certainly thriving.

Their father had a good job in a plumber's firm, but it seemed that they rarely saw him any more. He went out early and came in late. At the weekends he was supposed to have a half day free on Saturday, and Sundays off, but he often had to cover emergency callouts.

In October, the children were surprised to hear that their mother was pregnant again. Georgy had just turned eleven before this announcement and felt quite shocked about it.

'That means that by the time this baby starts school, I will have started work,' he said to William, when they were alone later.

'What of it?' replied his brother.

'Well, I'll hardly know them,' Georgy continued. 'It'll be like a different family, or something.'

'Don't be daft,' William said scornfully, punching his brother on the arm. 'You do talk a lot of nonsense sometimes!'

But Georgy couldn't get the idea out of his head. How would he relate to someone so much younger than himself? He couldn't imagine it.

The baby was due in March, so at least the worst of the winter weather would be over. This year the family were more prepared for it, but it was severe all the same. Being a smaller place than Halifax, it was easier to get around to school, shops, work etc. There were no street cars here, just good old traditional horse and carts, plus a smattering of the new automobiles. Supplies still struggled to get through at times, and it was just the goodwill of the community which ensured that everyone had enough food and firewood.

Arthur was born on March 18th; a large, healthy baby who bawled loudly from the moment he arrived in the world. Ellen was torn and sore and took a while to recover from the birth. For some reason she seemed disinterested in her new son, though she fed and changed him, dutifully. Georgy noticed that she paid little attention to Arthur and looked distracted. There was none of the cooing, singing and smiling that he had seen with previous arrivals. Having watched it three times already, he thought this was odd. Their father spent a few days with them all before going back to work and being absent again.

Georgy suddenly realised what the difference was this time: they had no family support. Before, there had been Aunt Mary and her family, Uncle Dick and Aunt Minnie, and even Grandma Goddard. He missed them all. He took to thinking about his cousin Nellie, wondering if she still wore her hair in pigtails, and how tall she was now. His memories of all her family, especially her bubbly mother, Aunt Mary, were clear and bright. What happy times they had had. All of a sudden, Georgy felt a bit homesick. He loved Canada, but he felt the need for a wider family. Maybe his mother was feeling the same. One day after school, he tried to talk to her about it.

'Mum, can I write to everyone back in England? I'd like to tell them all our news.'

'There's no need,' replied Ellen in a curt voice. 'I wrote to Uncle Dick the other day.'

'But what about Aunt Mary and Uncle Will?' persisted Georgy. 'Can I write to them?'

'They don't speak to us any more,' his mother said, 'because they didn't like us moving away.'

'But surely if I wrote...' Georgy began.

'You're not to and that's that!' Ellen snapped, her voice rising angrily. 'I won't have it!'

Georgy was shaken by her anger but anxious to find out more.

'Don't you miss them all, Mum?' he asked. 'I do.'

'Of course not,' she said. 'We have our own lives here, now. Do be quiet, Georgy.'

He could tell his mother was upset, so he left well alone. Later he confided in William, but he seemed to agree with Ellen.

'Can't say I miss grumpy old Grandma,' William remarked. 'Good riddance to the lot of them. Well, I suppose Nellie and Billy were all right, but we've got new friends now.'

'Mum doesn't seem herself,' Georgy said thoughtfully.

'She's just tired after having the baby,' replied William. 'She'll soon perk up.'

But a few weeks went by, and this didn't seem to happen. Coming home from school one day, Georgy noticed his mother's eyes were red as if she had been crying. He made a special effort that afternoon to help around the house and was glad to see that Ellen was smiling again later. It's probably nothing, like William said, he thought, and tried to forget it.

At the weekend, however, Ellen sat in the kitchen, staring into space, showing no interest in anything.

'Come out and see what we're doing in the garden, Mum,' called William, 'We're going to have a race.'

Their mother barely glanced at him. She just sat there listlessly, her hands in her lap. William grabbed her hand and tugged at her, but she seemed in a world of her own. A tear rolled down her cheek. William went back to the others, confused and annoyed.

'Mum won't talk to me,' he said. 'I don't know what's wrong.'

Georgy was concerned. 'I don't think she's very well,' he replied. 'Maybe we should fetch the doctor.'

Leaving Gilbert and Ethel to play outside, the two older boys went in to see their mother.

'Mum, are you all right?' asked Georgy. 'Can we get you anything?'

'Leave me alone!' she exclaimed. 'Children – that's all I see everywhere I go, always wanting more!' Then, just as suddenly she burst into tears. William put his arms around her and held her as she wept. Georgy felt useless for a moment, then he suggested he make a cup of tea.

'That'll make you feel a lot better,' he said and went off the put the kettle on the stove. He knew William was the best person to console their mother, but why she was so upset he couldn't fathom.

A hot drink and a lot of hugs appeared to restore Ellen's equilibrium, at least for a while. Some fresh air in the garden made the colour come back to her cheeks and her voice returned. Unfortunately, then baby Arthur started crying again and her face darkened. She went inside to feed him and didn't come back outside afterwards. They found her standing in the nursery, looking almost as if she hated the infant, her hands clasping and unclasping in an agitated manner.

‘We need to tell Father,’ Georgy said to William, after they had calmed and soothed their mother once again.

‘What good will that do? He’s never here,’ his brother replied.

‘That’s the point. Maybe he needs to be at home more. I’ll talk to him tonight after everyone else has gone to bed.’

Georgy was nervous of talking to his father about such a thing but being the oldest he felt it was his responsibility.

‘Good luck with that!’ remarked William.

To give Mr Huntingford his due, he cared very much about his wife, but he was working long hours to provide for his family and scarcely had time to think. After supper, when all his siblings were upstairs getting ready for bed, and Ellen was seeing to the baby, Georgy attempted to speak up.

‘Dad,’ he began, ‘I’m worried about Mum.’

His father looked at him in surprise. ‘What do you mean?’

‘She keeps crying, Dad, for no reason, and she doesn’t seem very interested in anything.’

It sounded a bit feeble, but it was all Georgy could think of to say.

‘Crying?’ his father said. ‘She seems fine to me. I haven’t seen it.’

‘I don’t think she’s very well,’ Georgy mumbled but his father wasn’t really listening.

‘Don’t be silly, son. Everyone gets upset at times. You know your mother is a bit emotional. She is perfectly well.’

‘Maybe she needs some help with the baby?’ Georgy suggested.

His father glared at him.

'Look son, I think I know your mother better than you do. She is perfectly capable of raising a baby. After all, she's done it four times already!'

Georgy faltered. 'Yes, I know but…'

'That's enough, George,' his father insisted. 'Now, isn't it time you went to bed?'

After Georgy went up, his father reflected on what his son had said. In bed that night with his wife he tentatively asked her if she was all right.

'I'm fine, dear,' she replied but it sounded hollow.

'How is little Arthur?' her husband enquired. 'I've not seen him a lot, unfortunately. I hope he's not being too much trouble.'

'Of course not!' Ellen cried angrily. 'Now let's go to sleep'.

Mr Huntingford decided to keep an eye on his wife for a couple of days. The weekend started and he made an effort to be at home as much as possible. Watching closely, he had to admit that she wasn't herself. The beds weren't made, meals were slapdash, the house uncared for. Of more concern were the emotional upsets. Ellen seemed to go from vacant and tearful, to angry and spiteful in a second. He noticed that the children were getting the worst of it, and he was worried.

On Sunday the boys held a secret conference after a difficult weekend.

'Look,' said Georgy, 'I don't know what's wrong with Mum, but I think we need to help out more. If we all did our bit around the house perhaps it would make her feel better.'

'I could help in the kitchen,' Gilbert volunteered enthusiastically. 'I like cooking.'

'You needn't think I'm doing cleaning,' declared William. 'That's women's work!'

'Well, you could help out with Ethel,' suggested Georgy, 'and run errands. I can do some cleaning up, and if we all make our own beds in the mornings that will help.'

A pact was made, and they did their best to stick to it. Meanwhile on Monday Mr Huntingford asked around at work and found out one of his colleagues had a wife who would be glad of some extra money. It was agreed that she would come in most weekdays to 'help out.'

Aileen O'Keefe was a kind, cheerful Irish lady who breezed in the next day much to Ellen's surprise.

'Your husband's asked me to come in and 'do' for yer, every morning. Now where do I start, ma'am? Oh, here let me see to the baby. He's a dear, ain't he?'

Ellen's initial feelings of resentment and anger gradually gave way under the onslaught of such good-humoured chat.

'It's a fine morning, to be sure,' remarked Aileen after an hour of working hard. 'Why don't we take a dish of tea out into the garden now, soak up some of that sunshine?'

With Mrs O'Keefe's morning visits and the boys' efforts after school, Ellen's spirits slowly improved. She was able to smile more, though she still found it hard to connect to baby Arthur.

It was now the middle of May and two years since the family had left England. Ethel was no longer a baby but a delightful little girl of three years old. Her birthday celebrations were held out in the garden, and the neighbours were also invited. Mrs MacNeil next door had a sprawling brood of five healthy children, all at school. Georgy was in the same class as her second son James and liked him very much.

'Have you visited the Bay of Fundy yet?' Mrs MacNeil asked. 'You really should see it.'

'What's there?' Georgy enquired.

'Why, don't you know? It's a wonderful piece of coastline with such high tides, you never seen. Beautiful it is.'

'Sounds great, but how would we get there?' William asked.

'Well, the train of course. Goes straight from Amherst to Truro, then there's a regular carriage ride to the bay. You can easily do it in a day.'

'Oh Mum, can we?' cried William. 'It sounds fabulous. You know how much I love the sea.'

Ellen smiled weakly. 'One day soon, dear,' she said, 'but I can't take you at the moment. I just don't feel up to it.'

The boys were disappointed.

'Can't we go on our own?' said William. 'We'd be all right on the train.'

'Certainly not!' their mother replied. 'Don't be silly, William.'

'Begging your pardon, Mrs H,' said Mrs MacNeil, 'but I'd be happy to take them all next time we go, if you like. A few more children don't make much difference when you got so many already.'

'Oh Mum,' said Georgy excitedly, 'please can we go? We'd be ever so good.'

'Please Mum,' begged William.

'Ethel's too little to go,' Ellen said.

'I'll stay and look after her,' said Gilbert. 'I don't mind.'

Ellen hesitated. 'Well, I don't know, maybe it would be possible. I will have to talk to your father about it, though.'

To her surprise her husband was very enthusiastic about the idea.

'I think it would be a great chance for you to have a day off yourself and relax,' he said.

'Relax!' Ellen exclaimed. 'I'm hardly likely to do that with a baby and two children to look after!' Her moods were still unpredictable at times. George stopped her tirade.

'I'll get Aileen over for the whole day, then she can look after all of them, while you rest. It will do you good.'

It was agreed therefore that the two oldest boys would join Mrs MacNeil and her tribe of children the following Saturday. The weather dawned bright and sunny, and they were very excited.

'They have the highest tides in the world there,' declared Georgy, 'and waves that go backwards!'

'How can waves go backwards?' said William scornfully. 'Don't be silly.'

'It's called a tidal bore,' Mrs MacNeil explained when they were on the train. 'The tides are so powerful that they run up the river estuaries and so they appear to go backwards.'

'See! Told you!' cried Georgy, sticking his tongue out at his brother.

The steam train rattled along until it pulled into Truro station where they piled out and grabbed the first horse and wagon that they saw. It took them to a place called Chignecto Bay, where they spent the day exploring. It was an amazing place with strange rock formations the like of which they had never seen before.

'They look like mushrooms,' said William.

'They're called the Flowerpot Rocks,' Mrs MacNeil told them. 'They're quite famous.'

'How were they made?' asked Georgy.

'The tides have carved them out over many years,' she replied.

'Oh look, there's some people over there fishing,' Georgy exclaimed. 'They're very brave to go out that far.'

'They're Mi'kmaq,' said Mrs MacNeil, then seeing he looked confused she explained: 'Native tribespeople. They've always done it.'

'Do they live in Amherst, like us?' asked Georgy.

'No dear, bless you. They live on a reservation.'

'What's that?'

'A special area for the natives,' she replied.

'Why don't they live with us in the town?' he persisted.

Mrs MacNeil was getting flustered, but just then her son interrupted and all was forgotten.

'I can see some whales!' cried James. 'Come and see.'

'Can we go in swimming?' asked William.

'Not really,' replied Mrs MacNeil. 'With these high tides it can be dangerous. You have to be very careful.'

'Besides,' laughed James, 'it's not that kind of beach.'

As the tide went down, they could see a vast stretch of mud, stretching as far as the eye could see, hardly a beach suitable for bathing, but instead dotted with exciting rock pools to explore, with sea creatures imprisoned within, until the next tide would free them. They pottered about for hours, seeing things they had never seen before. Eventually they had to leave to catch their train home.

'What a wonderful place,' remarked Georgy, 'but we didn't see the backwards waves.'

'Another time,' Mrs MacNeil said. 'You need to catch it at high tide. This is a place that is different every time you visit.'

'I'd like to come here every week,' declared William. 'It's brilliant!'

They returned home, satisfied and happy. It was a pleasure to find their mother waiting for them at the door, looking relaxed and cheerful. The day of rest had done her good. From that point on, things slowly improved. There were bad days of course, but the black despair had dissipated, replaced by a gentler melancholy which was easier to bear.

Chapter 15

1910

It was a day of mixed emotions for Georgy as he prepared to leave school for the last time in July 1910. He was one of the youngest in his year, as he hadn't yet turned fourteen, though his birthday wasn't far off. He was excited at the thought of the future but scared at the same time. Walking out of the school gates with his friend James MacNeil, he suddenly felt very nervous.

'Where do you think we'll be in ten years' time?' he wondered.

James laughed. 'I guess I'll still be here, working hard in Amherst, but who knows where you'll be, what with your family never staying put for long!'

It was true. The Huntingfords were on the move again over the summer, this time to a city called Moncton in New Brunswick. It wasn't far really, but it seemed like a world away from rural Amherst. Georgy knew he would miss the town he had come to love: the gentle farmland, the beautiful forests and lakes, and that amazing coastline. What times they had spent there, soaking up the spirit of the wild sea. Georgy sighed at James' words.

‘I’ll miss this place,’ he said, ‘and all of you, of course. It won’t be the same.’

‘Well, we’ll both be out at work anyway,’ said James, ‘and we won’t have time for much else.’

Georgy reflected sadly that this was all too correct. Whilst at school they had had time to spare to enjoy themselves, but now they had to put their childhoods aside. They were growing up; embarking on life’s journey, not knowing where it would take them.

Georgy had already experienced changes in himself which made him feel strange and vulnerable. His voice didn’t seem under his control any more. The pitch rose and fell as it pleased, leaving him croaking at times. As for his body, hair seemed to sprout from all kinds of places, and there were urges within which he didn’t understand. His emotions were less stable as well. He’d always been a level-headed boy, but now he was up and down as the day took him, sometimes in despair, other times full of anger or intense joy. He almost hated himself for it. Father told him that these things were normal, and so he clung to the hope that it would all pass sooner or later.

The reason for the move to Moncton had been explained to them all. When they had first come to Amherst it had been booming, with industry thriving, but there had been a dip in the town’s fortunes of late. Their father’s workplace was still doing a steady trade, but he thought he could do better. George Huntingford dearly wanted his own business again, if only to give his sons somewhere to work in the future. Therefore, he had bought a plumbing business in Moncton from someone who needed to give up due to ill health. Georgy was going to join him as an apprentice.

When it came to a career Georgy didn't really have that many options. Working in the lumber trade or on a farm didn't appeal, and at least he knew what the plumbing business involved; after all, he'd helped his father out enough times recently. It looked like William might join them as well in the fullness of time, though at twelve years old, he was a restless soul, never sure of what he wanted.

Consequently, they were all moving over the summertime again, so as not to disrupt schooling. Ethel had now turned five and was due to start school for the first time in September. Gilbert was nine years old, and Arthur, no longer a baby, was two. Artie, as he was often known, was a noisy and outgoing toddler, into everything and keen to explore as widely as Ellen would allow. He particularly liked to be outdoors in the garden, and he hated to be confined.

It was only a week later that they bade farewell to the MacNeils. Georgy was sad. Besides his friend James, he had developed a partiality for his friend's sister Johanna, a tall, black-haired beauty who he admired from afar. She scarcely noticed he existed, but still Georgy found himself strangely stirred when she was around. Still life had to move on.

Now it was off to Moncton. The boxes were packed, the furniture strapped onto the cart and the family on the train. Moncton was a vibrant and prosperous city, mostly due to its extensive railway connections. A previous ship-building boom had seen it flourish in the 19th century but then decline again until the advent of the rail links. Now, new buildings and businesses were springing up everywhere. Nevertheless, the area they were moving to, Lewisville, was out of the centre and was pleasantly rural in its way. Seeing it for the first time Georgy felt relieved. Big cities were all very well, but he preferred a quieter place to live.

Their new home was a comfortable Victorian residence with a garden and spacious rooms. Georgy was also pleased to note that Moncton was in a river valley, with the Petitcodiac river running through it, both broad and deep. It reminded him of the dear old Thames, back in England, so many years ago, or so it seemed. He struggled to think of England as 'home' now. He'd only been in Canada for four years, but he loved it. True the winters were fearsome, but he'd got used to them as time went on, and the feeling of wide-open space prevailed everywhere, even in the heart of the cities. England seemed small and cramped by comparison.

Remembering the Thames, however, set Georgy to thinking of the day when he had rescued Nellie's boat, and he felt a wave of sadness wash over him. If only he could have seen them all again. Maybe one day he would travel to England and visit. He knew his mother wouldn't approve but he was about to start earning his living and was on the verge of becoming a man. He would be able to decide his own life soon.

There was a week to get settled in, and then Georgy was horrified to be told by his father that he would be starting work the following Monday.

'But I haven't had a summer holiday yet,' he protested. 'Surely I don't have to start straightaway.'

'Look, my lad,' said his father sternly, 'you're not at school now, you know. It's a working life for you, just like the rest of us. There are no long holidays any more. School days are over.'

Georgy gulped. How would he get used to this new routine?

‘How long is the apprenticeship, Dad?’ he asked, hesitantly.

‘A minimum of four years if you do well,’ replied his father, ‘though it can go to five if necessary.’

‘Four years!’ exclaimed Georgy. ‘But I’ll be eighteen then by the time I’m qualified.’

‘That’s right,’ said his father. ‘That’s quite normal. At least you’ll get Saturdays off as an apprentice. I don’t. Think yourself lucky.’

Georgy felt shocked. When they’d talked about him joining his father, he hadn’t realised it would be like this. He wished he’d asked more questions.

‘What happens if I want to do something else instead?’ he asked glumly.

‘You’ll have to wait until you’re qualified, then you’ll have a trade to fall back on. After that you can do what you like.’

Georgy tried to cheer himself up by thinking that at least he would be getting a wage and have his own money at last.

‘Pull yourself together, Georgy,’ he told himself firmly, ‘everyone else is in the same position as you.’ But then the thought occurred to him: ‘Is this all there is, then? Work, work and more work. Don’t I have anything to look forward to?’

He felt depressed and unaccountably angry at the unfairness of life, and he took himself off to the garden where he mooched around, just needing to be alone. By dinner time he had managed to restore his spirits and even raised a smile for his family. Just got to bear with it, he thought, no point in moping.

On the Saturday before he was due to start work the whole family went out to explore the city centre. It was rare that Father was able to join them on an outing, and it was only because he hadn't yet started work. Husband and wife proudly walked along with Arthur in the baby carriage, whilst their other offspring went ahead. The city of Moncton was full of elegant buildings, mostly of wood and brick, some very newly built such as the Provincial Bank, which had opened earlier that year. They were surprised to discover how bi-lingual the city was, with French and English to be seen equally everywhere. Having learnt French at school, it was no hardship to the three boys, but Ethel and their parents were confused at times.

William was delighted to see that, just like Halifax, there was an electric streetcar which they could use to get around the city. It was his favourite form of transport.

The family navigated their way down the main street, stopping to look in shops and at roadside stalls. Georgy was finding it all rather hectic as the noise from the railway engines arriving and departing was constant. Moncton was a very busy station. He suggested to his mother that they find somewhere quieter to have their lunch and she agreed.

'Can we see the petticoat?' asked Ethel.

'Petticoat? What petticoat?' said her mother, confused.

'The petticoat river,' the little girl told her.

They tried not to laugh.

'You mean the Petitcodiac River, dear! Yes, let's go and have a look at that.'

'You can see the tidal bore there,' said Georgy knowledgeably, 'just like when we went to the Bay of Fundy. That's where the river flows backwards.'

They ventured to the riverside, but it was not as scenic as they'd imagined. It was a bustling place with barges and boats carrying cargo, and industry thriving along the bank. The river seemed to be used more for work than recreation and they were disappointed.

'I don't think this is the place for our picnic,' remarked Father. 'Let's find somewhere else.'

Georgy then spotted a sign which pointed to Victoria Park and Moncton Zoo, so it was resolved that they would go there. To their relief they found a delightful green space with colourful flower beds and tall, stately trees. After enjoying their lunch, William was keen to visit the zoo. Young Ethel was a bit scared of the idea, but Gilbert, ever her protector, promised to look after her, so it was agreed. They wandered happily over the grass taking in the sights. Baby Arthur had twice tried to climb out of his baby carriage, so in the end, Ellen took him out and allowed him to toddle around, holding her hand.

The animals were mostly local wild animals with a few more exotic specimens here and there.

'Come and look at this funny bird,' called Gilbert. 'He's so comical.'

Dutifully, they all followed and were transfixed by the antics of an ostrich. They had never seen anything like it. For a moment Ellen let go of Arthur's hand and stood there staring with the rest. It was only a few seconds but suddenly Georgy gave a shriek.

'Quick! Catch him!'

Arthur was toddling over as fast as he could to the next enclosure.

'Horsey!' he exclaimed, being the only animal's name that he knew. 'Horsey.'

However, it wasn't a horse at all, but something much more fearsome – a large, ferocious looking wolf, grizzled and somewhat grumpy, not overly impressed at the sight of a human youngster heading straight towards him. The growls were becoming immense, but Arthur took no notice and kept on going. Only the swift pursuit of his father and brothers prevented him reaching the fence.

'Horsey,' cried Arthur again and he screamed loudly as he was removed to a safe distance. Ellen turned very pale and had to sit down on a nearby bench feeling quite faint. They all felt shaken, and Ethel started to cry.

'It's all right,' said Gilbert soothingly to his little sister, and he hugged her.

'What were you thinking?' Mr Huntingford said to his wife in a severe tone. 'He could have been killed!'

Ellen promptly dissolved into tears as well.

'I'm sorry. I thought I'd got him. It all happened so quickly.'

Georgy stepped forward as peacemaker.

'There's no harm done,' he said. 'These things happen. Arthur's fine, Dad. Let's go and enjoy the rest of the day.'

Short tempers were soothed and tears dried. The excursion resumed, though on a subdued note. Georgy reflected on the way home that this would be his last day out for a while, but with times like these maybe it was just as well.

Monday morning arrived, and despite the 6am start Georgy was intent on being bright and breezy. If this was where life was to take him, then he would do his best to enjoy it, or at the very least, endure it.

Chapter 16

Moncton 1910 - 11

The gentle rains of mid-September were starting to fall when the news came. Ellen called them all together one evening, in a state of great excitement.

'We've had a letter,' she announced. 'We're not going to be on our own any more.'

They looked up, surprised. Georgy's heart leapt. Maybe Nellie and her family were going to visit.

'Your Uncle Dick is coming over to live,' Ellen continued. 'He arrives in October, and then if all goes well Aunt Minnie and the children will be following. Won't it be lovely to have some family around at last?'

They all agreed that it would be wonderful, though secretly Georgy was disappointed that it wasn't the other side of the family. He liked Dick and Minnie well enough, but he had no great love for his cousin Ralph. Young Ethel couldn't remember them at all, and she was thrilled to think that she had cousins, aunts and uncles.

'Where is Uncle Dick going to live?' she asked. 'Will he stay with us?'

‘No dear. He has some temporary accommodation booked for him in Quebec to start with, and then he is planning to move over here to be near us.’

‘I wonder if he will have to go into quarantine like we did,’ said Georgy. ‘That was a horrible time.’

Ellen shuddered. ‘It certainly was. I thought I was never going to see you all again.’

‘What’s quarantine?’ asked Ethel.

‘You were there. Don’t you remember?’ said William impatiently.

‘She was too young to realise what was happening,’ replied his mother. ‘Yes, you were there, Ethel, but I’m glad you’ve forgotten it. It wasn’t nice. We all had to be kept away from people in case we had an illness, but luckily, we were all right.’

‘It was like being in prison!’ declared William.

It seemed that Dick was a lot luckier than them, fortunately, as he arrived in Quebec safe and well on October 30th, without any excessive restrictions or mishaps.

A telegram arrived to tell them the good news and that he would be coming into Moncton by train at the end of the following week.

What excitement there was as he stepped off the train, though he looked so much older and greyer than when they’d last seen him. He was only three years senior to his brother George, but there seemed a vast difference. Their father clasped his hand in a hearty handshake, and Ellen hugged her brother-in-law fiercely. The children stood there, not knowing quite what to do or say. He seemed almost a stranger after all this time. Arthur screamed in protest at being ignored, and Ethel suddenly went all shy and hid behind her mother. As the eldest, Georgy decided he should make an effort, so he stepped forward and said, 'Welcome to Moncton, Uncle Dick.' He shook his uncle's hand quite formally and then fell back to allow the others to do the same.

'Well, you have all grown up, haven't you?' exclaimed Dick. 'Georgy, you're a real young man. Are you out at work now?'

'Yes,' replied Georgy enthusiastically. 'I'm a plumbing apprentice.'

To his surprise he suddenly felt proud of his job. He'd been there for nearly two months now, and the time had flown by. He'd been very nervous when he first started but he soon made friends with the other two employees, in spite of being the boss's son. They'd been taken on by his father as part of the ongoing business.

Sam was an elderly man, with a wealth of experience, a grizzled complexion and any number of humorous anecdotes. Georgy loved to sit and listen to him talk at lunchtimes. The other employee was a lad in his early twenties, who had finished his apprenticeship a year or two back. Joe was lively company, and by his own account, a bit of a one with the ladies. It made Georgy feel grown up to be with them both.

The work was tiring and even boring at times, but it was enlivened by his companions. His father kept him hard at it, secretly worried that to ease up on his son could be seen as favouritism. Often, he bawled his son out for doing something wrongly. One afternoon he made Georgy stay late and do the same task over and over again, until he mastered it.

Georgy had found this upsetting at first but soon got used to it. One day as they walked home after a particularly difficult day, his father spoke out.

‘I know I’m very strict with you, George, but it’s all for the best. I don’t want the men to think I’m treating you better than them just because you’re my son. I hope you understand.’

‘Of course, Dad,’ replied Georgy, quite touched by his father’s consideration, and he resolved to bear it like a man.

Uncle Dick managed to find a job at the Moncton Almshouse, as a maintenance man. It wasn’t well paid, but he hoped to able to set up a home ready for his family when they arrived.

November that year brought the usual winter storms, but this time with such a deluge of rain that parts of the river basin in the city flooded. The Petitcodiac was higher than it had ever been, and there were times when it was difficult to travel around. Georgy secretly hoped for a few days off due to bad weather, but it wasn’t to be. If anything, they were busier than ever.

The spring of 1911 finally arrived, bringing better weather and calmer seas. Joe kept trying to persuade Georgy to join him on a night out around the city taverns.

‘Come on George, you’ll meet all the ladies there, and have a real good time, believe me.’

But Georgy didn’t feel quite ready for all that and steadfastly resisted. Alcohol was generally frowned upon by the authorities, but that didn’t stop it being available all the same. He’d never tried it, and he knew that his mother didn’t approve. There was talk that it might be banned quite soon. Georgy was shocked, therefore, when his father invited him to come out with him and Uncle Dick to celebrate Dick’s birthday.

‘Me?’ said Georgy. ‘But what will Mum say?’

'You're a young man now,' his father replied. 'Time you were able to indulge in adult pastimes.'

Ellen ranted at her husband in private, making her views on the idea very clear, but George Huntingford stood his ground.

'He's so young,' she cried. 'It's not right.'

'He's working now and entitled to be treated like a man, not a child,' her husband said firmly. 'This is my decision and it's final.'

Ellen said no more. She knew when she was beaten.

That weekend Georgy went out with his father and uncle. Before he left, William railed at the unfairness of it all.

'Why can't I go? I'm only a bit younger than you. I always get left out!'

Georgy was nervous. He'd never been out drinking before, and he'd heard lots of terrible things about the dangers of alcohol. In a lot of ways, he'd have been happy to let William take his place, but it was not to be.

They entered a tavern on Main Street and ordered some beers. Georgy eyed the large glass of foaming amber coloured liquid before him, and hesitated.

'Cheers!' cried his uncle and they all took a gulp. It was a taste such as he'd never experienced before: bitter and strong, yet soothing and mellow. He wasn't sure if he liked it or not, but he took another slurp and began to warm to it.

By the end of the pint, he was convinced, and also a little intoxicated. Everything suddenly seemed hilarious, and he couldn't help laughing.

'Let's move on to the next place,' suggested Dick and they hit the fresh air, looking for another tavern. There were plenty down Main Street and Georgy lost count of how many they went in, or what he had to drink. His father winked at his brother. He'd been watering down the last few drinks for his son.

Everything was spinning and Georgy was unsteady on his feet as they arrived home. His voice was loud, and his speech slurred. It was late and everyone else had gone to bed.

'Shhh!' said his father. 'You'll wake them all up.'

Georgy giggled uncontrollably and then got the hiccups.

'Dad, Dad,' he laughed. 'I can't find my legs! How do I get to bed?'

Smiling, his father guided him upstairs, made him lay down and then took off his boots for him. Georgy passed happily into a deep drunken slumber almost immediately. His father gazed fondly at him for a minute, then went to bed himself. His son would, no doubt, have a hangover in the morning, but it was a rite of passage for a young man and best done with paternal supervision. He cherished the memory of his first drinking session with his own father and hoped that Georgy would one day feel the same.

Aunt Minnie and their cousins Ralph and Dorothy arrived in late March, after a rough voyage and a lengthy quarantine. Ellen was delighted to have another woman around, though Minnie being of a frail disposition, took some time to recover. On the first visit to their house, however, despite having grown up in age, Georgy and William discovered that Ralph had not improved in temperament. From a moody boy he had turned into an angry young man of fifteen, with a permanently sour expression.

The adults went off to catch up on old times, whilst the cousins were left to amuse themselves. Dorothy was only two years old, just a bit younger than Arthur, but of an altogether calmer disposition. Ethel played quietly with her and Arthur in the corner of the kitchen, sharing her toys and telling them stories. Gilbert, William and Georgy meanwhile were left to entertain Ralph. He sneered at Georgy when he heard where he was working.

'Plumbing! What do you want to do that for? I can't think of anything more boring. I suppose you're not up to working in an office like I do. Don't you have any ambition?'

William instantly stood up for his older brother.

'It's a good job, with a future, and lots of money!' he declared, which might not have been strictly true, but he didn't care. 'Only the best people can do it.'

'Huh, you mean the stupidest,' exclaimed Ralph.

William would have hit his cousin, but Georgy pulled him away.

'Don't, William. It's not worth it. He's only trying to annoy us.'

Just then Arthur started protesting because the story Ethel was reading had come to an end.

'Doesn't he ever shut up?' Ralph demanded. 'Typical of your family!'

'Leave him alone!' cried Georgy, feeling he must defend his little brother.

'Yes, or we'll make you!' threatened William.

Ralph laughed sarcastically. 'Oh yeah? I don't think so. You're just weaklings, you two. I could take you any time!'

Georgy felt a red-hot rage possess him.

'Yes? Well, let's see, shall we? Let's go outside!'

At that moment Aunt Minnie and their mother came in chatting happily and noticed something was amiss. 'What's going on?' said Ellen.

'They're going to have a fight, Mum!' Gilbert told her. 'Stop them!'

'A fight! Really boys, you know better than that. You should be ashamed.'

'Ralph,' said Minnie in her mild, ineffectual way, 'you mustn't you know. I think it's time we were going home.'

'Don't forget what I told you, Minnie,' Ellen said as they left, 'but remember, it's our secret!'

Ralph scowled and Georgy sulked, feeling cheated out of his right to defend his reputation.

'Don't think this is over,' he said to Ralph quietly. 'I won't forget this.'

'Suit yourself!' his cousin replied. 'I'm ready any time you are!'

With that he was whisked away by his mother, along with his little sister.

After his emotions had subsided, Georgy felt ashamed of himself. He wished he could have more self-control. Whatever had got into him these days? Ralph always brought the worst out in him, but even so, he shouldn't let himself be provoked.

It wasn't very long before Ellen's mysterious secret was revealed. She was pregnant again, the baby being due in October.

'Yet more babies!' said William to Georgy that night after she had told them. 'Why do they go on? Really, they should know better.'

Georgy was surprised as well. After all, their mother was over forty years old now and her health was never strong at the best of times.

‘At least Aunt Minnie is around now to help out,’ he remarked. ‘It won’t be like last time.’

‘Let’s hope it’s the last one,’ said William. ‘Enough is enough!’

Chapter 17

The summer of 1911 was a strange one. The family splintered like glass and went in different directions. Georgy felt increasingly disconnected from them all. Work kept him busy five days a week often until late in the evening, and at the weekends he was too tired to do much. Ellen was heavily pregnant and feeling the heat. Aunt Minnie invited Ethel to come and spend most of the summer break with them to keep Dorothy company, now that Ralph was working. It relieved the pressure which their mother seemed unable to cope with. This left William, Gilbert and Arthur at home over the school holidays. Gilbert did his best to amuse and chaperone his younger brother, taking him out and about whenever possible. There was nothing Arthur liked better than to be outdoors in either the garden, the park or (his first choice) the zoo. Gilbert was now eleven and being an amiable boy was more than happy to indulge him, though he missed Ethel. Meanwhile William mooched about, not knowing what to do with himself, until he took matters into his own hands and started running errands on a casual basis for some of the businesses down by the river, to earn a bit of cash.

Ellen begged him to stay home and look after the others, but he was having none of it.

'I'm not a nanny, Mum!' he declared. 'This time next year I'll be starting work!'

It was true the years were passing by, and he was no longer a child. He missed spending time with Georgy, though he saw him at the weekend, but it wasn't the same.

Georgy felt bad that he couldn't help around the house more. He knew his mum was struggling, and that William was lonely. This was to be his lot now, he thought gloomily, rarely seeing his family and with no time for himself. Would life always be this way? He understood now why his father hadn't been more involved with the family. It wasn't his fault; work just got in the way.

Trade slackened off; it seemed that people had fewer plumbing needs in the summertime. There were none of the burst pipes and frozen water supplies which kept them busy all winter. Even so, it was a complete surprise when Georgy's father suddenly suggested they close the business for a week to take a holiday. Sam and Joe were reluctant. No work meant no pay, and they couldn't survive without that. Sam grumbled loudly.

'T'aint right, Mr H, sir. I mean, how's the missus going to manage with no wages coming in? We still got to eat.'

Joe agreed. 'My mum will have a fit if I don't bring in my share,' he said. 'What's more I've promised my girl I'll take her to the Majestic Theatre next week. Tickets don't come cheap, you know.'

Georgy's father relented and compromised. The two regular employees could continue as normal. He and Georgy would take a few days off.

'I'll pop in each day to see if everything's all right, though,' Mr Huntingford told them, 'Just in case.'

'Checking up on us, more like!' muttered Joe under his breath, but luckily Georgy's father didn't hear. Georgy was only too glad to have some time to himself, and he wondered how best to make use of it. It was hot and dusty in the city. Even the trees looked thirsty, and the grass was brown.

If only I could get out in the countryside, Georgy thought, and then he had an idea. It was a suggestion that William got very excited about. Now it was just a matter of convincing Ellen.

'Mum,' explained Georgy, 'William and I are going to go camping for a few days. We will be out from under your feet, and it will do us good.'

Ellen was hesitant.

'On your own? But boys, it could be dangerous. Where will you go?'

Georgy had discussed it all with his brother beforehand and had all the answers.

'Just to the local woods on the outskirts of Moncton,' he said. 'There's a lake where we could go fishing. Lots of people go there. It's quite safe.'

'But where will you sleep? You haven't got a tent.'

'We've made one,' declared William. 'I got some old canvas from Fred down at the shipyard, and Georgy's bought some poles and rope. We've got everything we need.'

'I'll have to ask your father,' Ellen said firmly. 'I'm not sure he'll agree.'

But Mr Huntingford was only too keen for them to go.

'I think it's a great idea,' he said. 'It will help toughen them up. Why don't we ask Minnie if she can take Gilbert and Arthur for a few days as well, then we could have a bit of quiet time here, just the two of us?'

He smiled persuasively and Ellen relented. It was all arranged for two days' time. Minnie was only too happy to help out, and Gilbert was desperate to see Ethel again, so it worked out well for everyone. William was wildly enthusiastic.

'We can go fishing,' he said, 'and trap rabbits for dinner.'

Georgy frowned. He didn't like the idea of hunting animals. 'No,' he said firmly. 'No traps. They're cruel. We'll take some food with us. I don't mind doing some fishing, but no hunting.'

William protested but Georgy was adamant. He'd seen a rabbit struggling desperately in a trap once before, when they visited the Bay of Fundy and he had never forgotten it. William was out, laying in supplies when Georgy's father came up to him quietly and called him into the garden to speak privately.

'George, lad, I'm all in favour of this trip. It will do you both good. But just take care. There are bears out in the woods. I want you to take this with you, but don't tell William or your mother!'

With that he handed Georgy a shotgun which he had kept behind his back until then.

'Dad! Really, I can't. I don't know how,' stammered Georgy, shocked.

'I'll give you a lesson now,' said his father. 'It's only to be used in an emergency; just the noise should be enough to frighten off a dangerous animal.'

His father showed him how to load, aim and fire. Georgy was a hopeless shot, but he did his best.

'Always keep the safety catch on when you're travelling,' his father advised, 'and don't point it at anyone, not even in fun.'

Georgy felt that he could never face using it, but he took the firearm with him and hid it away in his baggage. Meanwhile William acquired fishing rods, bait, nets, a cooking pot, food and some other necessities.

The next day they were ready to leave. Laden heavily, they headed off by train to the woods just outside the city. Once they got off the train they hiked through the beautiful woodland until they found a glade near the lake which looked suitable. The sun shone brightly above, but here under the trees it was filtered. Shafts of light came down through gaps in the canopy, illuminating patches of ground below. The woods went on for miles until they became a deeper forest, on the foothills of the blue-grey mountains in the distance.

The two young men attempted to put up their tent, constructed out of canvas and wood. Eventually their best efforts succeeded in a strange looking, lopsided affair but they felt pleased with themselves. After arranging their bedding, it looked almost cosy. They crawled inside and enjoyed the novelty of it all. Then William suggested they try and catch some fish for their supper. This was not as easy as it looked. Nothing seemed to like their bait, and it was nearly dark by the time they had enough for the smallest of meals. Still, they lit a fire and cooked their meagre catch in the pot over it and swore they'd never eaten anything so good before.

An impenetrable darkness came down, and they lay in the tent trying to sleep, listening to the sounds outside. Georgy felt scared really but tried to pretend he wasn't. To take his mind off it he started to talk to his brother about anything that came into his head. In a way, being unable to see each other, made it easier to open up. The two boys covered many topics that night. William talked about what he wanted from the future.

'I don't want be an apprentice,' he said. 'I want to travel the world, to find adventure, maybe go to sea.'

'I'd like to go back to England again,' admitted Georgy. 'Not 'cos I don't like it here, but to see people.'

'People, what people?' asked William.

'Aunt Mary and her family. Nellie, Billy and yes, even Grandma Goddard! I miss them all.'

'Yes, I know what you mean,' replied his brother, 'but they'll have forgotten all about us by now. What's more, I doubt you'd recognise them if you passed them by in the street.'

Georgy reflected sadly that this was true. He could hardly remember their faces, and by now they would all have changed.

They fell asleep reminiscing about old times and happy days. Next morning they awoke at daybreak, wondering where on earth they were, then it all came back to them – camping!

Two glorious days of freedom and fun went by. Swimming, fishing, hiking – they enjoyed it all. Luckily, their skills at fishing and cooking both improved.

It was the last day. They were packing up and had already taken down the tent, ready to go home. Suddenly there was an enormous roar some way behind them. They turned to see a large, angry looking bear lumbering slowly in their direction. They froze.

'Don't move,' whispered Georgy. 'Stay still.'

'Not likely!' cried William, and he turned to run. The bear growled and got up speed, racing towards them. Georgy fumbled in his bag in panic, raised the gun and shot blindly in the general direction of the animal. It was their only chance. The gunfire echoed off the tree trunks, missing the bear by a mile, but it was enough to stop it in its tracks. It turned and ran off, back the way it had come, much to their relief.

'Crikey!' exclaimed William. 'Where did you get that? You could have told me.'

'Dad gave it to me,' admitted Georgy sheepishly, 'just for emergencies.'

'Phew! Well, I think that was one, for sure. Let's get out of here!'

Georgy was busy at work, fixing some pipes, on August 21st when Joe came up whistling.

'Well, that's it,' he said. 'The government's announced it at last. There's going to be an election.'

'About time, too,' added Sam. 'Now let's get rid of those daft Liberals. All that American nonsense, I ask you!'

Georgy was aware of what they were talking about, though he wasn't eligible to vote yet. He'd heard them grumbling about the way the Liberal party wanted to integrate with America more. People were feeling quite worried and annoyed about it. No-one wanted to be American. They were Canadian; whether that was British, French or other origins, it didn't matter. There was a lot of anti-American feeling around, resulting in protests and unrest. The Conservatives had fought hard against the integration issue and in the end an election became inevitable.

Public feelings ran very high for a few weeks, but in September the Liberals were voted out and things settled down again. Georgy was glad. He hated conflict, even if he wasn't involved.

Leonard Huntingford was born on October 15th, though Georgy saw little of the event. He was busy repairing a sink when William arrived to tell him and Father that Ellen had gone into labour.

'Can I go and see Mum, please Dad?' he asked but his father replied in the negative.

'What and leave a job half done? What kind of business do you think I'm running, George? You just stay and finish your work!'

Reluctantly Georgy carried on, and it was the end of the day before he could get home and see how things were.

The baby was healthy and strong. Another boy thought Georgy. Five boys and one girl – surely, they will stop now.

Luckily it was just before the winter storms set in, so Ellen was not isolated this time. Minnie came to stay for a while with Dorothy and then visited regularly afterwards.

Georgy barely saw his new brother until their short Christmas break came around, though several times he was woken in the early hours by the wail of a hungry infant, demanding to be fed. He had never realised how important it was to get a good night's sleep until he started work. Now he felt shattered the next day if he was disturbed overnight.

1912

The weather after Christmas was of a bitter coldness, even more extreme than normal, and the ice took a long time to retreat. As April dawned people began to talk of spring and warmer days, but it seemed the sea did not agree and persisted on clinging onto its icy character. This was to prove tragic for the ill-fated passengers of a luxury ocean liner, the Titanic, who dared to sail too close to an iceberg.

1,500 people perished: many bodies being brought ashore to Halifax. Georgy could never think of that lovely harbour in quite the same way again, and Ellen cried for days. The list of lost souls was quite shocking.

There was a crisis of a more personal sort later that year. It was the last weekend in July and William had just left school for the last time. Sunday morning dawned, hot and sunny, and Georgy luxuriated in bed, enjoying his chance to lie in. All of a sudden, he heard shouting downstairs, and he recognised the raised voices of Father and William arguing about something. A few minutes later William came charging upstairs to the bedroom they shared and started grabbing his belongings.

'What's going on?' asked Georgy sleepily. 'What's all the shouting about?'

'Father!' cried William. 'He wants me to be an apprentice plumber, just like you. I told him I won't do it! It's my life and I'm going to do it my way; not be tied to something for four years!'

'What did he say?'

'What do you think? Told me it was that or nothing; to get out. Well, I will. I'll show him. I'm off!'

William slung his bag over his shoulder and stomped out of the room. Alarmed, Georgy leapt out of bed and started pulling clothes on hastily. This seemed serious.

Downstairs he heard more shouting, and his mother crying. He hurried down half dressed, just in time to see William slam the door.

'Wait! Don't go!' Georgy called.

Their father's face was as black as thunder.

'That no-good waster! He doesn't want to work, the idle good for nothing boy. Ungrateful, that's what he is. I set him up with a job and that's how he repays me! Well, he can go. I don't care!'

'Please George,' pleaded Ellen tearfully. 'William needs time to come `round to the idea, that's all. Don't make him go.'

Mr Huntingford snorted and stormed off, followed by his wife, trying to make him see reason.

Georgy sat down, stunned. What should he do? He hurriedly pulled on his shoes and a coat. He had to stop William. Now, where would he go?

William had got a good head start and had hopped on the nearest streetcar to get as far away as possible. After an hour of fruitless searching, Georgy was in despair until he suddenly thought about the riverside and headed towards the water. He found his brother there, sitting dejectedly on a bench, his head in his hands.

'William! Thank goodness! Please come home.'

'Never!' declared William. 'I'd be gone now if I could get a passage on one of these boats, but they all turned me down.'

He sighed and a tear started to fall, but he fiercely brushed it away.

Georgy talked and talked: soothing, reasoning, persuading; eventually William agreed to come back and try again.

'But if he starts on at me again, I shall leave for good this time,' he told Georgy. 'I'm warning you.'

Meanwhile Ellen had done the same with her husband and had just about managed to calm him down. William was her favourite child, and she wasn't about to lose him.

The two teenagers returned to the house warily, but they needn't have worried. Ellen hugged William frantically and Father was too downcast to be annoyed any more. A compromise was agreed – William need not sign up to an apprenticeship, but he must find a job and stick to it. He could choose his own way, but he should face up to adulthood.

Later that evening, when they were alone, William admitted to Georgy that he was glad he'd come home.

'I don't really know what I'd have done, to be honest, but Father was so unreasonable, I couldn't stand it.'

'It's best not to do anything hasty,' said Georgy. 'Who knows where you might end up.'

'One day,' said William wistfully, 'one day I'll leave this place behind and travel the world. But for now, I guess I'll just have to find a job. Cheers for your help, mate, anyway.'

It was as close as William ever got to saying thank you to his brother for his intervention, but it was enough. Georgy fell asleep feeling happy again. Another storm was over, at least for now.

Chapter 18

1913

'Georgy, it's nearly 7 o'clock', called his mother. 'You'll be late!'

Georgy bounded down the stairs two at a time, trying (and failing) to button up his best jacket at the same time.

'It's all right Mum, it doesn't start till 7:30,' he said, 'but I better go. I'm meeting Joe in five minutes.'

Now that Georgy was seventeen, he'd started going out more in the evenings. There had been a few trips to the tavern with Joe, his work colleague, and even one occasion when he and William had visited the local music hall on their own. William had been fascinated by the dancing girls, with their colourful flounces and crimped hair, and had wanted to go and meet them backstage afterwards. Georgy said no, firmly. It wouldn't do to get a certain reputation.

William had developed into a handsome and charismatic young man, who only had to smile at a girl to make her blush and giggle. Georgy, on the other hand, was of a pleasant, but unremarkable, demeanour and still uneasy around the fairer sex.

Tonight, he and Joe were going out to a dance to meet Joe's latest girlfriend, Hélène, and her younger sister, Marie-Thérèse. Georgy felt as if he was being set up, but Joe begged him to come along.

'Hélène will only come to meet me if she has her sister as chaperone,' he told Georgy. 'So, you can do me a big favour and keep Marie out of the way. I've heard she's a nice girl. You'll enjoy yourself.'

The event was in fact a veillée, held in a nearby community hall. This involved music, dancing and storytelling and was part of the Acadian culture, for the two sisters came from a French-Canadian family. Georgy was aware that there was a large community of Acadians in Moncton. It was already a bilingual city with a strong French presence.

Joe embraced Hélène and introduced Georgy to Marie-Thérèse. Georgy was immediately struck by her beauty - hair the colour of autumn conkers with eyes as dark and skin like ivory. He could not take his eyes off her face. He was entranced. She greeted him shyly and lowered her eyes modestly. He suddenly felt awkward and didn't know what to say.

'Hello,' he stammered. 'How do you do?'

Joe led Hélène off to dance, and the two younger people were left standing there nervously. 'Can I get you a drink?' Georgy asked, and his companion smiled sweetly. It lit up her face, and Georgy fell under her spell. Somehow, they started to chat, first about families, then work, (she was a seamstress), school and more. Their joint nervousness evaporated, and when Joe came back, they found the two of them deep in conversation.

'You two should go and dance,' suggested Hélène.

‘Yes, let's please,’ said Marie-Thérèse enthusiastically. ‘I don't get out much.’

Ellen had spent the last week trying to teach Georgy how to waltz, but these dances were very different. The music was fast and lively, played on the fiddle and accordion, and involved a lot of stomping and twirling. Georgy was hopeless but did his best, whilst his partner effortlessly spun and glided in her delicate floral dress with her pretty ribbons in her hair, a vision of feminine charm. They ended up in a laughing heap at the end of it.

‘These dances are different to anything I've done before’, explained Georgy. ‘I'm sorry I'm so dreadful at them.’

Marie laughed. ‘It is fine. They are part of our heritage. And I've been brought up with them. So, I gather you haven't been to an Acadian dance before, then?’

‘No,’ said Georgy. ‘But tell me all about them. I'd love to know more about your culture.’

They talked and talked, and by the end of the evening, Georgy understood a lot more.

She told him about her family and their strong Catholic faith. She was one of ten children, and their father was a lumberjack. Hard work and prayer were the mainstays of their life. It seemed a world away from his own family, Georgy thought, but he was still fascinated.

The music subsided and soft lights began to glow as a storyteller gathered people around and began. Georgy was spellbound. The evening came to an end and Joe and Georgy escorted the two girls back to their family home, a basic wooden house on the outskirts of the city. By now Georgy felt he couldn't face not seeing Marie-Thérèse again and he had to ask.

'Can I see you again? Please. Maybe we could meet for a walk or something. Please.'

Marie-Thérèse hesitated. 'I'm not sure if I'll be allowed out,' she replied. 'Father is quite strict about these things. But you know where I work. Maybe we could meet one lunchtime. I have a break at 12:30 till 1 and I usually go to the park.'

'I'll be there,' promised Georgy. 'How about Tuesday?'

His heart was full of a beautiful new emotion as he walked home that night. What it was, he didn't understand. Was this what they called love? Or just a passing fancy? In bed that night, he couldn't sleep for thinking about her - her smile, her hair, her eyes, and her gently rounded womanly figure, soft and warm, full of promise. Tuesday came and somehow Georgy managed to squeeze in enough time to meet her at the park. Her delight at seeing him was evident and he felt reassured. Weeks went by of meetings - lunchtime and after work. Often Georgy would walk her home if he could finish work in time. But he was never asked in, which surprised him.

'Can I come and meet your family?' he asked. Marie smiled. 'One day, perhaps, not now.'

He was dissatisfied but tried to be patient. On the third week, Georgy felt brave enough to hold her hand as they walked in the park and she didn't pull it away. Her delicate palm rested there softly in his, and his joy was complete. Next time they met, he was delighted to be given an invite to the family house for Sunday lunch. Georgy felt that this was real progress.

At this stage, he hadn't told her how he felt, and although he had wanted to, he hadn't kissed her. As she left him this time after telling him the address, he suddenly plucked up the courage and kissed her on the cheek. She turned, surprised, and pulled away.

'I must be going now,' she said. 'I'll see you Sunday.'

At home that night, his mother called him aside to speak to him privately.

'I know you're keen on that French girl,' she began, 'but I think you should be careful.'

'I haven't done anything to be ashamed of!' exclaimed Georgy.

'No, I'm sure,' Ellen replied. 'But their ways are different to ours and you may find yourself getting hurt, that's all.'

'Marie isn't like that,' said Georgy. 'She's a fine girl.'

'Just look after yourself, that's all,' she warned.

Georgy didn't understand his mother's concerns and tried to dismiss it from his mind. Sunday lunchtime came and Georgy duly arrived at the house, clutching a bunch of flowers and wearing his best clothes. He was greeted politely but formally and introduced to many people. Marie shyly led him to the table, a huge, long affair with at least 20 people around it. Some were siblings, some cousins or friends, all speaking French rapidly, which he couldn't understand. At school he had learned some of the language, but amongst fluent native speakers he was lost and couldn't follow it.

To his dismay, he was not seated next to Marie-Thérèse, but on the far side of the table. She smiled at him from across the way, but he felt isolated and awkward. The meal consisted of dishes he had never tasted before - chicken fricot and potato dumplings. They were delicious and Georgy complimented their mother on her cooking, but she just nodded her thanks. The meal commenced and ended with prayers, all in French, which Georgy found embarrassing. He tried to join in at the right places and hoped he hadn't made a fool of himself.

Halfway through the meal, attention suddenly turned on him when the father started asking him about himself, his family, his work, and more. The barrage of questions felt like an interrogation and Georgy was uncomfortable. He did his best to answer cheerfully, but he was aware Mr Leblanc was not impressed.

'Your famille - they come from England, yes? Why did they come here? Did they have somewhere to live? What does your father do?'

Georgy talked of the journey over, the perils of the steamboat and the quarantine, but it was dismissed as nothing.

'Poo. This is not hardship. Your family come here expecting everything and they get it! How is that fair?'

Georgy didn't know what to say. He fell silent and the conversation dropped away. Mr Leblanc returned to speaking in French to his family and Georgy was ignored again. He was glad to escape at the end of the lunchtime. Marie saw him out.

'I don't think your father likes me,' he told her.

'Nonsense,' she said. 'By the way, there is another veillée next week if you'd like to come.' This cheered Georgy up. He'd been trying to persuade Marie to come out for an evening but every time she replied no, she must be in for evening prayers.

'What every evening?' Georgy had asked.

'Yes, it is our routine,' she explained.

So, he was pleased to know he would see her, and he made a note of all the details. On Thursday evening, he turned up, as promised, at a large barn near their home, which had been turned into a dance hall for the night. All the hay bales had been moved back against the sides, providing seating for the guests, and the musicians were there already, tuning up. Marie arrived with her oldest sister Jeanne, but they were accompanied by a young man who Georgy recognised from the dinner party.

'This is my cousin François,' said Marie-Thérèse. She seemed genuinely pleased to see Georgy, but she was dragged off by her sister, who was keen to control what she did that evening. The band started to play, and Georgy managed to grab her for a dance, but he was disappointed to discover that he would not be her partner for the whole evening. Jeanne insisted François take Marie on the floor for a major part of it. Georgy watched helplessly as the two cousins danced the French folk tunes effortlessly and perfectly. Finally getting Marie-Thérèse to himself again, Georgy tried to ask her what was going on, but the music was loud and the dance fast, so he couldn't catch his breath and talk at the same time. The music subsided and the lights fell, in time for the storytelling and this time Georgy managed to take a seat on a hay bale next to Marie-Thérèse. The storyteller was talking in French, which Georgy struggled to follow, but he didn't care. The magical atmosphere cast a spell on everyone, and Georgy slipped his arm around her. To his joy she leaned against his shoulder, and he felt at peace. Surely, she must like him, or she wouldn't have done that. Georgy decided that next time he saw her, he would tell her how he felt.

The next week in the park when they met, Georgy sensed Marie-Thérèse was sad. She was very quiet as they walked. They passed under a low tree branch and suddenly she gave a little cry.

'Ouch, my hair is caught! George, can you help me?'

The ribbon of her hair was tangled up with the tree branch and Georgy spent a few minutes undoing it. They were so close he felt breathless.

'Let me tie it up for you again,' he said and did so. This brought them face to face and Georgy could no longer resist. He took her in his arms and kissed her gently on the lips. She was warm and yielding, her mouth soft and wet, her eyes closed in bliss, but suddenly it was all over, and she pulled away.

'George, we mustn't,' she said. 'I can't do this.'

'Why not?' pleaded Georgy. 'You must know how I feel about you. Surely you feel the same. I know you do.'

'I like you, George,' she said seriously. 'But I can't see you any more. I was going to tell you today.'

'Why not?' he said, shocked.

'My father has someone lined up for me to marry. It's my duty.'

'But that's not right!' protested Georgy. 'He can't do that.'

'He can,' said Marie-Thérèse, 'and he will. And I must obey. Obviously, if I really don't like the person, then that's a different matter, but I must follow my father's wishes if I can.'

'Why?' spluttered Georgy. 'You don't have to, surely.'

'It's our tradition,' she explained. 'You wouldn't understand, but it's part of our culture.'

'I don't understand - you're right there!' he exclaimed. 'I love you. Doesn't that count for anything?'

Marie-Thérèse smiled sadly. 'I thought you knew, George, that it couldn't lead to anything between us. I was just enjoying your company for a while. I'm sorry.'

'Sorry!' exploded Georgy, now thoroughly upset. 'I suppose it's François, isn't it?'

'Yes,' she replied reluctantly. 'He has good prospects and he's a decent man. I've been promised to him for a long time.'

Georgy was aghast. 'So, all this time then you knew we had no future?'

'I'm sorry, George,' she repeated. 'You're a sweet person, but we have to say goodbye.'

She walked away, leaving Georgy feeling bereft. That night in bed, he reflected sadly on a love gone missing before it had even started. His mother had been right, he thought. What a fool he had been. He would be more careful with his heart in future.

Chapter 19

August 4th 1914

The mood at Georgy's place of work was grim that morning. It seemed that war was inevitable. Joe worked silently with gritted teeth, thinking of his latest sweetheart, and whether he would be sent off with the troops. Georgy felt waves of fear wash over him. What would it be like being at war? Last night they had heard that Germany had invaded Belgium and declared war on France. Britain had sent an ultimatum, and everyone knew that if they entered the war, so would Canada.

Discussing it at home with the family in the past few days, Georgy had been shocked to hear young Arthur (now six years old) say: 'Why should we go to war, just because Britain does? It's not fair. It's nothing to do with us!'

Then Georgy reflected that for one thing, Arthur was still a child, and for another, that he had been born in Canada. He had never known England. It was just a distant land across the sea, to which he had no connection. It was different for the rest of them, he realised. They could still remember their homeland.

He tried to explain this to his young brother.

‘We are part of the Empire, Artie. Canada is a dominion, ruled by Britain.’

‘I don’t see how,’ said Arthur stubbornly. ‘We’re separate to them. Well, I’m not fighting any battles for them, anyway!’

He stomped off moodily, leaving the others grinning.

‘I don’t think a six-year-old will really be called upon to help,’ laughed their father, ‘but you never know. Things could get desperate!’

‘Oh George,’ cried his wife, ‘don’t! I can’t bear to think of any of you being called away to fight.’

Her husband patted her on the arm soothingly. ‘Don’t fret, old girl. I’m too old for them to be interested in me, and the boys are too young. There’s no need to worry.’

By contrast with Arthur, William was keen on the idea of getting involved. War seemed an exciting adventure to him, and he made secret plans to join up.

The headlines of the newspapers that day rang loudly with the news that German troops had entered Belgium. Old Sam brought in the latest edition when he came into work, and they gazed at it gloomily. Eventually Mr Huntingford demanded that they focus on the job-in-hand, but it was hard to concentrate on anything, and little got done.

At midday, Georgy and Joe went into the city to find out the latest. People were gathered outside the newspaper offices, waiting, in case there was a special edition. There were rumours that anything could happen at any moment. Crowds took to the streets, roaming uneasily, unable to settle.

The afternoon dragged slowly on, with no news. The deadline that Britain had given Germany was due to expire at 6pm Canadian time. After an ineffectual day,

Mr Huntingford finally gave in and told them all to pack up early. At home, the family ate dinner in silence, a mixture of dread and excitement in the air.

Six o'clock came and they heard a commotion nearby. Church bells were ringing, and the streets were alive with people. The Huntingfords went outside to see what was happening. Instead of fear and despair, the atmosphere seemed to be one of celebration. War had been declared by Britain, and therefore Canada was now also at war. Yet there was singing in the streets, flags waving and people cheering. In the main square, in front of the ruins of the city hall which had burnt down only a few months before, speeches full of patriotic fervour were being made. The public were roused in support of their home nation. William was excited and ran off to join the throng, listening to the speakers as they motivated the people.

Georgy was surprised at such a keenness for war. He supposed it must be the right thing to do, but at what cost? True, you couldn't let someone go walking into another country to try and claim it for themselves. That should never be allowed. Britain had done well to stand up to the Germans, he thought, and he suddenly felt proud. But to celebrate the start of a conflict? Well, he wasn't sure he could go that far.

Ellen had tears running down her face, leading her younger children gently through the outskirts of the hubbub, though Arthur sulked throughout. Ethel and Gilbert went hand in hand, waving flags, though they weren't too sure why. It was a strange evening. The newspapers ran special late editions declaring '*Britain at War – Canada too!*' So that was that, thought Georgy.

It seemed so strange to be getting up the next morning, going to work as if nothing had happened. The world had changed and yet everything appeared the same. Georgy rose at 6am, just as usual, but he noticed a difference in his brother. William was normally reluctant to get out of bed and had to be constantly chivvied along to get him to work on time, but not this morning. He was up and dressed, before Georgy had barely risen. Whistling cheerfully, he rushed downstairs, grabbed a hasty breakfast and left the house before them all. Georgy was instantly suspicious. What was William up to?

Georgy and his father reached their place of work for the day to find a state of chaos. The householder who had requested the work no longer wanted it done and said so in no uncertain terms.

'Don't you know we're at war?' exclaimed the customer, Mr Briggs. 'I can't go paying out for luxuries like plumbing, when who knows what might happen. My son, he works for me, but today he's gone to sign up, so what's going to happen to my business, I ask you? Not to mention the shortages we're bound to have. I'm sorry, but I've got to cut back.'

Harsh words were said on both sides. George Huntingford always hated to be messed around. Eventually they headed back to their base, only to find no Joe. Sam was there and told them why.

'He's gone to the recruitment office, silly man. His girl's got it into her head that he's a coward if he don't, so there you go! I heard there's a queue a mile long down the street.' He turned to Georgy. 'Hope you're not planning to sign on as well, my lad.'

'Well, no, I'm not sure,' stammered Georgy. 'I hadn't thought about it.'

'I should think not!' said his father. 'You're far too young to be doing that. Anyway, they won't need Canadians, they've got a whole British army already.'

Joe came in at lunchtime and told them, rather sheepishly, that he would be leaving next week.

'We have to go to training camp for a few weeks first,' he said, 'then overseas later. That's if it's needed. It may all be over in a few months they reckon. I hope so, but at least this keeps Elsie, my sweetheart, happy.'

'I hope she's worth it,' remarked Sam sourly. 'I wouldn't have no woman telling me to go off and fight!'

Joe turned red. 'She's promised to marry me when I get back,' he replied, 'so of course she's worth it.' Then he said something which shocked Georgy. 'Saw your brother down there, trying to sign up.'

'My brother!' exclaimed Georgy. 'William?'

'Yes, but they didn't take him. He tried to pretend he was eighteen, but they saw right through him, knew he was too young.'

'Thank goodness!' breathed Georgy.

'That stupid youngster!' cried his father. 'What on earth does he think he is playing at? Just wait till I see him!'

'Father don't be too hard on him,' begged Georgy. 'You know he's always wanted adventure. It's in his nature.'

'I'll give him 'adventure'!' muttered his father ominously but said no more.

That evening at dinner, William moped in a gloomy silence.

'What's wrong?' asked Ellen anxiously.

'Nothing,' mumbled William.

'But you're so quiet,' his mother persisted. 'Are you all right?'

'I'm fine! Just leave me alone!' snapped her son.

'William!' his father said sternly. 'There's no need to be like that to your mother. We know you're disappointed that you couldn't sign up but think yourself lucky.'

'Sign up?' exclaimed Ellen. 'No, William, please don't do that! I couldn't bear to lose you.'

'Oh Mother, don't fuss,' William replied. 'They don't want to take me, anyway, said I was too young. I thought they wanted volunteers but obviously not.'

'You *are* too young,' George Huntingford remarked. 'You're only sixteen. The minimum age is eighteen.'

William turned and looked at Georgy.

'So why aren't you signing up then? You're nearly eighteen. Are you a coward?'

'William!' cried Ellen. 'That's not fair. Georgy, take no notice.'

Georgy was hurt by his brother's taunts but also confused. *Was* he a coward? He wasn't sure.

'If I have to go to war, I will do my bit,' he replied stiffly, 'but I don't see the need at the moment.'

'But Germany has invaded Belgium! Doesn't that mean anything to you?'

'William, that's enough!' cried his father. 'George is our eldest son and his place is here, working in the family business. It's a responsible job and he is doing valuable work.'

William pushed his plate away, stood up and left the table, saying: 'Well, I know what I would do. Just give me half a chance!'

With that he walked out of the room. The rest of the meal passed in an awkward silence. No-one knew quite what to say.

Upstairs in their bedroom that night, William and Georgy didn't speak. Usually, they chatted about the day's events, but not this time. Everything had changed.

It was later that week that even more pressure was applied to poor Georgy. Aunt Minnie came over with Cousin Ralph in tow, to tell them all the news that he had signed up.

'I'm sure he'll be a hero,' Minnie told them. 'He's so brave and strong. But I will worry about him all the time.'

Ralph looked bored by the conversation.

'I've told you, Mother, I'll be quite safe. I'm going to be an officer and make you proud. Just you wait till you see how many medals I bring home!'

'Won't you be scared,' asked Ethel, 'of all the guns and things?'

'Don't be silly,' said Ralph scornfully. 'I'm not a child any more.' Then the inevitable question came. 'What about you, then, George? Have you signed on yet?'

'No, not yet,' mumbled Georgy feeling embarrassed.

'Why not?'

'Well, I, er, I'm working and I'm not eighteen for a few weeks yet. I have to finish my apprenticeship first then I'll see what happens.'

'Don't you want to help out Britain? It is our homeland after all.'

'Well, yes, of course' said Georgy getting flustered.

Aunt Minnie seemed to think he should go as well. 'We must all do our bit,' she said. 'It's our duty. Ellen, you must make him go.'

‘My sons will not be made to go to war!’ retorted Ellen, hotly. ‘I don’t want them going off and getting killed. Georgy is quite right to stay at home and work. He is doing his duty right here.’

The subject dropped but Ralph spent the whole afternoon bragging about how it was a wonderful adventure for him. William couldn’t bear to listen and went out of the house. There had never been much love lost between the cousins anyway and things weren’t likely to improve now.

Two weeks went by, and the city began to empty out of young men. Joe said a sorrowful goodbye to them all and left to go to training camp. Ralph had been sent to officers’ school. It seemed that everybody was going away somewhere. The streets seemed eerily quiet, and many shops and businesses had lost employees. Women began to fill the vacant places, which Georgy found quite surprising. The newspapers continued to bring daily stories of German atrocities, fuelling the desire for vengeance, and inspiring yet more volunteers. William tried once again at the recruitment office, and would have succeeded, if it hadn’t been for a man he once ran errands for, who saw him and told the authorities that the boy was only sixteen.

With Joe leaving, the firm was short staffed and so Mr Huntingford managed to persuade William to join them as a ‘general help’ for a while. William’s other job had dried up, with the business owner himself signing on and closing down, so he reluctantly agreed.

‘It won’t be for long, though,’ he told them. ‘Just while you’re short-handed. I’ll be off as soon as I can.’

Relations between William and Georgy had eased, though Georgy was aware of his brother’s disapproval of him. Georgy’s eighteenth birthday came around, but he couldn't yet reconcile himself to the idea of being a soldier. His conscience troubled him frequently, but he knew how upset his mother would be, and he wasn't at all sure what he wanted to do. His apprenticeship had finally finished, which should have been cause for celebration, but everything felt different now, and it was scarcely noticed.

October 3rd was a depressing day. The first Canadian troops departed for Quebec to sail to England, and then on to destinations unknown. Joe and Ralph were among the thousands. It being a Saturday, Ellen insisted that the whole family join Minnie and Dick to wave them all off from Moncton Railway station. The crowds were enormous however, and they barely caught a glimpse of them as the trains steamed away. Minnie cried and waved her handkerchief frantically, and they all did their best to cheer the soldiers on their way, but Georgy reflected privately that Ralph and Joe probably hadn't even known they were there. William was as enthusiastic about the 'adventure of war' as ever, but his attempts to join up had been thwarted so far.

Still doubts continued to plague Georgy as to what he should do. On November 4th they saw in the newspapers, that the first Canadians had been killed in the war a few days beforehand. This made Georgy feel ashamed that he wasn't doing more to help his countrymen, but then, quite unexpectedly, Ellen announced that she was pregnant again, the baby being due in April 1915.

'That's it,' thought Georgy. 'I should be at home, just in case. I might be needed. And there's no point in making Mother worry about me all the time. It wouldn't be fair. It'll all be over soon, anyway.'

Chapter 20

1915

After the usual storms of the Canadian winter, the last snows finally petered out in early April that year. Georgy was relieved. At least they would be able to fetch the midwife when their mother needed her. She wouldn't be snowed in. Life was tense enough as it was. The city seemed to be dominated by troops moving through, catching trains taking them to their fate. Bad news kept pouring in, with casualty lists now a sadly regular feature in the newspapers. So-called 'enemy aliens' had been rounded up and interned, even well-known local shopkeepers who had lived in Moncton for many years. Georgy was shocked when he saw the nearby butchers closed down and boarded up. Apparently, Mr Smit was of Austrian origin and therefore of doubtful character. Moncton wore a severe and gloomy face.

At home, things weren't much better. Georgy's relationship with William was on a knife edge. William still longed to sign up, whereas Georgy was tormented by doubts, guilt and regret. Their mother was just weeks away from giving birth. It was clear that they were needed at home. Ellen had not fared well in her pregnancy this time. She was now over 40 years old and finding it very hard. Her back and legs ached, and she was frequently in tears. Her emotions were always close to the surface at any time, but now they were erupting. William, being her favourite offspring, was often able to soothe and comfort her, but he was inclined to lose patience and walk off, leaving Georgy to pick up the pieces. Father seemed to be withdrawing into his work again and they saw little of him at home. Gilbert and Ethel were working hard at school, and the two younger children seemed unaware of their mother's distress. So, responsibility seemed to fall more and more on Georgy. He worked long hours himself, but he did his best to support her when he could.

William's 17th birthday came around and if anything, it seemed to make him even more frustrated and angry.

'Why can't I sign up?' he demanded that evening when they gathered to mark the occasion. 'They need more men to fight the Hun. If only I was a year older! I bet it'll all be over by the time I'm 18. It's not fair!'

It was the 18th of April, and the expected new arrival could only be a matter of days away. Ellen started to cry again at the thought of William going to war. Her whole frame shook with sobs.

'Don't wish your life away like that,' their father said sternly. 'Look how you've upset your mother now. It's not right in her condition.'

Georgy put his arm around Ellen's shoulders.

'It's all right, Mum. He didn't mean it,' he said.

'Oh, shut up, all of you!' cried William. 'You don't understand.'

With that, he stormed out into the night, only to return much later. No more was said about the incident, but the whole family felt the stress of it. Tempers were frayed and conversations stilted.

On the 22nd of April, the war became much more personal. Aunt Minnie had arrived to stay with Ellen for the impending birth, but it was debatable which woman was the stronger. In floods of tears, Minnie told them all of Ralph's hardships on the Western Front, and when news came that many Canadian troops had suffered a savage gas attack from the enemy, she was almost inconsolable.

'I know he will be killed, I just know it,' she cried. 'He's such a hero. Always trying to help others.'

Ralph was one of the lucky ones, however. Minnie heard from him only a couple of days later, reassuring her that he was safe and well. Minnie's moods fluctuated wildly between joy and fear, and she did little to soothe Ellen's emotions, but at least she was there.

Georgy arrived at work on the 24th of April and was surprised to see Sam there, tears streaming down his wrinkled old face.

'Sam, what's wrong?' Georgy asked. 'Is there anything I can do?'

'There's nothing anyone can do,' the old man muttered bitterly. 'Look!'

He got out the newspaper he had with him and opened it at the casualties' page. Joe's name was among them. Such a small listing amongst the many, barely noticeable except to those who knew him.

'Silly young fool!' exclaimed Sam. 'I told him not to go. Just 'cos his girl wanted him to be a hero. Now look where it's got 'im.'

Georgy was stunned. He knew death was an inevitable result of war, but to think of someone he knew, someone he went drinking with, shared jokes with. Well, it was almost too hard to bear.

'Gassed!' Sam told him, 'In the Battle of Ypres. I ask you - what for?'

Feeling like the ground had been pulled out from under him Georgy sat down heavily, reeling from the news.

'Maybe it's a mistake,' he said hopefully. 'Surely it can't be true.'

'Oh, it's true all right,' declared Sam. 'I saw his old man on the way over here. They're sending his effects back along with a medal. Much good that'll do him now.'

Mr Huntingford and William caught up with the news at lunchtime when they all met up. These days there was little work in domestic properties. They were mostly working on businesses or public sanitation. The firm was often scattered around in different areas, but they usually met up once a day.

'At least he died a hero,' remarked William. 'Giving his life to defend his country.'

'He's dead all the same,' replied Sam sourly. 'It's such a waste.'

Leaving work that evening Georgy felt utterly downcast. Joe had been such a cheerful chap, always ready to have a laugh, but also happy to help and advise on work. Georgy knew he had learned so much from him during his apprenticeship and he felt his loss keenly. Guilt kept Georgy from his rest that night. Should he have been there with Joe to do his bit? Would Joe have still been alive if he had? He couldn't answer that, but it troubled him, nonetheless.

On the 30th of April, a healthy, gurgling baby girl was born. Ellen was delighted to have another girl and named her Hazel after the trees around their home. The birth was a difficult one, however, and resulted in Ellen being unable to have any further babies.

'That's a good thing,' thought Georgy when he heard. 'Mother's too old to keep going through all this strain. She's not strong enough.'

After an operation to repair her damaged body, Ellen was ordered to rest completely for some weeks. Minnie was on hand to help her with housework and cooking, having brought their cousin Dorothy over to stay as well, whilst Uncle Dick fended for himself at home. Mr Huntingford and most of the family were delighted at the new arrival. Ethel, now nearly ten, particularly liked to hold her baby sister and even got involved in feeding and changing. Young Leonard cooed and clucked at the baby constantly. Even William admired her begrudgingly. Hazel had an angelic face and smiled at everyone almost from birth. In spite of her illness, Ellen was besotted by her new daughter and showed her off proudly to anyone who was there. None of the family were aware of the kettle of simmering resentment in their midst - Arthur.

Gilbert, Ethel and Arthur always walked to and from school together. As Gilbert was now working hard on his final year exams. Ethel often took Arthur off to the park or woods on the way home. With the birth of Hazel, however, everything had changed. Ethel was keen to get back and see her new sister.

'We'll be such friends when you get older,' she told the little girl. 'You're my only sister and I love you so much.'

Hazel merely smiled and gurgled happily.

'Effie,' asked Arthur on the way home. 'Can we go to the park please? We haven't been for two weeks now.'

'Not today, Artie,' his sister replied. 'I told Mum I'd take Hazel out in her pram for some fresh air. You know Mum can't do it at the moment.'

'But that's not fair,' stormed Arthur. 'What about me?' His face was as black as thunder.

'We all have to make sacrifices now,' Ethel told him, having heard these lines from her parents. 'Hazel is the important one. She's so little.'

Arthur sulked all the way back and refused to speak to anyone, though he still appeared for his supper. He glared at the baby as he went past.

The next day, he tried again but was again given the brush off.

'I have to go to the shops Artie. Why don't you come with me?'

'Don't want to!' declared Arthur and said no more.

None of the family were aware of the young boy's rage and hurt, and so what happened next came as a complete surprise.

On May 16th, Ethel celebrated her 10th birthday, and as it was a Sunday they decided to have a party. There had been dreadful news on the war front recently with the terrible loss of the Lusitania, torpedoed and sunk by the Germans on May 7th. Ellen had been in tears and Georgy had been horrified by the scale of the deaths. Most of this had been kept from the younger members of the family, but a gloom had descended, nevertheless. It was one which their parents wanted to dispel, so a party was planned.

'We will invite all Ethel's friends and the neighbours, and turn it into a real celebration,' said Ellen enthusiastically. 'We can show off little Hazel and cheer everyone up. Dick can come over as well, then he can see Minnie and Dorothy again. After all, they've been here four weeks now. He must be missing them.'

Mr Huntingford thought it was a great idea and a good way to distract everyone from such a depressing time. The sun shone on the day, and people began to pour into the Huntingford's home and spill out onto the garden. Arthur had been mooching around quietly outside, but his peace was suddenly invaded by laughter and jollity.

'Come and join in with some games, Artie,' Georgy said to him, but his young brother just scowled and walked off. 'Strange,' thought Georgy.

As the sun went down, the youngest guests began to leave, accompanied by their parents, calling out their thanks as they went. This left the adults and close family. It was then that they noticed that Arthur was missing.

'Where's Artie?' asked Gilbert. 'I haven't seen him for a while.'

'Probably upstairs,' replied Ellen.

'I don't think he was enjoying the party much,' remarked Georgy.

'I'll take Leonard up to bed now,' said Aunt Minnie. 'The little chap's dead on his feet. I'll have a look for Arthur whilst I'm up there and send him down.'

'If he's asleep, don't worry,' Ellen told her. 'He's probably tired out.'

It was only five minutes later that Minnie came tearing downstairs, clutching a piece of paper in her hand. 'He's gone!' she cried. 'Arthur. He's run away!'

There was panic and consternation in the house. They examined the note.

I am leeving hom becos I don't like it heer any more and you don't luv me. You only lov the baby. Goodbye foreva Arthur.

'Oh, my goodness,' cried Ellen. 'How could he? Surely, he knows we love him. Where can he have gone?'

Plans were hastily made. Mr Huntingford, Georgy, William and Gilbert were to go and look for him. The others were to stay at home. Ethel started to cry.

'It's all my fault because of my birthday. I should have taken him to the park when he asked. That's all he wanted.'

'There, there, now,' her mother said. 'It's not your fault. I guess we've all spent a lot of time with Hazel recently and he's felt left out.'

The four searchers divided the local area and went off hurriedly in different directions. Gilbert, being the youngest, was sent to check out the park and the zoo. William went to the riverside, Mr Huntingford to the town, and Georgy to the nearby woods. His instincts told him that that was where Arthur would be.

It was getting dark, so they took lamps with them though they shone little enough light. As Georgy entered the woods, he felt apprehensive. What wild animals were there? How much of a head start had Arthur got? Where would he sleep?

The woods were quite extensive, stretching around the outskirts of Lewisville, a dense mixed forest, pleasant enough in the daytime, but tricky at night. He trod carefully through undergrowth which crackled and snapped underfoot, calling out Arthur's name loudly every few minutes. If the boy heard him, would he even want to be found anyway? Would he run the other way? Georgy had no idea, only hope.

Strange noises around him made him stop nervously. Birds hooted and Georgy thought he heard a growl. Bears! He couldn't think how a 7-year-old boy would be able to cope with an angry bear. He shuddered. On and on he went, deeper into the woods, and the darkness became thick and impenetrable as it got later. Georgy's tiny lantern scarcely made any impression. He didn't know what the time was now, but he had to carry on. Arthur must be here somewhere. He just knew it.

Water dripped off the branches overhead and filled the ditches on the path below. Georgy was getting cold, tired and very damp but he couldn't quit now. He wasn't even sure where he was or how he could get home anyway in the dark. No. He would have to keep searching and calling all night. It was the only way. The woods became eerily silent, and his voice echoed off the trees as he called desperately:

'Arthur! Arthur! Where are you? Please!'

Then, just once, he thought he heard a whimper, a faint cry somewhere nearby, but away from the path.

'Arthur, are you there? It's me, Georgy. Where are you?'

For a moment, there was nothing, and Georgy despaired. He'd imagined it. Or maybe it was an animal. But then he heard something again, and this time he felt sure it was a human voice. Georgy plunged off the path in the direction he thought the sound came from, calling frantically, but stopping to listen as well. Suddenly, he was sure he could hear words and what sounded like tears. It was Arthur! Where was he? The lantern barely helped, but he got steadily closer until he practically fell over Arthur in the dark, curled up and crying by the foot of a tree.

‘Oh Artie, thank goodness I’ve found you. You silly idiot! Of course we love you. Come here.’

Arthur fell into Georgy's arms, sobbing. He was cold, wet and scratched, but otherwise safe and well.

‘I’m sorry!’ he cried. ‘I thought everyone hated me. Oh, I've been so scared. I went off the path, and it got dark and then I didn't know what to do. I want to go home!’

Georgy comforted his young brother. ‘It's all right,’ he told him. ‘We’ll have to stay here until it gets light, then we'll be able to see our way back. It won't be very long now. Come and cuddle into me and we'll keep warm together.’

As dawn broke, the two tired brothers made their way slowly out of the woods. Father and William had also been searching all night and were still out there. Gilbert and Dick were hastily dispatched to fetch them home.

Many tears and cuddles later, the whole family were reunited, sitting down to a late breakfast. No one was any the worse for wear it seemed, thank goodness, thought Georgy, though he felt he could sleep for a week. There would be no work that morning for any of them. He looked over at the miscreant who was already fast asleep on the sofa. This would be a night they wouldn't forget to be sure, he reflected, and he mentally made a note to always try and make sure that the people around him knew that they were loved. After all, it seemed it was all too easy for someone to feel unwanted, when in fact, the truth was very different. He swore to himself that he wouldn’t make that mistake again.

Arthur and Georgy had never been close; Georgy having been at work so much that he hadn't seen enough of the lad to get to know him. He vowed this would change in future. Arthur could be difficult and wayward, but he was still family and that was what mattered.

Chapter 21

February 1916

Outside, the snow piled up, inch after inch so that no one could leave home. The younger children were delighted, of course - no school and time to play. Meanwhile, Mr Huntingford grumbled loudly at not being able to work and Ellen struggled to keep the house warm. Georgy, William and Gilbert were secretly relieved at not having to go out and happily lazed around by the fire, chatting. Gilbert was now working as a labourer at the shipyard, having not been inclined to join the plumbing firm. He was a quiet, steady worker who was respected by his fellow employees. William chafed slightly at not being able to see his latest girlfriend, but in reality, his relationships were never very serious. His good looks and charisma ensured him a regular swarm of female admirers, but he brushed them off easily and was mostly unmoved. Georgy had dated a couple of girls recently but couldn't seem to find someone to commit to. He was wary of the opposite sex these days. All these subjects and more were covered as they luxuriated in the rare pleasure of time to themselves. Then, of course, the thorny subject of the war arose.

The family had recently been shocked to hear of the Zeppelin raids on Great Britain on the 31st of January. Many people had died, and homes were destroyed in the Midlands. It was an outrage which could not easily be forgiven.

'How could they do that?' demanded William. 'Innocent civilians. I ask you!'

'Surely it's no worse than invading France or Belgium, though,' Gilbert remarked.

William scowled at him. 'Yes, but these are *our* people just going about their lives, minding their own business.'

'I hope Aunt Mary and her family are safe,' said Georgy. 'They're all very near to where it's going on. Anything could happen.'

'At least we're safe over here,' said Gilbert.

'That's a selfish way to go on!' declared William, roused to anger now. 'Don't you care about England?'

Gilbert got up feeling awkward and embarrassed. 'I didn't mean it like that,' he said. 'I just thought about us and, well, I.....' His voice trailed off.

'We understand,' said Georgy. 'Don't worry.'

'I think I'll go and see if Mum needs any help in the kitchen,' Gilbert said and disappeared out of the room.

'Really, William, you don't have to be so hard on him,' Georgy said to his brother. 'He's still only young.'

William sighed. 'Yes, I know, but it makes me so mad when people don't understand.'

He paused and calmed down. 'You know it won't be long until I'm 18?'

'It's not till April,' Georgy said. 'Two months yet.'

'Yes, but I've heard they'll take you on a month or so beforehand so I'll be there as soon as I can. The Hun has got to be stopped. Why not sign up with me? We could be in the same regiment then and go out together. They wouldn't separate brothers, and then we could watch out for each other.'

Georgy was caught off guard. 'Me? Sign up? Oh, I don't know.'

'Come on, George. It would be great. You and me, we'd be unbeatable.'

For a few moments, Georgy seriously considered it. Perhaps William was right. Certainly, the enemy had to be stopped. It was an unjust war with civilian casualties as well now. The other day Georgy had been given a white feather by a girl in the street, which had shaken him badly. Maybe he was being a coward. Should he try and prove himself? For the first time, he listened to what his brother had to say.

'I'll think about it,' he promised at last, and William was delighted. It was the first time that Georgy had made any concessions on this, and William felt sure that he would be able to persuade his brother in the end. A warm camaraderie developed between them for the first time in ages and the two young men sat at peace together. Further private conversations ensued in the following snowbound days. In his heart Georgy felt that his brother must be right, and he was strongly inclined to agree to the proposal though what his mother would say, he dreaded to think.

The wild snows of February finally subsided to an icy slush, and with it, Georgy's reluctance to sign up also melted away. He would do it! His mind was made up. It was his duty.

One evening he secretly told William that when he went to join up, he would go with him. His brother was over the moon and suggested that they both go along on the following Tuesday because that was a time when they were due to be working together at the same location. They would therefore be able to slip away unnoticed.

'But shouldn't we speak to Mum and Dad about it beforehand?' suggested Georgy.

'Not likely!' exclaimed William. 'You know they would try and stop us. Once it's done, there's nothing they can do.'

Georgy felt uneasy about the deception but went along with it. It was then that disaster struck. It was the Thursday beforehand. Their father was impatient to get back to work again after the enforced break. They had just been given a contract with Moncton Almshouses to renew their sanitation. The manager was now pressuring them to get on with the work. Mr Huntingford and his team arrived at the site to find ice, like sheets of glass all over the paths and walkways.

'Dad, this doesn't look safe,' said Georgy.

'It's fine,' replied his father. 'Let's get on.'

'It's bloody lethal, Dad!' said William in his usual forthright manner. 'Don't risk it.'

'Don't swear, son! Anyway, we haven't got any choice. The work has to be done.'

'Begging your pardon, boss,' said Sam, 'but should I go and get some grit to put down?'

'Yes,' Mr Huntingford agreed. 'Do, but we can't wait until that's arrived. It'll waste time. We'll make a start whilst you go and fetch it.'

'Dad, please let's wait a bit,' said Georgy, 'just till Sam comes back.'

But his father wouldn't listen and boldly stepped out, tools in hand.

'Come on, lads,' he said firmly. 'Time to start work.'

The first half hour went without a hitch. Everyone was very careful how they trod. It was then that Mr Huntingford realised he had left an item they needed back in the cart outside, and he went to get it. A few minutes later Georgy and William heard a loud crash and a shout of pain. Taking as much care as possible, they rushed over to where the noise came from and found their father sprawled in agony on the ice.

'My leg! Oh, I think it's broken. Help me.'

An hour later they were all gathered at the hospital whilst the doctors saw their father. Ellen and Minnie with baby Hazel and the three older sons. The younger children were at school and blissfully unaware at present. After some time, the doctor came out to see them.

'It's a bad accident,' he told them. 'The leg is broken in three places and will take a long time to heal, I'm afraid. We are putting it in a plaster cast at the moment. He's also very bruised and shocked of course. As soon as we have set the leg then he can go home and recover there. Is there someone who can nurse him?'

'Yes, of course, I can,' replied Ellen. 'But how long will it take till he can walk again?'

'About three months,' the doctor said, 'and he may still have a limp afterwards. It's difficult to say.'

Three months! Georgy had a sick feeling in his stomach. How could he go away now? They would have to change their plans. Later, they saw father in his hospital bed, looking pale and fragile. What a change there had been in him since the morning. All of a sudden, they saw his vulnerable side.

'I'm sorry,' Mr Huntingford said, 'I was a fool. Now look what I've done.'

'It's all right, dear,' Ellen said. 'You just need to get well again, that's all.'

'But what about the business?' Mr Huntingford said anxiously. 'Who will look after it? There will be no money coming in. If the work doesn't get done, then how will the family manage?'

He looked at Georgy as he said this, and Georgy knew where his duty lay, without hesitation. 'I can run the business, Dad. You've taught me all I need to know, and I'm fully qualified now. We can keep it going until you're fit again.'

William glared at Georgy but said nothing.

'Really. Oh, that's so good to know. Thank you, my sons. I know I can rely on you.'

Later, when they were alone, William turned on Georgy.

'How could you? Do you know what you've done? You know we're going to sign on next week.'

'No,' said Georgy firmly. 'I won't be going anywhere at the moment. My loyalty is here and so should yours be.'

'Me! You needn't think I'm fitting in with your plans. You're not going to ruin my life. What you do with yours is your own affair, but you can forget about expecting any help from me!'

'But William, how can I manage all the work with just me and Sam? We need you. Surely you can't leave us now. Mother is going through a hard enough time is it is. Please stay, we can go later.'

'Forget it!' cried William, and he walked out, slamming the door as he went.

Feeling that his brother would come round to his way of thinking shortly, Georgy tried not to worry too much about it. Surely William would not abandon them now?

On the planned Tuesday, however, William disappeared during the morning, claiming he had to collect some supplies from the yard. He had barely spoken to Georgy for the last few days, though he maintained an air of family affection with the rest of them. No one seemed to notice the frost that had descended between the two eldest, and even Georgy was hoping that things had resolved themselves.

Father came home but was bedridden and fractious, trying to give instructions and failing to rest. Eventually Ellen lost all patience with him and told him to sit still or else. Georgy soldiered on with the work that day, supported only by Sam. William failed to reappear. Trying not to feel angry, Georgy finally packed up for the day and headed home. As he came in the door, he could hear a commotion going on and he quickly guessed what it was all about.

Mother was crying hysterically and there seemed to be a shouting match going on in Father's sick room.

'Georgy!' cried Ellen in between sobs. 'William has only gone and signed up! Why has he done this? How could he?'

She was incoherent and inconsolable. Her face was covered in tears, her breath ragged and uneven, her eyes red and her hands shaking. Georgy held her in his arms, soothing her until she dropped with exhaustion into a nearby chair. Then he went into his father, where the two men were shouting loudly.

'How dare you?' shouted Mr Huntingford. 'Can't you see we need you?'

William fought back. 'I have to do this. It's my duty. I have to fight for my country. You don't understand. You never have!'

Mr Huntingford was nearly speechless with rage now. 'Get out!' he cried. 'I don't want to see you again.'

'Suits me!' William shouted and stormed out.

The younger children didn't know what to make of any of it. Ethel stood there looking shocked, with Gilbert trying to comfort her. Georgy was the only one to try and pick up the pieces. He made a cup of tea, got some food for the family, and put Ellen to bed. Later, he took stock of what had happened. How would he manage at work without William? Well, that was something he could sort out. They could take on someone to replace him and maybe cut down on a few jobs. As for the family? Well, he knew Ellen would recover with time. Maybe he should call Aunt Minnie over to help out again. She wasn't very efficient, but always kind and willing. For Father, perhaps he should get a nurse, though this would cost. His feelings about his brother were complicated. He both despised and admired him.

William returned in the middle of the night. Georgy heard him creep into bed but said nothing. In the early morning, they both rose to go to work.

'So, when do you leave?' asked Georgy.

'In two weeks' time,' replied William, 'to go to training camp for a few months first.'

'Will that be nearby?' Georgy said, hoping that maybe William would be able to live at home during that time.

'Camp Hughes,' his brother said, 'in Manitoba.'

'Manitoba! But that's over a thousand miles away! How long will it take to get there?'

'About three days by train,' replied William. 'They run special ones for the troops, you know.'

'So, you'll be off soon, then?'

‘Yes,’ said William hesitantly. ‘I wish you were coming with me, George. Won’t you change your mind?’

‘No, I'm sorry,’ Georgy told him. ‘Family comes first to me, William, you know that.’

William sat down suddenly, bowled over by shame and sorrow.

‘I'm sorry, George, I wouldn't go, but you know I have to. I’ll go mad if I don't and that won't help anyone. At least you'll save money without having to feed me as well.’ He paused. ‘Forgive me.’

Georgy patted his brother on the shoulder.

‘You know I will, you idiot! But you need to make up with Mum and Dad. You don't want to go off with all these bad feelings. Try and smooth things over at least.’

‘I'll try,’ promised William and he was as good as his word. The first thing he did was to go and give Ellen a big hug, and he spent an hour or more patiently and calmly trying to make her understand. He had some success, and at least their mother had stopped crying by the time he belatedly went into work. Father was another matter. But after a couple of days of avoidance, the two had a heart to heart on Sunday. Eventually, they agreed to disagree.

‘I will never understand your reasons,’ Father told him, ‘But I respect you for your courage, son. I just hope you will stay safe.’

‘Of course I will,’ his son replied. ‘Nothing will happen to me, I promise.’

Chapter 22

1916

William left home on March 25th 1916. Georgy watched him go with a lump in his throat, wondering if he would ever see him again.

'Where's William going, Mum?' asked Len.

Ellen choked back her emotion.

'He's going off to be a soldier, dear,' she told the child.

'Will he be back soon?' Len persisted.

'We hope so,' she replied.

Standing at the door, she continued to wave desperately long after William had disappeared from view.

'Come on, Mum,' said Georgy. 'It's time to go in now. He's gone on his way. It's what he wanted.'

The house was a sad and gloomy place for a few weeks, but gradually they came to accept it. Georgy found William's absence harder than he had imagined. His impetuous, often difficult, brother had amused and annoyed him in equal measures, but now he missed him more than he could say. There was a rip in the family blanket which could never be repaired.

Necessity focused Georgy's thoughts on work. Without Father and William around, he needed to get some extra help. The contract at the almshouse had to be fulfilled and there was no way he and Sam could manage to do everything. An obvious choice was Gilbert though he was not qualified in plumbing in any way. Gilbert, being an amenable person, was happy to agree once Georgy approached him.

'Are you sure?' asked Georgy.

'Yes, of course. I'd like to do my bit to help out,' Gilbert assured him, 'though I'm not sure how good I'll be at it.'

'It doesn't matter,' Georgy told him. 'Just a general help will be great. That's all William did after all.'

Nevertheless, Georgy reckoned that another person would still be needed, and so he placed an advert in the local shop window. The number of replies were minimal, many men having left to go to war. One reply caught his attention, however: '*Harry Wilson, experienced in home plumbing. Eager to learn, hard worker, reliable.*' Sounded very promising.

Georgy decided to find out more and invited them to the house for a chat. The appointed time came, and he opened the door to a surprise. A middle-aged woman stood there, sturdy and robust, dressed in men's trousers and looking quite unladylike. Georgy didn't know what to say.

'Can I help you?' he managed at last.

'Harriet Wilson applying for the plumber's assistant job,' she replied. 'Is this the right place?'

'Yes,' stammered Georgy and let her in. After his initial shock, he found out all about her. Harriet had been brought up in a family of plumbers and was married to another who had gone off to fight. She wasn't qualified but knew a lot about the trade.

'My father and brother were in business together, then they took on an apprentice who I ended up marrying! My father's dead now and my brother and husband have joined up. So, you see,' she explained, 'I'd like to do my bit to help whilst my man is away, and also if I'm honest, I need the money. I have two children, and the army pay isn't enough to keep us all fed.'

'But what about the children when you're at work?' asked Georgy.

'They're both at school but my mother is living next door, and she can look after them until I get home.'

Georgy was impressed and suggested a suitable working schedule so that Harriet could still manage to see her children as much as possible.

'That's kind of you, sir,' she said gratefully.

'Family are very important,' Georgy said and went on to tell her why they were looking for help.

'So, it might only be for a few months then?' Harriet said.

'Well, yes, it's possible, but we'll have to see how it works out. My younger brother is also helping out for a while, but he might want to do something else in the future.'

'That's all right,' said Harriet. 'I'm quite happy with it anyway.'

So, it was settled, and Georgy felt happier. At least now the business would continue until his father was able to pick things up again.

About a month later, the family received a letter from William.

"Dear all, having a fine old time here in Camp Hughes. I've made a lot of friends with some decent

chaps, all very jolly and respectable, you'll be glad to know! The camp is really like a big town with all sorts here. There are shops, churches, a post office, a tobacconist and even a swimming pool! It also has its own newspaper.

We're all sleeping in tents though. I've never seen so many. All in neat rows like mini ant hills. I have to say it's pretty chilly at night, but it's to get us used to what it will be like at the Front. I'm sharing with Jimmy; he snores a bit but is a good bloke otherwise.

We started off by learning how to clean and maintain our weapons. I won't say what sort they are in case this falls into the wrong hands. They say there are spies everywhere so we have to be careful.

Next week we're going to be digging trenches and using them for exercises. We're all getting very fit now, taking part in drills and long distance runs every day. The officer here is a complete tyrant and won't let us rest for a moment. All he does is shout at us from dawn to dusk. We have to be up and dressed in our army kit by the time it gets light each day, but we always had to get up early for work anyway, so that's not really a hardship.

Anyway, I hope you're all keeping well. Don't worry about me. I'm loving it here. It's just what I needed.

Yours, William."

Ellen was delighted to hear from her son and read the letter over and over again. Father snorted derisively though.

'That boy still thinks it's all a bit of fun. He'll find out the hard way soon enough.'

It seemed that Father was right because William's next letter a couple of months later was less enthusiastic.

"All we do is crawl around in trenches all day! When it's sunny, they're so dusty that we are choking, and when it rains, we're up to our knees in mud. Then there is grenade training, which is hell - so loud and quite dangerous. One of the chaps got injured last week because he didn't get out of the way quick enough. He's lucky he didn't lose his leg.

The only good thing these days is that they're going to teach us to ride. The horses are coming in next week."

Three months went by since Father's accident. His plaster cast was removed, and he cautiously started walking again, but it would take time to get his strength back.

'I want to get back to work,' Father said irritably, just days after this. 'It's my firm and I need to be there.'

'George, be patient,' said his wife. 'You know everything is fine, just take your time and don't worry.'

'How can I not worry?' grumbled Mr Huntingford, 'when it's being run by two boys, an old man and a woman? Why George took her on, I don't know.'

'My dear husband, you know there aren't many men left in the workplaces now. It was a sensible thing to do. Women are getting the vote now as well, I've heard.'

'Humph!' grunted her husband.

Meanwhile, Georgy had enjoyed managing the business with his team of Sam, Gilbert and Harriet. Harriet had proved to be strong, capable and knowledgeable, besides having a raucous laugh and a wicked sense of humour. They all worked well together.

A letter of a different sort arrived in June that year from England. It was many months since Ellen had last heard from her parents over there, but this time there was sad news. Her brother Fred, who had been helping run the alehouse, had died quite suddenly of heart failure, aged 41, leaving Grandma and Grandpa Goddard struggling on their own. Ellen was sad to hear about Fred though she hadn't seen him in many years, and it turned her thoughts to her family. She wondered how the rest of the Goddards were getting on.

'I suppose Nellie and Billy will be grown up by now,' she mused that evening. 'I wish we'd kept in touch more, really, but Mary and Will didn't approve of us moving away.'

Georgy sighed. 'I often think of them,' he told his mother. 'I miss them all.'

'Do you?' she said, surprised. 'Well, I suppose you were quite close, weren't you?'

'Maybe I could write to them,' Georgy suggested, but his mother frowned.

'No, I don't think that's a good idea,' she said.

Secretly Georgy resolved that he would do it anyway. His mother was sure to come round if she heard from them. After all, she hadn't actually said he mustn't.

Mr Huntingford slowly went back to work, gradually rebuilding his stamina. Just as he was about to give Harriet her notice, old Sam was taken ill. He was over 70 now and getting quite frail and his wife was keen for him to stop work. After his many years of faithful service, Mr Huntingford was happy to award Sam a small annuity to help him cope. Therefore, the old man finally, and sadly, left the firm. Mr Huntingford was quick to notice Harriet's efficient and hardworking manner and soon found her indispensable in spite of his reservations. Seeing that the business was safely back in his father's control, Georgy toyed with the idea of signing up again. News of the war continued to be thoroughly horrifying each day.

Another letter came from William, and this time they detected a strong note of annoyance.

"I don't know when we're going to get to this war. We just seem to keep doing the same training over and over. I'm getting bored with it all and can't wait to get started. Surely, we would be better used on the front lines instead of doing endless rifle practice?"

'Perhaps William will leave if he doesn't like being a soldier any more,' said Ellen hopefully, after reading the letter aloud to the family.

'Ellen dear,' said her husband, 'you can't just leave the army, you know. It's not like a job. Once you've signed up, that's it.'

'Yes,' agreed Georgy, 'and if you go 'absent without leave' then you could be court-martialled and shot.'

'Oh dear!' exclaimed Ellen. 'I didn't know that.'

In August that year, Minnie came dashing round to see them all, fretting about Ralph.

'He's been injured,' she cried. 'Shot in the knee. They've had to operate to remove the shrapnel, but he's going to come home soon, thank goodness. I don't intend letting him out of my sight again!'

'Oh, I do hope William will be all right,' said Ellen. 'I wish he hadn't signed on.'

'They all have to do their bit,' replied Minnie, looking pointedly at Georgy. He blushed but said nothing.

One Sunday in early September, there was a knock on the door, and there stood William, resplendent in a crisp army uniform.

'William!' cried his mother, 'You're home!'

She flung herself at him in a wild embrace.

'Steady on, Mum,' William said, disentangling himself. 'I'm afraid I'm here on embarkation leave.'

'What's that?' asked Ellen. The rest of the family gathered round, keen to see him.

'Embarkation Mum. It means I'll be heading off overseas very soon. My training is finished for now and I'm off to England on the 25th of September. Then maybe to France or wherever they send me. We get a couple of weeks leave beforehand.'

'Overseas!' said Ellen, distressed. 'Oh William, don't go! You mustn't.'

'I have to, Mum. I've got orders now. I'm going to be in the 5th Canadian Mounted Rifles.'

'Do you have to ride a horse?' asked Arthur, fascinated.

'Yes, indeed. I will tell you all about it.'

The two weeks flew by. William found time for all his family whilst he was there, taking the younger children out on excursions, talking at length with his parents and Georgy about his experiences and even visiting old Sam in town. Georgy took a few days off work, with agreement from his father, and spent time with his brother. They even had a night camping in the woods, just like they had done five years before.

That night in the tent, they talked:

'I'm sorry, I haven't signed on yet,' said Georgy. 'I will do when things settle down again.'

'George,' said William, seriously, 'it's up to you, mate. Who am I to say what you should do? It's no picnic even doing the training, I can tell you. And when I think that I will be doing it all for real soon, well, I don't know how I will cope.'

'Are you scared?' asked Georgy. There was a pause.

‘I suppose I am, if I'm honest, but we've been taught not to think too much about it. We won't be at the Front all the time. It's two weeks on, then two weeks further back doing supplies and maintenance, and then there are some rest periods as well. But yes, I am scared of dying, but I'm more scared of letting everyone down.’

‘What do you mean?’ asked Georgy.

‘Well, if I was to run away, not follow orders, or not back my comrades up, I'd feel so ashamed.’

‘You're very brave,’ said Georgy. ‘You always have been. You won't let anyone down. I know it.’

‘I certainly don't intend to,’ William said. ‘But who knows how anyone will react under fire, with guns blazing and tanks coming towards you?’

‘You're no coward,’ said Georgy. ‘You'll be fine.’

William left to join his regiment on September the 24th on the train to Halifax. He was to sail on the Tuscania over to Liverpool and then travel down to Shorncliffe in Kent for final preparations. They all went to see him off at the station. Ellen cried and everyone felt very emotional. This was it, the next stage of William’s journey to war.

Even William had suspiciously moist eyes as he hugged them goodbye. In the last six months, he seemed to have suddenly matured and become more understanding.

‘I’ll write,’ he promised, ‘whenever I can. I love you all. Take care of yourselves.’

They waved and waved as the train steamed out, until it disappeared, leaving just a wisp of smoke hanging in the air. William had gone.

Chapter 23

1917

Cousin Ralph was discharged and came home in late January, much to Minnie and Dick's delight. His knee had been badly injured by gunshot, and he was considered medically unfit, at least for the time being. He was due to be re-assessed in two months' time.

He was sitting, looking very pale, with his leg bandaged and raised on a stool, when the Huntingfords came to visit. Not that it was the whole family. Ellen had brought baby Hazel, and Georgy had gone with her to look after them in the snow. The sun was shining out of a pure blue sky, but it was bitterly cold, and the drifts from a few days ago were still piled high. Father had volunteered (a bit too eagerly, Georgy thought!) to stay at home with the rest of them. No more snow was forecast that day, so it was a good chance to get out.

Minnie fussed around her son, plumping up cushions and fetching him drinks.

'He's such a hero,' she told them. 'He saved the life of three men. They're going to give him a medal!'

'So, you're still here, then?' Ralph sneered at Georgy when he saw him. 'Not signed up yet?'

‘No, not yet,’ replied Georgy. ‘Father’s not been well. I’ve been looking after the firm.’

But your dad’s well again now, isn’t he?’ asked Minnie. ‘He seems to be back on his feet.’

‘Well yes,’ muttered Georgy looking embarrassed.

‘Then there’s nothing stopping you,’ said Ralph. ‘William’s gone, I understand.’

‘Yes,’ Ellen said sadly. ‘He went overseas to France at the end of October, though we don’t know where exactly.’

They had heard from William a couple of times, though one, a letter, had been heavily censored, and the other was just an official army postal card, stating he was well. They had sent over a food parcel and some small essentials and were hopeful that he would receive it.

‘Well at least he’s doing his duty,’ Ralph commented, looking at Georgy. ‘It’s down to all of us, you know.’

Georgy flushed scarlet. ‘Yes, I know.’

‘So, stop making excuses and get out there! Or are you a coward?’

‘A coward! How dare you?’ cried Georgy. ‘I’m no coward and I’ll prove it. I shall be signing up this week!’

‘Georgy!’ exclaimed Ellen, shocked. ‘No, please don’t. Not you as well. I can’t bear it!’

Georgy realised what he had said but couldn’t back down now.

‘Mum, I have to. Ralph’s right. I have to do my bit.’

‘Good to hear,’ said Ralph smugly. ‘It’s about time. Conscription’s coming in soon anyway. It’s already started in England. I’m sure you’d rather be a volunteer than a conscript, wouldn’t you?’

It was true. The government had been debating the issue lately, but it had proved to be very divisive. Georgy couldn't see it happening any time soon.

Ellen was silent as they picked their way carefully through the snow laden streets, but as soon as they got home, she turned on Georgy.

'You mustn't do this, Georgy,' she cried. 'We need you here. Take no notice of Ralph. He's just trying to provoke you.'

'I know,' replied Georgy, 'but seriously Mum, I've been thinking about it a lot lately, especially with William having gone. The only reason I didn't go earlier was because Dad would have to find someone to take my place at work and that's not easy these days.'

At that moment his father came in and overheard part of the conversation.

'What's going on?' he asked.

Georgy reddened.

'I want to sign up, Dad,' he told him. 'I'm sorry. I know it will leave you in the lurch.'

His father was quiet for a minute, then he said: 'I think it's a good idea, son. Don't worry about the work. If that's what you want to do, then you must do it. Business is pretty slack these days anyway, if I'm honest. I'll be proud of you.'

Georgy was amazed. 'Thanks, Dad,' he said.

'George!' exclaimed Ellen, at her husband. 'How could you? We've already let one son go. How can we part with another?'

Her husband looked at her. 'Really, Ellen, this is a cruel and unjust war with civilian casualties. How can we stand by and do nothing? It's true I was angry at William for leaving when we needed him, but I understand now. If I was young enough, I'd go myself. Now that's an end to it!'

Ellen was speechless and Georgy was in awe. His father rarely put his foot down, but when he did, there was no denying him.

9.30am Wednesday 7th February 1917

Outside the recruitment office, the line of new volunteers waited in nervous anticipation for it to open. The numbers were far fewer now than the early days when the queue had stretched around the block, but still there were a dozen or so. The sky was grey with more snow threatening and Georgy stood there shivering, half from cold and half from fear. He knew he had to do this for his own sake if nothing else. He couldn't go on feeling ashamed of himself forever.

The doors opened and a brisk, uniformed officer shepherded them in. The morning disappeared in a blur. First there was registration, then they had to fill in the attestation form with all their details. Then came the oaths. Georgy felt a big responsibility laid on him when he had to sign to affirm loyalty to King George V and then swear an oath of allegiance to the crown. It suddenly seemed very serious and life changing.

A medical examination followed, though to be fair, it was sketchy at best. As long as you could stand, and preferably see, you were likely to be declared fit to serve. All the volunteers that morning were passed and after an officer had signed their papers, that was it. Georgy was now a member of the Canadian Expeditionary Force. He was stunned by the speed and simplicity of it all and left the recruitment office in a daze. He had been told to report to the local base on Friday that week to be fitted for his uniform. Then about ten days later on the 19th of February, he was off to Camp Sussex for training.

The town of Sussex was only about 50 miles from Moncton and on the direct rail line, so Georgy was hopeful that he might be able to go home sometimes whilst he was training. This would soften the blow for his mother as well. Since his father's forceful statement on the matter, Ellen had tried hard to cover her feelings, but Georgy knew she was struggling. Leaving the family for the first time was hard for him, too and it was a wrench when his train moved out. He watched their figures disappear from view as the engine gathered speed.

Two hours later, he arrived at the camp and was relieved to see that recruits no longer had to sleep in tents but now had wooden barracks. It would still be winter for another couple of months, and Georgy knew from experience how severe the Canadian weather could be. As it was, flakes of snow hit him in the face as he assembled with the rest of the new intake on the parade ground. Several hours of drills and physical exercise later, after a basic meal, Georgy fell onto a narrow wooden bunk and tried to sleep. The wind howled around the hut and blew into every nook and cranny. The army blankets were hard and scratchy and the mattress wafer thin. It was an uncomfortable night, but it would be the first of many, designed to prepare the men for the conditions at the Front.

Camp Sussex was not like Camp Hughes in many ways. It was much smaller and had none of the leisure time facilities that William had enjoyed. It was designed for a shorter initial training of about eight weeks, before undertaking more advanced training in England.

In the first week, Georgy quickly bonded with some of the other new trainees who had bunks next to his. There was Walter, a man in his 30's, who had a wife and children, but who had recently lost his business.

'Have to make a living somehow,' he told Georgy. 'Might as well get paid to do this. It's as good as anything else.'

Then there was young Gordon, just turned 18 and keen on the idea of an adventure. Though he had little in common with either of them, Georgy found them good companions, all of them blundering their way through drills, rifle training, bayonet practice and worst of all, trench building. The weather that year in March was atrocious. They were up to their ears in mud for much of it. If it wasn't that, it was long distance route marches through the countryside until they were so tired they were fit to drop.

'I wish I had just found another job,' complained Walter, one evening in the barracks. 'What was I thinking? I must have been mad!'

'I think my feet are dissolving!' remarked Gordon. 'They've been wet the whole week.'

'I know,' agreed Georgy. 'I feel the same. I wish I was sat by the fire at home.'

This made him feel sad and he fell silent. He had managed to get back to his family on a couple of occasions, but it was strange being there. No one knew what he was going through. They all wanted him to be the same as he was before, but something had changed in him. He wasn't sure what.

Gas training was one of the worst experiences. They had to be able to fit their masks on in a matter of seconds and were fed unpleasant, though not toxic, fumes in an enclosed area to encourage them to do just that. Georgy always fumbled with the straps and was one of the slowest. The officer shouted at him: 'You'll be dead if you don't speed up, Huntingford! Get a move on!'

'I think I've had it if we're gassed,' remarked Georgy to his friends. 'I'm too slow. I just can't get the hang of the blessed thing!'

'At least you can handle a rifle,' replied Gordon. 'When I aim, I always miss.'

It was true. Georgy had a good eye for shooting, and it was decided to place him in the artillery pool. In the evenings, if they weren't too tired, the three of them sat there in the bunkhouse playing cards, sometimes for small amounts of money, though they were careful not to let the officers know. Gambling was strictly forbidden. The light was dim, but somehow, they managed to see until darkness finally fell.

At other times, if they were allowed, they ventured into the nearby town for a drink. Sussex was happy to have the troops there and welcomed them, though it made the area much busier these days. There were 250 men in the barracks and little privacy, but the camaraderie between the three men eased the tension and dispersed the gloom. Georgy barely got to know any of the rest. There were just too many people, and they were all kept so busy they had little time to chat. They were just unknown faces adrift in a sea of humanity.

Eight weeks flew by in the blink of an eye and all of a sudden it was time to depart. First there would be two weeks embarkation leave and then they would all be heading for England. Georgy had been thinking about this for a while, and despite his mother's disapproval, had sent a letter to Aunt Mary asking whether he could visit sometime if he got the chance. He had no idea what the response would be, or even if he would get a reply.

Georgy was sad to say goodbye to Walter and Gordon, but he was hopeful they would see each other again in England. Gordon's enthusiasm for adventure had rapidly declined as the training went on, and it seemed likely he would go into the Infantry department as a private. Walter had fared better, becoming cheerfully resigned to the hardships. Like Georgy, he was destined for the artillery as a gunner. Georgy let the title roll around inside his head: 'Gunner Huntingford' - it sounded good, but could he do it?

Dressed in fresh, crisp army uniform, the three men went their separate ways back to their families for leave. Like all the men at Camp Sussex, they came from the New Brunswick area and so it wouldn't take long before they were back with their loved ones.

It was the end of April when Georgy arrived home. The snows had ended, and spring flowers were beginning to poke their heads up cautiously. The family were expecting him and there was a delightful celebration. Georgy was just pleased to sleep in a soft, comfortable bed and to have dry feet for a change. Whilst he'd been away, there'd been another letter from William, this time saying that he'd been in hospital with scabies but was all right again now.

Ellen had heard of scabies but wasn't quite sure what it was, so when she visited Minnie next, she asked Ralph if he had come across it.

'I should say I have!' he exclaimed. 'Everybody gets it out there. It's horrible. The worst thing is thinking about that nasty little mite borrowing into your skin.'

Ellen shuddered.

'But the itching is so bad it nearly drives you mad and then you scratch yourself to pieces trying to ease it, but it doesn't help. I've seen men with badly infected sores because they just couldn't stop scratching. One chap I know even used a burning cigarette, to try and stop it!'

'How do they cure it?' asked Ellen.

'Mostly sulphur ointments and the like,' replied Ralph. 'They smell dreadful, but at least they seem to work.'

When Georgy heard all this, he wondered if he would catch it as well when he got to the Front. It was down to so many men living together in cramped and dirty conditions apparently, and hard to avoid. He hoped his brother hadn't suffered too much with it. At least they knew William was alive and well.

Another letter had arrived whilst Georgy had been away - a note from Aunt Mary to him, telling him he would be welcome any time. Nellie was working as a telephonist in London and Billy had started an apprenticeship. When Georgy told Ellen he had had a letter, however, she became quite annoyed with him.

'Why did you write to them?' she demanded. 'You know they don't like us any more.'

'I thought you'd be glad to hear how they are,' Georgy said. 'You know how much I miss them. I want to go and visit them when I go to England.'

'Visit!' exclaimed Ellen. 'No Georgy, I don't want you to do that. They don't approve of us, and I don't want them to know anything about our life here.'

'All right, Mum, if that's the way you want it,' Georgy said, pacifying her. 'I'll forget all about it.'

But even as he said this, he knew he wouldn't. The draw was too strong.

Two weeks flew by and before he knew it, Georgy was saying goodbye again. He hugged them all.

'It won't be long until I get some more leave and then I'll come home again,' he promised. 'It's just more training to start with, so there's no need to worry. I'll write soon.'

Climbing on board the troopship at Halifax, Georgy reflected that this would be the first time he had left Canada in over ten years. He watched from the deck as they roared past the islands in the harbour, remembering their days of travel and of quarantine. How long ago it seemed now. England was a distant memory, but it was just about to get a whole lot closer.

Chapter 24

England 1917

Aunt Mary cried out in joy when she opened her front door and saw her nephew standing there.

'Oh, Georgy! How wonderful. Come in.'

Then she enveloped him in a huge bear hug.

Three weeks earlier, Georgy watched as Liverpool docks slid into view beside their ship. It was noisier and busier than ever before, with troop ships arriving and departing all the time. It was 23rd May and after a brief stop at Liverpool, the soldiers travelled onwards by train to their various destinations, some like Georgy to further training, some to embark for the Front. Georgy was shocked to see great numbers of wounded men also coming and going, even with some amputees among them.

'My goodness,' he thought, 'how bad have things got? I hope William is safe.'

This time Georgy was headed for Witley Camp, near Godalming, for advanced artillery training. To his delight he met up with Walter again on the train and they discovered that they would be at the same place.

'Gordon has gone off to Shorncliffe in Kent,' Walter told him. 'He was on the same ship as me coming over, so we had a chance to chat. He's going to be in the infantry.'

'A foot soldier – that's no picnic,' remarked Georgy. 'Poor lad. He was so keen as well.'

Georgy wasn't too sure how he would feel when he saw England again after ten years, but travelling down to London by train he saw the countryside in all its newly green spring glory, and he remembered how he loved it. Canada was beautiful with its forests, lakes and mountains – a land of extremes – but England was gentler with a subtle beauty all its own. The late May sunshine bounced off the sparkling rivers and the rolling hills, coming to rest in the farmer's fields and orchards. 'I'm home,' he thought.

Witley Camp was not so very different to Camp Sussex, except that the newer recruits were in tents, rather than wooden huts. The climate was kinder here though, so the nights were not so chilly, at least. There were more recreational facilities on offer including a number of shops (which the men affectionately called 'Tin Town') and a magazine, but the daily routine was similar. Drills, route marches, long distance runs and lots of artillery practice. Here they were taught to use, load and maintain all the different sorts of weapons, from a pistol to a howitzer. Those big guns overawed Georgy with their sheer destructive power. How could he dare to use these on another human being?

It was June 14th. On the way to Tottenham, where his aunt lived, Georgy had been shocked to see London city. A massive air raid the previous morning from the German Gotha aircraft had left behind smoking ruins and devastation. They'd all heard about it down at the camp, of course, but nothing had prepared Georgy for the sight. 162 people had died, including many young children at a primary school in Poplar. The East End had been particularly badly hit but everywhere had felt the effects. People hurried past, a hunted look in their eyes, some openly distressed. Windows were shattered and buildings destroyed. The emergency services were still trying to clear up and restore order, but it was a hard task. Georgy saw a policeman reduced to tears whilst trying to tow away the wreckage of a number 25 bus which had been the site of a number of fatalities. It was with a great deal of relief that he finally arrived at his aunt's house and fell happily into her arms.

All week, Georgy had been tormented by the knowledge that he was deliberately going against his mother's express instructions by visiting his aunt and her family. It was the first time in his life that he'd ever done anything Ellen would disapprove of, and he felt bad about it. But somehow, he reasoned his way through it and decided to follow his own inclinations for a change. Now here with his Aunt Mary, he had no regrets. They drank tea and tried to catch up on all the news of the last ten years. Georgy was disappointed to hear that Cousin Nellie was out. He had really been hoping to see her again.

'She'll probably be back very soon,' Mary told him. 'She worked last night and said she would stay on for a while in the morning. She's going down to the East End to see if she can help in any way. They caught the worst of it yesterday, you know.'

Two cups of tea later, Georgy was just getting ready to leave, when the front door was flung open by a young woman, at once familiar and yet strange to him. The pigtails had gone. In their place, a cloud of wavy fair hair surrounded a face, keenly alive, strong but sensitive. Her grey-blue eyes shone with joy as Nellie realised who was there.

'Georgy!' she exclaimed and rushed to embrace him. 'Oh, I've missed you.'

Then she suddenly stepped back, looking slightly embarrassed at such a display of affection. Georgy, however, was delighted to see her.

'Nellie! How wonderful to see you. How are you? Tell me what you've been doing.'

The reunion was all too brief for Georgy had to get back to camp, but he promised to return very soon. On the train, he reflected on his visit, but all he could remember were Nellie's sparkling eyes and luminous face. What a beauty his cousin had turned into, he thought, but then he had always known she would.

Somehow Georgy found an excuse on his next free weekend to visit again. This time Nellie was at home and the chat flowed freely. Anecdotes and memories, laughter and hardships - all intertwined as they caught up on the missing years. The weather was fine and Aunt Mary suggested they sit in the garden and relax while she did the ironing.

'Don't you think it seems so strange sitting here whilst others are giving their lives to defend our country?' Nellie said thoughtfully.

'I know what you mean,' replied Georgy. 'I keep thinking of William and hoping he will be safe. He's reckless at the best of times, as you might remember.'

Nellie laughed. 'Yes indeed. I remember him wanting to dive in and rescue my toy boat that time. But you were more sensible and got it done anyway.'

Georgy smiled at the sweet memory.

'Maybe I shouldn't be so sensible,' he said. 'I always think things through too much.'

His face fell. 'That's probably why I didn't sign up before this, if I'm honest.'

He didn't know why he was telling his cousin all this, but it was easy to talk to her.

'I suppose I'm a coward, really,' he continued. 'I feel ashamed.'

Nellie reached out to touch his hand reassuringly.

'No, Georgy, not at all. People have been too hasty in going to war. It's not something to be taken lightly. You're no coward, I know that.'

Georgy felt very close to his cousin and took to visiting regularly whenever he could. His colleague Walter teased him about it.

'Off again, are you?' he said. 'I reckon you're in love!'

'Don't be silly,' replied Georgy, reddening slightly. 'Nellie's my cousin.'

'Oh, a cousin – well, yes that's different, isn't it? Just family.'

'She's like a sister to me,' replied Georgy, but as time went on, he realised that this wasn't quite true. Should he ask her on a date, he wondered, just as friends?

Next time he was at the house he suggested that perhaps she might like to go to the city, for a meal or a show. Many theatres were still open despite the possibility of further air raids. Attacks still occurred around the country, but after the June atrocity, London seemed to have been mostly left alone again.

Nellie hesitated.

'Well, I'd love to, but of course I work most nights on the telephone exchange.'

It was true. Nellie was awake all night, keeping vital phone lines running and connecting important calls for the military. She'd been working there since she turned eighteen and felt that she was contributing to the war effort. Georgy admired her determination and courage.

'Maybe we could meet for lunch then?' he suggested. 'How about Lyons Corner House? You can show me where you work.'

If Aunt Mary was surprised at the two cousins going off to meet up together, she never showed it. On the contrary, she positively encouraged them.

'It's so good to see you two together again. You've always been like brother and sister,' she said.

The lunch date was a great success. Georgy found Nellie so easy to chat to, both funny and sensitive at the same time. It seemed that she understood him better than anyone he'd ever met. Nellie, in return, still secretly idolised her cousin as much as she had whilst a child. Her eyes sparkled with admiration for him though Georgy was blind to this.

At the Corner House, they enjoyed a delicious chicken casserole for lunch and delighted in listening to live music and browsing all the exciting foodstuffs for sale, though things were getting more expensive each day as the war went on. There was even talk of rationing if it carried on much longer.

At this point Georgy and Nellie acted purely as cousins and friends, enjoying each other's company and nothing more. After all, Nellie was quite a bit younger than Georgy. One lunch date led to others, however, and as the weeks passed by, they drew ever closer.

The hardships of army training did its best to interrupt Georgy's peace of mind, along with the constant threat that they might be sent overseas at any time. Route marches were long and arduous, but at least Georgy could think whilst jogging, and what he thought about mostly was Nellie. Her bright and lovely face, her kind grey eyes - they were in his head all the time.

From time to time, he remembered his family, and in particular his brother William, fighting somewhere, he knew not, where. Regular letters arrived from Ellen, keeping Georgy up to date with their news. Gilbert had had a bad cold recently and Arthur was causing concern again by taking every opportunity to go off into the woods on his own. Some things never change, thought Georgy.

In return, he wrote and told them as much as much as he was allowed to about the camp and their daily routine, but with no mention of Nellie or her family. He felt guilty keeping it all secret, but he knew his mother's feelings on the matter and didn't want to upset her. It appeared that William had been in a field hospital sick with a fever lately but was well again now and back at the Front. How long would it be until he too was out there, thought Georgy. Surely it couldn't be long now. No one told the recruits anything, so a sense of nervous unease pervaded the camp.

It had been a particularly wet summer that year and Georgy was fed up of being cold, damp and muddy all the time. In September Nellie had a few well-earned nights off from her job and so he suggested that they go to the theatre whilst they had the chance. '*Carminetta*', a musical comedy, was showing at the Prince of Wales Theatre in Coventry Street and Georgy hoped it would be a nice distraction for them both. Nellie happily agreed.

Georgy's feelings were in turmoil at the moment. He tossed and turned in bed at night. Surely, he couldn't be in love with his cousin. These things were frowned upon. Indeed, he didn't even know if it was legal.

Anyway, the chances of Nellie thinking of him in anything other than a brotherly way were slim, he reckoned. Georgy fought hard to keep his emotions in control, but he couldn't help it. Every time he was near her, he just wanted to take her in his arms and kiss her, but he didn't dare. What would she say or do? Occasionally he touched her hand or brushed her arm, and he always felt a thrill go through him. Once, as he did so, Nellie turned and smiled deeply into his eyes, and he almost gave in and embraced her, but he swallowed hard and forced himself to move away. He thought that maybe Nellie looked disappointed, but probably he was just imagining it.

September 4th, 1917, was a clear, bright evening. There was a faint hint of autumn in the air as Georgy met Nellie at the station, to go to the theatre. She was wearing her best dress, a deep blue crepe de chine, and her hair softly curled around her face in a most becoming way.

'You look beautiful,' said Georgy impulsively, then wondered if he should have said it. Nellie blushed slightly and thanked him demurely.

'You look very smart as well,' she replied.

Georgy had his best dress uniform on. They weren't allowed to wear civilian clothing even on days off, which seemed a shame. This emphasised the fact that their life was the army now and nothing else.

She took his arm, and they promenaded along to the Prince of Wales Theatre.

'It looks so grand,' said Nellie in awe. 'I've been past the theatres often enough but never been to a show. This is a real treat!'

'You deserve it,' Georgy told her. 'All that night work. You are very brave to go out at that time and work. Don't you get scared?'

'No, not really,' replied Nellie. 'All the raids have been in the daytime anyway and I feel I'm doing my bit to help in a small way.'

They took their seats in great excitement. The plush red velour seats were set in circular tiers before the grand proscenium arch and stage. An ornate ceiling and curtained private boxes added the final touch. The theatre was a vision of ivory, gold and deepest red. Georgy bought them both a cone of ice cream and they settled down to enjoy the show.

They had a wonderful time together. The operetta was light and amusing with memorable songs, and a romantic theme. Sitting next to Nellie in the seats, Georgy found he seemed to brush up against her frequently. His arm longed to creep around her shoulders. But should he?

The show finished and Georgy was reluctant to let the magic end. As they left the theatre, he suggested that they walk by the river for a while. The sky was clear with stars shining down, and it seemed a shame to waste the beautiful night. Nellie wrapped her shawl closely about her and joyfully went along with Georgy's suggestion.

They reached the Victoria Embankment and started to meander along by the river. Suddenly there was an enormous roar, and out of nowhere, it seemed, German Gotha aircraft appeared in the sky. Bombs started to fall all around them with flashes of light and fire.

'Run!' cried Georgy, grabbing Nellie's arm. 'Let's get to some shelter.'

A terrible sight met their eyes as they fled. Some other like-minded people, strolling by the Thames, had been struck down and killed. There were screams and cries all around. The two of them stumbled along the embankment looking for a safe haven.

'Quick! Up this street!' cried Nellie. 'It goes to the underground station.'

They headed up the Strand, as buildings around them, succumbed to the furious onslaught from above. Dust, rubble, fire - it was terrifying.

'There's Charing Cross. Let's go in there!' shouted Georgy.

As they neared the entrance to the station, however, a massive high explosive bomb landed right next to them. They were torn apart and flung to the ground, covered in shattered bricks and dust. The blast knocked Georgy out, and when he came to, he couldn't see Nellie anywhere. The building opposite was aflame, with a ferocity he could not have imagined. Broken glass was everywhere, and people lay on the street, injured or dead - he didn't know. Where was Nellie?

Georgy was frantic and started searching.

'Nellie! Nellie!' he shouted, staggering through the ruins, searching the bodies on the ground in terrible fear that she was among the casualties. Tears ran down his face. Panic overwhelmed him. He felt desperate. Anxious minutes went by. Suddenly, he heard his name called feebly from nearby. He turned and there she was, covered in dust, her beautiful dress in shreds and her hair full of dirt. She staggered towards him, dazed but uninjured.

'Nellie!' He rushed to her. 'Oh, I thought I'd lost you forever,' he cried. 'Oh Nellie. I love you so much. I couldn't stand to lose you!'

He held her in his arms and kissed her again and again, not even thinking what he was doing. To his joy, she responded eagerly. Suddenly Georgy came to his senses and realised what had happened.

'Nellie, I'm sorry. I didn't mean to. I just - oh, I love you - I'm sorry.'

'Don't be sorry, Georgy,' Nellie responded breathlessly. 'I love you too. I always have done. Don't ever leave me. But please, let's find somewhere safer!'

They stumbled into a nearby underground station, arms around each other, not wanting to let go. In the muted dim light below, they waited with many others until the raid finally subsided an hour later. In a quiet corner, they took their time to caress, to kiss, and to consider their situation. Should they tell anyone? What would Aunt Mary say? What should they do next? They didn't know. All they knew was their newfound love.

Chapter 25

Time was running out. Georgy could tell from the repetitive daily routine at the camp that their intake of trainees had learnt all they needed to know. Now they were just marking time until they headed to the Front. Why was there such a delay? he wondered. Surely fresh troops were needed. New recruits had arrived at intervals, but none had departed for quite some time. Georgy had heard a rumour that it was just too dangerous for ships to cross at the moment, because of the threat of enemy attack. Not that he was in any hurry to go, since having discovered his feelings were returned by the lovely Nellie. The waiting and wondering, however, continued to nag away at him.

September had been a blissful time for them both once they had recovered from their stressful night-time ordeal. They hadn't yet revealed their relationship to Nellie's family, or anyone else. It continued to be their secret. They just didn't know how the news would be received. From what he had heard, Georgy realised that public opinion was against cousins courting, though he couldn't think why.

One morning on the parade ground, Georgy's unit were called together to receive a briefing. His heart sank. Was this it? Would he be parted from his love now? Georgy knew that it was inevitable, but he dreaded it all the same.

The officer spoke: 'Now chaps, I know you've all been wondering when you will get to have a go at the Hun, so I'm here to give you some good news.'

Georgy groaned inwardly.

'Due to poor sea conditions in the Channel, we are delaying the next departure until December. In the meantime, you will all be getting four weeks embarkation leave starting on the 1st of November.'

There were cheers from everyone except Georgy, who felt stunned. Four weeks! That was great but meant that he had enough time to get back to Canada to see his family. It would be arranged for them, so there was no way he could stay here with Nellie. It sounded like after that, they would finally be on their way to the war.

'You will report for duty again on 10th of December at Shorncliffe Camp in Kent,' the officer continued. 'From there you will then sail for France. Those of you travelling to Canada for your leave will join the troopship SS Megantic to return on 24th of November from Halifax. If you miss this ship, you will be considered AWOL and dealt with accordingly.'

Two gloomy days passed before Georgy was able to talk to Nellie about it. It was hard trying to be happy about going home when he really wanted to be with Nellie instead. Indeed - where was home? Canada or England? He wasn't sure he knew any more.

Nellie realised something wasn't right as soon as she saw Georgy.

'I can see by your face,' she said, 'something awful has happened. Are you leaving?'

‘Yes,’ replied Georgy. ‘But not to go to war just yet; to go on leave.’

‘Leave?’ said Nellie. ‘Won't that mean we can spend time together?’

‘No,’ he replied glumly. ‘We're being shipped back to Canada for a couple of weeks from beginning of November.’

Nellie sighed. ‘Surely it'll be nice for you to see your family again, won't it?’

‘Yes, I suppose so,’ he admitted, ‘though I'd rather be with you.’

‘We knew you'd be leaving soon in any case, and it's better to be going home than to war, surely?’

‘Yes, yes, of course. But after that we have to report back to Shorncliffe Camp in Kent to prepare for shipping out to the Front.’

Nellie swallowed hard, and Georgy realised that she was trying to be brave for his sake.

‘I don't want to think about that,’ she said. ‘I can't bear to think of you in danger.’

‘It's not the danger,’ replied Georgy. ‘It’s just that I don't want to be parted from you.’

They held each other tight and if tears were shed then no one would have blamed them. ‘Let's make the most of the time we have,’ Nellie said at last. ‘We have a few more weeks yet. We must make every moment count.’

The days flew by, though Georgy and Nellie took every chance, no matter how slight, to be together. Georgy wrote to his mother to warn her of his impending visit, and gradually he came to feel happier about seeing them all again. After all, they were his kin, and he had spent all his life until now with them. He loved them, undoubtedly. It’s just that he had another focus now, his beloved Nellie.

1st November came and Georgy had one day free before he had to catch the train to Liverpool. He wanted to spend it alone with Nellie, but her mother had other ideas.

'We've hardly seen Georgy lately,' Aunt Mary told her daughter. 'You've been keeping him all to yourself. We must give him a proper send off. Tell him to come here and we'll have a family party. It's the least we can do.'

Reluctantly, Georgy and Nellie did as they were told. There was no arguing with Aunt Mary once she had made up her mind.

Despite his regrets, Georgy found it was a fine get together. Uncle Will was there, along with young Billy, now a strapping lad of 15. Not only that, but Charlie, Will's eldest son from his first marriage, came with his wife and child. Charlie was a lot older than the rest of his siblings, nearly 30 now, and he worked with his father in the carpentry business. He had wanted to volunteer, but the pleas of his wife Ann kept him from doing so.

All this, Georgy learned as he chatted to them all. What a lovely family, he thought to himself. Everyone asked after his own family, wanting to know all the news, especially about Ellen. Will had been close to his sister when they were young and he missed her. He regretted them falling out.

'Georgy,' said Aunt Mary, seriously, when she got him alone for a minute. 'Please can you give your mother a message from us when you see her. We want her to know we are sorry for our hasty words before she left. We admire you all for making a go of things over there. We were wrong and we apologise. Please tell her.'

Georgy nodded, embarrassed. The only problem was that his mother didn't even know he had seen them. But still, maybe he could explain. He hated keeping secrets and telling lies, but it had seemed the only way. Perhaps now was the time to open up.

Then, to his surprise, there were two more unexpected guests. Grandma and Grandpa Goddard appeared. They looked much frailer than he remembered, but it had been a decade since he had last seen them, and age had taken its toll.

'Grandma,' he exclaimed. 'How lovely to see you. I thought you were living in Essex still. Did you come all this way to see me?'

Grandma Goddard smiled. 'We've just moved back to Edmonton, dear, though we would have come to see you anyway. We had to give up the pub. It's been too much hard work since poor Fred died. You've grown into a fine young man now. How is your mother? She must be very proud of you.'

Georgy did his best to update them all on his parents, on William's volunteering, and all the rest of his siblings, many of whom they had never seen.

'It's such a shame', said Grandma. 'Grandchildren that I will never meet.'

'You might one day,' Georgy replied. 'They may come back to England for a visit or something.'

He felt suddenly fond of his grandparents. He'd always thought of them as distant and a bit scary but now he saw that they were vulnerable and fragile. Life's struggles had finally caught up with them.

As the family members slowly drifted away at the end of the day, Georgy hugged them, each and every one, vowing to keep in touch. Addresses had been exchanged, and he promised to write. Aunt Mary had invited Georgy to stay overnight, and Nellie was going to see him off at the station the next day. He was dreading saying goodbye to her. In his head, he had rehearsed over and over what he was going to say. He loved her, but he couldn't expect her to wait for him. It wouldn't be fair.

The next morning, after an emotional goodbye with his aunt and uncle, Georgy and Nellie travelled to the station in near silence. There was over half an hour before the train was due, so they adjourned to the station cafe for a cup of tea.

'Nellie,' said Georgy awkwardly, 'I need to say something, but I don't really know how. Can you please bear with me?'

Nellie nodded silently and reached out her hand to touch his.

'As you know I'm going away soon, I know this time it's only on leave, but when I get back, I guess it will be the real thing. I'm sure you know how much I love you and I know you love me, but it's time to let go.'

Nellie gasped. 'No,' she stammered.

Georgy held up his hand to still her protest. 'Please, Nellie, it's for the best. You must forget about me or think of me just as a friend.'

'No!' cried Nellie. 'Don't ask me to do that. I can't.' There was a pause. 'Will you forget me then?' she challenged him.

Georgy's eyes met hers. 'No,' he admitted. 'I never could, but it's not fair of me to ask you to wait. I might not return.'

'Oh, don't say that!' begged Nellie.

'It's true, though,' Georgy continued resolutely, 'and you will meet other young men who will also love you, though I doubt anyone could love you as much as I do. You must be free to love them if you want to.'

His voice started to break with emotion. 'I won't ask you to wait, but if I return safely and you still feel the same, then we could start again.'

Tears welled up in his eyes and he looked away.

Nellie was crying too.

'No Georgy,' she told him. 'I've waited 10 years for you to love me, and a bit more waiting won't hurt. You're the only man I want. I'll always feel the same.'

Georgy gazed deep into her eyes and saw that she spoke the truth.

'You'll always be my love, Nellie, and I'm happy that you feel this way, but I still think it's a lot to ask.'

'I'd rather wait an eternity for you than take up with any other man!' she declared.

They embraced over the table, sending teacups flying in all directions. Laughing through their tears, they promised to write regularly.

'We'll have a telephone soon as well,' Nellie told him. 'I'll let you have the number when I know it. Then we can keep in touch when you're in Kent.'

There was no escaping the passage of time, however. Georgy's train was waiting to whisk him away. They kissed on the platform then Georgy reluctantly clambered aboard. As the train pulled out, he watched as Nellie, waving frantically, disappeared from view. He had tried to set her free, he reflected, but she didn't want to go, and for that he was profoundly grateful.

Boarding the ship with Walter and the rest of their unit at Liverpool Docks, Georgy finally began to feel excited about seeing his family again. It had been six months since he'd been home, and he wondered how they'd been getting on. As the ship steamed on over the waves, his thoughts of them all became stronger until he felt desperate to see them.

It was with a shock, when Georgy disembarked at Halifax, that he remembered the severity of the Canadian winters. After a long period of mild rainy weather in England, the extreme cold here made him gasp. Flakes of snow were drifting in the icy air, though nothing serious as yet just a few playful flurries. Pulling his army great coat around him, Georgy collected his baggage, said goodbye for now to Walter, and headed for the train back to Moncton.

Arriving at the family house, Georgy had expected a welcome of some sort but was sorely disappointed. Most of his siblings were at school or work, and his mother was nowhere to be seen. Eventually, he tracked her down, lying on the bed in a darkened room upstairs, with little Hazel asleep at her side.

'Mum, I'm home,' he called, but all Ellen did was wail.

'Georgy, Georgy, we've had such terrible news! William went missing and now we hear he's injured and in hospital. I'll never forgive myself for letting him go. It's all too much. I can't bear it!'

Ever the practical one, Georgy made tea and spent time with his mother, finding out the details and pacifying her. It seemed that after a traumatic telegram telling them that William was 'Missing in Action', the family had, a couple of days later, received better news that he was in the 17th Casualty Clearing Station, though with what injuries they didn't know.

Ellen had taken to her bed and refused to be consoled until she knew her son was all right. The rest of the family were just trying to manage the best they could. Ethel was doing all the cooking and most of the childcare, whilst the others did their bit to help where they could. Father, it seemed, had refused to discuss the matter at all, leaving his wife to her misery.

Not much of a homecoming then, Georgy thought to himself, but maybe he shouldn't have expected it. William had always been Ellen's favourite and things weren't about to change.

Chapter 26

Moncton Canada

Georgy was feeling annoyed. Numerous telephone calls and telegrams from the local office had failed to elicit any information about William's injuries or whereabouts. Standing in the telegraph office, he tried once again to contact the 17th Casualty Clearing Station, wherever that might be, by cable. Twice it had already been rejected, but this time something appeared to have gone through.

'You'll just have to wait now,' the agent told him. 'The reply could take some time. We will send it to your house once we get it.'

Reluctantly, Georgy gave in and left it at that. He'd done all he could. His mother had begged him to find out something for her, so he'd done his best, but it was like wading through treacle.

It was a strange interlude for Georgy; he was having trouble adjusting to home life again. All his siblings seemed to have grown up so much lately, even just in the time he had been training, and he wondered how different he would find them when (and if) he finally came home for good. Gilbert was still working with Father and Harriet, but next year, if the war continued, he would also be old enough to fight. Ethel was twelve now and fast becoming a purposeful and energetic young woman. Arthur was as wild and unpredictable as ever, but the two youngest, Len and Hazel, luckily seemed unaffected by the war or the family separations. Georgy realised that they barely knew who he was, and that made him sad. He made a determined effort to spend time with them whilst he could.

Spending time with his younger siblings was a pleasant distraction, though the weather was frightful and outdoor excursions were infrequent. He helped the boys build a route for their toy trains around their bedroom and spent time reading stories to little Hazel.

Dreamily he thought that maybe one day he and Nellie would have children of their own. But then he stopped himself. That was jumping just a bit too far ahead!

Nellie had sent a letter to him, giving him their telephone number and sending all her love. Georgy realised now that he should tell his mother at least something of his contact with her family. Ellen still spent most of her days in bed, moping and worrying, with little regard for the rest of them. Towards the middle of his visit, Georgy decided to try and talk to her. He sat down on the bed.

'Mum, I've got some news of your family in England.'

'My family?' she said, sitting up and paying more attention.

'Yes, I bumped into Aunt Mary whilst I was in London, and she invited me over to her house.' Georgy had decided it was best to be economical with the truth for the time being.

‘I hope you didn't go!’ Ellen exclaimed.

‘Well, I did, Mum, it was hard to get out of it, and it was lovely to see them all again. I saw Grandma and Grandpa as well. They've moved back to Middlesex now.’

In spite of Ellen’s antagonism, she was keen to hear more about her parents and her brother. Georgy told her all the news and then proceeded to tell her what Mary had said, with her apology.

Ellen was mollified by this.

‘Well, it's about time,’ she said, ‘but it's nice to hear. Maybe it was a good thing you met up after all. How were Nellie and Billy?’

Georgy was encouraged and (whilst leaving out the details of his and Nellie's relationship), gave his mother an update on them both.

‘Perhaps I’ll write to Will and Mary,’ Ellen mused.

Georgy was pleased to hear this. If they started communicating again, that would hopefully make life a lot easier for him in the future.

A couple of days after Georgy had sent the telegram, a reply arrived, but it wasn't very satisfactory.

“Pte Huntingford W, 832429 is not currently a patient at this location.”

That was all. There was no mention of where he might be now or his state of health. There were so many unanswered questions that, in spite of the weather, Georgy dashed back down to the telegraph office and sent another cable, asking for more detail. This time, the reply arrived within a few minutes.

“Information restricted.”

Restricted! What did that mean? Had William gone back to his unit again, been moved to another hospital, or worse? Telling Ellen and the rest of his anxious family, Georgy put a positive spin on things.

'I'm sure this means that William has gone back to the Front again,' he told them optimistically. 'That's why it's restricted. They can't give away information on troop movements.'

To his relief, his mother and siblings seemed to accept this version of events, though privately Georgy felt very anxious about his brother. His father sat there saying nothing, but later he caught up with his son when they were alone for a moment.

'George, son, tell me the truth, do you think William is all right?'

Georgy hesitated. He could bluff the others, but not his father.

'I don't know, Dad,' he replied. 'I am worried about him, I must admit, but don't tell Mum.'

His father sighed. 'I thought as much but didn't say anything. You're right to give the others something to hope for. It will be very hard on them all otherwise.'

He paused. 'Please take care of yourself when you're out there, won't you?' he added in a slightly husky voice. 'We need you, son.'

He walked away, leaving Georgy feeling quite choked up.

Thankfully, Ellen now emerged from her self-imposed bed rest and took up her household duties again, relieving poor Ethel, who had been valiantly holding the fort.

'You look tired,' Georgy said to her. 'I'm sure it's not been easy, what with school and everything else.'

His sister just smiled, however. 'It's no problem,' she said. 'I'm used to it. I like looking after people. Len and Hazel are little angels, but Arthur, well, that's a different matter!' She laughed. 'He certainly knows his own mind.'

'Yes, indeed,' laughed Georgy.

Just before the end of his leave, Georgy decided to go into the city. He wanted to catch up on the news at work and run a few errands. It was strange being free to go out and about around the town again.

First, he went in with Gilbert and Father to see where they were working at the moment. Harriet was still there, but a resigned melancholy had descended on her, as her husband and brother had both been killed in action a few months earlier.

Georgy wanted to express his condolences but wasn't sure what to say.

'Harriet, I was very sorry to hear your news,' he began.

'It's all right,' she replied, though her eyes were suspiciously moist. 'I'm over it now. We just have to grin and bear it. Nothing else we can do.' Her voice quivered slightly. 'At least I have this job,' she added. 'Your father has offered to keep me on, so I will be able to feed the children.'

'Won't you get a widow's pension?' asked Georgy. 'Sorry, none of my business, really!'

'Yes, but it's not much. Just about enough to pay the rent, so this helps.'

Georgy felt proud of his father for looking after Harriet in her hour of need. He often seemed stern, but George Huntingford had a kind heart.

It was a novelty to Georgy to stay at work for an hour or two. Plumbing seemed almost alien to him after months of army training. He was pleased to see Gilbert, now nearly 17, working well as a plumber's mate.

'How do you like this business?' he asked his brother whilst alongside.

'It's fine,' Gilbert said, 'but not really what I want to do. I'll be more than happy to return it to you again when you're back, or William, of course.'

'What *do* you want to do?' asked Georgy.

'I love cooking,' replied his brother, 'but I don't suppose I'll be able to make a living at it. If the war carries on, I'll join up when I'm 18. Do you think they would let me fly an aeroplane? I think they're fantastic.'

'I expect it takes a long time to learn to fly,' said Georgy, 'but I guess it's the future. Germany has been using aeroplanes to bomb London lately. I was caught up in one of the raids. It was quite terrifying.'

He shuddered at the memory of that night but then had to smile to himself when he remembered the outcome.

After a bit of shopping in the city, Georgy also found time to visit Aunt Minnie. Uncle Dick was at work in the alms-house and Ralph was back in hospital again, having further surgery on his knee. Minnie was delighted to see her nephew, but very emotional when talking about William. Georgy reassured her as best he could.

'We think he must have gone back to his unit again,' he told her. 'He's not in the hospital any more.'

'That's good news,' his aunt said. 'I just wish this dreadful war would be over. All these young men killed - it's awful!'

Georgy remembered when Aunt Minnie had been very enthusiastic about everyone signing up. It seemed that her opinion had changed. The reality of war was coming home to roost.

The last of Georgy's freedom ebbed away and too soon it was time to depart again on the morning tide from Halifax. His only consolation as he left his family on the 24th of November was that maybe he would see Nellie once more before they were sent overseas – a slight hope perhaps, but a chance, nevertheless.

As they left, the harbour and city of Halifax were glistening with ice, though a weak sun made everything shine like silver. It had a beauty all its own.

It was a rough crossing this time, with wild, angry seas and a bitter cold for much of the journey. The troops huddled down below, looking forward to a milder climate ahead. They were all relieved when the SS Megantic pulled into Liverpool docks on the 8th of December.

They poured out into the city and headed for the train station, which was where they were shocked to see the newspaper headlines.

"*Halifax Explosion kills 2000. Read all about it!*"

The stunned Canadian soldiers, including Georgy, grabbed copies and read the story of a terrible disaster. Two ships had collided in the Halifax harbour, it seemed. One caught fire and was unfortunately carrying vast amounts of high explosives, which caused a catastrophe.

Georgy couldn't believe his eyes. To think they'd all been standing there only a few days beforehand. The docks were devastated, as was much of the city. Buildings had collapsed and thousands of people were homeless. The death toll was up to 2000, with many others injured. Though rescue teams were busy arriving from all areas of Western Canada, including Moncton, a severe snowstorm was now hampering their efforts. Some of Georgy's fellow soldiers were in tears, one or two frantically trying to phone or cable their loved ones who lived there.

Thank goodness my family are a safe distance away, thought Georgy. To think it's not even to do with the war - just bad luck, fate, he supposed. How awful.

On the 10th of December, Georgy and the rest of his Canadian colleagues reached Shorncliffe Camp on the coast near Folkstone. The camp was of the now familiar style - wooden huts to sleep in, cold and uncomfortable, with the usual routine. This time they would be practising their embarkation drills, which Georgy realised gloomily meant they would be leaving soon.

The first chance he got, he phoned Nellie. It was strange talking on the telephone, especially as it was inside a shop with people passing by. He wasn't used to the implement and found it difficult to express himself properly. He was relieved, however, to hear her voice and know that she was safe. Further night-time air raids had taken place whilst he was at home, and he had feared for her. Likewise, Nellie had heard about the Halifax explosion and was worried. They promised to write or phone whenever they could. Would he get the chance to see her again before he departed for France? Georgy just didn't know.

Chapter 27

Shorncliffe Camp, England

To his disappointment, Georgy was not billeted in the same hut as Walter this time. His nearest companions were a sour-faced, taciturn conscript from Toronto called Tom and a larger-than-life Scotsman, Jamie. He did his best to get along with both of them, but it wasn't always easy. Tom understandably resented being there, whilst Jamie was wildly enthusiastic about the whole event. Consequently, arguments frequently broke out, which Georgy did his utmost to avoid without much success.

On another dreary route march through the muddy lanes of Shorncliffe, however, he suddenly found himself near his old comrade and was able to exchange a few words whilst stamping along.

'Did you hear about poor Gordon?' Walter asked him.

'No. What?' Georgy exclaimed. 'Not dead, surely?'

'Sadly, yes,' replied Walter. 'But you know what? He never even got to the Front. He bought it right here.'

'Here! But how?'

'Damned German air raid back in the summer. Killed a few here at the camp and the poor lad was one of them. He's buried in the cemetery over there. I went there yesterday.'

'Really. How dreadful! What bad luck for him. I must go and visit.'

It was a sombre afternoon for Georgy the next day, standing there gazing at the grave of his fellow trainee. What a waste, he thought. Not even to have made it to the Front. Poor Gordon had so badly wanted to be a hero, yet surely this wouldn't count. It was unlikely to generate him any medals, which somehow seemed so unfair. The cold December air wrapped around Georgy's lone figure as he placed some flowers on the greedy earth.

Returning to the hut later, he could hear Tom and Jamie arguing again.

'I don't see why I have to be here,' cried Tom. 'It's not my war. Let `em get on with it without me!'

'Och, you don't know what you're saying, laddy,' retorted Jamie. 'This will be the greatest adventure you'll ever have.'

Horrified at his friend's death, Georgy felt he had to intervene.

'You two are both wrong! For one thing, if innocent civilians are being bombed and killed for no reason then that *makes* it our war. I was in London in September and witnessed it myself. Burning buildings, bodies everywhere - just innocent people enjoying a night out! And you, Jamie, you should be ashamed as well. It's no picnic being on the frontline, you know. My brother is currently wounded, and I don't even know where he is. Adventure? Don't talk to me about it, because it just won't wash!'

With that, he flung himself down on his bunk and turned away. There was an awkward silence, then both men muttered their apologies and sat down, feeling embarrassed.

On December the 18th, the unit was suddenly called together for a briefing. The next day at 6:00 am, they were going to be sailing for France! There was a rush of preparation, and the hut became a centre of frantic activity.

Many men wanted to phone loved ones for the last time and the queue for the camp telephone seemed endless. Eventually it was Georgy's turn, and he dialled Nellie's number, but as he might have guessed, she was out at work. Maybe it had even been her putting his call through at the exchange, he thought, only to be told by his aunt, that she wasn't there. He left a message and chatted to Mary for a short while but couldn't say what he was really feeling. Mary wished him lots of luck and said they would all be thinking of him. There was no more he could do. Then he wrote to his family, updating them on developments and sending all his love. As a final task he also wrote to William in the hope that he would get it and let him know how he was.

His outfit gathered on the parade ground at 5:00 am, backpacks loaded and guns at the ready. The weather was wild and stormy and the skies still dark. They waited and waited for an officer to arrive, wondering what was going on. Finally, a sergeant major came and informed them that they would *not* be departing today after all, due to inclement weather conditions. Everyone groaned. The build-up had been so nerve wracking and intense that it was not so much a relief, as an anticlimax. Now they would have to go through it all again.

Two further days passed with endless drills and practice trench building. Tempers were frayed and bickering was frequent amongst the men. Then on the 22nd December they were called together for another briefing. This is it, thought Georgy. We must be off tomorrow, or very soon anyway. Over Christmas as well - that's great!

To his surprise however, the officer informed them all that there was to be a delay now until the New Year and that they were all being given Christmas leave from the 24th to the 28th of December. Four days thought Georgy. But what do I do? I can't go home in that time. What will it be like staying here? Could I possibly see Nellie?

That evening, Georgy walked into the nearby village to use the public telephone kiosk at the shop. The one at the camp seemed to be in use all the time. He just hoped that Nellie would be at home this time, and to his joy, she was.

'Georgy, where are you? I thought you were on your way to France!'

He explained that it had been delayed and that he now had some leave over Christmas.

'I was wondering if we could meet up if you're not working.'

Nellie exclaimed in delight.

'Oh yes, why not come for the whole Christmas? You could stay with us. You know we have room.'

'I think you'd better talk to your mother about that first,' replied Georgy.

'Oh Georgy, she won't mind. I'm afraid she knows about us now. I got so upset when she told me that you were leaving that she asked what was wrong, so I had to tell her. I'm sorry!'

'How did she take it?' asked Georgy.

‘Well, she wasn't too happy at first,’ said Nellie, ‘due to us being cousins. But she's accepted it now, I think. Please come and stay for Christmas. It would be lovely.’

‘Not until you've asked your mum,’ Georgy told her firmly. ‘Look, go and talk to her and I'll phone back in half an hour.’

Half an hour later Georgy had his answer. Everyone would love to see him. He speedily made arrangements for his travel and returned to camp a happy man.

It was a warm welcome at the Goddard household for Georgy when he arrived on Christmas Eve, but he thought he discerned a certain awkwardness from Aunt Mary.

‘Nellie, Billy, go and take old Mrs Sharp next door those biscuits I baked, will you? Stay and have a cuppa with her. You know she gets lonely at this time of the year.’

Nellie's eyes met Georgy's in alarm. Something was going on, but there was nothing she could do.

Having disposed of her children, Aunt Mary settled down beside Georgy on the sofa.

‘Now I need to talk to you, George,’ she began. ‘Nellie has told me all about how she feels about you, and she says it's the same for you.’

‘It is!’ Georgy assured her.

‘Please listen a minute. I don't doubt your sincerity, but it won't do. You’re cousins and it’s not to be encouraged. Yes, I believe it is legal these days, but to my way of thinking it shouldn't be. It’s not right. You're too closely related. What I meant to say is that we're all very fond of you, Georgy, but I really can't encourage this thing with Nellie. You're welcome here as part of our family, but there will be no ‘goings on’ whilst you are in my house. You will be chaperoned every time you are together. You will not see Nellie alone. Is that clear?'

'Yes,' muttered Georgy. 'I understand.'

'What does your mother think about this?'

'She doesn't know,' he replied.

'I thought as much. I don't think she would approve either.'

Aunt Mary paused and eyed her downcast nephew. She softened.

'Look, I don't mean to be unkind, Georgy. We want you to enjoy Christmas with us and we wish you well. I know it's a very emotional time with the threat of the war, but you must treat Nellie just as a friend, or a sister even.'

Georgy said nothing for a while, but sat there, his head hanging down in his face, burning. Eventually he said: 'Of course. I'm just happy to be here with you all and I wouldn't want to do anything to upset you.'

Aunt Mary put her arms around him then and gave him a hug.

'Good lad,' she said. 'It's the sensible thing to do. We'll say no more about it.'

'I think I'll get some fresh air,' said Georgy and went out into the garden where he tried to get his emotions in order. He was surprised by his aunt's reaction. He was aware that some people thought that cousins shouldn't be sweethearts, but he hadn't thought that she would be like this. Half an hour later, he had mostly managed to reason things out. It was, after all, just a few days. Who knows what would happen in the next few months? There was nothing to stop Georgy and Nellie corresponding, even if that had to be in secret.

It was unlikely that he would see her for quite a while after this anyway. Her mother needn't worry.

He made up his mind to just enjoy the festive season with the family and to gaze at the lovely Nellie from a distance. It was enough to be in the same room as her. That was certainly a fine Christmas gift for him.

Nellie looked at Georgy anxiously when she returned, aware that she had been deliberately 'got out of the way'. He tried to smile reassuringly and did his best to behave normally. That night, as he lay in the spare room unable to sleep, he realised that he must tell Nellie. He wrote a brief note and slipped it under her bedroom door.

"*Dear Nellie, your mother has told me that she isn't happy about our relationship and will be watching us during my stay. If I don't seem as affectionate as normal to you, I hope you will realise why. Be assured that my love for you remains the same as ever. Love, Georgy.*"

Feeling better about the situation, he finally dropped off and was happy to awake to jollity and family warmth on Christmas morning. Nellie nodded at him as they made their way down to breakfast, and Georgy knew that she understood. She brushed his hand under the table, and a thrill went up his spine.

It was a merry day of eating and celebrating in the way that only families can. Georgy wondered how the rest of his family were getting on, especially William, but there was no way to contact them. He had debated sending a Christmas message to Canada, the day before, via telegram, but thought the arrival of such an item would only cause fear and alarm. No one wanted telegrams at the moment. They were nearly always bad news.

On Boxing Day Nellie suggested that they could go out for a walk as the weather was cold but bright. Aunt Mary agreed but said that Billy should go too.

Billy groaned. 'I don't want to go,' he complained. 'It's cold out there!'

'You're going!' said his mother firmly and packed them all off to the park. Out of sight of the house, Nellie took Georgy's arm and clung closely to him. Billy grumbled most of the way.

'Billy,' suggested his sister. 'Why don't I give you some money and you can go and get a cup of tea at the cafe. We can catch up with you later, but we won't tell Mum. She doesn't need to know.'

Billy was happy and headed off, giving the young couple a bit of time to themselves. They sat on a park bench and talked, Georgy telling Nellie what her mother had said.

'We'll have to keep things secret again,' he said, sighing. 'I guess I may be off abroad shortly anyway.'

'Do you think it will be soon?' asked Nellie.

'I don't know,' replied Georgy. 'Everything is so uncertain.'

'I could come and visit you down in Kent,' Nellie suggested, 'and stay at a guest house nearby. There's a friend of mine who lives in Southend. I could pretend to Mum that I was going there.'

'That would be nice,' said Georgy, 'but please don't get yourself in trouble with your mum over this. Let's wait and see what happens in January.'

They kissed and cuddled up to each other, making the most of every moment. Eventually Nellie remembered Billy.

'We better go and collect him,' she said.

Billy wasn't stupid. When he saw them arrive at the cafe holding hands, he was surprised but not concerned.

'Oh, so that's what's going on, then,' he said, laughing. 'No wonder you wanted me out of the way.'

'Sorry, Billy,' said his sister. 'Do you mind?'

'Mind? No. Why should I?'

'Listen, Billy,' said Georgy seriously, 'Your mum isn't too happy about it. So can you help us out by keeping quiet about this please?'

'Hey, no problem.' said Billy. 'My lips are sealed!'

They returned to the house and Mary was luckily none the wiser. The next day Georgy left to go back to camp, wishing them all a fond farewell.

'What sort of Christmas did you have?' he asked Tom when he returned.

'Well, I suppose it was all right,' the lad said begrudgingly. 'We all put some money in and had a pretty good Christmas dinner – Turkey, pudding and a pint each. The best laugh was having the officers serving us, you should have seen it! We had a rare old sing song in the evening as well, though I heard that one unlucky unit had to ship out on Christmas Day. Would you believe it?' He shook his head in disbelief. 'Then me and Jamie went to the pub on Boxing Day. He's not such a bad chap really when you get to know him. Not that I agree with his views on the war, mind.'

Georgy smiled. Good to see them getting on.

Camp life went back to its normal drudgery – marches, artillery practice, trench building - often in the cold and wet - plus the constant threat of embarkation looming.

January 13th, 1918: Georgy was on the parade ground when his name was shouted out.

'Gunner Huntingford, 2099931 - report to the office, on the double!'

What was going on now? People didn't usually get called on individually. Was he in trouble? Nervously, Georgy knocked and entered the office. Two stern looking military policemen were there to see him, their bright red caps making their status immediately obvious.

'Come with us Gunner Huntingford,' they ordered. 'We have some questions for you.'

Once in a secluded area, he was told to sit down. 'My name is Major Connors of the MFP,' the older man said, 'and this is my assistant, MFP Sherwood. I expect you know why we are here.'

Confused, Georgy replied: 'No, I have no idea.'

'Your brother, Pte William Huntingford 832429 - have you seen him lately?'

'No, why? How could I have seen him? He is serving on the frontline somewhere. I wrote to him recently, but he hasn't replied.'

MFP Sherwood pulled Georgy's letter out of a pocket. 'Yes, we have it here. We want to know if he has been in touch.'

'But why?' cried Georgy. 'As far as I know, he was injured in November and in the hospital. I tried to find out if he was all right, but they said he wasn't there any more. Where is he now?'

'We're asking the questions!' declared the major. 'That's what we want to know. Don't you realise that he has gone AWOL – absent without leave? This is a very serious offence, and if you are involved you could also be in big trouble.'

'AWOL!' exclaimed Georgy, 'but William would never do that, he's no coward! I haven't heard from him at all. As I said, the last thing we were told was that he was at the 17th casualty clearing station.'

'He went AWOL from there on the 11th January,' MFP Connors informed him. 'We believe he may be on his way to see you.'

'Well, he's not!' Georgy cried. 'He wouldn't! You've got it all wrong!'

'We have evidence that you have been contacting him,' MFP Sherwood continued. 'You have sent him telegrams and letters. Were you trying to arrange to meet up?'

'No, of course not!' declared Georgy angrily. 'William knows his duty and would never shirk it. He signed up as soon as he could, just before his 18th birthday.'

'People change,' Major Connors told him coldly. 'Under fire, men lose their nerve. He has not returned to his battalion, and he is not in the hospital, so where is he?'

'I don't know!' insisted Georgy. 'Really, I don't!'

'Just to remind you that the penalty for desertion is court-martial and death by firing squad. Those who help or shelter absentees will also be dealt with severely. It is in your interest to tell us anything you know, no matter how slight.'

'Yes, yes, I will of course,' Georgy replied desperately, 'but I don't know a thing!'

The questioning went on for hours, until the military policemen finally left, satisfied, for now, that Georgy was telling the truth. The first thing that he did that evening, his mind reeling, was to phone Nellie. His distress was obvious in his voice and she reacted accordingly.

'I'm coming down,' she cried. 'I'll get somewhere to stay in Folkestone and be there by Saturday. Meet me at Victoria Pier at 7, that evening, and we'll talk then.'

Chapter 28

It was cold standing by the entrance to the pier, waiting for Nellie to arrive. The January winds whipped around Georgy's shoulders, making him shiver. The pier was closed up at present, partly due to the time of year and partly due to the war. It would have been an easy target for bombers with all its lights on and amusements running. Suddenly, out of the darkness, Nellie appeared, her face alight with love and concern. It warmed him immediately.

They retreated to the residents private drawing room in the London and Paris Hotel, where Nellie had managed to secure a room for herself for the night.

'There aren't many places open at this time of year,' she said, 'and some have even been turned into hospitals for the troops. Oh, I hope you won't end up in one of those!'

Georgy held her hands in his and murmured reassurances as best he could.

They seated themselves in a quiet corner, behind a screen of potted palms and ferns. In the centre of the room a gentleman in evening dress tinkled gently on a grand piano. There were very few other guests. An elderly couple and a sad-faced, middle aged lady listened to the music, the lady fiddling absentmindedly with her string of pearls. Bereaved, thought Georgy. A husband, brother, son? Who knew? We all have our troubles.

The gentle ripples from the piano acted as a shield for their conversation, which they conducted in hushed tones.

'Tell me all about it,' invited Nellie, 'I'm here for you, my love.'

Georgy recounted all the details of his interrogation, ending with his fears for his brother.

'The worst thing is,' he said, 'if William is not AWOL, then where is he? If he's not in the hospital any more, does that mean that he's dead?' His voice trembled as he said the last words. 'I can't bear the thought of it, but I know he's not a coward, so he can't be a deserter!'

Nellie attempted to comfort him.

'Maybe he's lost his memory or something and is confused, or perhaps he's unconscious and they don't know who he is. When he comes to, then everything will be sorted out.'

'I hope you're right,' said Georgy earnestly. 'William wouldn't desert. He's never been scared of anything in his life!'

'I can't remember him that well now,' Nellie said, 'but he was always impulsive, that I do know. Maybe he's on some secret mission behind enemy lines.'

'Yes, that would be just like him,' Georgy remarked and smiled a little. 'He's always so keen to be a hero. That's why I just can't go along with the idea that he's a deserter. I know some men do, and who can blame them when they're under fire? What's to say how I will behave when it comes to it? But William, he's been out there for over a year and stuck it up till now. Why would anything change?'

'Do your family know?' asked Nellie.

'I don't think so,' replied Georgy, 'unless someone has contacted them recently.'

'Perhaps you should write to them and warn them,' she said.

'Yes, I'll do that,' said Georgy. 'Last time I wrote I thought I was about to embark for France. They will think I'm in the thick of it all, when in fact, I'm still here dealing with all this!'

A stifled sob broke loose from him. Nellie held Georgy close and soothed his distress as much as she could. Her warmth and love enveloped him, and he let his feelings flow. It was such a relief.

'I'm sorry,' he said after a while. 'I've just been holding it all back till now. You are so good for me.'

'You don't need to be sorry,' Nellie replied, brushing the tears from his face. 'It's only natural. Look, I have tomorrow free, but I have to go home in the evening. Why don't we spend the day together doing something nice?'

'Yes, I'd love to,' Georgy said. 'Sunday is our day of rest so I can come into town for a few hours. Now, what's the time? I have to be back at camp by 9:15 pm. Oh, ten past eight - I'll have to go soon. Where shall we go tomorrow?'

They agreed to meet for a walk along the Leas Promenade in the morning. Luckily, although the weather was cold, the sun was shining, and the wind had dropped. Georgy took Nellie's arm proudly and they strolled along the coastal path. Beautiful gardens and even a band stand were on the inland side of them, and the open water looking across to France, on the other. It seemed just a stone's throw away.

'To think it's only a short voyage over there,' mused Georgy, 'to war and all its horrors.'

'Please don't,' said Nellie. 'Let's not think about that today.'

'Sorry,' Georgy apologised. 'Yes, let's try and forget it all and relax.'

The walk was bracing but enjoyable and left them with a clean feeling of fresh air in their lungs. At lunchtime they retired to a local cafe for pie and mash.

'What a feast,' said Georgy. 'So much better than the usual stuff we get.'

The day was a beautiful interlude, but all too soon it had to end. Georgy had to get back to camp, and Nellie had to catch her train.

'It's so hard saying goodbye every time,' he told her. 'I wish we could be together forever.'

'I'll wait for you, Georgy,' she promised. 'Come back to me when you can.'

They shared a lingering kiss and went their separate ways, promising to phone and write when they could. Somehow, they both knew that this would be their last chance to spend any decent period of time together before Georgy's departure. The date of that was still unknown but could not be very far away now.

That evening, Georgy sat down to write his family a letter. It was so hard to know what to put. How could he tell them that William was considered a deserter? He assured them that he was well himself and then attempted to describe the visit from the military police. Trying to make light of it, he simply said that they weren't sure where William had gone after the hospital and that they were looking for him. Georgy neglected to mention the threats made to him and to William. Least said, soonest mended, he reckoned.

By the time Georgy's letter arrived in Canada, however, the family already knew what was going on.

The Canadian winter was at its height, a snowstorm raging outside, when a heavy knocking sounded on the front door.

'Who on earth can be out in this weather?' exclaimed Ellen, going to answer it. To her surprise, she saw two policemen on the doorstep. One was the local man who she recognised, but the other wore a different uniform with a red cap, which confused her.

'Hello PC Stevens, what can I do for you?'

The man looked embarrassed. 'Can we come in, Mrs Huntingford, please? We need to talk to you about something serious.'

Ellen gasped. 'There hasn't been an accident, has there? My husband, the children - are they all right?'

'Yes ma'am, it's nothing like that,' PC Stephens assured her, and she breathed a sigh of relief. 'This gentleman here, Major Downs, is a military policeman and he is inquiring about your son William.'

'William?' said Ellen. 'He's at the Front serving his country. He's not been well lately.'

Major Downs spoke: 'Madam, we want to know if you have heard from him recently.'

'Well, we've had letters fairly regularly,' replied Ellen, 'but we've not had anything since September now. We had a telegram to say he was missing and then that he was in the hospital. I wrote to him at Christmas, but he hasn't replied yet.'

'Are you sure you haven't seen him?' asked MFP Downs sternly. 'Be honest now. It will be better for you in the long run.'

‘Seen him? No. Why should we? He hasn't had any leave for a long while.’

‘Madam, you must know that he has gone AWOL, surely?’

‘AWOL,’ Ellen repeated. ‘What's that?’

‘Absent without leave. It's a very serious offence. He could face the firing squad for it.’

Ellen turned pale and started to feel faint. ‘Please, I need to sit down,’ she said.

‘Of course,’ said PC Stevens in a kindly manner. ‘This is a lot to take in.’

Once seated, she felt a bit better and tried to answer their questions.

‘Where is he, madam? Please tell us. Has he written or called?’

‘No, he hasn't,’ Ellen protested. ‘I don't know why you think William has done this AWOL thing you talk about. He wouldn't!’

‘Madam, he's a deserter and deserves to be punished. Anyone found to be shielding or helping him could also be penalised. We have spoken to your other son George, and we are suspicious of him. He often leaves camp and won't tell people where he is going or who he is seeing. It may be that he is meeting up with his brother.’

‘George and William are law abiding citizens!’ cried their mother. ‘They wouldn't do anything wrong!’

‘Let us know if you hear anything from either of them as regards to William's whereabouts, madam. If he has not returned by the 11th of February, he will be officially declared a deserter, and his army pay will be stopped.’

Ellen was stunned after they left. When the children returned from school, they found their mother in tears.

Ethel ran to her and gave her a hug, and even Arthur was concerned, though Len just seemed mostly confused. Ellen explained what had happened as best she could, making Ethel very annoyed about the policeman's treatment of their mother.

'It's not fair to come here accusing you,' she cried. 'I bet Dad will be really cross when he comes home. We should complain!'

George Huntingford certainly was angry when he heard about it, and the next day he marched into the local police station to vent his wrath.

'How dare you speak to my wife in that way!' he berated PC Stevens. 'And to malign both my sons like that. It's not to be borne. I demand an apology!'

PC Stephens muttered some excuses and retreated into a back office. He returned with MFP Downs in tow.

'Sir, this is a serious business. You must allow us to do our job. I apologise if your wife is upset, but deserters must be pursued and punished.'

'My son is not a deserter!' stormed George. 'It's the last thing he would do. You don't know him.'

'To be fair, sir, *you* don't know how he would behave under enemy bombardment. It can turn men from heroes to cowards in an instant.'

'Just leave my family alone!' cried George, and he marched out, slamming the door behind him.

Privately, George's thoughts went through much the same arc as his eldest son's. If William wasn't AWOL, then where was he? Was he injured or dead? He dreaded to share these thoughts with his wife as he knew her mental state, fragile at best, would never cope with the idea that her favourite child was lost forever. Ellen had now naively convinced herself that

William had indeed run away from the army and was on his way home to her. She started to look out for him every day. Her mood was buoyant and hopeful but guarded in case the policemen came back. She took to making plans for William's return.

'Ellen dear,' her husband reasoned, 'we don't know what is happening at the moment. I doubt he would risk coming here anyway. It's the first place they'd look for him. Let's just be patient.'

Georgy's letter finally arrived, and they heard the account of his ordeal at the hands of the MFP.

'At least we know George is safe and well,' said Father. 'It's good of him to write.'

Georgy was safe for the moment, but time was running out. Not long after his day out with Nellie, all visits out of the camp were cancelled for his unit. Embarkation was looming and so the officers wanted to ensure all men were always present. Sundays were still a day of lighter duties and time to go to church, but the other days were taken up with intensive training. Occasional phone calls with Nellie were the only things that relieved the monotony.

February 11th. Returning to the barracks at the end of a hard day's training, Georgy was unpleasantly surprised to see Major Connors waiting for him.

'Gunner Huntingford: I am here to inform you that Private William Huntingford has now been AWOL for one month and is hereby officially declared to be a deserter. Do you have any information for me?'

Georgy shook his head. 'Very well then, so be it!' the major said and walked out, leaving Georgy lost for words. He knew his brother would never have deserted, which could only mean one thing - he was dead. The idea chilled him to the bone.

The following morning there was the announcement that his unit had been dreading. They were to sail for France on the 14th of February, just two days' time, from Folkstone. This time they knew the details of the ship they would be travelling on, so it was unlikely to be delayed again. Nellie was dismayed to hear the news, but adamant that she would be there to see him off.

'I don't know if we'll have time to speak,' Georgy told her. 'But it will be nice to know you're there somewhere.'

The sun was just starting to come up as Georgy's outfit rose and gathered their belongings. Packs were loaded, rifles checked, ammunition stored. It all seemed quite unreal, almost like a bad dream. Georgy went through the actions they had rehearsed so many times, mechanically, without thinking. Then the officers came round to check everything. Orders were shouted and reprimands given to the men who had tried to take too much with them. Personal possessions were strongly discouraged. A photo or two was allowed, but no more. Georgy had a photo of his mother, and one of Nellie. They were very precious to him, and he wasn't about to leave them behind.

Then came the march to the port. The cold morning air hit them in the face and shocked them into reality. Their breath steamed out in clouds behind them. Walter was nearby and smiled grimly at his friend as they stamped along.

Reaching the port, Georgy was surprised to see a gathering on the dockside, plus a military band. The people cheered as the long line of soldiers came into view and the band started to play. He felt choked with emotion - fear, excitement, patriotic fervour and more.

The troops came to a halt on the quayside and were given the order: '*At Ease*'. A brief moment to relax whilst horses, artillery and provisions were loaded on the ship. An officer gave them a final briefing with details of which ships they were allocated to. Then they were allowed to mingle with the public for a short while. No one was to leave the area under any circumstances.

The crowd surged forward to see their loved ones one last time. Desperately Georgy scanned the multitude for a face he recognised. Suddenly he saw them - Nellie and her mother fighting their way through to get to him. Despite Aunt Mary's protests, Nellie flung her arms around him and kissed him passionately.

'Nellie! George!' cried Aunt Mary, shocked. 'Please stop this at once. It's not proper!'

Nellie turned to her mother. 'No Mum, I'm sorry. I love Georgy and you can't change it. Now either put up with it or go away!' She clung to Georgy again, her eyes full of tears.

'I'll leave you alone for a while then to say your goodbyes.' Aunt Mary said in a subdued voice. 'George. I just want to say that we wish you well and will be praying for your safe return. We all love you, you know. God bless you.' With that, she wandered off along the quay.

What Nellie and Georgy said in those last few moments together was too intimate and emotional to be repeated, but neither of them would ever forget it.

The horn sounded and the men wrenched themselves away from their families and sweethearts and re-assembled. Packs were shouldered and guns were glistening in the cold bright sunlight as the troops now made their way up the gang planks onto the ships.

Georgy's heart was thumping. Once aboard, they stowed their belongings and then stood to attention on deck whilst the band played rousing tunes. The throng moved as close as they could to the edge of the quay and Georgy was sure he could see Nellie and Mary waving to him. The sun was in his eyes and maybe that's why they were watering so much, but who could say?

The ship's horn blew once more, and the gang planks were pulled up. There was a salute of gunfire, and the anchors were weighed. The troops stood motionless, each man with his own private thoughts and emotions. Slowly, oh so slowly, they heard the engines roar into life and felt the ship starting to move. This was it. They were off!

Chapter 29

The Western Front, France 1918

It had been a day of utter horror. Georgy slumped against the wall of the trench and attempted to have a 20-minute snooze. The images in his head were too intense and shocking though, to allow him any rest. His mind roamed back to the start of it all. The jam-packed ship, the long journey by foot and train to the reserve trenches, the noises and the smells becoming ever clearer. Then the mundane but arduous tasks in the support trenches, with the ever-present sound of shellfire and the stench of rotting bodies, accompanied by scenes of total devastation - ruined houses, burnt out villages, dead farm animals, the skeletons of trees blasted to pieces. What atrocities had been done in the name of war?

After a relatively quiet period, there was the night-time march through the long communication trenches to the Front, in complete silence, for fear of the enemy hearing their movements. Now here they were, in the thick of it.

It was April 1918, and it should have been springtime in France, but there was no sign of it in this wasteland. Last week had been the first time Georgy had fired at living human beings. He had watched as his machine gun fire had cut down a line of advancing German soldiers. Even from a distance, it was hard to take the knowledge that he had wiped them out of existence.

But it was the same on both sides. Shells rained down on their own trench, so feeble a protection from such mechanical savage power. Men serving just a few yards further down from him on the line were blown to pieces. One moment Johnny Brown was standing there, the next he was gone, parts of his body scattered in the mud. Sickness had nearly overwhelmed Georgy then, but heeding the advice of more war seasoned soldiers than himself, he tried not to look.

'Ain't no good dwelling on it, lad,' Sergeant Evans told him. 'We just have to get on with the job and do our duty.'

Walter was alongside Georgy, loading and firing in a similar intensity of action. They had orders to bombard the enemy with as much artillery as possible in order to allow their line of infantrymen to advance later, hopefully in greater safety. There had been a sudden renewed attack from the Germans around the end of March onwards. A 'spring offensive' the sergeant reckoned, to try and end the war. The rumour was that things were going far from well for the Germans and that this was a last big push. The Allies, it seemed, had been making good progress until recently, but under such a persistent and ferocious bombardment, they were now struggling. General Haig sent a message out to the troops:

"Every position must be held to the last man; there must be no retirement. With our backs to the wall, and believing in the justice of our cause, each one of us must fight on to the end."

So, reinforcements were brought forward, including Georgy's unit.

Today had been worse than most. Walter was busy loading the giant howitzer when suddenly a shell exploded near him in the trench. There were a flash and a terrible scream from Walter which made Georgy drop what he was doing and rush over to his friend. Walter was covered in blood and worse, his left leg was mangled beyond repair.

'Stretcher bearers!' shouted Georgy, 'Quick!' He knelt beside Walter, staunching the blood flow as they'd been taught and trying to soothe him.

'It's all right mate, you'll be fine. It looks worse than it is,' he said, as reassuringly as he could. Walter groaned and passed into unconsciousness. The stretcher bearers arrived and carried him off whilst Georgy went back to his post. He stumbled over to the big gun and fired it at the enemy with a vengeful anger that surprised him.

'Take that, you swines!' he cried, then felt ashamed of himself. What was he becoming? He was covered in Walter's blood and shaking all over.

'Huntingford,' Sergeant Evans ordered, 'take a break – now!'

So here he was, trying to cope with all he had seen and heard and preparing for the next bout.

Weeks of terror went by until Georgy felt numbed by it all. He moved almost in a dream, loading and firing, loading and firing, over and over again. He heard that Walter had lost his leg but was now being shipped home.

Lucky blighter, he thought, but then realised that it wasn't so lucky for his friend after all.

Letters filtered through from time to time, some from home, some from Nellie. They were a great source of comfort to him, but also a form of torture. All those anecdotes of normal life - so far removed from him - it was so trivial and yet precious as well. Nellie's letters were always full of her love for him, but at times he struggled to remember the moments they had shared. It all seemed so long ago. Georgy attempted to reply to his loved ones when he could, but soldiers' letters were heavily censored, and he couldn't express what he was going through anyway. He often thought about William, but there was no news of him from home, and he doubted he would hear anything of him out here.

The German's 'spring offensive' had been making headway, and the Allies had had to retreat in places. The troops kept having to move and dig out new trenches and assemble more defences. Many men were lost, especially in the infantry who were mown down in their multitudes by German guns, but they kept following orders. Georgy realised that once you got out there, that was all there was - no time to think; probably just as well.

In early June, a letter from home reached Georgy with some surprising news. It seemed that William had been awarded the Military Medal, even though no one knew where he was. The medal had been given for '*valour on the field of battle*,' sometime during 1917 and yet he was still being classed as a deserter. How could that be? wondered Georgy, reading his mother's letter in amazement. Can you give a medal for bravery to a deserter? It doesn't make sense. It had even been noted in the London Gazette list of honours. Georgy was confused.

Back in Canada, Ellen felt more and more certain that her son was alive, and what's more, a hero. This proved it, surely. After all, why give a medal to someone the Army was ashamed of? It must be that he was working on some special secret mission behind enemy lines. The whole family was stunned by this development. Even Father thought it was very odd, although he'd heard of posthumous medals being awarded often enough and he hoped it wasn't the case this time. He wisely kept his thoughts to himself. Whilst his wife was happy then the family home continued on an even keel and for that he was thankful.

On the Western Front, the tide of war began to turn. The German troops were hungry and short of supplies. When an inspiring new French general was appointed to the Allies, victory came in the Second Battle of the Marne, and the Germans had to retreat. Georgy, however, had no real idea of how the war was progressing. He could tell they were moving again, but this time forwards instead of backwards. The officers, when they saw them, were full of encouragement and hope, but the troops on the frontline were weary and battle scarred. Periods of intense action interspersed with extreme boredom continued. How much longer would this go on?

In June, the Americans joined the war and fresh soldiers arrived who had not had time to get tired or disillusioned. Georgy met some of them during the summer that year. They were brash and inexperienced but tough fighters.

'Hey,' said Dave, one of the new recruits. 'So, you're Canadian. That makes us neighbours. We need to team up!'

Georgy found them lively and fun to be around, and it brought an energy into the trenches that hadn't been there before. There had always been banter and comradeship amongst the battalion, but this seemed different.

They played cards together, in spare moments, though Georgy invariably lost. In return, he tried to teach them English football, without much success.

'Gee, this is a crazy game!' declared Dave. 'I don't know how you guys make sense of it.'

In August, the Allies scored another victory in Amiens, by breaking through part of the Hindenburg Line and things began to look promising.

'One last big push, men. That's all that's needed,' claimed the major when he visited. They scarcely dared to hope, but it did seem as if it might be possible.

One night, Georgy dreamed as he lay on his uncomfortable bunk, listening to the rats scurrying around, of going home - back to Nellie, back to his family, back to all the things he knew. But he woke in the morning to the sound of gunfire, which depressed him greatly. Soon, he told himself. It must be soon now.

Georgy's birthday came around on the 6th of September and fell in a welcome break between actions. After an intensive attack on the Droucourt-Queant line, the Canadian corps had emerged victorious, with the Germans retreating still further, leaving large areas undefended. The Canadian artillery had worked hard, starting with a fierce barrage, followed up by tanks and then infantry. Georgy was both fascinated and terrified by the might of the tanks ploughing over the battlefield, crushing everything in their path: soldiers, horses, corpses, buildings, barbed wire and more. This was one asset that the enemy lacked, and it worked well to the Allies' advantage. The losses were still many on their side, however. Georgy didn't know the numbers of dead, but he saw the bodies strewn over the ground they had just gained. When the fighting ceased, they went out to recover their fallen comrades. Some were so young, Georgy doubted whether they were even eighteen. What a waste, he thought. He shed no tears any more though. He was past all that. There were just too many to mourn.

After this operation, the division rested, waiting for new orders. They all knew that another big battle, (maybe the last one), was looming. On his birthday, Georgy was even able to relax a little in the late summer sunshine. Some of the officers organised a sports day and he was happy to join in, taking part in a relay race and the tug of war. There was welcome laughter in the air, despite the circumstances. It was a brief respite; a moment for the tired and wounded to recover and time to bury the dead. A letter and a food parcel arrived from his mother, wishing him a happy birthday. It seemed so out of place here, but it made him remember other birthdays - parties and outings with the family, last September in London with Nellie. The memories made him smile, but they also made him sad. Was he the same person now? He doubted it.

On the morning of the 20th of September, the division was called together to receive new orders.

'Our objective is to capture Bourton Wood,' the major said. 'To do this we will need to cross the Canal du Nord. As you know chaps, the enemy has destroyed the bridges and flooded a lot of the land around here. However, we are encamped here by the only dry passage over to the other side. Our orders are to secure the canal and build a temporary bridge allowing our troops to cross and attack the enemy on the far bank. The artillery will provide covering fire for our chaps to get this done. Any questions?'

Nobody ever dared to ask questions. They knew better. Orders had to be followed and that was all there was to it.

At 5:20 am on 27th of September, it all started. Georgy was manning one of the 18 pounder field guns which he handled with deft precision. His artillery section performed a creeping barrage just ahead of the infantry who were crossing the canal. Hours went by and temporary bridge sections were brought into place which allowed the whole division to cross the canal and attack. Things were going well for the Allies despite some casualties. Bourton Wood was easily captured and then they were ordered to advance further the next day.

'We've got them on the run, chaps,' the sergeant assured them.

The 4th division, Georgy's unit, were ordered to progress to and capture Tilloy village.

'There are no Germans there any more,' the sergeant continued. 'It's all empty countryside, easy pickings.'

Unfortunately, this wasn't quite the true picture as they found to their cost. Advancing on the 28th of September, they met resistance from pockets of enemies who had not been expected. The artillery worked hard to defend the troops, but many men were killed. Nevertheless, the village of Tilloy (or what was left of it) was eventually secured. Exhausted and discouraged, the troops rested again, only to hear they were to move on once more, in the next few days to Cambrai.

Georgy sighed when he heard this. How much more could they take?

30th of September: The Allied troops were advancing on the area of Cambrai when they were set upon from all sides by the enemy in a last desperate stand. Georgy was striding forward with his machine gun in hand, trying to give covering fire to his comrades, when suddenly he heard a pop and felt a burning pain in this thigh. He fell to his knees.

His first thought was sheer surprise. He knew immediately that he'd been hit but tried to stagger to his feet and carry on. I must get out of this, he thought. I must survive. If I stay here, I'll die. It was a useless attempt, however, and he collapsed again, blood running down his leg. For a moment, he contemplated crawling, but he couldn't seem to make his limbs move.

His vision began to blur, and he started to feel faint. All around him the war carried on, and he realised how insignificant he was. But suddenly, a concerned, friendly voice jolted him back to reality.

'Come on mate, let's get you out of here.'

The speaker half carried, half dragged him away from the battlefield. Georgy was barely aware of who it was or how he got to safety. He tried to mutter some thanks, but his words made no sense, then he passed out.

Chapter 30

Georgy came to and found he was lying in a narrow wooden bed, in a very large tent which smelt strongly of disinfectant. As his eyes got accustomed to the gloom, he realised he was in a field hospital. The beds stretched away as far as the eye could see, and nearly every single one was occupied. Nurses bustled around like ministering angels. He tried to sit up but suffered an agonising pain all the way down his leg as he did so, causing him to let out an involuntary cry. A nurse came rushing over and scolded him severely:

'Gunner Huntingford, lie down immediately! You will do more damage and pull the dressing off. If you start it bleeding again, I won't be responsible for the consequences!'

Obediently, Georgy lay down quietly.

'Sorry,' he said. 'Where am I? What happened?'

He knew they were idiotic questions, but his mind was fuzzy, and he couldn't think what to say.

'You're in the 14th casualty clearing station, just behind the front lines at Cambrai. You were brought in yesterday with a gunshot wound. Luckily, it's only your leg, but you need an operation to remove the bullet. We were just waiting until you could be moved to the base hospital in Boulogne. Now that you're awake again, we'll get some transport sorted out.' She smiled. 'Don't worry. We'll soon get you sorted out.'

'Who was it that rescued me?' Georgy managed. 'I'd like to thank him.'

The nurse's face clouded over.

'It was an American, Pte Dave Reynolds, but he's in here, himself now, I'm afraid. Brought in this morning, in a very bad way.'

'It didn't happen whilst he was saving me, did it?' said Georgy anxiously.

'No,' replied the nurse. 'He was hit by a shell just after dawn, today.'

'Can I see him?' asked Georgy.

'Sorry, you're not to move at the moment,' she replied, 'besides he probably wouldn't know you were there, anyway.'

'Please,' begged Georgy. 'I need to tell him I'm grateful.'

The nurse took pity on him then.

'I tell you what,' she said, 'I'll wheel your bed over next to his, then you can talk to him from there, but no getting up, mind, and only for a minute.'

Georgy was shocked to see the state of his saviour, Dave. His face was bloody and battered, one eye nearly gone, his abdomen and legs heavily bandaged. It looked very serious.

'Dave, mate,' Georgy called out. 'It's me, George. How are you doing?'

Dave turned his head slightly and appeared to look at him. He tried to speak but could only make a few sounds.

‘I just wanted to say thank you,’ Georgy continued bravely, ‘for saving my life. I'd have been a goner if I'd been left there. I'm very grateful.’

Dave managed to move one hand and gave him a thumbs up and Georgy realised that he had understood.

‘Well, you just get well, mate, they'll fix you up, I'm sure.’

‘Come on now, that's enough talking,’ said the nurse. ‘Let's move you back again now.’

‘Chin up Dave, mate,’ called Georgy, as his bed was wheeled off. ‘See you soon.’

The next morning Georgy asked after his friend but was told that Dave had sadly passed away during the night. The doctors had tried their best to save him, but it was useless. His injuries were too severe. Tears poured down Georgy’s face when he heard the news. He’d seen so much death and suffering recently and had thought he’d become immune to it, but this affected him deeply.

‘That’s not fair!’ he cried. ‘He was a hero - my lifesaver!’

The nurse just patted him on the arm and left him to grieve.

Later that day, they came to move Georgy to the hospital in Boulogne. It was then that he suddenly thought of something as they wheeled him out to the ambulance.

‘You haven't told my family that I've been wounded, have you? I don't want them to know. They will only worry.’

‘Well,’ the orderly said, ‘we were about to send a telegram, but we can leave it if you'd rather.’

'Please,' said Georgy. 'My mother's had enough to deal with lately. My brother is missing in action, you see, and I don't want her to be upset again.'

Georgy couldn't bring himself to say that his brother was dead, or a deserter. Neither seemed a very good option.

'Very well, we can omit it as long as you are happy, but you'll need to sign a form.'

'That's fine,' replied Georgy. He felt relieved that his family would not be troubled further and wondered if they'd heard anything about William. Thinking of his brother made him feel sad again. Georgy could hear the sound of continuous shell fire in the distance and wondered how the battle was going. He had once thought that it would be a relief to be away from it, but it wasn't. He felt guilty. He should have been there! He had let them down.

'How is it going out there? Do you know?' he asked the orderly.

'Very well, I believe,' the man replied. 'I hear they've got them on the run. Quite right too! Mind you, the casualties keep coming in, unfortunately. It's not over yet.'

'Let's pray that it will be soon,' said Georgy fervently. 'It's been going on too long now.'

The journey in the army ambulance was a rough ride to say the least. It was a ramshackle vehicle, and he was crammed in with several other wounded comrades on hard, uncomfortable stretchers. The van rattled along over rutted and pot-holed roads which were little more than tracks in the dirt. His leg ached, in spite of the morphine they had given him, and he felt quite sick with all the swaying and rocking by the time they finally reached Boulogne.

Georgy awoke after the operation feeling sore, but it was a new kind of pain – cleaner, fresher – a sharp cut which would heal. The burning, sickly pain of an alien object embedded in his flesh had gone. Now all he wanted to do was to get back to his unit and help finish the job. He felt that he should be with his comrades for the final onslaught. It was not that he was thirsty for battle, just that his sense of loyalty was nagging at him.

It was only a couple of days later that Georgy was moved to a more general hospital at Hardelot to recover.

'I thought I'd be going back to the Front,' he said a few days after he arrived there. 'I'm better now. really.'

The French doctor frowned at him. 'Now look Gunner Huntingford, you've had a nasty gunshot wound and a big operation. Give yourself time to heal. There are stitches which will have to come out later, and the muscles need to get strong again. Don't be too hasty or you'll be back here again before you know it.'

'But they need me at the Front!' protested Georgy.

'From what I've heard,' the doctor said, 'it's all over bar the shouting. Haven't you heard? The Bulgarians have surrendered, and they say the Kaiser has begun negotiations for peace.'

'Oh, that's wonderful!' cried Georgy. 'I do hope that's true. Maybe I can relax then, after all.'

Whilst he was in the hospital Georgy had plenty of time to think. He wrote letters to both his family and Nellie, assuring them that he was safe and well.

"I had a slight injury," he told them. *"But nothing to worry about. It sounds like the war may be over soon and then we can be reunited. I miss you."*

There were times in his days of recovery when Georgy was haunted by memories of the past few months. Images of death and fire filled his sleep and gave him nightmares. He awoke from these, dripping with sweat and terrified. The gentle light of dawn and the calm of the hospital soothed him, though the faint sound of gunfire could still be heard regularly.

News from the Front became even better. Some German soldiers were refusing to fight, and German civilians were rioting in their towns, protesting about the war. The Kaiser had become very unpopular, and it seemed his own people wanted him to go.

On happier days, Georgy reflected on the future. He desperately wanted to see his family and Nellie again, but he knew that even when the war ended, he would still have another six months to serve, because his sign-up papers had committed him to this. What would he do when it was finally all over? he wondered. Could he face going back to plumbing? If he was to return to Canada, how would he be able to see Nellie? These questions and more ran around his head and he found no answers.

A letter reached Georgy in the hospital from his mother with worrying news. A new virulent strain of influenza was rampaging through the country, attacking young people in particular, killing many. Gilbert had been infected and was dangerously ill. Georgy's mother begged him to come home but he could barely walk down the hospital corridor, let alone travel. Letters often took at least a couple of weeks to get to them, so there was no knowing how Gilbert was by now.

Worried sick, Georgy came up with an idea; a way to find out some information.

'Is there any way I can send a telegram please?' he asked one of the nurses. 'My younger brother is very ill, and I need to contact my family, but they're in Canada.'

'Canada!' exclaimed the nurse. 'Well yes, we can send someone to the telegraph office for you, if you write out what you want to say. I'm not sure how long it will take to get a reply, though.'

Georgy hastily composed a note to his family sending all his love and asking for news of Gilbert. His recollections of his brother were fond ones. Gilbert was a quiet, hard-working, gentle soul who never troubled anyone. He'd taken on Georgy's role at the plumbers without a second thought, even though it wasn't what he wanted to do. It was a relief to receive a reply from Ellen the next day assuring him that Gilbert was now on the mend and out of danger, though it had been touch-and-go. It appeared that London was also being badly hit by this Spanish flu, and Georgy worried about Nellie being in the midst of it all, but there was nothing he could do.

The days went by, and Georgy began to get more mobile again, exercising gently whenever he could, around the ward and sometimes outside. His leg began to recover its strength and he felt better. Around the 5th November they all heard the news that both the Ottoman and Austro-Hungarian empires had recently surrendered to the Allies. Germany was becoming increasingly isolated but still fought on. Then on the 7th November Georgy was told that he was being transferred back to Boulogne hospital again for final convalescence and physiotherapy to prepare him for duty once more. He was eager to be back to full fitness and so was encouraged by this, though going back to the war now seemed an unattractive option. After nearly five weeks away, he wasn't sure how he would face it.

A couple of days later, he woke in the morning, after a restless night, feeling thoroughly uncomfortable. His legs itched like mad and though he scratched frantically it didn't seem to help. The feeling spread to his whole body and when he opened his shirt, he was horrified to see sores appearing. Oh no – scabies!

'Nurse,' he called. 'Please help. I think I need some treatment.'

She took one look and hurried him off to a hot bath full of a solution designed to cure it. His skin felt as if it was being stung by a thousand wasps and he was glad to get out, but he wasn't allowed back to the ward. His bed and clothing were disinfected, and he was speedily removed to a hospital in Écault which specialised in infections.

Once there, he was treated with foul smelling sulphur ointments and more baths in strange solutions. A couple of his sores became infected, as he couldn't stop scratching despite his good intentions. Georgy felt irritated and miserable. He could only think that he had picked up the mites from one of the hospital beds in Boulogne or Hardelot. Ironic, he thought, to go somewhere to be healed and to catch something else!

On the 11th November however, everything changed. The war finally stopped at 11am that day and the whole place was alive with celebration. The armistice was signed in the Forest of Compiègne very near to the town of Écault, and so they were among the first to hear the news. The guns fell silent and church bells rang out, in joy and relief that it was all over. Meanwhile the soldiers still in the trenches just listened to the eerie quiet in disbelief and were grateful to be alive.

There was singing and flag waving in the town and the hospital, with all the staff joining in. Not all the patients felt so cheerful, however. Those with serious injuries, or had lost eyes or limbs, or seen awful scenes they would never forget – they lay there silently trying to take it all in.

Peace – everyone had hoped it was coming, but the day itself seemed unreal, a dream. Georgy felt wildly happy, but emotional at the same time. Now he would go home again, see his family, see Nellie, maybe even find out what had happened to William. He was in turmoil, even though he was glad. There had been so much death and suffering – had it been worth it? Was it truly finished?

Telegrams were flying around the world, and Georgy was anxious to send his own, both to his mother and to Nellie. The telegraph offices were so busy that in the end they didn't get sent until the next day. All he put on both was:

"The war is over! Looking forward to seeing you again soon. All my love, Georgy."

He just couldn't think what else to say. It was all too much for words.

In two separate homes far away from the Western Front, Georgy's telegrams were received with pleasure, nonetheless. The celebrations in England and Canada were still ongoing, and the public mood was buoyant. There was a feeling of optimism in the air and hope for a new era of peace.

Nellie dreamed of being reunited with her love, and of holding him close again, whilst Ellen planned a party for her eldest son's homecoming and stubbornly refused to contemplate the possibility that her favourite son, William, might not be returning. The future looked bright.

Chapter 31

On the 17th of November, Georgy rejoined his unit, his scabies cured and his wound healed. They were now stationed in overflowing camps waiting for demobilisation. His current duties were very different but still challenging and at times dangerous.

As part of the artillery pool, one of his main tasks was to recover and remove shells, (some unexploded), ammunition of all sorts, and make the area safe for civilians to return. It was hazardous to say the least.

Three days after their outfit started this job, Georgy was busy clearing and storing such items when he heard a massive explosion nearby. Everyone rushed out and were horrified to learn that one of their number had unfortunately met his maker when coming upon an unexploded mine. They returned to their work in a sombre mood, Georgy reflecting that such armaments were lethal at any time, not just in battle.

As the days wore on, the unit were called on for other duties as well. Removing and identifying the remains of their fallen comrades was another unpleasant, though necessary activity. They did their best to treat the dead with respect but often it was difficult to know who the mangled, and now rotten, body parts belonged to, which somehow made it seem distant. Georgy didn't feel emotional whilst undertaking this. It was so hard to connect these collections of raw meat with human beings.

The task that Georgy found most positive, if such a term could be used, was that of helping French civilians get back to their normal lives again. His outfit helped clear away the destruction of war and build anew; reconstructing roads, bridges and public buildings whilst encouraging the locals to return and start afresh.

In a small village near Arras, he came across a French family staring at the burnt-out ruins of their farmhouse and he felt for them. A solitary cow remained in the fields.

'Monsieur, what can we do?' The farmer asked him. 'How can we come back here? We have nothing now.'

Georgy had no answers but did his best to help. With a couple of comrades, he rigged up a temporary shelter, fed the cow, organised some food and got the well working again. It was a day's work, but one that he looked back at with pleasure. A small gesture, but a personal one that made a difference to real people. The family were so grateful for his help and couldn't thank him enough, but he felt humble and just pleased to be of service.

It was the middle of December when a detachment of Georgy's unit was ordered over to a nearby field hospital. Some men were instructed to help the wounded to get to the main hospitals whilst others, including him, were to clear up and dismantle the medical station. Listening to the instructions from the major, Georgy was stunned to hear which hospital they were going to - the 17th Casualty Clearing Station!

That's where William was supposed to have been. Perhaps he could find out some information whilst he was there.

As soon as he arrived at the location, Georgy set about this in earnest.

'Excuse me ma'am, can you check your records for me, please?' he asked the nurse on duty. 'I need to know about a wounded soldier who passed through here.'

The middle-aged woman was not too keen to help.

'Do you realise how many hundreds of casualties have been here?' she said.

'Yes, of course, I realise that;' said Georgy as politely as he could. 'But surely you have kept names of them all?'

'Well, we have if we knew the names,' she replied. 'But many haven't been identified.'

'Could you look for this name, please – Pte William Huntingford 832429? Around the beginning of November 1917,' he begged.

Grumbling, the nurse disappeared off into a back room to search through the archives. It seemed a very long time before she reappeared, but eventually she did, clutching a large logbook.

'Here is the month you mentioned. There is an entry here for William Huntingford, but then it is crossed out and another name is substituted.'

'What does that mean?' asked Georgy, confused.

'It probably means that there was a mistake and that the soldier was wrongly identified.'

'But how could that happen? We all have ID tags.'

The nurse looked at him with contempt. 'When men are badly injured in battle, these forms of ID aren't always available. Haven't you seen shell casualties?'

Georgy realised what she meant. Too often the remaining parts of the wounded were unrecognisable, and their uniform blown to pieces.

'So does this mean that Private Huntingford was never here?' he said.

'I don't know,' the nurse replied. 'He may have been at some point, but not in November 1917, or so it appears. Now please, I have work to do and I can't spend all this time answering your questions. I must get on.'

'My apologies,' said Georgy and left her to it. So, was that it? Was William never there at all? If so, what did that mean? Was he dead? Surely if he had been alive, they would have heard from him by now. He made a mental note to write home and tell them what he'd found out. He wasn't sure what his mother would think, but it was best that she knew.

Christmas arrived, as it always did, bringing a period of restrained festivities to the troops. Now that they weren't fighting a war any more, they were all allowed to relax and enjoy themselves. A fine Christmas dinner of turkey, plum pudding and ale was served to the men by the officers, then there were entertainments with singing, comedy and a military band, though Georgy got quite emotional when they all sang '*The Maple Leaf Forever.*' For those inclined there were sports, but many preferred to just rest for a change.

It was a jolly time for all, with much hope for the coming year. 1919 held promises of joyful reunions and homecomings, though the Canadians knew it would be a while yet. They had been informed that they wouldn't be shipped out until at least the spring, due to the logistics of enabling mass transportation across the ocean. When they were told this, the men complained loudly, but were pacified by the promise of leave in the meantime.

With the war over, the army postal service had much improved, and Georgy was delighted to receive several Christmas letters and parcels. Ellen had sent a long letter from home, and the whole family had added their own individual message to him. This touched him greatly and made him long to see them all again. Nellie had sent a letter full of her love and hope for the future. Georgy tried to remember her face and her voice but struggled. He was sure it would be all right once he saw her, which he hoped would be soon. To his surprise there was a third letter, along with a hand-knitted pair of socks, from Grandma Goddard, wishing him well and inviting him to stay whenever he liked.

January came and the troops began to get despondent at the delays in going home. There was much unrest in the ranks. Rumours of soldiers going on strike in Britain reached their ears, which unsettled them even more. Georgy felt it too and decided to apply for leave. He hadn't had anything since the previous Christmas, and as he had relatives in England that he could stay with, he was a prime candidate. His request was granted and on the 18th January he headed off towards Blighty. There would not be enough time to get to Canada and back, so England was the only option. Georgy was happy about this since it gave him a chance to see Nellie again. He longed to be back in her arms once more.

Nellie was overjoyed when she received Georgy's letter, and she hastily arranged a few days off from work so she could spend some time with him. Her mother still disapproved, but Nellie was adamant that nothing would stop her.

Georgy arrived at his grandparents' house to a hero's welcome. Patriotic bunting was flying gaily in the cold January wind, and a big banner proclaimed: "*Welcome Home!*" He cringed with embarrassment. Though it was kindly meant he didn't feel he deserved it. Grandma Goddard hugged him and brought him into the sitting room, where he was surprised to find several other elderly ladies sitting around.

'These are my neighbours, George,' his grandma explained. 'They all wanted to meet you and hear about your adventure.'

Georgy flushed scarlet. 'No, I can't,' he muttered. 'Sorry. I can't tell you anything.'

'Don't be shy, George. We know you're a hero. You're among friends here. Tell us all about it.'

'No,' he said firmly. 'I can't.'

Images of shell fire and dead bodies filled his head, and he knew he couldn't put that into words, certainly not for these genteel ladies.

'Can I go and lie down?' he asked. 'I feel tired after the journey.'

Lying on a soft bed after months of sleeping on everything from sandbags to wooden planks seemed un-natural, however, and he got little rest.

Later, after the visitors had reluctantly gone home, he tried to explain to his grandmother how he felt.

'It's too hard to talk about it, Grandma. I'm sorry if I let you down, but I can't put it into words. Sorry.'

Grandma was not best pleased at having been embarrassed in front of her friends, but she did her best to understand.

'Well, maybe later,' she said. 'I don't really know why you can't. After all, it's man's duty to go to war. I would think you'd be happy to share it with us.'

Georgy sighed. What could he say?

Standing on Nellie's doorstep, waiting for her to answer his knock, Georgy suddenly felt nervous. He hadn't seen her in nearly a year, and so much had happened in that time. He'd seen such horrors and it had changed him as a person. Would he still feel the same for her? Would she still want him?

Nellie shrieked with delight when she saw him and reached out her arms to enfold him in an embrace. Georgy tried to respond, but it felt strange.

'Come in,' she cried. 'It's so lovely to have you back again.'

He noticed everything about her as if he was seeing her for the first time - her fair hair cascading around her face, her shining grey eyes, the smell of her perfume. It was all so lovely, and yet it seemed untouchable. They sat awkwardly in the parlour with Aunt Mary, drinking tea and making small talk. Georgy realised he wasn't used to being in a house any more after months of tents, trenches and wooden huts. He hardly knew how to act. His legs and feet didn't seem to want to perch politely on a chair. They were more inclined to sprawl in an ungainly manner. He did his best to control them.

To Georgy's relief neither Aunt Mary nor Nellie asked him about the war. They inquired how his leg was now, what the journey over had been like, and talked about the weather. All harmless chatter but he felt disconnected from everything. He did his best to ask how everyone was but embarrassed himself by forgetting what Nellie's young brother was called. 'Billy. Yes, that's it, I remember,' he said.

'Shall we go for a walk?' suggested Nellie.

'Good idea,' agreed Aunt Mary. 'Perhaps you two could go to the baker's shop for me. I need another loaf.'

Grateful to be doing something, Georgy accompanied Nellie outside. As they went, she slipped her arm through his and drew close. He was silent, however, as they walked, his mind a blur. Nellie chatted to start with but got little response and eventually fell silent as well. The loaf purchased, Nellie guided Georgy to the nearest park and after a short stroll, suggested they sit on one of the benches. The weather was cold and damp, but still they sat there, each with their own thoughts.

'I've got some days off,' said Nellie. 'We could go into London or wherever you like. I don't mind.'

'Yes,' replied Georgy absently. 'That would be nice.'

'Where should we go?' she asked. Realising that she was waiting for him to make a decision, he made an effort to pull himself together.

'Yes, London. Let's meet at the Corner House like we used to, then take in some sights.'

Nellie was pleased that they had made some arrangements but was surprised that when Georgy left, he only kissed her on the cheek. Something was different, she thought. What could she do?

They met at the Corner House as friends, with a gentle hug and a smile. Wisely, Nellie decided it was best to keep things light and fun for now. She sensed her love was going through something she couldn't share and needed time to himself. Nellie told Georgy about her job, her friends, her family – anything to keep his mind away from his troubles. Georgy only half heard her but was comforted by the normality of it. They paid a visit to one of the museums, now re-opened in the new era of peace, and admired the statues and artefacts. They stopped by a painting of an enormous battle, with heroic figures striding along gloriously. Georgy stared at it, hardly able to believe his eyes.

'War!' he suddenly exclaimed. 'That's not war. It's a lie!'

He was shaking with a mixture of fear and anger. Nellie took his hand and dragged him away.

'Let's go and look at something else,' she said.

'Leave me alone!' he suddenly snapped. 'I have to get out of here!'

He rushed out onto the street, not knowing what he was doing. Nellie dashed after him. Nearby, a car suddenly backfired loudly, sounding like a gunshot and Georgy's mind was instantly back in the middle of the trenches, filled with dreadful images and noise. He sank to his knees with his head clutched in his hands, living it all over again.

'Watch it, mate!' shouted a man nearby, who was hurrying past. 'You bleeding cuckoo or something?'

Nellie grabbed Georgy and pulled him to his feet, then gently manhandled him into a nearby cafe. Her arms were around him, enveloping him whilst he trembled violently.

'Can I take your order, miss?' the waitress asked. 'You can't sit in here without buying something, you know.'

'Two teas then, please,' said Nellie, annoyed. 'Then leave us alone!'

The comfort of Nellie's arms gradually soothed Georgy's distress and he began to feel more like himself. He was ashamed to be seen acting like this in public, but grateful for Nellie's assistance. Eventually, he spoke:

'I'm sorry, I don't know what came over me. I didn't mean to shout at you.' He looked up at her and saw the love and concern shining out of her beautiful face. He raised his hand to touch her cheek softly. 'I love you, Nellie, but it's going to take time. I'm not the same man that I was. You probably won't love me any more.'

'I will always love you,' she replied quietly. 'But let's just be friends for now. I think that's what you need more than anything.'

He hugged her and they clung together, but in companionship rather than passion.

The two weeks slipped quickly by. Grandma Goddard had given up on trying to show Georgy off to her neighbours and just allowed him to relax, which helped. Her husband Bill was mostly to be thanked for this.

'Give the poor lad a rest, Martha,' he had told her, 'He's been through a lot.'

'But I'm proud of him,' she said.

'I know,' Bill replied. 'But this isn't the way. Let him be.'

Georgy didn't know why he had behaved that way at the museum. Something deep inside him had sparked it off. He wished it hadn't happened, and he did his best to make up for it.

The young couple spent time together, but friendship was what was healing Georgy. He couldn't commit to anything more at present. When he left to go back to France again, he promised her that he would write and kissed her on the cheek. Nellie's eyes were sad. Had they lost the love they had found or was it just temporarily mislaid? Only time would tell.

Chapter 32

1919

The overcrowded camp was beginning to thin out when Georgy returned in February. Men were slowly being sent home, but influenza had hit badly and many had died. Isolation and barrier techniques had come into force and Georgy found himself being used to clean and disinfect bunkhouses, kitchens, latrines and more, along with his comrades, though they all had to wear masks and wash thoroughly each day. As he scrubbed floors and cleaned down surfaces his mind was full of Nellie. How could he have pushed her away? He needed her so much and yet he'd been distant to her. She was very precious to him, a shining beacon of love and light. Would he get an opportunity to make things right?

He tried to write a letter to her, but the words sounded trite and meaningless when he re-read them. Nevertheless, when Nellie received it, it gave her hope. Georgy had said he was sorry and wanted to try again.

"*We need a fresh start,*" he wrote, "*time to get over this. Please forgive me. You've been very patient and I am grateful. Maybe we can pick up where we left off?*

All my love, Georgy xx"

Hearing that Georgy was a plumber by trade the authorities now put him on reconstructing the sanitation facilities in the area. It felt good to be using his skills again and made him think of future employment. The other thing that many soldiers were taking part in was the 'Khaki University,' an education programme set up to give the bored Canadian troops something to do, whilst they waited for demob. Georgy attended a few maths lessons. He'd never been that good with numbers, and it helped to get his brain going again. His nightmares had decreased of late, and he was beginning to sleep properly. If only he could go home.

In the middle of April, they were informed that they were all going to be shipped back to England to prepare for demobilisation. There would a month or so at Witley Camp before finally being taken home to Canada. The whole unit rejoiced and there was a party atmosphere in the barracks. Men were singing to themselves and writing to loved ones. All the weeks of waiting were coming to an end at last. Georgy was overjoyed to know that they would have some time in England before departure to home. He had another chance to see Nellie, to make amends, but what then? He would soon be travelling to the far side of the briny deep, away from her again. He didn't like to think about that too much.

It was pure pleasure to pack up his few things and depart French shores for good. Georgy respected the French people and had been happy to help but now it was time to get his own life back on track. The ship steamed into Folkestone harbour, accompanied by rousing tunes from a military band. There were a small number of people waiting to welcome them. Being

Canadian, their main celebration was yet to come when they reached their homeland. The troops disembarked two by two, whilst the band played on. Then they formed up into a parade for the officers to inspect them. All the while, Georgy could see Nellie and her brother Billy watching and smiling at him, amongst the crowd. He couldn't respond but that was understood. Military discipline was still to be maintained. As the outfit marched off to get the train to Witley, Georgy managed a brief secret smile at them as he went past. Nellie's face lit up.

Settling into Whitley camp again felt strange, a case of déjà vu, but now the atmosphere was different, joyful, positive. Though the men were scarred mentally and physically by their experiences, the one thing they all wanted was to go home. The month would be spent handing in equipment, having medical checks, signing paperwork, all to get them fully demobilised. Georgy telephoned Nellie as soon as he could and arranged to meet. A month - a glorious month! All the troops were on light duties and allowed to go out every evening and weekend if they wished. They could even wear civilian clothing again. Georgy resolved to make the most of it.

To his delight, Georgy ran into some people at the camp who he hadn't seen since he was at Shorncliffe. Tom and Jamie, his bunkhouse companions, were both there waiting for demob and happy to see him as well.

'Great to see you made it through, laddie,' said Jamie. 'How you doing?'

'Fine,' replied Georgy. 'And you?'

'Och, we'd have been goners if it hadn'a been for young Tom here. He's a fine chap. One of the best to have by your side, I tell you.'

Tom blushed.

'Go on, Jamie. You know we got through it together.'

Georgy was pleased to see they were getting on so well. In fact, they were now best friends. Tom was even travelling up to Scotland with Jamie once they got out.

'I'm going to see these Highlands for meself,' Tom said. 'See if this 'ere chap knows what he's talking about!'

He laughed. It was obvious a bond had been formed. They were due to leave next week and Georgy wished them well. It was so good to know that some other people had survived the horrors and were happy. It made him feel that he must make the most of his opportunities now.

The first time he saw Nellie again, he rushed to her and held her in his arms. His feelings were overflowing and he kissed her again and again. Then they happily went off to walk around London in the spring sunshine. All was going well until they were about to cross a busy road and they saw a ragged looking child run out, in front of an omnibus. Nellie screamed, but Georgy reacted. He leapt into action, scooping up the child in the nick of time and depositing the boy safely on the pavement.

'Don't do that again', he scolded. 'You might not be so lucky next time.'

The child just laughed and ran off leaving Georgy feeling stunned. Nellie ran over to him.

'You were marvellous,' she cried. 'Such a hero!'

The word 'hero' struck Georgy hard and brought back bad memories. He exploded with emotion.

'Hero? I'm not a hero! I wasn't even there when the end of the war came. I was in hospital with scabies. That's not heroic. That's downright stupid! All I did was my job. I didn't save anyone or do anything special. Someone rescued me and just look where it got him!'

He sobbed as he remembered Dave.

'You're *my* hero,' she told him. 'No matter what. Why don't you tell me what happened if you can? It might help.'

Bit by bit, she got it out of him - his wound, the rescue, his shame at not being there in the final battle. It all came out. Nellie didn't comment or judge, simply listened. The burden was lifted just by being shared.

'You're the only person I've told any of this to,' Georgy said. 'I love you, Nellie, and that's why I can talk to you. You understand me. I will tell you more, but not yet.'

'There's no rush,' she told him. 'I'm not going anywhere.'

As much in love as ever, the two of them spent every available moment together for the month. Aunt Mary did her best to discourage their relationship, but all in vain. They went to concerts, visited galleries, walked in the parks and more, all the while chatting and laughing. That's not to say that things were always easy or perfect, but if Georgy was withdrawn at times, Nellie tried not to take it personally. She knew there was pain deep within him that would take time to heal, if it ever did.

The day came when Georgy and his unit had finally completed all their demob preparations and were given a date for departure in one week's time on 28th May. Until that day they were free to do whatever they liked. When he heard the news, Georgy was in turmoil. What an awful choice to have to make - to stay here with Nellie or to go home to his family. Ellen kept writing enthusiastically to her son, looking forward to the day when he was home with them once more. He couldn't let them down, but he couldn't bear to part from Nellie.

When he saw Nellie the day after he got the date, he told her the news with trepidation. Her face fell.

'Oh Georgy, so we're to be parted again. Will it be for good this time or will you come back? I knew it would happen, but even so, I foolishly hoped it wouldn't.'

Georgy took her hands in his. 'I have to go, Nellie, my love, but I promise I'll come back. Or you could come and visit me.'

'In Canada?' she said in surprise. 'But it's such a long way. I don't think I could afford it.'

'I could send you some money,' said Georgy, 'once I get what I'm owed for my army service. You would love Canada. The countryside is amazing. I'd love to show it to you.'

'That would be great,' said Nellie, doubtfully. 'But what would your family say? You know, my mother isn't keen on us being together. I don't suppose your family will be either.'

'Maybe we wouldn't need to tell them,' Georgy replied. 'Well, not at first anyway. Just let them get to know you for a while and then we can break it to them later.'

'But I wouldn't want to stay there too long,' she said anxiously. 'My home and family are here. I'm sorry. It's all I've ever known.'

'I understand,' said Georgy, his heart breaking.

'You know that I'd do anything to be with you,' she said. 'But this is such a big step. I suppose I'm scared.'

'I'll come and visit you then,' promised Georgy. 'It's the only way.'

‘Oh, why did we have to start this?’ exclaimed Nellie. ‘All we get is more pain every time we part. We should have known that it couldn't work with us both the opposite sides of the ocean!’

She cried then, and Georgy held her, comforting her and promising he would return.

‘My love, my love,’ he murmured. ‘We must be strong. Things will work out somehow. We couldn't help starting this. It was just too much for us to resist.’

He stroked her hair, which was damp from her tears.

‘I wish I could stay,’ he said. ‘But with William missing, most likely dead, I must return for a while at least. It's only fair.’

‘I know, I know,’ sobbed Nellie, ‘and I love you for it, but it's so hard to bear.’

The last few days were sombre ones for them both. Most of Georgy's companions were longing to be home, but his heart was torn in two. Nellie came down to the harbour on the day of departure to see him off. She tried to smile.

‘We seem to be making a habit of this!’ she said brightly. ‘We really should stop it.’

Georgy kissed her gently.

‘I promise this will be the last time we say goodbye,’ he said. ‘I'll write and let you know when to expect me. In the meantime, take care of yourself, my love. Goodbye.’

‘Farewell my love, safe journey,’ she managed, then turned and walked away so that Georgy wouldn't see her cry. Swallowing back his emotions, Georgy boarded the ship and stood to attention one last time on deck as they steamed out of port with bands playing and flags waving. They were on their way home.

As he travelled over the foaming waves, Georgy cursed himself. Why hadn't he asked Nellie to marry him and come to Canada as his wife? It was the obvious solution. He knew he wanted to be with her for the rest of his life. How stupid he had been! Now what would she think of him for leaving her once again? He swore to himself that next time he saw her, he would propose. He just didn't know when that would be.

A week later, they were back in Halifax, viewing the devastation and ruins of 1917's disastrous explosion. The docks had been speedily restored, but everything else would take time. Georgy was shocked by the sight. The troops were whisked off by train to a final base camp to hand in their uniforms and be medically checked once again. Declared fit, Georgy was finally released – demobbed, a free citizen, not under army orders any more. His spirits rose as he boarded a train for Moncton. He couldn't wait to see his family again.

Chapter 33

Moncton, Canada

The civilian suit that Georgy had been given during demob fitted him badly and chafed his neck, but at least he was finally out of that dratted army uniform. There had been only one outfit for the whole year, and Georgy dreaded to think what it smelt like. Now he felt clean and new, ready to face the future.

He stepped down onto the platform at Moncton hoping that someone might be there to greet him. The Canadian sun was shining, and the summer flowers were blooming brightly, so different to the desolation of the battlefield. He was dazzled by it and stood there blinking in the light. There was a shout – 'Georgy!' – and he turned to see his mother and Gilbert rushing towards him. It was a grand reunion which rather overwhelmed him.

'Father gave me the day off to come and meet you,' Gilbert told him. 'I said I would escort Mother. The others are all at school of course, except little Hazel. Aunt Minnie is looking after her today.'

Gilbert had grown into a fine young man and even sported a small sandy coloured moustache. Georgy was shocked by how grown up he looked. Thank goodness the war had ended, otherwise his little brother would have had to go and fight.

Ellen hung onto Georgy's arm as they walked home, chatting non-stop about the family. Later he realised that she had never asked him how he was.

It was delightful seeing everyone again when they came home from school. Len looked at him warily, as if he was a stranger, but Arthur and Ethel welcomed him warmly.

'Can we go out to the forest again, Georgy?' asked Arthur. 'I want to camp overnight, but Mum won't let me.'

'We'll see,' Georgy replied, smiling.

Ethel was fourteen now and just about to leave school. She was a capable, sensible girl who was very good with the younger ones. Georgy sensed that she had also spent a lot of time looking after their emotionally fragile mother.

There was a fine dinner that night to celebrate Georgy's homecoming, but he was rather shocked when Ellen said: 'Of course, we'll have a proper party when William comes home.'

Everyone exchanged furtive glances around the table.

'Have you heard from him then?' asked Georgy, confused.

'No, not yet,' his mother said enthusiastically, 'but when he comes out of hiding, he'll be in touch, I'm sure.'

'Hiding?'

'Yes, because he ran away,' Ellen explained. 'Those men told me he could be arrested if they catch him, so the only way is to hide until all this is over.'

'But William wouldn't run away,' Georgy said. 'He's not a coward.'

'I know he's not,' replied Ellen, 'but it's the only thing he could do. He'll be back soon.'

At the head of the table Father sat there looking embarrassed. He changed the subject abruptly.

'So, George, your job's there waiting for you. Gilbert is going back to the shipyard and Harriet is giving up work now, so if you can start on Monday, I'd be grateful. I expect you're keen to get back to normal again.'

Georgy swallowed hard. So soon?

'Father, I, er, I'm not sure I'm ready for that yet.'

His father frowned.

'It's the best thing you can do now, George. Just put the war behind you and move on.'

'Yes, I agree,' his mother joined in. 'It'll be good for you to get back to work.'

Georgy sat there in silence. It seemed that no one understood the enormity of what he'd been through. How could he explain it to them? He had dreaded having to tell them all about it, but now it seemed that everyone wanted to forget it had ever happened. He found his voice eventually.

'No, Father. I'm sorry. I need a few more days yet. I'll come back to work the week after.'

'But I need you,' his father protested. 'We've got a big job to finish. You can't let me down like this.'

'Harriet said she could do one more week,' Gilbert piped up. 'Why don't you ask her?'

Grumbling, their father reluctantly agreed, and Georgy breathed a sigh of relief. He just needed a few days to adapt.

Later that evening, he seized the chance to have a quiet word with Ethel.

‘How has Mum been?’ he asked. ‘About William, I mean.’

His sister frowned.

‘It's not been easy,’ she said. ‘Mum just can't accept the fact that he's not here any more. She has convinced herself that he will be home soon.’

‘How did that happen?’ asked Georgy.

‘Well, it all started when those men came `round saying he was a deserter. Then when you found out that he hadn't been in the hospital, that just reinforced it.’

‘Oh dear,’ sighed Georgy. ‘So, it's partly my fault. I wish I hadn't told her, but I thought she ought to know.’

‘You’re not to blame,’ replied Ethel. ‘Mum would have been like this in any case, I think.’

‘Can't we try and talk some sense into her?’ he said. ‘Reason with her.’

‘No, I don't think that's wise. She's in complete denial that anything might have happened to him. It's best to humour her. One day she will realise he's never going to come home. At least she's happy. You know how low she can get when she's not.’

Georgy knew only too well, remembering her previous bout of nerves after Arthur's birth.

After a couple of days at home, with Father and Gilbert at work and the youngsters at school, Georgy was beginning to feel stifled and claustrophobic indoors. With only his mother and little Hazel for company and four stone walls around him, he felt closed in, almost trapped. He still wasn't used to a house and needed fresh air. This was when he suggested to Ellen that he take Arthur camping in the woods that weekend.

‘We could leave on Friday afternoon straight after school,’ he suggested, ‘and return on Sunday. It would do him good and get him out from under your feet for a while. You know I'll look after him.'

'But couldn't you wait until William gets back?' said Ellen. 'Then you could all go together.'

'We can go again later,' Georgy said, humouring her. 'But this will keep Arthur happy in the meantime.'

So, it was agreed, and Arthur was delighted. Ever since Georgy had found him when he was lost in the forest, they had been close, despite the difference in their ages. The weather stayed warm and dry, and the two of them had a great time. They hiked through the forest to the foothills of the mountains where they set up camp. Georgy showed Arthur how to light a fire and cook on it, and they spent time fishing at a nearby lake. Arthur was naturally good at all these things, and Georgy was amazed how quickly he learnt. They saw a bear in the distance but luckily it never came close.

'Can we follow it?' Arthur asked, but Georgy put his foot down.

'No Arthur. Bears are unpredictable and dangerous. Never approach one if you don't have to.'

The boy was sensible enough to listen to his older brother's advice, but he was still fascinated by all the Canadian wildlife.

'One day I'm going to go out to the Yukon,' he told Georgy. 'That sounds the place for me. Wild and free.'

'I think it's rather cold, though,' Georgy remarked, smiling.

'I don't care,' declared Arthur. 'Just you wait and see what I do!'

After the weekend, Georgy set about completing some other things he wanted to do. Firstly, he wrote a long letter to Nellie to say he was home safely and telling her all about his camping trip. Then he organised a day to go and visit his old friend Walter in New Brunswick.

Approaching Walter's front door, Georgy felt nervous. Would he find his friend much changed? How would he be able to talk to him? To Georgy's relief, however, Walter opened the door, smiling, leaning on a crutch and bidding him welcome.

'It's great to see you again,' said Walter. 'How are you doing? Did you come through unscathed?'

They sat and talked of old times and Georgy gave him all the details about the end of the war.

'It was a mess,' he said. 'But I missed most of it due to my leg injury.'

They shared their reminiscences and their feelings of guilt at not being there for the final push. Only other servicemen would have understood. It was good to be able to talk about the horrors.

'No one outside can really know what we went through,' Walter remarked. 'Unless you were there, you wouldn't believe it.'

'True,' said Georgy. 'My young lady does her best, but it's hard to explain. At least that's better than my family. They just want to pretend it never happened.'

Walter sighed. 'My wife Sarah, she's a fine woman, but she's found it hard to deal with me losing a leg. She has to work more now doing laundry. I feel bad about it. I wish I could provide for her like I used to.' He paused. 'So, you're courting then? Good for you.'

'I am,' said Georgy, 'but sadly she's over in England and I'm here. I don't know what to do.'

'Do!' exclaimed Walter. 'You have to follow your instincts. mate. Don't hang around here in Canada if you love her. If you're not careful, you'll lose her.'

Georgy knew his friend was right and was determined to tell his parents that he would be moving back to England. He knew this would be difficult though, and he wasn't looking forward to it.

On the Saturday before Georgy was due to start work again, they were sat down to dinner when Father suddenly asked:

'So, you're all ready to come back on Monday morning then, George, now that you've had your holiday?'

Georgy swallowed hard. Now was the time to break the news.

'Yes, Dad,' he said, 'but only for a while. I'm going to move back to England again soon.'

There was a stunned silence around the table.

'What?' demanded his father. 'You can't. Why would you do that?'

'What do you mean?' cried Ellen. 'You've only just come home. Why?'

'I've fallen in love with an English girl, Mum,' Georgy confessed, 'and I want to be with her. I'm sorry. I'll come back and visit, I promise.'

'Fallen in love!' his father said sarcastically. 'What are you, a silly young fool? You don't even know the meaning of the word.'

'Who is she?' asked Ellen.

'Her name's Nellie,' replied Georgy, 'and she works in London as a telephone operator.'

'The same name as your cousin then,' said Ellen. 'That's a coincidence.'

'Yes,' said Georgy, blushing, 'the same name. I met her whilst I was doing my army training.'

'Does this mean we can't go camping again?' asked Arthur angrily.

'Well, maybe some time,' said Georgy awkwardly.

Arthur stood up and stormed out the room, banging the door as he went.

'Surely you can stay until William returns,' said Ellen. 'It will be so nice to have the whole family together again.'

'I'm sorry, Mum,' Georgy mumbled. 'I'll wait a few weeks, but that's all.'

The rest of the dinner time passed in an uncomfortable silence, but when Georgy left the table, his father followed him.

'George,' he said sternly, 'I want a private word with you.'

Once they were alone, his father continued.

'This isn't fair on us, son. Your mother needs you here. Surely you can see that. The rest of us know that William is not going to come home again, and once she realises that she's going to need all our support.'

Georgy knew his father was right and reluctantly conceded.

'Look, Dad, I'll stay till the end of the year, but that's it. I need to get back to England.'

His father huffed in annoyance. 'So be it!' he declared. 'We'll see how things are then.'

The conversation ended with both men feeling dissatisfied and irritated. Georgy wrote to Nellie that evening, telling her what had happened and begging for her patience until the end of the year. He prayed that she would wait.

The routine of daily work took some getting used to, but Georgy struggled on. He missed Nellie so much. Sometimes he couldn't sleep for thinking of her. Months went by and the end of the year was just around the corner. Ellen continued to wait for William to arrive, and the family were beginning to think that nothing would ever change. The first anniversary of the Armistice appeared, the newspapers carried stories of the war again, and memories were stirred. One particular news story focused on the soldiers who had returned home; wounded, shell shocked or with amnesia, who still resided in hospitals or sanatoria in England. Sometimes no one knew who they were.

Reading this, Ellen suddenly declared.

'That's it. That's where William is, in a hospital in England. I need to go and find him!'

'Don't be stupid, Ellen,' her husband said firmly. 'There's no point in dashing off over there.'

'I could take her, Dad,' offered Georgy. 'I'll be going soon anyway.'

His father scowled at him.

'Your duty is here, George,' he said. 'Besides, look at the weather. Do you really want to go overseas in this?'

The Canadian winter was at its height once more, with frequent ice and snow making travel difficult. Sailings were few and far between and even the railways were struggling to get through.

'As soon as the winter is over then,' said Georgy defiantly. 'Mum and I can go to England.'

'And who will look after the children?' demanded Father. 'What about Hazel and Len?' 'Maybe I could help out,' began Ethel, but stopped when Father glared at her.

'The children, yes,' said Ellen. 'Well, let's all go as soon as the weather improves.'

'What? Just throw everything up and leave!' exclaimed Father. 'Are you mad, woman? What about my business? The house? The children's schooling? Is that really what you want - to ruin us?'

Ellen went off to the bedroom crying, and it seemed that the subject was at an end. Just after Christmas, however, a letter arrived which added more fuel to the fire. Ellen's father had suffered an apoplectic fit and was now bedridden and frail. Grandma Goddard was struggling to cope and begged Ellen to come home.

For several nights, Georgy heard arguments raging from his parents' room as he lay in his bed. He couldn't make out the words, but both of them looked tired and miserable in the mornings. It seemed that they were barely speaking and there was an unpleasant atmosphere in the house. Christmas came and went and Georgy started to plan for his escape. He had to get back to Nellie. In her last letter, she had sounded disappointed in him, he thought, though she didn't say as much. He felt he was letting her down.

January 6th came around - Twelfth Night: a time for new beginnings. The family were called together by Father for a surprising announcement. They waited expectantly. Father cleared his throat.

'Well,' he said, 'we're all moving back to England again as soon as the weather clears up. I've booked a passage for us all in May on the SS Grampian. That gives us time to pack up the house, sell the business and sort out new schools. Mother is going to search for your brother and help look after her father. I know it will be a wrench for some of you, but it can't be helped. We have to do this.'

'No!' shouted Arthur. 'I won't leave. You can go, but I'm staying!'

'Arthur, you will do as you're told,' their father said forcefully. 'We are all going and that's an end to it.'

Arthur flung a vase across the room where it smashed noisily, then turned and ran out. Georgy found him in his room later, crying his eyes out.

'It's all your fault!' Arthur cried. 'It was your idea. I don't want to leave Canada!'

'I'm sorry,' said Georgy. 'I didn't think we would all go.'

He was stunned by the news but pleased as well. At last, he would be reunited with his love. He couldn't wait to tell her.

Chapter 34

Late May 1920

Georgy stood on the deck of the steamer SS Grampion and reflected on the past few months. Emotions had been running high lately. There had been his mother's anxiety to start the search for William, Arthur's tantrums and attempts to run away, his own eagerness to be with Nellie again, her sadness at the delay, his father's anger and resentment, and much confusion from Uncle Dick and Aunt Minnie. They just couldn't understand why the family would want to return to England.

'What's wrong with Canada?' demanded Dick of his brother. 'You've got a good life here - a business, a family. Why throw it all away?'

Father just shook his head and refused to talk about it. He knew it was the only way to pacify his wife, but it certainly wasn't what he would have chosen.

Georgy regretted leaving Canada as well. It was a land of beautiful contrasts – lakes, mountains, forests, rivers - differing greatly from the cities with industries such as the railway, shipyards, lumber and more. He loved it but it wasn't home. He realised now that his true home was in England, preferably beside Nellie.

Looking out across the dark ocean the memories came rolling back to Georgy like waves on the sea. This was the first time the whole family had travelled by ship together, since leaving England in 1906. Much had changed since then. New family members had arrived, and one had been lost. Georgy vividly recalled himself and William running around the decks of the steamer all those years ago. He smiled at the vision but then felt sad again. His brother's absence had left a huge gap that could never be filled. The longer Georgy spent in the family home, the more keenly he felt it, and he could sympathise with his mother's feelings. William and Georgy were different in just about every way but despite this, they had still been close. He missed him.

Like any mother, Ellen was keen to hear more about her son's sweetheart. Georgy had told her as much as he could, but without mentioning the family connection. Judging from Aunt Mary's reaction, he had a feeling his mother would not be pleased if she knew the truth.

It was almost a full year since Georgy had sailed away from Nellie and he was desperate to see her. He had hoped that she would be at the station to meet them as their train arrived from Liverpool, but his eyes searched the platform in vain. In retrospect, he realised it would not have been a good idea. His mother and father might have recognised her even after all these years. Though she had blossomed into a beautiful young woman, she still retained some of the features of the child they had known. Georgy was disappointed, nonetheless.

Their first port of call was Grandma Goddard's house, where they stayed for the first week. It was chaos.

Adding two adults and six offspring to the Goddard's tiny cottage made it cramped to say the least, but Ellen wanted to see her parents and until their new home was ready, they had nowhere else to go. Everyone slept top to tail on the floor or the sofa, wherever they could. The younger children loved it all and ran around screaming a lot. Father grumbled incessantly, and Georgy was keen to escape whenever he could. Ellen spent time tending to her father, who was now very frail, allowing her mother a much-needed break. Georgy noticed how worn and tired his grandma looked now, so different to the last time he had visited her. The spirit seemed to have gone out of her.

'Thank you, dear Ellen,' said Martha Goddard to her daughter. 'It means a lot to have you here again. Will and Mary have helped out as well, of course. I know they would love to see you. Maybe we can arrange something.'

Ellen was reluctant, however. She still remembered how they had reacted to their decision to emigrate. Grandma Goddard was keen to reunite her family, but Ellen made sure the Huntingfords were too busy to attend any get-together. Excuses were made and disagreements left unresolved.

The first thing that Georgy wanted to do was to telephone Nellie, but when he did so, he was disappointed.

'Sorry, George. She's gone out with someone from work,' his aunt told him. 'I don't know when she'll be back. I'll tell her you called.'

Undeterred, Georgy called back a couple of days later at a different time but received much the same answer. When this happened, for the third time in a row he realised that he was being given the brush off. Was this from Nellie, or from her mother? He was anxious to know.

Meanwhile their belongings slowly caught up with them, landing in the house they had rented in Tolworth, Middlesex. The Huntingfords moved into their new home, much to everyone's relief, and life began to settle down. They were glad to find it was a fairly quiet, rural area with plenty of sedate Edwardian houses. It helped make the transition from the beautiful Canadian countryside somewhat easier. Father started working for a local plumbing firm; the younger children went back to school and Ethel and Gilbert looked for work. Georgy's task was to escort his mother around to look for William. He knew it was a futile mission, but hopefully it would lead to some kind of healing for her. There were only a couple of weeks to go before the children broke up for the summer, so Ellen was keen to get started. She knew she would be busy once the holidays arrived.

Their first step was to visit the Red Cross Centre in London. Georgy and Ellen spent hours poring over the list of soldiers currently known to be in hospitals around the country, but there was no Huntingford to be found. However, there were many unidentified inpatients, which gave Ellen grounds for hope. Buoyed up by visions of finding her dear son among them, she took a note of all the locations that she intended to visit. Georgy was shocked at the widespread distribution of all the hospitals and sought to dissuade her.

'It will take a long time to get to Nottinghamshire, Mum,' he said. 'Let's start locally at least.'

To his relief, his mother agreed happily and they planned a trip in the next few days to the Ex-Servicemen's Welfare Society in Putney.

His head in a whirl, Georgy decided that before he went off on a jaunt with his mother, he would write to Nellie. It was possible the messages he had left weren't getting through. Surely a letter would. Pouring out his heart and his joy at being able to see her again, he finished off with his address and telling her he would phone as often as he could. As he put the missive in the post box, he hoped with all his being that she would respond.

The hospital in Putney had only been open a few months when Georgy and his mother visited, and it was gleaming white and fresh. On the way they travelled across London and Georgy showed Ellen where the bombs had fallen on that fateful night when he and Nellie had been so nearly injured or killed. Ellen shuddered.

'I never realised they came so close,' she said. 'How dreadful.' Then she asked: 'When will we meet your young lady? You must bring her to visit.'

Georgy stammered his way through some excuses. 'Yes, yes, of course. But she's very busy working at the moment.'

'Well, wait till William's home again and then we can all meet her. I wonder if he's got himself a lady friend. He's such a handsome boy.'

There was nothing Georgy could say to that, so he didn't attempt it.

A matron showed them around, Ellen peering anxiously at every patient. There were men sat in chairs staring into space whilst well-meaning nurses tried to engage them in basketwork, crafts or other activities. Many inmates were severely disabled with limbs missing or eyes blinded. Some just wandered around talking to themselves.

‘We have a therapeutic approach here,’ the matron told them. ‘Lots of gentle, creative activities for them with fresh air and exercise. Then as they become fitter, we get them ready for the workplace.’

It was certainly an impressive centre, with workshops, gardens and a bustle of positivity. Ellen, though, was shocked by the severity of the patients’ injuries (both physical and mental) and was in tears by the end of it.

‘He’s not there,’ she moaned to Georgy as they left. ‘I thought we would see him. I know William’s out there somewhere.’

‘It may take some time,’ Georgy told her. ‘Or it’s possible we may not find him at all.’ He spoke gently trying not to hurt his mother, but to instil a vestige of reality into her mind. However, Ellen snapped back immediately:

‘Of course we’ll find him! We just have to keep looking.’

A visit to another hospital, this time in Golders Green, was planned for September.

Three weeks had gone by since Georgy had written to Nellie and there was still no reply. His telephone calls went unanswered and he began to despair. Had he lost her forever? What could he do? His longing for her was so intense, it was painful.

Now that his younger siblings had started their school holidays Ellen was very busy entertaining them, in-between helping to care for her father. This gave Georgy more time for himself and he devised a plan to try and see Nellie. He had to find out how she felt, once and for all. This uncertainty was killing him.

It was evening when Georgy reached Victoria Telephone Exchange where Nellie worked. He knew her shifts usually ran from 8pm to 8am, so he hung around outside at about quarter to eight, hoping to see her as she came in. Lots of young women passed into the building but not Nellie. Eventually Georgy asked a young woman with a friendly face, who was hurrying along.

'Nellie Goddard – yes, she`s my friend. Why?' she asked suspiciously.

'I need to see her,' Georgy replied desperately. 'I've come over from Canada and I….'

'Canada!' interrupted the girl. 'Don't tell me you're Georgy! She talks about you all the time.'

'Yes, Georgy, that's me! I've phoned and written to her since I got here, but she hasn't answered. Now I'm worried that she doesn't want me any more.' He hadn't meant to tell the unknown person all that, but it just came out.

The girl smiled. 'I don't think you need to worry about that,' she said. 'Look, she's on shift at the weekend, this Friday, Saturday and Sunday. Why not come along on one of those mornings after she finishes, then you can catch her on the way out. My names Doris, by the way. I'll tell her to look out for you.'

'I'll be there,' promised Georgy and went home feeling happier. He still didn't know why Nellie had ignored his calls, but at least he could see her.

It was 8 o'clock on Saturday morning and the sun was already shining brightly as Georgy waited nervously outside the telephone exchange. He'd had to rise especially early to get there, but he didn't mind. It would be worth it to see Nellie again.

The first flush of employees departing came and went, and for a moment Georgy thought something had gone wrong. Then suddenly there she was, excited and happy to see him.

'Georgy!' she cried. 'You're here at last!'

They hugged and kissed despite the disapproving looks of passers-by.

'It's been so long,' said Nellie. 'I thought you were arriving in May.'

'I did,' Georgy said. 'I phoned your home many times and I wrote to you. I thought you'd changed your mind or something.'

'Phoned?' said Nellie. 'But I never heard about it, and I haven't had any letters. Are you sure?'

'I spoke to your mum on several occasions,' Georgy told her. 'She said you were busy.'

'My mum!' cried Nellie. 'You wait till I see her. She never said a word about it. I didn't know, Georgy, really, I didn't.'

Overjoyed to be together again, they sat down to talk.

'I'm over here for good now,' said Georgy. 'No more partings. We can be together whenever we like.'

'That's wonderful,' Nellie replied. 'But I'm a bit worried about my mum. I know she doesn't approve, but I didn't think she'd stoop this low.'

Happily, they arranged another meeting, this time to go out for lunch, but when Nellie arrived a week later, she seemed very downcast. Georgy sensed it immediately.

'What's wrong? he asked. 'Are you all right?'

'It's Mum,' Nellie told him. 'She's not at all happy about us seeing each other. She's told me it's got to stop.'

'Why?' exclaimed Georgy. 'Just because we're cousins?'

‘Yes, she thinks it's wrong. I've told her that I don't care what she thinks, but I’m only 21 and I still feel I have to go along with their wishes.’

‘That's not fair,’ said Georgy. ‘What can we do?’

Nellie sighed. ‘Well, I'm not going to stop seeing you,’ she replied, ‘but I think we will have to keep it as quiet as possible.’

‘Yes, you're probably right,’ agreed Georgy. ‘I haven't even dared to tell my parents for the same reason. It's very hard because I love you Nellie, and I want everyone to know, but we must be sensible and discreet.’

Georgy's intention had been to ask Nellie to marry him, but on thinking about it he realised that it would be best to wait until they could get her parents’ consent. They were unlikely to get it at the moment, it seemed, so patience was called for.

The planned visit to the First Home of Recovery in Golders Green turned into an episode of frustration. Unknown to Georgy and his mother, the hospital which regularly treated cases of neurasthenia (shell shock), had recently been given to the RAF to treat their own servicemen for the same reason. After an hour of wandering around the wards, workshops and gardens, they realised it was a pointless exercise and retreated.

Ellen was extremely irritated by this and ranted all the way home. Apparently, there were other similar homes in places further away that they could try, but Golders Green was a non-starter.

‘What a waste of time!’ Ellen exclaimed. ‘They're just trying to stop me finding my boy. This proves it. It's a conspiracy. Something is going on.’

‘Mum, be reasonable please,’ begged Georgy. ‘This is bound to take time.’

But she wouldn't listen, and it was many hours before she calmed down. By the time Father and Gilbert got home from work, the younger children were either crying or sulking. Ellen had shouted and stormed at them all without cause. Eventually Georgy heard Father tell his wife firmly that if she didn't stop this behaviour, he would no longer allow her to search for William. This brought tears from Ellen, but restored calm at last.

These days, Ellen's moods varied between wild enthusiasm, bitter anger and deepest depression. It was never easy to tell which it was likely to be, but several more fruitless visits around London hospitals with Georgy didn't help. Meanwhile, Georgy and Nellie continued to meet as and when they could, discreetly, using subterfuge when necessary. Nellie's friend Doris was often made the reason for her frequent visits to London which, as yet, Aunt Mary had not seen through. Time, however, was slipping by and things were about to change.

Chapter 35

Tolworth, England, Christmas 1920

'Guess what?' said Ellen at dinner one evening in December. 'Your Aunt Mary and Uncle Will are coming over for tea on Sunday, as it's nearly Christmas.'

Georgy gasped. This was the last thing that he wanted. If his mother and Aunt Mary chatted there was bound to be trouble. Ellen kept asking Georgy to bring his sweetheart over to meet them, but he kept putting her off. Furthermore, as far as Aunt Mary knew, he and Nellie were no longer courting. What might be exposed if the two mothers got together, he hated to think.

'I thought you didn't get on,' he said cautiously to her.

'Oh well, they sent me a Christmas card recently, so I invited them over. It's time we buried the hatchet,' she replied.

The dreaded Sunday came and Georgy was a nervous wreck. He'd not had a chance to talk to Nellie about it, but he expected that she would already know. To make matters worse Georgy remembered that he hadn't even told his mother about all the occasions when he had been at Aunt Mary's house: the Christmas in 1917 that he'd spent with them, the countless visits for tea and cake, the times they had seen him off - oh dear, it would all come out now.

The first hour passed by without incident and Georgy was beginning to think that everything would be all right. Aunt Mary looked sharply at him when she arrived but said nothing. The two husbands retreated to the kitchen to have a crafty beer whilst the children amused themselves and the mothers talked in the front room. Georgy tried to stay in the background. There was much chatter about how all the family were doing, and reminiscences of the past. All quite safe so far. Then suddenly Ellen asked Mary:

'And how are your children? They must be so grown up by now.'

'Oh yes,' said Aunt Mary. 'Charlie is married with two children now, Billy has just started an apprenticeship, and Nellie is working at a London telephone exchange.'

'What a coincidence!' said Ellen. 'Georgy's young lady works in one of those places. I wonder if they know each other. Her name's Nellie too.'

Mary looked horrified. 'Have you met her yet?' she asked.

'No, not yet. I keep asking Georgy to bring her over, but she's very busy.'

Mary stood up. 'Georgy, where are you? Come here!'

He approached warily.

'How dare you, Georgy!' his aunt cried.

'What's going on?' asked Ellen, confused.

Mary turned to Ellen. 'Your son has been courting my daughter, his cousin. I've told him countless times that I won't have it. It's not right!'

'No, that can't be true,' said Ellen. 'He hasn't even seen Nellie.'

'Oh yes he has!' Mary replied grimly. 'He's been visiting our house, taking her out, spending Christmas with us, and it's all been going on behind our backs!'

'Georgy!' Ellen cried. 'What does she mean? Is this true?'

Georgy's face was flushed red and he could hardly answer. 'Yes Mum,' he mumbled, 'but I love her.'

'She's your cousin. She should be like a sister to you! This is wrong. It must stop at once. How could you have lied to us all?'

'Nellie may have been like a sister to me when we were young,' he tried to explain, 'but then you took us away and I hadn't seen her for years. It's all different now.'

'I don't want your excuses!' Ellen raged, her voice at a dangerous pitch. 'Get out of my sight! Go to your room and wait there until I can bear to talk to you.'

Georgy fled, glad to be away from the two irate mothers. It felt like being a naughty child again, being sent to his room, but he wasn't about to argue.

Hours later Ellen came upstairs to see him. Georgy could tell she was still annoyed and upset.

'George – your aunt has told me everything. How could you go behind my back and visit them? You know I didn't want you to do that. You betrayed us all.'

'I'm sorry, Mum. I didn't think there was any harm in it,' he replied brokenly.

'But then to start seeing your cousin as a sweetheart – that's disgusting. You should be ashamed. I won't allow it!'

'I love her, Mum, and one day I want to marry her, though I haven't told her yet. I'm not ashamed of the way I feel. Nellie is beautiful. She has helped me through a lot of things recently.'

‘Marriage!’ his mother shouted. ‘Over my dead body, my son. Don’t you realise that the offspring of cousins are deformed or imbeciles? You’re too closely related. It’s an offence against nature and against God.’

‘But it’s legal to marry your cousin these days, Mum,’ pleaded Georgy. ‘There’s nothing wrong in it.’

‘You will not talk back to me like this,’ screamed Ellen, now thoroughly worked up. ‘You will write a letter today, which I will oversee, saying you cannot see her again.’

‘No Mum, I can’t do that,’ cried Georgy. ‘Don’t make me, please.’

‘You will do that,’ his mother repeated, ‘or you will leave this house and never see any of us again. Do you hear?’

There was silence whilst Georgy took in what his mother was saying. Would she really turn him away from the family for good? It seemed so. He realised that his only option was to go along with it, and to hope that everything would calm down again soon. Maybe she would forget about it all if he did that.

‘All right,’ he said at last. ‘I understand. I’ll do what you suggest.’

If he had hoped to get away without writing or sending the letter, his hopes were dashed, for Ellen sat over him, dictating it. Then she sealed it, addressed it and went to the post-box herself to post it. Georgy was horrified. What would Nellie think? Would she believe it? If only he could get to the telephone to warn her.

His mother had forbidden him to go out anywhere, except with her.

‘I don’t trust you any more, George,’ she said. ‘You lied and deceived me all along.’

However, there were times when Ellen was busy with the children, or resting on the bed, and so Georgy hoped for an opportunity despite this.

A chance came just after New Year when Ellen had to see one of the teachers at school about Arthur. He'd been causing trouble again, being disruptive in class. Georgy walked to the school with her and promised to wait outside. Just over the road, he knew there was one of the new concrete public phone boxes. As soon as his mother was out of sight, Georgy headed straight there. He hoped and prayed it wouldn't be Aunt Mary answering. To his relief he heard Billy's voice, home early for once. 'Hello.'

'Billy!' said Georgy. 'Don't say anything. It's me, Georgy. Is Nellie there? I really need to speak to her, but please don't tell your mum.'

'Hold on,' said Billy. 'I'll get her. Don't worry. Mum's gone to the shops.'

When he heard Nellie's voice, Georgy knew she'd been upset.

'Oh Georgy, thank goodness! I got your letter, but I knew it wasn't you writing that. I could tell. My mum has told me to write to you as well, so take no notice if you get something. I still love you.'

'What can we do?' said Georgy. 'I still want to see you.'

'I'm forbidden to go anywhere except work,' said Nellie. 'But Mum doesn't always know what shifts I do. Maybe I could pretend I have to work, then meet up with you. Doris would probably let me stay at her house overnight. What do you think? You could write to me at her address as well.'

'That's a good idea,' replied Georgy. 'I think I can probably get away with going out for an evening here and there. I could say I'm going out for a drink with my army friends. Oh Nellie, I love you so much and I can't bear to be parted from you. This is terrible!'

'We will make this work Georgy, I promise,' she said. 'Don't worry.'

Once Georgy and Nellie had written letters to their mothers' satisfactions, Ellen and Mary relaxed, thinking the affair was over. This was far from the truth, of course, but at least life became calmer again and the pressure was off.

In the meantime, there was another surprise at home when Gilbert announced he had signed up to join the RAF. No one had any idea that he was thinking about it. He'd kept it all to himself, in his own quiet way. Ellen was distraught - another son was going away - but it was too late. Gilbert's training would be starting in a month's time and that was that. Georgy admired his brother's steady determination and wished him well.

'At least we're not at war any more, Mum,' he said to Ellen. 'Gilbert will be quite safe, and he'll learn a lot of useful things. It's better than just being a labourer.'

Ellen had to agree but was sad all the same. Georgy distracted her by starting to plan their next hospital visit. Now that they had visited all those in the London area, they needed to travel further afield if they were to continue.

'Do you really want to go all the way to these places, Mum?' Georgy asked. 'We don't have to carry on with this, you know.'

Ellen glared at him. 'I will never stop looking for William,' she declared. 'Of course we will carry on.'

Many difficult months went by. Georgy and Nellie sneaked in time together whenever they could, but it was tricky. Now that Ellen and Mary had reconciled, they visited each other from time to time, though Georgy always made himself scarce on these occasions.

Aunt Mary introduced Nellie to a young man from her father's workplace and insisted that they go out together to dances and other events. Andrew was a decent man, but Nellie didn't love him and never would. She didn't think he cared much for her either. There was no chemistry between them. They were just being pushed together by their parents.

One evening, as they sat in the dance hall awaiting their next dance, Nellie suddenly felt she had to be honest with him.

'Andrew,' she said, 'I'm sorry, but I can't love you. I'm already in love with someone else but my mother doesn't approve of them. You're a nice man and you deserve better than me.'

Andrew smiled gently.

'Nellie, you're a fine young woman, but to tell the truth, I know we're not suited. We don't even like the same things. We can be friends though, can't we?'

'Yes, of course,' said Nellie. 'Let's just leave it at that.'

Nellie's 22nd birthday came round in the autumn that year and Georgy braced himself to pop the question. He had wanted to be with her on the day but that was impossible. Aunt Mary had organised a party at home and invited many friends. Georgy knew that Andrew was taking Nellie out to a dance the following evening and he decided to gatecrash. For the last few months, he had wondered what Andrew was like and he couldn't help feeling just a bit jealous on some occasions. Tonight, he saw Nellie with a thick set, brown haired young man of ordinary height and build. Nellie sat there looking bored whilst Andrew chatted to a young lady on his right-hand side. It seemed that he was more interested in her than in Nellie.

When Nellie saw Georgy approaching, she squealed with delight and ran to him, embracing him. Andrew didn't even seem to notice, and Georgy realised he had no cause to worry.

'Georgy, how wonderful to see you!' Nellie exclaimed.

'Let's go for a walk,' he suggested.

Nellie briefly told Andrew where she was going, then went outside with Georgy.

'Doesn't he mind you coming out here with me?' Georgy asked.

'No, we're just friends,' she replied. 'He likes that girl next to him. He told her that I'm his sister!' She laughed. 'It keeps Mum happy if I go out with him.'

'I came to wish you a happy birthday for yesterday,' said Georgy. 'Here, let's walk through these gardens.'

It was dark, but a full moon was shining brightly, and the air was still pleasantly warm. The chill of winter had not yet arrived. They sat on a wooden bench and kissed, then cuddled up closely. Georgy could feel his heart pounding. This was the moment he had been rehearsing in his mind, over and over. He felt so nervous he started to tremble.

'Why, Georgy, what's wrong? Are you cold?' asked Nellie.

'No, I, er, I wanted to ask you something,' he said.

She smiled at him, encouragingly. 'Yes?'

Georgy took a deep breath. This was it, for better or worse.

‘I love you, Nellie. I know we've been through a difficult time lately, and that I don't have a job at the moment, and our families don't approve, but in spite of all that, well, what I wanted to say was, will you marry me?’

He gazed at her, fearing a reply in the negative, but Nellie didn't hesitate for a moment.

‘Of course!’ she cried. ‘I love you Georgy and it's all I want, though I don't know how our mums will take it.’

They kissed again, passionately.

‘Maybe we should elope,’ Georgy said, ‘then no one could stop us.’

They sat there mulling over ideas and wondering what to do.

‘I have to take Mum to the last hospital on the list in a couple of weeks’ time,’ said Georgy. ‘After that I need to get a job. There have been so many trips around recently, all of no use. This has to be the end.’

‘How do you think she'll take it if she doesn't find William this time?’ asked Nellie.

‘I don't know. Badly, I think. But Father has said this is enough now and I agree. We've done all we can. I've spent the year running around with her, but now I need to find work so that we can get a house.’

‘But I can work,’ said Nellie, ‘And you'll find something soon enough. You have your qualification in plumbing.’

‘I know,’ said Georgy. ‘But I can hardly ask your father for your hand in marriage if I can't support you. Besides, as your husband, it's my duty to provide for you. You shouldn't have to work.’

‘I don't mind,’ she said, ‘if it means we can get married.’

‘I would never stop you doing anything you want to do,’ Georgy said. ‘But I want to take care of you and any little ones we might have!’ He laughed and they kissed again.

‘Let's not tell anyone until you have a job then,’ said Nellie. ‘If you've got that, then Father will have to say yes. I just hope both our families will forgive us.’

‘I will start looking for work as soon as this trip is out the way,’ Georgy promised. ‘The sooner the better.’

They returned to the dancehall and let the music carry them away in each other’s arms. Georgy had never felt so close to another human being, and he loved the feel of Nellie’s warm body next to his. Soon, he thought, soon she will be mine forever.

Chapter 36

November 1921

A cold November wind wrapped itself around their legs as Georgy and Ellen made their way to the recovery home in Leeds. Hours of travelling on a cold and dusty train through a bleak wintry landscape had done nothing to raise their spirits. The proposed visit had been postponed from their original plan of an October trip, due to Gilbert arriving home on leave from the RAF. Everyone was delighted to see him, looking well and so fine in his uniform. Ethel, in particular, had missed her brother. They had always been very close, and whilst he was at home, he took Ethel out to a dance, which she loved. She so rarely got the chance to go out.

Georgy was surprised by how confident and mature his younger brother seemed and admired him greatly. The only member of the family who appeared uninterested in Gilbert was Arthur, who at thirteen years old, was a loner; wayward and angry at times. Only the other day Georgy had heard him say:

'Why did you bring me to this horrible country? I hate it here! I'm going to go back to Canada as soon as I can.'

'Well, first you need to finish school, find a job and earn some money,' Father told him. 'Then when you're old enough you can do what you like.'

'I will!' declared Arthur. 'You don't need to worry about that!'

Now here they were, Georgy and his mother making their last visit to a depressingly familiar type of facility. The home was large and built of grey stone, blending into a grey smoky background. Factories and mills churned out fumes and soot, and the air felt grimy, even worse than London. Briefly Georgy remembered the gorgeous scenery of Canada – the fresh rivers, the tree covered mountains – but that was in the past now. Their lives had changed.

Wandering through the wards and workshops, they peered closely at every patient. At the far end of an almost empty ward sat one young man on his own, staring at the wall. Ellen gave a sudden cry and rushed towards him: 'William!'

For a moment Georgy's heart gave a leap. The man looked so much like his brother. Could it be him? Ellen was convinced and didn't hesitate for a second. She reached the man, shouting: 'William! William, my son. It's me, your mum.'

But then the man turned scowling and Georgy could see that it wasn't William after all. Disappointment nearly overwhelmed him, and he felt embarrassed.

'Mum,' he entreated, 'it's not him. Come away, please!'

But Ellen couldn't see it. She so badly wanted it to be her son that she had fooled herself into believing it.

'William,' she repeated. 'It's Mum. Talk to me.'

The man stood up, glaring angrily at her.

'I ain't your son, lady. Clear off! You're just some crazy old woman. Leave me alone!'

'William,' she pleaded and approached close – too close. The man shoved her hard and she stumbled. Georgy caught her and pulled her away, whilst she collapsed in floods of tears. How he got his mother back to the station and onto the next train, he never knew. Ellen had become almost paralysed with grief and could hardly walk. She mumbled words to herself at times, but nothing coherent. Georgy tried to get her to eat and drink, but the most he managed to get down her was half a cup of tea.

At home Ellen went straight to bed. Ethel, who now worked mornings in a laundry because that was the only work that she could find, made dinner and looked after the rest of the family. She frequently picked up the children from school these days, since Georgy and Mother had been off on their longer trips away. Arthur usually walked the younger ones to school but could not be relied upon to be there at the end of the day, often leaving early or playing truant.

Father was naturally concerned about his wife and asked Georgy what had happened. He sighed when he heard.

'Perhaps this will put an end to it at last,' he said. 'Maybe it's for the best.'

It certainly didn't seem like the best over the next few weeks. Ellen lay in her bed most days, crying, barely eating and hardly talking to anyone. There was little anyone could do.

Though he felt a bit guilty about it, Georgy seized the chance to meet up with Nellie again. Once the rest of the family went off to their respective places, his mother just slept all day and was unlikely to miss him.

Nellie told her mum that she was seeing Andrew, meaning that she was none the wiser and they were able to enjoy each other's company once more. They enjoyed visiting the picture palaces, where they saw some of the latest comedy films from Charlie Chaplin, and Nellie's favourite, Harold Lloyd.

Now that electricity was beginning to be rolled out, the streets of London were brightly lit, and many shops and theatres had a gaiety to them that hadn't been there before. Georgy was surprised at the change in the city since he'd been there in wartime. Cars, lorries and omnibuses were beginning to make their presence felt, even though horse drawn trams and carts were still the norm, to say nothing of the cyclists who weaved their way amongst them all. It seemed a dangerous combination to Georgy, as the horses were easily spooked by the sound of the new vehicles and prone to take fright.

Fashions had changed as well. Nellie now wore simpler, shorter dresses and her wavy hair was styled in a new way. Georgy always found her beautiful no matter what, but it was true that the old way of life was changing.

On December 13th an official looking letter arrived, addressed to Mr and Mrs Huntingford. Father was at work, but Georgy took it straight up to his mother in her room.

'Mum, this looks important,' he told her. 'It's from military HQ, I think.'

Ellen sat up immediately and took notice.

'It must be about William,' she said eagerly. 'They've found him at last.'

It was indeed about William but was not the news that she had been hoping for. It informed them that his desertion had finally been cancelled and that he was now officially MIA.

'Missing in action,' said Ellen, 'but what does that mean?'

'Mum, I hate to say it, but it usually means that a person has been lost on the battlefield, and that they never found any trace of them.'

Georgy avoided using words like 'killed' or 'body' as he didn't want his mum to be upset any more than could be helped.

'At least his name has been cleared now. I knew he wouldn't desert. William was always very brave.'

'Missing,' mused Ellen. 'But that means he will be found one day. That's good news.'

'To be honest, Mum, I don't think it is really. People aren't usually found after this.'

'How do you know?' she snapped. 'Are you an expert? Go away!'

Georgy fled.

It wasn't long before Ellen left her room again, in one of her happier moods. Georgy was partly pleased but also alarmed at his mother's denial of the truth. She approached Christmas with a manic enthusiasm, arranging everything from food to party games and decorations. She even got her old bicycle out again and started riding it to the shops. Most of the family were happy to see this, but Father and Georgy were privately worried about her. These bouts of wild happiness were usually followed by a very low mood afterwards. This time would prove to be no exception.

May 1922.

Georgy sighed as he joined yet another queue for the employment exchange. The line stretched in front of him, and he despaired ever getting to the desk by the time the office closed. So many people all looking for work - what had happened to the country? The air of positivity that had been around immediately after the war ended had evaporated, leaving strikes, unrest and mass unemployment in its wake. Men came back from the front line expecting their old jobs back, only to find they had been replaced by others or by the dreaded automation. Less people were needed now, and with the partial addition of women to the workforce, there just weren't enough places for everyone.

It had been a difficult year so far. In spite of what had been said previously, Ellen had expected to go out looking for William again. When Georgy refused, she ranted and raged at him, screaming abuse and crying. Father intervened, putting his foot down and at last, Ellen listened. A deep melancholia ensued, which had only recently given way to something lighter and more cheerful.

William's birthday in April was always a particularly difficult time, these days. The family would have suffered badly if it hadn't been for dear Ethel's care of them all with Georgy's help. Gilbert was now away, flying missions to places they could only imagine. Arthur was due to leave school soon and Father was busy trying to find him an apprenticeship, much against Arthur's wishes.

Months of looking for work had been depressing for Georgy. His only consolation was that having an excuse to go out and about, it was much easier to see Nellie. Aunt Mary had finally relaxed her restrictions on her daughter, thinking that there was now nothing to worry about. A few days of casual labouring here and there had helped bring in a few pennies for Georgy, but there wasn't anything more permanent at present.

With Nellie's help, he had knocked on the doors of many local businesses, asking if they needed anyone, but always the same answer: sorry, no. Now the employment exchange seemed the only solution, but it was proving tortuously slow. If he could only get some secure work, then he could marry Nellie.

Ethel's 17th birthday was approaching and their mother had worked herself up into a state of enthusiasm, planning a family celebration. Ellen cycled around to the shops, collecting up food and gifts. Georgy took a few days off from his job search to help as well. It was good to see his mum in better spirits again.

The day fell on May 16th and the weather was fine and dry. Everybody felt in a good mood, even Father. Ethel was busy opening her gifts in the evening after work when the late afternoon post arrived. It was nearly 5 o'clock. An official looking letter dropped on the mat with a government address on the back. It was addressed to Father. They were all itching to know what was in it, but they had to wait until he came home at six.

'George, quick,' Ellen said as soon as he arrived. 'Open this! It's important. I'm sure it must be good news about William.'

'Give us a minute, woman!', he declared. 'Let me get through the door first.'

The family gathered around nervously as Father opened the letter. His face fell.

'I'm sorry, my love, it's not good news. Quite the opposite, I'm afraid.'

He handed it to Ellen, who took one look, let out a scream, and then dropped to the ground in a faint. Georgy grabbed the piece of paper as it fluttered down and read what it said:

"*Re William Huntingford, Private, 832429.*

We regret to inform you that the above person, for official purposes, is presumed to have died on or since 1/11/17."

It was a shock to see what they had all feared written down in black and white at last. Even Georgy felt it. It was so final. The authorities had made their decision. And yet - and yet - it still sounded so vague. '*Presumed*', '*on or since*' - it wasn't clear at all. Ellen was carried off to bed and a doctor was called, poor Ethel's birthday quite forgotten in the commotion. Len and Hazel were far too young to remember William, but the rest of the family sat around glumly trying to come to terms with it.

'Aren't we going to play any games now?' asked Hazel. 'You said we could.'

'I want to have some cake,' cried Len. 'You promised!'

Arthur just looked confused.

Georgy and Ethel took charge as best they could whilst Father tended to his wife and spoke to the doctor. Later that evening, the younger ones in bed and Ellen having been given a sedative, Father, Georgy and Ethel sat down to talk. They all felt exhausted but needed to unwind together.

'Father,' said Ethel, 'do you think we should go into mourning for William?'

Father hesitated. 'I'm not sure,' he replied. 'I mean, we've all known this for quite a while now, apart from your mother that is.'

‘Should we wear black armbands,’ asked Georgy, ‘as a mark of respect?’

‘I think it will just upset your mother more,’ said Father thoughtfully. ‘Maybe we should just leave well alone.’

‘Couldn’t we get a memorial done for him?’ asked Ethel.

‘Yes, he needs to be remembered,’ added Georgy. ‘We can’t just let him disappear as if he never existed.’

‘I agree with you both,’ said Father, ‘but we’ll have to see how your mother bears up. I don’t know how she will cope.’

‘Perhaps it would bring her some comfort,’ Ethel suggested, ‘if she had a place to visit and put flowers.’

‘Yes, we could have a service for him,’ said Georgy, ‘to honour his life. I’m sure the vicar would say a few words.’

‘We’ll see,’ Father replied. ‘If your mother is up to it, then I think it would be a good idea.’

But it was two weeks before Ellen could even get out of bed. Two weeks of tears and screaming, alternating with drug induced sleep. She lost so much weight that she was little more than a skeleton by the time she finally emerged.

Georgy and Ethel spent all their time looking after her and encouraging her to eat and get well, but it was hard work. Then one morning at the start of June, she suddenly got up, though rather shakily, and staggered into the kitchen to try and make breakfast.

‘Mum,’ said Georgy, ‘it's good to see you up again. Take it easy though, you've not been well.’

The hysteria had gone at last, but in its place was a deep, still pool of sadness where pebbles of family conversation barely stirred a ripple. Ellen moved around quietly, mechanically, in a world of her own. Meals were made and tables set, but often she was found sitting, staring into space, barely noticing any of them.

Father did his best to cheer her and a couple of weeks later he ventured to suggest that they have a memorial service for William.

'Memorial?' Ellen repeated, her interest piqued at last. 'Yes, that's a good idea. I'd like that.'

The family gathered around a small, enclosed patch of grass and a temporary wooden plaque in the nearby cemetery, whilst the parson did his best to commemorate the life of someone he had never met. Ellen's tears still fell but they were gentler now and softer. It wasn't just her that was feeling it, they all did. Even the younger children were solemn and quiet knowing that something serious was taking place.

It occurred to Georgy that it was four and a half years since they had first heard that his brother was missing in action. What a long, drawn-out period it had been, not knowing whether to mourn or to hope. At last, he now felt that they had laid William's spirit to rest, if not his body, and that this should bring peace and acceptance for all of them.

Chapter 37

July 1922

July arrived like a bird in full flight, all blue skies and fluffy white clouds. Len and Hazel were excited at the thought of the summer holidays to come shortly, and even Arthur looked forward to spending more time outdoors. Meanwhile Georgy trawled around the streets of nearby Surbiton, trying to find a job and becoming increasingly frustrated by his failure to do so. How would he ever be able to marry Nellie?

Father and Ethel continued their daily work, whilst Ellen remained quiet, calm but deeply saddened. She functioned normally providing meals, caring for the children, keeping the house clean etc but something had gone out of her. Her spark had been quenched. Twice a week she cycled to the churchyard to put flowers on William's memorial. No-one tried to stop her. They hoped it might help.

July 26th

'I'll be home for lunch, Mum,' said Georgy. 'I've got someone to see about some possible plumbing work in Kingston, but I'll be back by then.'

‘That sounds encouraging,’ his mother replied. ‘I hope you get something. I’m just going to visit William and then go to the shops, so I’ll see you later.’

He kissed her on the cheek and went off in an optimistic frame of mind. Three hours later he returned, somewhat depressed, and was surprised to find that his mother was not in. Ethel had arrived home after her shift at the laundry and was busy making lunch.

‘Where’s Mum?’ asked Georgy. ‘Isn’t she back yet?’

‘No,’ replied Ethel. ‘She must have got held up somewhere. I thought she’d be home by now.’

They waited for her return. Half an hour went by, and lunch was beginning to get rather overdone. Georgy went to the front door and looked down the road, but there was no sign of her.

‘Maybe we should have our lunch,’ suggested Ethel. ‘It’s getting a bit dried up.’

Putting Ellen’s plate aside, they sat down reluctantly to eat. Another half hour went by.

‘I think I should go out and look for her,’ said Georgy anxiously. ‘She’s not usually as late as this. Perhaps something’s wrong.’

‘She’s probably just got delayed at the shops,’ replied his sister. ‘Let’s wait a bit longer.’

It was now 2 o’clock and their mother was always home before that. She liked to have lunch promptly at one. This was out of character and Georgy was worried.

‘No,’ he said. ‘I’m going out.’

He was putting on his shoes and coat when there was a heavy knock at the door. They rushed to open it thinking it was their mother, but a policeman stood there looking very serious.

'Mr Huntingford?' he asked. 'Can I come in, please?'

'I am Mr Huntingford Junior,' Georgy told him. 'Did you want me or my father? He's at work, I'm afraid.'

'Your father, really,' the policeman replied, a bit flustered. 'When will he be back?'

'Not till 6 o'clock this evening. Can I help?'

The policeman looked at the two young people before him and seemed to come to a decision.

'Are you the children of Mrs Ellen Huntingford?' he asked.

'Yes, that's us. Is Mum all right? She hasn't come home yet.'

The man hesitated.

'I'm afraid I have some bad news,' he said. 'You might want to sit down.'

They did so in trepidation.

'What?' cried Georgy. 'Please tell us!'

'Yes. What is it?' Ethel exclaimed.

'Your mother has been in an accident, I'm sorry to say. She was knocked off her bicycle and fell under a motor lorry. They took her to the hospital, but it was no use. Her injuries were too severe. There was nothing they could do.'

There was a shocked silence.

'She's dead?' managed Georgy eventually.

'Yes, I'm afraid so.'

Ethel let out a little cry. 'No, surely not! That can't be true!'

'I can't believe it,' said Georgy, his mind reeling from the news. 'Not gone, not dead - she can't be!'

'I'm so sorry. Please accept my condolences,' the policeman said. 'Her body is at Surbiton Hospital if you would like to make the necessary arrangements.

She will need to be formally identified. Perhaps you could tell your father and the rest of your family.'

Once he had left, the two of them fell apart. Sorrow and shock overwhelmed them. It seemed unreal, and yet it was sadly only too true. Ethel curled up in a little ball on the sofa, hugging herself and crying bitter tears. Georgy sat there, numb with grief. Their dear mother, gone forever in an instant. It just wasn't right.

Eventually they realised it was time to collect the younger ones from school and that the dreadful news would have to be shared. Together, the brother and sister made their way there to collect them. Arthur instantly knew that something had happened and demanded to know what it was. Georgy had already thought about where the best place to tell them would be. He was aware that Father would not like any of them to be seen crying in public, but the children were anxious to know what was wrong.

There was an enclosed area in the nearby recreation ground with hedges around it where they could not easily be seen, so this seemed like the best idea. As expected, there were lots of tears and everybody hugged each other. Ellen may not always have been the perfect mother, but she was much loved by all. After that they somehow managed a solemn and dignified procession homewards.

'What about Father?' asked Ethel once they were indoors. 'He should be told as soon as possible, shouldn't he?'

'Yes,' agreed Georgy. 'I know where his place of work is. I'll go and see him whilst you look after things at home if you like.'

It was a terrible task to have to do; to tell a husband that his wife was dead. His father was stunned, just like the rest of them, but appeared to take it with fortitude. He wasn't prone to showing his feelings usually, and this was no exception. As they walked home, however, Georgy saw his father's face was grey and lined with pain.

The family sat in the kitchen feeling shattered. Nobody knew what to say, only 7-year-old Hazel, who kept saying 'Where's Mummy? I want Mummy.' Then she started crying all over again. Ethel put her arms around her and rocked her back and forth, which seemed to bring some comfort.

'I'll make some tea,' offered Georgy, not knowing what else to do. They barely tasted it, but the warm liquid began to bring them back to life. Father stirred.

'We should tell some people' he said, brokenly.

'Oh my God!' cried Georgy suddenly. 'Gilbert! He doesn't know yet. How do we get in touch with him?'

'We could telegraph the RAF base,' suggested Ethel.

'Yes, but the office won't be open now,' Father said. 'It will have to wait until tomorrow morning. Then there's Mum's parents, and Will and Mary.' He faltered, grief overcoming his words, but swallowed hard and went on. 'Could you help me, please, George? I'm not sure I can do it all.'

'Of course,' agreed Georgy and then realised how desperate he was to speak to Nellie.

'I could phone Aunt Mary. I have her number.'

He ran to the public phone box by the school and put in the call, his hands shaking. As he began to tell Aunt Mary the dreadful news, he broke down and only managed to impart it in-between his sobs. He hoped that no one outside would notice. Mary was similarly shaken by the information but promised to tell Grandma and Grandpa, as well as her husband, Will, and their offspring. She offered to come over, but Georgy turned her down.

'No, I don't think we can cope with any visitors at the moment,' he said. 'No offence. Please can I talk to Nellie though now? I need her.'

Mary wasn't too pleased really but couldn't deny a bereaved son's request. Nellie came on the line as comforting and helpful as ever. Georgy felt better just to hear her voice. He couldn't quite define why he loved her so much. She was beautiful, kind and intelligent but so were lots of girls. He just felt complete when she was around.

The next day was a dismal one, full of unpleasant chores. After a sleepless night, the family arose to a breakfast they barely tasted.

'George,' said Father, 'I have to go to the hospital this morning to see Mother and to make the arrangements. Would you come with me please? You don't have to see your mum, just keep me company.'

Georgy had never heard his father so needy, and it touched him greatly that he had asked for his support.

'Of course, Father, I'd be glad to. And if you don't mind, I'd like to see Mum. I can't quite believe it until I see for myself.'

'It may not be very pleasant,' said Father, 'but you're welcome to come.'

On the way to the hospital, they stopped off at the telegraph office and dispatched a telegram to Gilbert via the RAF camp to tell him the awful truth.

Georgy had seen many dead bodies in the war, but seeing his mother lying white and still on a hospital slab was something entirely different. Luckily her dreadful injuries had been covered up, so all they saw was her face. She almost looked serene, but it was strange how all personality seemed to have left her. The spirit had fled, leaving only a vacant shell.

Father shed tears as he held his wife's hand for the last time. Georgy too, couldn't help but show emotion. Now it was only too real; too horrible. He exited the room abruptly leaving his father alone to say goodbye to the love of his life.

As they came out of the morgue, a nurse called them over to see a man waiting at reception. 'This is the driver of the lorry that was involved, gentlemen. He would like to speak to you.'

The man was clearly very upset.

'I just wanted to say how sorry I am,' he said. 'Her bicycle came flying out of the road from the cemetery and she was wobbling all over the place. I never had a chance to stop. I'm so sorry. I tried to swerve, really, I did.' He paused.

Father spoke gently.

'It's not your fault, sir. These things happen. My wife was not the best of cyclists.'

The man continued. 'I stopped and tried to help, but there was so much blood. She was caught right under my wheels. I'm not going to drive again – ever!'

A gulping sob broke from him. Father patted him on the shoulder and then walked away, unable to bear any more. Georgy followed. He'd have liked to try and comfort the driver, but he knew his father wouldn't have approved.

Gilbert arrived home later that day, looking pale and drained, having two weeks compassionate leave. Ethel hugged him and they cried together.

No-one went to school or work for the next week or more. Aunt Mary, Nellie and Billy visited the following day, and Georgy sought solace from his sweetheart. No-one challenged them when they went out to the garden to talk in private, though there was more crying than talking done. Georgy was grateful for Nellie's arms around him, holding him tight. It was the only thing that made this bearable.

The funeral was a restrained and sombre affair. Ellen's simple wooden coffin was transported to Surbiton Cemetery by horse drawn hearse. The family and other mourners walked behind it; Father and Georgy, as eldest son, leading the way. Next came Gilbert in his finest RAF uniform, complete with black armband, and Ethel, who clung to his arm for support. The rest of the children followed solemnly, Arthur carrying a bunch of wildflowers, which he later put on Ellen's grave. Georgy had talked to the children beforehand about how they should behave.

'I know we are all very upset about Mum,' he said, 'but on the day we have to be dignified and respectful; that means we should only cry in private.'

'But I miss Mummy,' cried Hazel. 'I can't help it.'

'We all miss her,' explained Georgy gently, 'but she wouldn't want us to make a big fuss about it in public. We should grieve at home where nobody can see us. We must be very brave now.'

They did their best and it was a sedate, quiet procession to the graveside. Grandma and Grandpa Goddard brought up the rear, though Grandpa was in an invalid chair, being pushed by his son, Uncle Will. Aunt Mary, Charlie, Nellie and Billy were also there, along with Ada Potter, one of Ellen's married sisters who they hadn't seen in years. Everyone wore dark colours, or black armbands, and Grandma Goddard had a black veil over her face to hide her distress.

They stood around the graveside, so close to poor William's memorial, as the vicar recited some prayers and words intended to comfort the bereaved. Georgy found his mind drifting to thoughts of his mother at her best – laughing, playing games, loving them all. She had been the centre of his life from the moment he was born, and he could hardly believe that she had gone forever. The last couple of years clouded his memories, but he didn't want to remember her that way. He preferred to recall the good times.

Family life began again but it was different. Ethel kindly offered to leave work to look after the children and keep house for Father. Gilbert returned to his RAF camp, whilst Georgy stayed at home until the children went back to school in September, helping to keep them occupied. There could be no lively activities or fun for them in this period of mourning, however. They spent their time in quiet reading, walks and regular church visits.

Nellie visited often and helped console them all. She was a great support, giving Ethel a much-needed break from the chores. Georgy loved her even more for her quiet kindness. The two of them did nothing to hide their obvious affection for each other, but now no one seemed to care. Father had lost interest in anything these days; still working, eating, sleeping but distant from the family as if all that had ever bound him to them was his wife. He was a broken man, though he didn't show it. He spoke little and rarely smiled.

Aunt Mary took over the increasingly heavy duty of supporting Grandpa and now, Grandma Goddard. The trauma of losing her daughter in such a way had affected Martha Goddard badly. She had become frail and ill. Consequently, Mary didn't notice that Georgy and Nellie were spending all their spare time together. They couldn't be seen to be going out enjoying themselves at dances or picture palaces, but they walked out often to the park or by the Thames, and it greatly soothed Georgy. Meanwhile, Arthur reluctantly started an apprenticeship in carpentry and did his best to remain calm and respectful, though privately his older brother doubted this would last.

After the school holidays had finished and the young ones had returned to their lessons, Georgy began the search for work again, though he always found time for Nellie. In November, a local plumber took pity on him, seeing that he was in mourning, and gave him a few days' work as a plumber's mate whilst one of his employees was off sick.

It was good to be back at his old trade again and Georgy worked hard, anxious to please. He was full of hope that it might lead to something more permanent, but the employee returned and sadly the job ended. The boss, Reg Smith, was impressed with Georgy's level of skill and professionalism, however, and promised to keep in touch should a position open up. It was the most encouragement Georgy had had since he had returned to England.

As the year came to a close, it was decided by the family that they would start afresh. Six months was the standard period of mourning, and they had completed that. Now it was time to get on with their lives again. Things would never be the same without Ellen but nothing they could do would change that. They all hoped for better things in 1923.

Chapter 38

1923

Returning from another unsuccessful trip to the employment exchange, Georgy was surprised to hear that there was a message for him.

'Someone called Reg Smith came by this morning,' Ethel told him. 'He asked if you could drop in and see him.'

She handed him a piece of paper with the address of a plumbers' firm in Surbiton. Pleased and hopeful, Georgy wasted no time in visiting. He found Reg in a small office, busy ordering some supplies.

'Oh, Huntingford, good to see you again. Are you still looking for work?'

'Yes indeed,' Georgy assured him.

'Well, Pete is giving up this week due to poor health. You can start next Monday if you're interested. The job's yours.'

'What really?' asked Georgy. 'Is that permanent?'

'Of course,' said Reg. 'I know you're a good worker. So do you want it or not?'

Georgy readily accepted. A job and a regular wage at last; he would be able to marry Nellie. That's if she still wanted to. He realised it had been a long time since he had originally asked her. They had talked about the future, of course, but had avoided making definite plans. Now things had changed for the better.

They met up as usual later that week and Georgy told her the marvellous news.

'Oh, that's so exciting!' Nellie exclaimed, her eyes shining with joy. 'I'm so pleased for you, Georgy.'

'Nellie, I wanted to ask you something,' Georgy said seriously. 'A long time ago, I asked you to marry me. I still want that more than anything, but if you've changed your mind or have any doubts, I'll understand. Please be honest.'

'Don't be silly, Georgy,' she cried. 'Of course I'll marry you. I've never had any doubts.'

Safe in each other's arms, they started to make plans.

'The first thing I need to do is ask your father's permission,' said Georgy. 'But I'd like to wait until I've started the job and settled in. Then we can set a date and organise the wedding.'

'Maybe we could get married in the summer,' suggested Nellie. 'It would be a beautiful time for it.'

The two of them floated through the first month of Georgy's new employment on a wave of happiness. Nothing could go wrong now.

One Sunday in March, Georgy dressed in his best suit and set off to Tottenham to see Nellie's father. He was nervous, as any young man might be, about to ask for permission to marry his daughter. However, with a decent secure job now and good prospects, he was full of hope. Nellie knew he was coming and had contrived to get her mother out of the way for a while, by suggesting that Grandma needed her.

Uncle Will was pottering around in his garden shed when Georgy arrived. Nellie let him in, then disappeared.

'Hello Georgy,' said his uncle. 'Good to see you again. How are the family now?'

'Fine, sir,' he replied, 'slowly getting over our loss, I think. I wanted to talk to you about something.'

'Oh yes, how can I help?'

'Well, as you may know, Nellie and I have been very close for some time. I'm in work again now, I'm pleased to say, and I'd like to marry your daughter if you don't object. I love her and she loves me and we really think we will be happy together. Can we have your permission please?'

Will beamed with delight.

'Of course. How wonderful. I had no idea. You've certainly kept it quiet, you two. Go and get Nellie. Let's celebrate!'

It was a lovely hour whilst the three of them laughed, talked and planned but everything changed as soon as Aunt Mary returned.

'Mary,' called Will to his wife as she came in. 'Guess what? Good news! Nellie and Georgy are going to get married.'

Mary's face was a picture of fury. 'What? No, they can't. They're cousins. I forbid it!'

Will looked confused. 'But Mary, my love, there's no reason why cousins can't marry. Why, I've given them my blessing. I can't see a problem.'

'Problem!' exclaimed Mary. 'It's one big problem. It's unnatural. I won't allow it!'

She turned on Georgy. 'You've even got the same names as your parents. How is that right?'

Georgy hadn't thought of that before, but he couldn't see it was relevant. Dismayed by her reaction, he said: 'I'm sorry you feel that way, Aunty, but it's not going to stop us. We're adults now, able to decide for ourselves.'

'Your mother wouldn't have approved!' Mary continued.

'My mother isn't here any more, so don't bring her into it!' Georgy retorted, his voice raised in anger.

'Mum, please,' pleaded Nellie. 'I love Georgy and that's all there is to it. I'm of full age now and this is what I want more than anything in the world.'

'Yes, Mary, there's no harm in it,' Will intervened meekly. Mary turned on her husband.

'How dare you give them your blessing? You should have checked with me first.'

'Mum, leave Dad alone,' begged Nellie. 'He understands how we feel about each other.'

'Shut up!' shouted her mother. 'I can't bear to listen to you. You're a disgrace!'

Nellie couldn't help losing her temper then.

'Mum, you've gone too far! I'm going up to my room to pack and I'm moving out. If you want me, I'll be at my friend Doris's house until the wedding. Georgy, come and help me with my bags please.'

The young couple left the house with the shouts of Aunt Mary still ringing in their ears.

'I won't be coming to your wedding. Don't think that I will! And I'll be seeing the vicar to try and get it stopped. You mark my words!'

Nellie was able to hold back the tears at first, as she was so angry, but when they eventually got away from Tottenham and onto the train to the city, she cried bitterly on Georgy's shoulder. He had managed to get them an enclosed compartment for privacy, and he did his best to comfort her.

'I'm so sorry about this,' he told her. 'I hope it won't change your mind about our marriage.'

'Never!' declared Nellie. 'That will never change. But how could she be like that? I thought I knew her, but obviously not.'

Doris was more than happy to let her best friend stay as long as she liked and was very pleased to hear their news. After Nellie had calmed down, Georgy suggested that they visit his home the following week to tell his family.

'I hope we won't have a bad time with them as well,' Nellie said anxiously.

'I don't think we will,' answered Georgy. 'But either way, nothing can stop us now.'

Then Nellie suddenly thought of another thing that brought her great distress.

'Oh, no! Who will walk me down the aisle and give me away?' she cried. 'It should be Father, but I bet Mum won't let him. And what about Billy and Charlie? Will they be able to come to the wedding? Oh, I'm so unhappy and it's all Mum's fault.'

'I'll go and talk to them,' Georgy promised. 'I'm sure your brothers will be sympathetic. Perhaps Charlie could give you away instead if your dad really can't. Give your mum a bit of time and she'll probably come `round to it.'

It was the following Sunday afternoon when Nellie visited the Huntingford family home so that they could share their news. Georgy had managed to persuade everyone to stay in that day though Arthur grumbled loudly.

'It's my only day off and I want to go down to the river to watch the birds. I've seen Nellie loads of times. Why do I need to stay in and see her again?'

Georgy insisted, and to his surprise Ethel backed him up.

'It will be good for us all to spend some time together,' she said firmly.

Nellie arrived and they all sat down to a cup of tea.

'I've got an announcement,' Georgy began nervously. He took Nellie's hand in his and looked at his family, who were waiting expectantly.

'Nellie and I are getting married,' he said. There was a pause.

'I thought as much,' said Ethel. 'About time, too. I thought you'd never get around to it.'

Father looked surprised but stood up and shook his son's hand.

'Congratulations son,' he said gruffly, 'and to you, dear Nellie. Please accept my best wishes for your future happiness.'

Nellie was so overcome that she flung her arms around her future father-in-law and kissed him on the cheek.

'Thank you, Uncle,' she said. 'That means a lot.'

It was a time of much rejoicing with all the family. Even Arthur lost his frown and joined in the celebrations. Georgy wished that Gilbert had been there too, but he resolved to let him know as soon as possible. He'd been thinking about who to have for the best man, and Gilbert seemed the obvious choice.

Plans for the wedding went on apace. Though Nellie was not currently living at Tottenham, they opted to be married there in St Ann's Church as that was where she had been baptised. It was a beautiful building with an elegant spire, which would be a perfect setting for their special event. The curate, Reverend Brooks, was a kindly man and listened to their tale of family woe.

'There really is no reason why you can't marry,' he said. 'Maybe I could go and talk to your mother. Perhaps she would see reason.'

The date was set for June 9th and the two of them started looking for a house to rent. They found a small, terraced cottage in Tolworth, just right for newly marrieds on a small but regular income. It wasn't far away from Father and the rest of the family so they could be around to help out if needed.

Time was going by and the big day was getting nearer. Doris was going to be maid of honour and Gilbert had accepted the role of best man. Clothes were bought and flowers ordered. Still, Georgy was aware that his bride-to-be was very sad about her lack of family support, and he decided to go and sort something out.

Firstly, he visited Uncle Will and Charlie at their workplace. Georgy had begged a half day off from Reg as a special favour due to wedding preparations and his boss had kindly agreed. Reg was a fair man and a good employer. Georgy enjoyed working for him.

Will was busy smoothing down a large plank of wood when Georgy approached.

'Uncle Will,' he said. 'I'm sure you know why I'm here. We need your help.'

Will wasn't sure he could influence his wife to change her mind, but when Georgy told him the date and place of the wedding, he promised that he would be there no matter what, to give his daughter away. Georgy was delighted. Then Charlie arrived and he was able to invite him and his family to come to the ceremony. Charlie answered in the affirmative. He was fond of his little sister and liked Georgy. He couldn't understand his stepmother's reaction at all. He promised to make sure Billy knew about it as well. Nellie was glad when Georgy told her the news, though she still wished that her mother would see sense.

The invitations went flying out and the replies were all very encouraging. To their surprise, even Grandma and Grandpa Goddard were intending to be there. Everyone, in fact, except Aunt Mary.

Meanwhile, Mary had been learning a few bitter lessons. Her husband came home after seeing Georgy and for once stood up to her.

'Mary, I am going to their wedding,' he told her firmly. 'What's more, I am going to walk my daughter down the aisle and if you don't like it then so be it!'

'Will!' she exclaimed. 'How can you betray me like that? Charlie, Billy, listen to your father! Can you understand it?'

'Actually Mum, yes, we can! We're both going to attend. We love Nellie and we want her to be happy. You're the only one who doesn't,' Charlie replied.

Mary stared at them, stunned at such disobedience.

'But boys,' she pleaded, 'surely you can understand my point of view.'

But Mary was left increasingly isolated from the rest of the family. A further shock occurred when Grandma Goddard informed her that they were also going to the wedding.

'I'm so excited,' she said to her daughter in law. 'Come and help me choose something to wear.'

'But Martha, why? It's wrong.'

'Nonsense,' said Martha firmly. 'Lots of cousins have married over the years. Gosh, if it's good enough for royalty, it's good enough for us. Besides, anyone can see they're in love.'

Slowly, oh so slowly, Mary's views began to change. Truth to tell, she missed having her daughter to talk to and the thought of being left out of the celebration was becoming hard to bear. But still, she wouldn't give in. She'd made her stand and needed to stick by it.

Mary saw Doctor Greene when he came to visit her father-in-law and seized the chance to ask him something.

'If cousins marry and have children,' she said, 'won't the babies be deformed?'

'Rubbish,' the doctor said, laughing. 'That's just an old wives' tale. They are no more likely to have problems than any other babies. Where did you hear that?'

'I've been told it lots of times,' Mary stammered, uncertain now for the first time.

'Well, it's all a load of nonsense, I can assure you,' the doctor said. 'Nothing to worry about.'

That night, Mary tossed and turned in bed, unable to sleep. Was everything she had believed a lie? Had she been mistaken? It seemed so, but how could she back down now? It had all gone too far.

It was the next day, only two weeks away from the date of the nuptials, when the vicar visited her.

'I've just come to see how you are, Mrs Goddard,' Reverend Brooks said. 'You must be looking forward to your daughter's wedding, I'm sure.'

Mary swallowed hard. 'I'm not going, Vicar,' she said. 'I don't approve of cousins marrying. It's against God's law.'

'Where did you read that?' the vicar asked. 'I don't recall it being in the Bible, my dear.'

'It's not right,' Mary persisted. 'Surely you must agree.'

'It's perfectly legal,' Reverend Brooks told her. 'In fact, it always has been. Cousins have married many times over the centuries. It used to be very popular and it's only recently that it's gone out of fashion. As far as I can see, if they love each other, which these young people most certainly do, then there's nothing to worry about.'

Mary started to cry.

'Oh Vicar, what have I done? I've turned my daughter away and I've fallen out with my whole family over this. How can I make things right again? Help me.'

'My dear lady,' the vicar said gently, 'it's never too late to say you're sorry. There's still time before the wedding to make amends. Why not do it today?'

Georgy and Nellie were sitting in the Huntingford's kitchen discussing their plans when they were surprised and a little alarmed to see Mary arrive at their front door.

'Yes, Mother?' said Nellie coldly, expecting more abuse. 'What can we do for you?'

To their utter amazement, Mary broke down in tears, pleading with them to forgive her. 'I love you Nellie, and I can't bear to be a stranger to you. Please come home and be married from there. I promise I'll support you all the way. I'll even help you do your hair and put on your wedding dress like a mother should. Please!'

It was a beautiful moment of reconciliation. The final obstacle had been overcome. Nellie, Georgy and Mary made their peace and looked forward to the special day. Nellie collected her things from Doris's and returned home for her last few days of spinsterhood. Her father and brothers were overjoyed and the family were reunited.

On June 9th, Georgy stood waiting nervously in his pew with Gilbert beside him as the wedding march started and Nellie walked up the aisle on her father's arm. As she reached him, they smiled at each other tenderly, full of hope for the future. In the rows behind him. were the whole of the family, Goddards and Huntingfords, delighted and eager to see them wed. Aunt Mary had tears in her eyes but this time of joy, and even Father was smiling broadly. Georgy's only regret was that two of his loved ones were no longer around to share his joy, but some things could not be changed.

The sweethearts made their long-awaited vows with great love and seriousness, gazing into each other's eyes. Georgy knew that he'd never been so happy, and he thanked the heavens above for bringing him and Nellie together. After all they'd been through, this was the moment they'd been waiting for, both an end and a new beginning.

Finally, the vicar smiled and said those immortal words:

"I now pronounce you man and wife. You may kiss the bride."

Epilogue

George A P Huntingford senior died in 1930. Ethel continued to care for him and the younger children until she married, when she found him a housekeeper to take her place.

Georgy and Nellie had a very happy marriage and are remembered fondly by all the family. They had two children and eventually retired to Canada in the 1950s where they passed out the rest of their days. Their descendants still live in Canada and the USA.

William's body was never found. He has three memorials: one on the Ypres Menin Gate in Belgium, a personal plaque in Surbiton, plus he is also named on his parents' gravestone, again in Surbiton Cemetery. (The fictionalised story of what *might* have happened to William is explored in the short novella '*Someone Else*', also available).

Ethel and Gilbert married another brother and sister – the Uptons. **Gilbert** joined the RAF in 1921 and served for 8 years. He married Eva Upton in 1926 and eventually became a chef with ABC Restaurants. They had one child. Gilbert emigrated to Australia when his wife died, to be with his son. He also had a companion in later life, called May.

Ethel married Leslie Upton in 1926 and had three daughters. They all moved to Cornwall in the 1950's. It was said that at age 80 plus, Ethel was still climbing up on the roof to fix a missing tile!

Arthur returned to Canada in1928 and spent the rest of his life there apart from occasional fleeting visits to the UK. Family legend has it that he lived in the wilds and was a guide in the Yukon. Tales were told of him trading with local native Americans and stealing fish from wild bears! Some people who met him said that he was a very cultured man, whilst others said he could hardly use a knife and fork. How much is true is anyone's guess. As far as we know he never married or had children.

Leonard married Violet Pearcy in 1934 and had one son, David, who is the author's father. They all moved to Devon in the late 60's.

Hazel married Leonard Mendham in 1952 but had no children.

Dick and Minnie remained in Canada until they died in the late 1940's and are buried there.

Ralph went back to his job as a railway clerk, after the war. Later he married and also served in WW2. He remained in Canada with his family.

Martha and Bill Goddard both died in 1925.

Main Families in the Story

THE HUNTINGFORDS 1
George Arthur Prideaux Huntingford b 1869
Married to Ellen (nee Goddard) b 1870

CHILDREN
George (known as Georgy) b 1896,
William b 1898
Gilbert b 1900,
Gladys, Ellen & Ethel (triplets) b 1904
Ethel b 1905,
Arthur b 1908
Leonard b 1911,
Hazel b 1915

THE HUNTINGFORDS 2
Robert Richard Prideaux Huntingford (known as Dick) b 1866 (brother of George Sr)
First wife: Bertha, died in childbirth, baby also died at birth
Second wife: Julie Minnie (nee Horder, known as Minnie) b 1873

THE HUNTINGFORDS 2 continued

CHILDREN
Ralph b 1896
Irene b 1903
Dorothy b 1909

THE GODDARDS

PARENTS
William Goddard (known as Bill) b 1846, married to Martha b 1845

CHILDREN
William b 1868 (known as Will), married to Mary b 1871
Ellen b 1870 (married to George Huntingford Sr)
Frederick b 1875
Adelaide (known as Ada) b 1879

CHILDREN OF WILL AND MARY GODDARD
Charlie (from Will's first marriage) b 1887
Ellen Elizabeth (known as Nellie) b 1899
William (known as Billy) b 1901

Bibliography and References

WEBSITES
Find My Past
Canadian Library Archives
General Register Office
Chatgpt.com
Wikipedia

BOOKS:
Through the Great Canadian Wilderness, Readers Digest, 1995
Introduction to Canada, Marchant, G., Hodder & Stoughton, 1991
Nova Scotia, New Brunswick & Prince Edward Island, Lonely Planet, 2000
The Usborne Introduction to the First World War, Brocklehurst, R. & Brook, H., 2015
Canada, Haley, C., Brompton, 1988
Journeys Into the Past, Life in the Twenties and Thirties, Readers Digest, 1998

DVDs
The Great Canadian Wilderness Volumes 1 – 3, Readers Digest, 2005
Wonderful London, BFI, 2012

About the Author

Alison Huntingford is a writer with a deep passion for family history and storytelling. With a background rooted in the rich traditions of the Huntingford family, Alison seeks to honour the stories passed down through generations. She is the author of a successful series of works that explore historical and personal narratives. She is an only child of two only children and so has always felt a distinct lack of family. This has inspired her work.

After an upheaval in her personal life, Alison achieved a degree in humanities with literature through the Open University which helped to give her a new start. A teaching career followed which then led naturally to writing. She is now retired from full-time work, but busier than ever.

In her spare time, she enjoys spending time with her husband and their pets, listening to music, going to the cinema, and gardening on her allotment. She also runs the South Hams Authors Network, a local writers collective based in South Devon.

Also by the Author:

The Glass Bulldog 2019
revised edition 2025
Someone Else 2020
A Ha'penny Will Do 2022
Revised edition 2026
Dance a Fearful Jig 2024
Editor: *Grasping the Nettle, Quirky Tales from the South Hams Authors Network* 2023
Editor: *Longtimber Tales, South Hams Authors Network* 2025

For more information:
website: alisonhuntingford.com

www.ingramcontent.com/pod-product-compliance
Ingram Content Group UK Ltd.
Pitfield, Milton Keynes, MK11 3LW, UK
UKHW022126080326
468770UK00001B/332

9 781068 388514